Five Real Friends

What is a real friend?

Published by
Accent Digital Publishing, Inc.
2932 Churn Creek Rd
Redding, CA 96002

ISBN 978-1-60445-031-6

Cover Art Francesco Sideli
Cover Design Tim Chattman

Five Real Friends

What is a real friend?

By
Ray Mossholder

Dedication

To Georgia Mae

You are my wife, my best friend, my prayer and ministry partner, and my partner in everything we do.

You burned the midnight oil with me night after night, week after week, month after month, reading and re-reading this book, to be certain Goober, Alfonso, Tracey, Willie, and Pee Wee, would be happy about every word written in it. Now I'm sure they are.

I LOVE YOU.

And to Joanie and Terry Benton, who brought Georgia Mae and me to live in Fort Worth, Texas.

You are our spiritual daughter and son. We love you and your family.

You brought us to Gateway Church too. It's a world-changer. We'll never get enough of you and it.

THANKS

VI

Acknowledgements

To Pastors Bill Johnson, Kris Vallotton, Danny Silk, Dann Farrelly, and the magnificent leadership staff at Bethel Church. Jesus Christ through each of you has given me my life back. THANK YOU.

To Terry and Joanie Benton who have brought Georgia and me to our new home in Fort Worth, Texas. You have given us brand new adventures in Christ that will continue into eternity. We love you. THANK YOU.

To my longtime mentors and friends - Dr. Jack Hayford, Dr. Tommy Barnett, Dr. Loren Cunningham, Dr. Pat Robertson, and to all of my friends at CBN Television Network in Virginia Beach, Virginia, to Russ Bixler, that mighty man of God who is undoubtedly now doing television in heaven! To Norma and all my friends at Cornerstone Television Network in Pittsburgh, Pennsylvania and to Dr. Jim Bakker who gave Christian television its start. This book and my whole ministry were birthed out of the solid biblical foundation and ministry advancement each of you gave me. THANK YOU.

To my own two great pastor sons Tim and David and Tim's wife Kelly. Your major passion like Tracey Dare's and mine is bringing others to know Jesus Christ and then helping them grow in Him. And to my amazing daughter, Elizabeth Hinson (the mother of five children – two sets of twins! – and a conference director at a major university!) and her multi-gifted husband, Todd. Each of you has a devotion to Christ and me that blesses me beyond words. THANK YOU.

To my step-son David Gerke who built the very computer on which I've written this book. Your talent with computers boggles my mind. By the way, you have an awesome mother! THANK YOU.

To my Granddaughter, Becka Hinson, who first read a very rough copy of this entire book and told me "Grandpa, you rock!" And to my equestrian Granddaughter, Kaelyn Mossholder, who helped me describe Willie's adventure with Firewall because of her great skill with horses. THANK YOU.

To all my grandchildren – Becka, Elliott, Avery, Ian, and Chloe Hinson, and Brennon, Kaelyn, and Braden Mossholder – I couldn't be more proud of you. Brennon and Braden you could play on Willie's baseball team ANY TIME and Elliott, Avery and Ian, you'll soon be ready to join them. And Kaelyn, Becka and Chloe, you're the prettiest cheerleaders anywhere and like Tracey you could play ball too. Talking with each of you eight Grandkids is like talking with the four friends in this book. You are truly GRAND KIDS! There are parts of each of your personalities in each of them. THANK YOU.

To my spiritual daughters, Celia Horton and Diane Griffith, and Larry Jack, my spiritual son, who grew up as teenagers in my home. And to Dr. Jo Del Rio who began to spiritually grow in my home as an adult. Your lives are all very different now, but your zeal for Christ is a joy to behold. Diane, thanks for my wonderful Grandkids – Windra, Robert and Virginia. And Larry and Renee – thanks for yours too – Danielle, Anika and Samuel. They are already winning Minnesota to Christ! Each one of you is in my heart forever. THANK YOU.

To my brother Ron. I love you, and am so very proud of all you've achieved in your life. Our conversations mean a lot to me. THANK YOU.

To our spiritual son, Adam Allison. During your three years at Bethel's School of the Supernatural you spent most of your Thursday nights at our home having dinner with Georgia and me. Your spiritual growth throughout those years has been remarkable and made you wonderfully contagious. We have grown in more and more revelation knowledge of God's Word and ways through you. You are like a son to us and I'm seldom at my computer without thinking of something more you taught me about using it. THANK YOU.

To my newest spiritual son and daughter Jimmy and Ashley Gingerich, and to my three God-children: Israel, Gabriel, and Makayla Areal. You have greatly honored Georgia and me in making us such a special part of your beautiful family. THANK YOU.

To Morgan and Shirley Fisher my awesome publishers who believed in Georgia and me from the very beginning of our amazing adventure in coming to Bethel. THANK YOU for your overwhelming love, your Taco Tuesday Nights and your generous loving hearts. Like your son Bradley you keep bringing your own kind of magic into our lives. Your passion to get God's Word out through books should excite every Christian writer. You're the best. The Mossholders and Fishers will be great friends eternally. THANK YOU.

To our precious friends, Dana Fisher and Marjorie Muir. Morgan and I know we couldn't have gotten this book printed without your tender love and care. THANK YOU.

To Torsten Wimmer my Audio Engineer, one of the most patient young men that I have ever known. You have brought this book to life making Georgia Mae and me sound wonderful. Five Real Friends has become an amazing audio presentation because of you. Your proffessional skills are profound and you made our work fun. THANK YOU.

To Francesco Sideli. Your name is already becoming greatly known thoughout the world for the creative genius and artist that you are. Your Goober on the back cover of this book is Goob all right. And only you my friend could have painted his picture so perfectly. THANK YOU.

To Dr. Craig Lamb, C.E.O. of International University in Tulsa. who has been my a spiritual son to me for many years and has now dedicated himself to fully restoring me to ministry and releasing Being Goober Boober everywhere.

May God reward all your hours of work on my behalf abundantly with non-stop salvations and healings through both of us. The old Ray died. The new Ray is thrilled to be running with Christ every day. Again and again amazing grace! THANK YOU.

To Dorothy Bakker who has been a precious friend to me since the never-to-be-forgotten days of PTL. You painstakingly examined every single word I wrote in the very first manuscripts of this book making welcome corrections. Thank God for e-mail and cell phones! I was in Redding, California, and you were in Charlotte, North Carolina, but there was never any distance between us. THANK YOU.

To Bethel Elementary principal, Don Mayer, a real encourager to me, who had some of your students evaluate my book. And to teacher Debi Armstrong whose sticky notes in a couple of the chapters you read gave me still greater insight into kid's today. THANK YOU.

To my kid's panel - those young people who read a nearly final manuscript of this book before it was complete and for their valuable comments that have helped me write this book – Ashliegh Gillie in Australia, Isaiah and Elijah Wimmer in Nicaragua, Elise Tkacyzk from Norway, Sasha Hollenbeck in Alaska, and my Granddaughter, Becka Hinson, in Maryland. And these outstanding students from Bethel Elementary School – Emma Gore, Bailey Morris, Julianna Stoker, Grant Bradbeer, Cameron Vollmers, and my spiritual Granddaughter, Charissa Humble. THANK YOU.

To the adults who read earlier manuscripts of this book as well – my daughter, Elizabeth Mossholder; my cousin, Jane Johnson; Milton and Anne Gillie in Australia and Lynn Streitzel in Taiwan and now at Bethel. THANK YOU.

To Jim and Carole Boersma, who believed in me no matter what I did. For four years you "sozo" ministered to me on the phone weekly. I owe my sanity to what the Lord did through you with your counseling and prayers. Your ministry like your friendship is profound. THANK YOU.

To Reverend Dick Joyce, my precious friend, extraordinary pastor in Mexico City and powerful fellow evangelist during the Charismatic Movement of the 70's and The River now. You would not let me go. We spent a year and a half before my recovery e-mailing back and forth daily to each other. Then you connected me with our mutual friend, Reverend Bill Johnson. The rest is history. THANK YOU.

To Dr. Vern Erwin my Southern California friend and dentist for nearly forty years. You and your beautiful wife Jena literally saved my life last year by gifting me with extensive dental surgery. And to Dr. Ron Trombley, my Northern California dentist. You gifted me with all eight teeth to replace those that had been extracted. Because of you, I opened my mouth and God filled it! THANK YOU.

To my great buddy and teaching colleague Stephen Collar and his wife Pam. Stephen you are the greatest "seer" I've ever known. No wonder angels constantly surround you. You and Pam are a total joy to me and most treasured friends. Our weekly co-teaching at "The Gathering" and our weekly supernatural meetings with two of God's greatest women – Anne Kalvestrand and Sarah Larson - and greatest men - Adam Allison - in our "New Brains" group - praying for autistic and brain damaged children and seeing God's miraculous results was above all I could ask or think. Stay totally well my friend. This world needs you SO MUCH and so do I. THANK YOU.

To the amazing mother and still other teaching colleague at "The Gathering" – Lynne Wimmer. I can hardly wait to hear you speak each week. And when anyone tells me kids are too immature to say the things Goober and his pals say in this book I'd like to have them spend ten minutes with your two sons - Isaiah and Elijah. They would totally change their minds! Your husband Scott is just like you and so is Torsten. What an amazing family! WOW! THANK YOU.

To all of you who attended our weekly Bible study "THE GATHERING". It was pure joy to watch you grow in Christ and to watch "THE GATHERING" grow. THANK YOU for the honor of your close friendship. We love and cherish each of you. THANK YOU.

These following friends have also been Georgia and my cheerleaders in the last three years any time the road seemed roughest. You have deeply impacted us with your friendship and specific words and deeds that we will remember all the days of our lives:

Our overseas friends (thank God for Skype!): Diana Boeva in Bulgaria, Milton and Anne Gillie in Australia, and Bruce and Julie Forlong and Doug and Clare Vallance in New Zealand.

And nearer home: Kathie and Dean Vanaugh and Gwen and Frank Rogers whos giving helped keep us going.

To Bethel friends: Darlene Johnson, Gene and Nell Niccolet, Mary Chico, Sal and Carol Girdano, Glen and Cheryl Loder, Ian Zedwick, Van Mason, Michael and Kristy Joyce, Robin and Hannah Hall, Joanie Dragland, Ryan Smerber, JP and Laci Lyons, Norm and Doris Lavell, Glen and Tammi Callendar, Curtis and Carol Neitsch.

And our e-mail, Facebook, letter, cell phone, and visiting friends: Kathy Kurland, Betty Moser, Dorthy Bakker, Bob and Jan Claus, Dr. Tom and Patrica Brussat, Dave and Joan Crissman, Jim and Doris Costopulos, Dee Patrick, Wendy Arelis, Ben and Denise Charles, Wease and Mike Bever, Joe and Sandy Graffi, and Jane Johnson and Ken and Rosamond Wallace. THANK YOU.

To Juaquin Evans. You've given me far greater understanding regarding healing and also the joy of being part of your mighty healing team. And to Steve DeSilva whose knowledge regarding financial management has been priceless to Georgia and me. Your graciousness to us has made you a very treasured friend. THANK YOU.

To four great ladies: Those who make Bethel's Eagles Nest Bookstore happen – Phyllis McCorison, Missy Niswander, and Deborah Parsch; and Bethel's receptionist who makes all the right connections – Amber Primm. You are such hard workers, forever fun, warm and friendly. As busy as you stay, it's always a joy to talk with you. THANK YOU.

I began to write acknowledgements for ALL the people who have become close friends to Georgia and me since we came to Bethel or who remained close friends during my dark years. But when I began writing the second hundred names and I still remembered more I realized that if I included ALL who are our friends it would require a book as least as large as this one. You know who you are. So do we. We are SO thankful for you, and our hearts are linked forever. THANK YOU.

And to my champion and role model, Dick Mills. If I can just catch your mantle without you having to die I will be blessed above all men. THANK YOU.

Introduction

Few joys in my life have equaled the joy of writing Being Goober Boober. I love Goober, Tracey, Alfonso, Willie, and Pee Wee. They are as real to me as any humans are. Now every time Georgia and I go to church for one of its many services I keep expecting to find the five friends sitting all together there. They'll wave and ask us to come sit with them because that's just the way they are. And we'll be thrilled to join them.

If I say this book was written even in part by the Holy Spirit I'm sure I'll be accused by some of arrogance. It wasn't written like the Bible was written that's for sure. But I have marveled often as I've been writing this book to hear the Holy Spirit directing me to take twists and turns I had in no way intended to take with this story. It should require no stretch of any Christian's imagination to realize that if we who love Christ can be "Spirit led," then our writing certainly can be "Spirit led" as well.

Seven of the people who grace this book are real people, and Georgia and I are SO GLAD they are. They include Pastor Wendell McGowan at the River Church in Redding, Kevin Dedmon, Cris Gore, Cris Overstreet, the biker usher – John Graham, and the greeter at the sanctuary entrance, Ron Spencer - all vital parts of Bethel Church, also in Redding. Randy Clark, whom Tracey quotes, is a magnificent Bible teacher and ministers powerfully in healing worldwide.

Although the major characters in this book are fictional, Bo Branders particular healing style is patterned after healing evangelists in my past that I have known or seen and greatly admired.

The fictional Wake Up, California, is patterned after a real city too. And Amazing Grace Church is just like a church I know well and also greatly admire. In this book,

Tracey Dare actually describes only a tiny few of the miracles that have happened at this church recently, or through its outreach. Christ's miracles continue constant there, and constant wherever the pastors, staff, or the revivalists they train for every nation, go. People regularly fly in from all over the world to be there with sicknesses, diseases, infirmities, and terminal illnesses and after they've been to this church a thrilling amount of them return home whole and completely well. Recreative miracles – the Holy Spirit either restoring body parts or instantly creating new ones - are a regular occurrence at this church.

So why aren't I naming this church I know so well? Because this church is one of a constantly growing River of churches like it throughout America and the world that are releasing more and more joy in the kingdom of God, bringing salvation, healing and awesome miracles, that Jesus Christ loves doing. The River works with all denominations and non-denominations. It tells pastors and Christians NOT to abandon their own denomination or church to join "our" movement. Instead it invites them to be totally open from now on to everything the Holy Spirit wants to do in and through them to bring Christ's love, Word, and power to the streets of their own city and to the uttermost parts of the world. How else could the body of Christ honestly and joyfully say we are KEEPING CHRIST FIRST DAILY in our lives?

In Matthew 6:10, during what is often called by all Christians "The Lord's Prayer', Jesus Christ teaches us to ask God to bring heaven to earth. There is no sickness and there are no messed up lives in heaven. That means Christ's offer of salvation, restoration, healing and miracles should be totally transforming people not only in churches but in each church's city as well as all over the Earth. The River is VERY SUPERNATURAL because GOD is VERY SUPERNATURAL. As Tracey Dare quotes, 'The real church service should begin when the congregation goes out the church door'.

From the waitress's miracle healing while being prepared for surgery to the cheerleader being healed at a football game and thirty students coming to Christ during that game to the transformation salvation makes in teenagers that creates in them deep spiritual hunger - these are NOT make-believe happenings, but events that have already happened and continue to happen at this church I know so well. This church and those church's now swimming in The River of the Holy Spirit expect such things to happen regularly because God in His Bible has said they would.

My favorite remark from one of the kids that read a recent manuscript of this book is: "THIS BOOK is God's powerful answer to Harry Potter!" Miracles, signs and wonders should be a part of every Christian life including yours. As Bo Branders quotes in his great message to the kids – Luke 1:37 – "NOTHING is impossible with God."

Though I wrote this book for the enjoyment of young people I wrote it too for people of ALL ages. "Unless you change and become like children you cannot even find the entrance point to the kingdom of God." (Matthew 18:3 paraphrased).

Ray Mossholder - Redding, California

Foreward

Ray is one of my closest friends. To hear him teach the Bible is pure joy and a constant learning experience. He is a true Bible scholar.

Ray is also a man of great integrity who knows what it is to take a long bumpy ride on the Potter's wheel after 34 years of international ministry. He thought his ministry years were over while he rode there, but God NEVER thought that. Ray hasn't only been restored, he's been made new by Jesus Christ for far greater ministry in this 21st Century.

Ray has the rare quality of being able to see into the hearts of God's children of all ages. People know they're loved by God and him wherever he is. His writing transforms his readers in the power of Christ that very same way. His characters aren't just people on a page. Get ready to fall in love with Goober Boober, Alfonso Guitterez, Tracey Dare, Willie Radner, and Pee Wee Fritz - straight from God's heart. By the time you've finished this book you'll know God, or know Him and His ways better than you ever have before.

Happy reading!

Steven Collar - Redding, California

Five Real Friends

Contents

Five Real Friends

Chapter One

Goober And The Bomber Brothers

"There are times when just to be alive is to be winning." That was the thought being flipped around in Goober Boober's brain as he slowly dragged himself to school.

Goober was thirteen, short for his age and skinny. "I could look right through you!" Grandma Ritchie had told him.

Goober had "dirt brown hair", according to his dad, freckles that didn't know where to land on his face, big bushy eyebrows, and a nose that at this moment was just too big. And though he would grow to be a handsome young man, he was, and he knew he was, an ugly duckling at thirteen.

Goober's eyes were brownish-hazel and he wished they were any other color so that he'd look like something Tracey Dare might like. Tracey was the first girl Goober ever really recognized was a girl. She was the cutest girl he'd ever seen. Goober thought of himself as very plain, "As plain as chewing gum", as his dad had told him many times.

But it was what his mother had said three times that morning as he ate his bowl of Cheerios with whole milk that troubled him. He wished he could be anywhere but on his way to Thomas Edison Middle School in Wake Up, California. He knew the wretchedly awful Bomber brothers were waiting there to torture him to death.

Was what his mom, Mimi Boober, said true? Was just being alive enough to make you a winner? Goober laughed out loud in spite of himself. No. Right now he'd rather be in the morgue on a cold slab, lying silent and no longer able to think, than to be facing whatever latest torture the Bomber brothers had planned for him. He didn't know what it would be, but they'd told him it would be hideous. Then they'd laughed.

The Bomber Brothers, Morty and Tinker, were 14 and 15, older by at least a year than any other student in their classroom. And since they'd come to Thomas Edison a month ago they'd found Goober their favorite toy. They'd dumped his head in the toilet of the boy's bathroom in front of all the other guys. They'd stripped him down to his underwear and thrown him in front of the girls in the schoolyard - including Tracey Dare. They'd torn up his report on the history of Star Wars. And they'd locked him in the gymnasium for one long and horrible night. And now the Bombers had planned some new ghastly surprise to make him wish what he wished now.

"I wish I was dead," Goober said to himself. Then immediately, Goober, being really honest about all this, realized he didn't seriously want to be dead like he'd never be able to come back and feed his goldfish, Henry. But dead like you could be dead, then alive again when you touched your nose. Touch it and you were dead so nobody could hurt you. Touch it again and zap! you're back at home again with a big bowl of chocolate ice cream ready to be devoured. He didn't want to die for all time - just for any time the Bomber brothers were able to get to him.

Fourteen-year-old Morty Bomber was six foot three in his stocking feet. He had bulging biceps from working out with weights, steel-blue eyes, a crooked smile, and two jagged teeth in front that made him far less handsome than his brother.

Fifteen year-old Tinker Bomber was six foot four. He had a great set of teeth and a smile that made girls swoon.

Both of the Bombers wore designer jeans and bright colored shirts that always made their red hair look extra bright and caught everybody's eyes. Girls wished they were the Bomber's girlfriends because the Bombers were so "cool".

But these brothers had made younger guys lives hideous wherever they'd gone from the time they were seven and eight. It started one day when they put a whole bottle of Listerine in Freddy Dool's Fruit Loops. The Listerine blended beautifully with all those colors of the Loops. Freddy hadn't noticed it. He'd hardly looked at his cereal before he took a huge bite. He gasped, choked, ran to the bathroom, and threw up. He was home sick for the next two days.

The Bomber brothers had watched this whole event with laughter. They thought it was hilarious. As Freddy threw up they gave each other high fives. From then on they had dedicated their lives to making smaller kids cry, and Goober was exactly their kind of victim.

Goober's real first name was Throckmorton. He hated that name and gladly accepted a nickname. It was his mom who began calling him 'Peanut', because she said he was small and hadn't come out of his shell yet. But his dad said, "A peanut is a goober, and that's what he really is. I'm going to call him 'Goober'." The name stuck.

It was OK when he was four. He really didn't begin wondering about his nickname until he started school and the rest of the students thought it was hilarious. So did all the teachers at the school. Whenever any of them looked at Goober, his name made them laugh. But they only talked with other teachers about how silly a name it was when Goober couldn't hear them. So Goober simply wondered why the teachers laughed as he walked by. He hoped it was because he made them happy.

Goober was a bright student, quick to learn. He had loved school until the Bomber brothers became part of his class. Morty sat directly in front of Goober, and Tinker sat directly behind him, trapping him like a sardine in a can.

One day Goober wore a bright shirt, thinking it looked kind of like what the Bomber brothers wore and maybe it would make him look more like one of them. It was pink and blue with green zigzags and yellow polka-dots all over, and it had purple stripes around the collar. The truth is, neither of the Bomber brothers would have been caught dead in such a shirt.

Mrs. Plumpff, his teacher, took one look at the back of Goober's shirt and said, "That's not a proper shirt to wear to school young man." The whole class laughed as his teacher sent him home to change it.

Before he left the classroom, Goober tried to explain to her that his mother hadn't had time to iron a shirt and had simply pulled this one out of the back of his closet and handed it to him. Mrs. Plumff said, "Go home and change it anyway. That is a completely inappropriate shirt to wear AT ALL."

At home, before he left for school, Goober and his mother had only looked at the front of his shirt. They had forgotten entirely about the large ripped hole in the back. "I'll rip up your next one too," Tinker sneered as Goober walked by his desk on the way to the classroom door.

Goober was afraid to talk about his horrible ordeal of being locked overnight in the gym. But one day, in a moment of despair, he finally did tell his mother about it. She put her arms around him to comfort him and he completely broke down crying and told her all the rest of the things that the Bombers had done to him. Mimi Goober was furious. She said "I'm going to your principal, Mr. Hirkshire, and I'm going to tell him everything they've been doing."

But when she told Goober's dad, Rex, that night about it, Rex said, "You're not going to do any such thing. Two things that the Boobers aren't are tattle-tales and mommy's boys. Goober just has to learn to take care of himself."

When Goober tried to explain to Rex that he didn't stand a chance against two evil giants like the Bombers, his dad answered him, "I always fought and won my own battles in school. You can do it too."

Rex was more than six feet tall and had been muscular as long as he could remember. Fighting was second nature to him. From the first grade on, Rex could push down and sit on any boy in his classroom. Later he seldom had to fight because of his size.

Mr. and Mrs. Boober had lived in Wake Up, California, for twenty years. Nearly everyone who graduated from Thomas Edison went on to John Kennedy High School where Goober's older brother, Clyde, had already graduated. Clyde was tall and built much more like his father than Goober was. He didn't fight often. With his build he scared away those who might otherwise have challenged him, just as his father had.

Wake Up had been a very small town when the Boobers moved there. Now it was a small city. Goober remembered with sorrow the day the Bomber brothers first came to class. The fatal date was September fourteenth. Today was October twenty-first. "October twenty-first," thought Goober. "I'm going to die on October twenty-first!"

Goober did have a best friend. His name was Alfonso. He spotted Alfonso walking just a block ahead of him. "Hey, Al, wait up," Goober shouted. Immediately Alfonso looked back at Goober, smiled, and waited for him.

Alfonso's dad was the manager of Winco Foods Grocery Store in Wake Up. After college, he and his wife had gone to Mexico City where Alfonso was born. They moved to Wake Up when Alfonso was seven. Goober and Alfonso immediately became best friends when they began first grade. Alfonso was a bit taller than Goober but skinny too. He had jet black hair, and beautiful brown skin that once made Goober ask him how any American could be racially prejudiced against Mexican people and then lie out in front of swimming pools or on beaches all summer trying to get a tan as great as Alfonso's. "I don't know," Alfonso answered. "Some people are funny that way."

Goober ran to where Alfonso had waited for him. He greeted his friend. "What's new, Bugaloo?" This was a special "hi" just between these two friends that they often gave each other instead of just saying hello.

"Nothing much," Alfonso replied. But Alfonso saw the worried look on Goober's face. "I'm sorry I ran away yesterday when the Bombers were chasing you. I should have stayed with you and helped you fight them off."

Goober smiled, "It's OK, Al. I'd have done the same thing. I was really scared. But Tinker just caught me and held me, and he didn't do anything more. Morty did it all with what he said. He got real close to my eyes and stared into them like he was looking right through me. Then he said, with that voice he uses when he's getting ready to kill, 'Tomorrow, Tinker and I are going to take you to the roof of the school building and leave you there. Better carry dinner with you. You're going to be there a long, long time! We've got one other surprise for you too, but we won't tell you what it is until tomorrow. Telling you would spoil our fun, and you wouldn't want to do that would you? Oh, and if any of your dimwit friends try in any way to help you by telling a teacher or someone else, or try to get you down from the roof, they'll wish they hadn't. We've got great plans for gruesomely torturing anyone who does that too!'"

"What are you going to do, Goob? This time I swear I'll stay and die with you if I have to."

"No!" said Goober solemnly. "I don't want you to do that. Live. Then tell everyone that I was your best friend. Think about it. There's nothing I can do. Once the Bomber's grab me, I'm dead meat. You'd be dead meat too if you were with me."

As Goober and Alfonso entered the schoolyard both boys felt sick. Alfonso knew as much as he liked Goober that he would run away again when the Bomber's got near them. Alfonso was faster than Goober and he knew he could get away while they were catching his friend.

Goober knew he would be forced to go to the roof right after school. He didn't stand a chance of getting away. "What are they going to do to me THEN?" he silently agonized.

The night he'd spent in the gym was horrible. He'd tried to get out every way he could think of, but nothing worked. He was cold and miserable all night long. Finally the custodian, Mr. Bozznobber, let him out in the morning after asking, "What on earth have you been doing in there?" Goober couldn't tell him. He knew the Bomber brothers might even hurt Mr. Bozznobber if he did.

Then Goober walked home to find his parents had been up all night. They'd even called the police. His mom was worried sick. But what surprised Goober most was that even his dad seemed to have worried through the night. However, he stopped worrying the moment Goober explained where he had been and why. Then he got mad and gave Goober a very loud, long, and angry lecture for not stopping the Bombers from locking him in. Mimi just sat in the same armchair where she'd been throughout the night saying, "Oh my! Oh my!"

Clyde laughed when he heard what happened and mockingly told Goober, "You really are a wimp, Shrimp!"

Goober and Alfonso entered their classroom. Most of the kids were in their seats and first bell was about to ring, but Morty and Tinker weren't there. Hope leapt into Goober's heart as he saw their empty seats. Alfonso pointed to both seats where the Bomber's usually sat and gave Goober a big smile.

Mrs. Plumpff began by saying, "Turn to page forty-seven in your math books." A half hour passed. Still there was no sign of the Bombers. Alfonso kept smiling at Goober and once in awhile pointed again to the Bombers' empty seats. Goober was more and more hopeful as still another fifteen minutes went by. But fifty minutes after class had begun, Morty and Tinker walked in. Goober saw them as they entered the classroom and his heart did the limbo, sinking to the lowest place it had ever been. All his hopes were dashed in one split second. He knew again that this would be his doomsday.

On hearing her classroom door open, Mrs. Plumpff turned and saw the Bomber brothers enter. Everyone looked up too as Tinker and Morty made a spectacular entrance. They wore bright blue shirts and their flame-red hair looked brilliant. As soon as they saw Mrs. Plumpff, both of them dropped their heads and acted very sorry for being so late to class. Mrs. Plumpff asked them, "Just where have you two boys been?"

Morty lowered his head and answered, "We're really sorry for being late, Mrs. Plumpff. As our mom was driving us to school her car ran out of gas. We had to walk a long way to a gas station and then bring a gallon back to her. Mom said she'll give us a note for you that we can bring tomorrow."

"Yes, do that," their teacher told them. "I'm glad you were able to help your mother. Both of you take your seats."

As Mrs. Plumpff turned to write something on the chalkboard she didn't see the huge grins the Bombers gave each other. Walking to their seats they smiled even wider at Goober. Morty whispered, "We've got big plans for you after school, Smallfry!"

At exactly 11:17 a.m., while Mrs. Plumpff had her back turned away from her class again to write some new spelling words on the chalkboard, Goober felt a piece of paper being stuffed down the back of his shirt. He knew it was a note from Tinker. Tinker had written many ugly notes to him in the past month and delivered them exactly this way. With great dread, Goober reached to the back of his shirt and retrieved the note. It read:

I hope you brought a BIG dinner you little cockroach because my brother and I are really going to be hungry after school. We can hardly wait to take you to your roof party. You're not going to like your surprise. Tinker

Goober had thought the Bombers might not wait until after school, but actually grab him during lunch hour. At least now he knew he might be able to eat something before his awful march to the roof!

The hands on the clock moved oh so slowly. Suddenly a song came into Goober's mind. It was from a really old western movie he and Clyde had seen on TV. The movie was called *High Noon*. He remembered the hero of the movie, a sheriff back in the days of the Old West. A bad man wanted to shoot the sheriff. In the big showdown the good sheriff and the bad guy faced each other to duel on the main street of town. Goober pictured himself facing the Bomber brothers that same way. "I could outdraw them and get them both before they got me." And then Goober shook his head and said to himself, "Why even think about that when I don't have a gun and I wouldn't use one anyway?" Finally, after what seemed like an eternity, the lunch bell rang and everyone filed out of class.

The Bomber brothers were waiting right outside the door where Morty whispered in Goober's ear, "See you right after school, you little zero!" Their jeans were at half mast and they swaggered away laughing like hyenas.

Alfonso went with his sad friend to the lunchroom where he downed a hamburger, large French-fries, and a milkshake. Goober had ordered a hamburger too, but only took two bites. It tasted like cardboard in his mouth. He was silent and just stared into space. Alfonso tried to cheer him up, "Hey, Goob, they weren't there at the beginning of class today. Maybe they won't come back after lunch."

Goober answered, "Yes they will. They wouldn't miss their roof-party for anything. I may as well face it. My life is over as soon as school is out today!"

Alfonso couldn't stand to see Goober so down. He thought a moment and said, "I've made up my mind to help you no matter what happens to me. You're my best amigo. I can't let you go through this alone."

Goober was moved by his friend's vow and knew Alfonso meant it. But Goober told him, "No. You can't do that. I've thought a lot about it since you got away from them yesterday. I told you I would have done the same thing if I was you. Let's face it. The Bombers are too big and too strong. They've sworn they'll gruesomely torture anyone at all who tries to help me. That's why I didn't tell my mom. If they tortured you because of me I would hate myself forever."

Alfonso asked, "Why didn't you tell your dad? He's stronger than both Bombers put together. Or tell Clyde? He's big enough to stop them."

"Because," answered Goober, "my dad would just laugh and tell me to beat them up. He wouldn't help me. Clyde would be worse. He'd be glad to watch it happen. He'd probably grab me for Tinker and Morty so that they could take me to the roof. Al, as much as I know you are my best friend, I'm going to have to go through this alone. But thanks for caring."

The two boys walked slowly back to their classroom. Neither spoke as they walked. They stood silent outside the classroom door until the second bell was about to ring. The Bombers were no doubt already inside. When they walked in, there they sat. Both winked at Goober with a smirk and sneered as Goober grimly took his seat.

Mrs. Plumpff began speaking and Goober daydreamed again. He was Superman. When the Bombers grabbed him he conveniently said, "Please excuse me. I have to make one phone call!" He slipped out of their hands and jumped inside a phone booth. (There really wasn't one at Edison.) He took off his outside clothes, and then and there he became the caped man with the letter S on his chest. He stepped out of the phone booth and was up up and away, grabbing both Tinker and Morty. He smiled as he dropped the Bomber brothers in the middle of the ocean. "Goodbye forever," he called, and waved to them as he flew away and they sank to the bottom of the sea.

Goober suddenly came out of his daydream when he felt yet another note being jammed down the back of his shirt. Retrieving it he read:

Be ready to be with Morty and me just as soon as school is out. We'll be waiting right outside the door. Don't try to run or you'll REALLY get hurt. Tinker

Goober read the note and then dropped it on the floor, grinding it with his right foot. Neither Morty nor Tinker saw him do it. But he wished that it was both of them he was mashing like that.

Minutes dragged by like hours. Each hour seemed like ten. He knew Mrs. Plumpff was teaching, but he couldn't hear her. The worst Halloween House of Horrors didn't hold as many monsters as Goober's imagination did.

Finally it was five minutes til three. Goober thought, "If only I could become invisible I'd slither out under the door and go home safe. They'd never see me leave." But even as he thought that he realized how totally impossible it was. "I'm visible," he thought in this moment of miserable surrender.

Although it wasn't at all a hot day, a bead of sweat appeared on Goober's forehead. He wished he could hold the clock hands still so that it never would become 3 o'clock. But he knew that was impossible too. There was just no use pretending. All at once the bell rang and Goober nearly jumped out of his skin.

Goober heard a low mocking laugh behind him. Tinker had seen him jump. "Scared, Jerk?" Tinker whispered menacingly. He added, "Poor little baby!" in a way that let Goober know that the more scared he was, the happier it made Tinker. Goober just sat there and tried to act calm. There was nothing he could say or do that would change a thing. He hoped Tinker couldn't hear his loudly beating heart.

Tinker got out of his seat, bent down, and still in an evil tone, tauntingly whispered in Goober's ear, "See you outside, Goob. I don't think you're ever going to want to smile again!" He joined the leaving crowd of kids and winked at Morty as they both strutted out the door.

Alfonso spoke to Goober as soon as the Bomber brothers were outside. "Let me walk out with you, Goob. This time I promise I won't run."

Goober knew his friend meant it, but he told him, "Don't even think about it. Just remember, you were the best friend I've ever had."

Alfonso couldn't think of any way to help him. He felt sick for Goober as Goober walked slowly toward the door.

Outside, the Bomber brothers were doing just what they'd promised. They were waiting eagerly for Goober. As soon as he stepped through the doorway, Tinker grabbed him and pushed him up against the wall. He put a hand on Goober's left shoulder and Morty put a hand on his right. Goober was now pinned against the wall like a dead butterfly pinned in a scrapbook.

"Now you little freak," Tinker growled, "you're going up to the roof. But we're going to wait here until Mrs. Plumpff leaves the room. We don't want to upset her when she finds her dumbest student isn't going home tonight!"

It seemed forever before Mrs. Plumpff came outside. Alfonso was walking with her. "Is everything all right boys?" the teacher asked them.

"Oh yes, Mrs. Plumpff," lied Morty. "We're just having a friendly chat with Goob. We're getting to be good pals. Isn't that right, Goob?"

Goober could do nothing else but nod his head. That seemed to satisfy Mrs. Plumpff and with no further words she walked on. Alfonso walked on too.

"Well, Maggot," Tinker growled again, "looks like your best buddy isn't really your buddy at all. He's yellow as mustard. Did you see him run away from the three of us yesterday? He looked like a track star he ran so fast. I'll bet he left a yellow streak behind him wherever he went."

"Yeah," added Morty. "He probably sounded like the little pig that cried 'Wee! Wee! Wee! all the way home!' He's so chicken, Colonel Sanders will feed him to somebody for dinner!" Tinker and Morty both roared with laughter.

When they stopped laughing, the Bomber brothers let go of Goober's shoulders and with no one in sight, picked Goober up - Morty at his head, Tinker at his feet - and began carrying him towards the gymnasium.

After entering the gymnasium they continued carrying Goober up on to the stage. No one was there but the three of them.

"OK, Morty, on the count of three," Tinker said. Then he counted, "1, 2, 3," and both boys let go of Goober at the same moment. WHAM!

Goober's body struck the hardwood floor so hard it knocked all the wind out of him. When his head hit the floor he got an instant headache. But the Bomber brothers laughed again at the sight of Goober hurting. Morty said, "Hey, Goob, you do a really good floorshow!"

"Not so much noise, Stink," Tinker scowled, though Goober hadn't said a word or even let out a sound, except the sound of all his air leaving him at once.

Tinker barked, "Where's that dinner you were supposed to bring, Squirt? I told you we'd be hungry." When Goober didn't answer, Tinker put his right foot hard on Goober's stomach and shouted, "Hey, Dummy, I asked you a question. Answer me or I'll put my foot right through you!"

"I didn't bring one," Goober answered quickly.

"What?" Morty asked, "You didn't bring us any dinner? Are you trying to make us starve? You're so cruel. Oh well, never mind. You aren't going to be able to eat anyway after what we do to you. In fact," he laughed, "you may never eat again!"

Tinker stared down at Goober and asked him, "Did you ever lose a tooth?" Goober nodded one quick nod, remembering his trip to his dentist and having to have one pulled. He remembered how much he hurt afterwards. "Well, here's your surprise: Tonight you're going to lose them all!"

Immediately Morty picked up a frighteningly large pair of pliers he'd hidden behind a stage curtain. "Yeah, you ugly little twerp," Morty snarled, "you didn't know we were dentists, did you? You are really disgusting to look at and we've been getting sick every time we've seen you smile. But, don't worry, we're your very best buddies and we're going to fix your smile for you! You'll look lots better without any teeth. Won't that be nice?"

When Goober didn't answer, Tinker shouted at him, "My brother asked you a question, Stupid. WON'T THAT BE NICE?"

Goober knew he had to agree or maybe he'd lose his teeth right then. "Uh huh," Goober said, knowing that the Bombers could do anything they wanted to do to him because they were so much bigger and stronger than he was.

"Well," Morty said, "get up, Jackie boy. We're going to climb this beanstalk!"

Goober rose, and Tinker shoved him to a tall ladder saying, "Girls first." Goober put his hands on the first rung and began pulling himself up the ladder.

As terrible as this was going to be, Goober tried not to give the Bombers any *more* pleasure by seeing how much he really was afraid. That night he'd been locked in the gymnasium, Goober did cry because he felt so all alone and scared. When he had told his mom about it, she told him, "There is nothing unmanly about boys or men crying. It just shows they have deep feelings, Goober. That's why you cried."

Goober could never tell his dad or Clyde that he had broken down sobbing during his dark night in that gym. They would have laughed at him if they had known. They would have started calling Goober a "crybaby". And Goober knew the Bomber brothers would make things even worse if he let go of the terrified feelings that were inside him now.

After Goober was a little way up the ladder, Tinker, holding the pliers, grabbed hold of both sides and hoisted himself up below Goober. It would only be a few minutes more now and Goober knew he'd lose all his teeth on the gymnasium roof. "What if I kicked Tinker in the face and knocked him off this ladder? Maybe Morty would fall too, and I could scramble...."

Then he stopped thinking that way. Reality seized him and he knew his little foot, compared to Tinker's quick big hands, would be no match for each other at all. Tinker would just grab his foot and probably pull Goober completely off the ladder. Besides, there was no place to run where they couldn't easily catch him again. There was no way out, just up.

Goober shuddered and ran his tongue over first his top teeth and then his bottom teeth. He wondered how he'd look to people tomorrow with no teeth at all! Tracey Dare would NEVER want to look at him again. And he could just imagine the pain inside his mouth that would never stop.

Suddenly Goober heard Morty yell loudly, "Hey! Let go of my foot! Who are you?" Goober was now a long way up the ladder and he had never liked heights until this very moment. But now looking below him he saw that his dad, Clyde, and his mom, were standing there along with Mrs. Plumpff, Mr. Hirkshire, and Mr. Bozznobber. He was shocked to see them. It took a moment for his mind to adjust to the miracle that was happening that would set him free.

Finally, looking directly at the bottom of the ladder, he saw a police officer bringing Morty off of it and Tinker coming off right afterwards. The police officer immediately took Tinker's pliers and then handcuffed the brothers to each other. It was only then that Goober saw the smallest member of the crowd. Alfonso was there too, grinning the biggest grin Goober had ever seen him grin!

"What's new, Bugaloo?" Alfonso happily shouted to Goober as Goober began his way back down the ladder.

Goober shouted back, "Not much now I guess!" Soon his foot touched the stage and his mother ran and hugged her son. "Oh my! Oh my!" she said.

Everyone was talking at once. Goober stood there with his mother's arms around him, trying to figure it all out. How did any of them know where he was? Or that the Bomber brothers had taken him to that ladder on the stage of the gymnasium? Why did both his dad and Clyde even care? Then it all became clear.

Rex Boober, Goober's dad, suddenly said, "Yes, those are the two thieves who stole computers from my store this morning!"

Morty yelled, "No we didn't. We were in school today, all day. Isn't that right, Mrs. Plumpff?"

Mrs. Plumpff answered, "No, Morty, it isn't. You both came in almost an hour late. Mr. Boober explained why. He said two redheaded boys who looked exactly like you and your brother came into his store about 9 a.m. and ran out several minutes later carrying two brand new computers that they hadn't paid for. That accounts for your late arrival in my classroom."

Police Officer McNair told Morty and Tinker, "You are under arrest. You have the right to remain silent and the right to legal counsel. But anything you say now, can and will be used against you in a court of law."

Tinker spoke up, "You can't prove we took those computers. Lots of guys look like us."

Mr. Boober smiled and answered, "Lots of guys your age have flaming red hair and dress like they've just stepped out of a fashion magazine?"

Morty tried again, "But Mrs. Plumpff, don't you remember that our mom ran out of gas while she was driving us to school? That's why we were late."

Mrs. Plumpff said, "That won't work, Morty. I've already phoned your mother. She said this morning was the third time you and your brother have taken her car without asking and driven away. And, of course, at your ages, you have no driver's licenses!"

"It was easy to find the computers, boys," Police Officer Rafferty explained. "We did that an hour ago. You forgot to lock your mother's car. I reached inside and removed a blanket from the back seat and what do you know? There they were, two computers, just like Mr. Boober had described them."

Morty and Tinker looked at each other in desperation. Then Morty got another idea. He said, "Officer, I've told you that my brother and I didn't go near a computer store this morning. I guess maybe when we left Mom's car unlocked, whoever stole those computers stuffed them under our blanket in there to hide them. We'll be glad to help you find out who really did this."

Officer Rafferty answered, "You won't be needing to do that, Son. When we got those two computers to the police station your fingerprints were all over them!"

Morty and Tinker began to shake. "Oh," added Officer Rafferty, "and this wasn't the first stealing you've done. You actually used guns to rob two 7-Eleven's last week. And you'll be happy to know you both looked real handsome on their store's security cameras!"

Custodian Bozznobber told them, "I knew you two were no good when last Wednesday you walked all over my favorite Petunias. You stomped on every one of them. I knew it was you because I recognized the footprints. No other students in this school wear clodhoppers as big as yours!"

Tinker did one last thing. He whispered to Goober, "Just wait til we get back to school and grab you again! We'll pull more than your teeth! You'll wish you'd never been born!"

Principal Hirkshire heard Tinker. He smiled and said, "Tinker, you won't ever be back to this school. Both your brother and you are expelled!"

Officer Rafferty piped in, "Besides boys, you'll be going to a new kind of school. When I was your age they called it 'Reform School', and you boys have A LOT of reforming to do. You'll be spending a very long time at Youth Authority."

The walk back to the Principal's office was a thrilling one for Goober. He had a grin on his face that matched Alfonso's. Mimi Boober was beaming too, but completely unaware how close her son had come to having to gum all his food!

Everyone but the police officers and the Bomber brothers went into Mr. Hirkshire's inner office. The brothers remained handcuffed and were put in the back seat of a police car. Officer McNair got into the passenger side of the front seat and Officer Rafferty drove all of them away.

When Goober, his brother and parents, Mrs. Plumpff, Alfonso, and Mr. Bozznobber, entered the Principal's office, Mr. Hirkshire said, "Why don't we all sit down and take a deep breath. This has been quite an ordeal for Goober." Everyone sat and breathed deeply.

Goober broke the silence. "I have a question. How did any of you know the Bomber brothers were taking me up that ladder to the roof to yank out all my teeth and then leave me on the roof overnight?"

Mrs. Boober looked at her son in horror. "What were they going to do?" she gasped. "Oh my! Oh my!"

Mrs. Plumpff spoke up. "Goober, I saw you drop a note on the floor near the end of classtime today. Then you ground it with your foot. I'm so glad I didn't do what I almost did. I almost shouted at you for littering our classroom. But just as I was going to speak I saw a very mean look on Tinker's face. That made me stop and think that I'd better see exactly what was written on that note. After you left the classroom I went to the note, picked it up, and read it. I was shocked by what Tinker had written. Then Alfonso came to me."

"Alfonso?" Goober gasped.

"Yes, Goober, Alfonso came to me and told me that those awful brothers were going to leave you on the roof all night. I was horrified. But we took deep breaths too, and then walked outside and saw Tinker and Morty leaning against you. I knew how brave you were trying to be. I wanted to stop them right then and there, but I knew I needed Mr. Hirkshire's and Mr. Bozzknobber's help to do that. So, Alfonso and I came to this office at almost the same minute your parents and brother arrived to tell us about the stolen computers, and they joined Alfonso to come to your rescue."

"Wow!" Goober exclaimed.

Mrs. Plumpff continued, "There's only one thing I feel badly about. When our class was in the gymnasium two days ago, Tinker asked me where that square panel in the ceiling led. I told him. I wish I hadn't."

Goober tried to make his teacher feel better, "Oh, don't worry about it, Mrs. Plumpff. Those brothers could have pulled all my teeth out anywhere!"

Goober's mother said, "Oh my! Oh my!"

Mrs. Plumpff answered, "Yes, I suppose that's true. But you owe us finding you so quickly to your friend Alfonso."

Alfonso squirmed embarrassed in his chair. He said, "Oh, it was nothing special."

"Yes it was," Goober spoke emphatically. "You knew the Bombers said they'd gruesomely torture anyone who helped me. That's why I didn't even tell you, Mom."

Mimi once more said, "Oh my! Oh my!" And then, "Thank you, Alfonso. You are such a fine boy."

Mr. Boober stood and said, "Well, I thank you too, Alfonso. That was very brave of you. Goober really would look strange without any teeth!"

You know who once again said, "Oh my! Oh my!"

Goober's dad said, "I've got to get back to my store, but I owe a great deal of gratitude to you, Mr. Hirkshire, and to you, Mr. Bozznobber. Goober told my wife about the Bomber brothers stomping out your prize Petunias. I'd like to pay whatever it takes to give you back those flowers."

"Well, thank you, Mr. Boober," Mr. Hirkshire responded. "But you really don't owe us a thing. Goober is a fine student and we're glad to have him at Edison."

"Nevertheless," Rex Boober told him, "I'd really like to replace those flowers." Then Goober's dad motioned for Goober to stand, and when he did his dad went to him. "Goober," he said, "you were very brave. I'm extremely proud of you."

Goober swallowed hard. He had never heard his dad say anything even remotely like that before.

"You know, Goober," his dad said to him, looking straight into his eyes, "I remember a similar time to this when I was just about your age. Only there weren't two brothers I was going to face. It was just one really tough kid. He was a bully and I knew that once I got to school I was probably facing the only fight I couldn't win. So guess what I did?"

Goober asked, "What, Dad?"

Mr. Boober answered, "I ran away, Goober! Instead of going to school I went and hid in our neighbor's barn. As I lay there in some straw it came to me. 'Rex Boober, you CAN'T run away from this or you'll be running all your life.'"

Goober asked, "So what did you do then, Dad?"

Rex answered, "I stood up, brushed the straw off me, and I went to school. Sure enough, when the final bell rang and I started home, there he was - Fuzzy Felton - the toughest kid I ever saw. He challenged me. He called me chicken. And then he started to hit me. I grabbed his hand and pulled him to the ground. We rolled and hit and slapped and punched until both of us were covered with blood and our clothes were torn. You know what's funny? I never felt any of the pain he gave me until I was lying in bed that night. I've always told you I won every fight I ever fought. Well, Goober, that wasn't totally true. That one fight was a draw. It took more than an hour for both of us to finally lie exhausted on the ground, too tired to fight anymore. And you know what we did that day at the end of that fight?"

Clyde was glued to his dad's story too and blurted out, "What, Dad?"

Mr. Boober answered, "We laughed and laughed. I knew that day that nothing would ever be so big again that I couldn't face it. Fuzzy later told me he'd learned the very same thing that day because he was so surprised at the strength I'd put into the fight. Goober, that's what I've tried to make you see all your young life. Today, with those cruel Bomber brothers trying to take you to that roof, you proved to me that you now know what I've been trying to teach you since you were born. I know that nothing will ever break your spirit. I love you, Son. I love you very much."

With that, Goober's dad pulled his son close and hugged him. He'd never ever hugged him before that Goober could remember. Goober smiled the biggest smile he'd ever smiled and knew that he was growing up.

Five Real Friends

Chapter Two
The Birthday Party

Tracey Dare was having a birthday party. That was the good news. The bad news was that Elsie Dare, Tracey's mother, insisted Tracey could only invite her "seven closest friends".

"Just seven, that's all. No more than that can come," Goober moaned. "Doesn't Mrs. Dare know there are twenty-seven students in Tracey's class? And if you add Clovella Stimple to her list, her best friend after school every day, what chance do I have of ever getting invited to her party?"

"I think you'll get an invitation, Goob," Alfonso encouraged. "Larry Beale told me that Tracey says you're a hero. Tracey told him you stopped the Bomber brothers all by yourself. And she said you weren't even scared when you did it!"

With that news, Goober laughed. "Wow, do stories get twisted. YOU were the real hero, Al. You saved my neck."

"It was nothing a best friend wouldn't do for his amigo," Al humbly responded.

Goober continued, "Well, you did save my neck, Al, and all my teeth." Goober pulled his lips over both his upper and lower teeth and made a face at Alfonso to show how terrible he would have looked without them. Then both boys broke into a hearty laugh at the thought of a toothless Goober!

It was Saturday. In the morning Goober had mowed the lawn and trimmed the rose bushes for his mom. Alfonso had cleaned the living room at his house; vacuuming, dusting, and making sure everything looked nice.

47

Now it was afternoon and the boys lay on the floor of Goober's bedroom just hanging out together.

"Just think, we'll be graduating this year, Al. I'm sure glad we get to go to high school together. I wouldn't like it half as much if you weren't there."

"That's how I feel too, Goob. Let's live right next door to each other after we grow up."

"Close buddies forever," Goober smiled. Then Goober stood up, picked up his baseball glove and said, "You want to go outside and throw some high ones?"

Alfonso was up on his feet in a flash. "Sure, Goob." And they did.

Monday at school, Goober walked into his classroom and the first person he saw was Tracey Dare in a beautiful new pink dress. Tracey had the prettiest blonde hair and the sea-bluest eyes that Goober had ever seen. She was only a hint of the beautiful woman she would later become, but turning thirteen a week from tomorrow, she looked like a pretty Princess.

Goober looked at Tracey and his mouth went dry! He tried to swallow and couldn't. He had felt the beginnings of love for her from the day a month before when he had found her crying outside Mr. Hirkshire's office. She had tried not to let him see that she was crying and turned away from him. But Goober would have none of it. "What's wrong?" he asked her. "Would you like to talk about it?"

Tracey blew her nose on a Kleenex and said, "Aunt Cheryl died this morning."

Goober had no idea in the world who Aunt Cheryl was. All he could see in Tracey's grief was that Tracey had loved her aunt very much. Goober said three words, "I'm so sorry." Then Goober took out a freshly-ironed handkerchief from his pocket and handed it to Tracey so that she could wipe away even more of her tears. Goober's mother always insisted he carry a handkerchief in both front pockets, even though he knew no other boy in school who ever used one.

To Tracey, no boy had ever been kinder to her or done more of the right thing for her, than Goober did at that very moment. She thanked him, and for the very first time their eyes met. Neither Goober nor Tracey had ever thought of having a boyfriend or girlfriend. Of course they'd heard those words, but such a thing seemed ridiculous to both of them because neither had ever thought they'd want one. Neither could in their remotest imagination at that moment imagine themselves wanting to be kissed by anyone but their mother. People who kissed on TV were "mushy" in both of their minds. When they saw the actors do it they both thought "Yuk!", though they'd never heard the other one react that way because they lived totally apart.

"I guess your Aunt Cheryl meant a lot to you," Goober said, obviously already knowing the answer.

"Yes, she did," Tracey agreed. "I love her, and I'm going to miss her SO much." With that, Tracey began to cry again.

Goober wasn't the least bit embarrassed by her tears. He remembered when his dog Brutus got run over by a car and died, and how he had cried himself to sleep night after night for awhile, missing him so much because Brutus had always slept at the end of Goober's bed. Only Goober's mom sympathized with him. His dad and Clyde just told him to get over it.

"Where did your Aunt Cheryl live?" Goober asked, trying hard to help Tracey get through this awful moment.

"Right next door," Tracey sobbed. "I always went to her house if Mom was out for some reason."

Goober somehow felt he should put his arm around Tracey. He in no way wanted to do anything more than comfort her. But he didn't put his arm around her because he was afraid she might misunderstand.

"Maybe I should just shut up. I guess I'm not helping you. I didn't mean to make you cry."

"Oh, I don't want you to shut up at all, Goober," Tracey answered quickly. "I'm so thankful that you're here. I feel so lonely just thinking about Aunt Cheryl being gone. I don't want to be alone right now at all. And I'm so thankful that you care. Could we walk for awhile and I'll tell you about Aunt Cheryl?"

Life contains certain marvelous moments which the one who experiences them remembers as long as they live. So often those moments have no announcement at all before they come. That was what happened in the next forty minutes in the lives of both Goober and Tracey. Both of them knew they were supposed to have returned to class after recess. Neither of them would have ever skipped a class on purpose. But for some totally unexplainable reason, they knew Mrs. Plumpff would approve of their being outside while Tracey told Goober about Aunt Cheryl.

Another thing totally unusual about this moment was that Goober and Tracey walked in the schoolyard without anyone else in sight. Just the two of them walked alone together.

Tracey talked on and on, telling happy or moving stories about Aunt Cheryl. Goober just listened, laughed, or was quiet at appropriate moments. Looking back it seemed really odd to Goober that no one interrupted their beautiful walk. And because Mr. Hirkshire had already told Mrs. Plumpff about the death of Tracey's aunt, she never asked either of them where they had been.

"Are you a Christian, Goober?" Tracey asked him as they finally walked back to their classroom.

"No, I'm not," Goober admitted. "I've never even been inside a church."

"Oh, being a Christian isn't about churches, Goober. It's about knowing Jesus Christ."

"Is that really important, Tracey?" Goober asked in complete sincerity.

"Oh yes," Tracey assured him. "Getting through the death of Aunt Cheryl is going to really be rough. But God will help me. I know He will. And I can't imagine what I'd do if I didn't know that Aunt Cheryl is in heaven now. She must be having a ball!"

"I guess if it helps you to think that way, then your church is a good thing for you," Goober told her. "I've just never thought much about it. My mom and dad and my brother aren't interested in religious things at all. So I haven't been either."

Tracey said, "Oh, I'm not at all religious, Goober. I'm a Christian."

Their conversation ended at that moment. Goober figured it was just as well. He had no idea what she meant about her not being religious. "After all," he thought to himself, "aren't Christians 'religious'?"

Goober was still thinking about the last thing Tracey had said at the end of their conversation a few days later when he was with Alfonso, "Al, do you think maybe God cared about Tracey so much that He wanted her to be able to get all that out about her aunt by talking with me?"

Alfonso answered, "Maybe. Who could know about such things?"

Goober and Alfonso went to the funeral service of Tracey's aunt at Amazing Grace Church. Alfonso had gone a couple of times to a Catholic Church in Wake Up with his father and mother, but this was the first time Goober had ever gone into a church or attended a funeral. Both boys were very surprised by many things about the church. For example, when they both first walked through the front door they were surprised to see the church had a coffee house. It was closed and a locked metal gate stood in front of it. But they could see a big sign on the wall above the shop that read "IS REAL". They wondered what that meant.

The boys were ushered into the sanctuary by a well-built man dressed in a Harley-Davidson T-shirt and black pants. He had "Security Guard" written on his shirt. His hair was gray and pulled back into a pony tail. "Wow," Goober whispered to Alfonso, "this guy looks like a biker!"

They were again surprised to see not only many rows of seats, but bleachers too. The usher took them down the center aisle to the first two seats on the right in the seventh row. That put them behind everyone else who was already there.

Those gathered for the funeral were Aunt Cheryl's relatives and friends. Goober could see Tracey on the front row and knew she must be sitting with her mom. He wondered where her dad was.

Neither boy had been formally invited, but somehow Goober felt they should be there for Tracey's sake. Alfonso's dad and mom had said it would be fine for their son to accompany Goober. Both boys wore black suits and dark ties, the only suit and tie each had. They would have preferred to wear jeans and a shirt, but both mothers had insisted, "Only dark suits and dark ties are proper for funerals." The boys accepted their fate, though both found their suits "itchy".

After they were settled, the boys began to look more closely at the people gathered there. Nearly all of them were wearing very casual clothes. That made Goober and Alfonso squirm all the more because they already felt out of place. Alfonso whispered to Goober, "You know, Goob, our moms must have gotten it wrong about our needing to wear suits. Look at these people."

Goober said, "Yeah." But then a pastor walked to the pulpit. The two boys suddenly grinned at each other. The pastor was wearing a suit. Goober nudged Alfonso and still in a whisper said, "Hey, Al, look at that guy. I guess our moms must have gotten it right after all. We look more like him, and he's the speaker!"

Goober was amazed to see the pastor smiling. He had always thought preachers at funerals would be sad. The pastor greeted everybody from the pulpit so happily that it almost made Goober forget this was a funeral. This pastor talked about "celebrating Aunt Cheryl". He soon had a bunch of people join him at the pulpit to tell fun and interesting stories about this lady who had just died. The first time Goober actually laughed during one of the stories he threw his hand over his mouth because he had always thought no one could ever laugh in a church, especially during a funeral. But everyone was laughing and the boys got used to it.

Tracey went to the pulpit and shared too. She told a really funny story about Aunt Cheryl when they'd gone Christmas shopping together the year before. Then Tracey's mom came to the microphone and shared that her sister had been a Christian who attended this church. She said, "I'm not a Christian and I want to thank Pastor Smith for letting me share about Cheryl." She then talked about her sister and how wonderful it was that she had lived right next door to Tracey and her. Tracey's mom seemed really nice.

By the time all the people told their stories, Goober understood even better why Aunt Cheryl had been so special in Tracey's mind. He realized he would have liked to have gotten to know Aunt Cheryl too.

Pastor Smith finished the funeral "celebration" by saying, "You know, Christians are the only humans on Earth who NEVER have to say goodbye. Soon we'll talk again with Aunt Cheryl."

"I wonder what he means by that," Goober whispered to Alfonso. "Doesn't he know that Aunt Cheryl is DEAD?"

After the funeral was over and people were leaving the church building to go to the gravesite, Tracey noticed the boys. She said nothing, but gave a quick smile as her mother, holding her hand, led her outside to a long black car. And that was that.

Now a month had passed since Goober and Tracey had walked together. During that month Tracey had smiled at Goober once in awhile from her desk, or when passing him in the cafeteria. But they hadn't talked again. The problem was that Goober couldn't think of something that made any sense to say. He felt really awkward. He knew he couldn't walk up to her and ask, "Well, how are things now that you're favorite aunt is dead? Got any more aunts that might die so that we could go for another walk?" So Goober said nothing to Tracey and Tracey said nothing to him. And now he stood looking at her in that new pink dress and he thought to himself that she must be the most beautiful girl who had ever lived on planet Earth.

Lunch hour came and Goober and Alfonso made their daily walk to the cafeteria. They stood in line and got spaghetti and meatballs, tossed salad, and a little scoop of strawberry cheesecake ice cream. Then they found a table and sat down. The moment they sat it happened. Tracey Dare walked straight to Goober, handed him a small pink envelope, and smiling said, "Goober, I hope you can come to my birthday party. It's at 5 o'clock a week from tomorrow."

"You bet I'll be there," Goober gasped. "I've really missed talking to you." Then he thought, "I sound stupid and Tracey must think I'm a nerd!" But she didn't.

"I've missed you too, Goober. I really have. I hadn't ever had a walk like the one we took and I think about it a lot!"

"You DO?" Goober gasped again. "Gosh, I never talk to girls, but I sure like talking to YOU!"

Alfonso was the only one to recognize what to say next. "Tracey, would you like to sit down and have lunch with Goober? There's lots of room."

"I'd like that very much," Tracey smiled.

Goober asked her, "Can I get your food for you? I'd be glad to bring it to the table."

"Well," Tracey suggested, "why don't we go through the line together and you can carry my tray back here."

"I'll guard your seats, Goob," Alfonso volunteered. "You know how crowded this place can get!"

"How have you been since that walk we took, Goober?" Tracey asked.

"Oh, just great" Goober answered. He tried desperately to think of more to say, but he was speechless. He just looked at her. She was so pretty that her smile made him melt.

Tracey knew Goober was ill at ease. "Anything wrong, Goober?" she asked.

"No, Tracey, everything's about as right as it could be now." He realized he had been staring at her. "Uh, it's just that, uh," he said, stumbling for the right words. "Tracey, you're the prettiest girl I've ever seen." Then Goober blushed because he'd said that.

Tracey didn't blush. Instead she said, "Goober, thank you for saying that. You really are nice."

Some of the awkwardness in Goober left after she said those words. She added, "I know what the Bomber brothers tried to do to you. That must have been terribly scary. You were so brave."

Tracey and Goober moved through the food line and Tracey handed Goober her filled tray. "You're very strong, Goober," Tracey said as he carried her tray back to their table. Goober blushed again. Then as Goober sat down next to Tracey he suddenly remembered he hadn't even introduced her to Alfonso. He quickly said, "This is my friend Al. And Tracey, if you want to know who REALLY stopped the Bomber brothers, it was him. We're good buddies. And, Al, this is Tracey."

"Of course," Tracey said, "I know you from class. You're Alfonso Guiterrez. You're the one who helped Mrs. Plumpff and the others find Goober so quickly."

"Yes," he answered her. Alfonso was embarrassed because he didn't like to have any fuss made over him.

Tracey continued, "I want to thank both of you for coming to my Aunt Cheryl's funeral. That meant so much to me. Goober, you told me when we walked that you had never been in any church before. Tell me the truth. Did you feel uncomfortable being there?"

"Oh no," Goober told her. "It was great. I would never have expected a funeral to be 'great'. We were just there for you."

Tracey was moved by Goober's words. "Thank you, Goober, and you too, Al. That means so much to me."

"How have things been for you since then?" Goober asked.

"Harder," answered Tracey truthfully. "I loved my aunt and I was at her house probably as often as I was at mine except to sleep. You would have liked her too. She loved the Lord and she had a great sense of humor. She always kept me laughing."

"Yep," Goober mused, "after what you shared with me, and you and the others shared at the funeral, I know I would have liked her a lot."

The conversation drifted from one subject to another, each of the three contributing, and the lunch hour passed so quickly that all three jumped when they heard the first bell to go in. They quickly rose, cleared their trays, and headed for their classroom.

"That was a really special lunchtime," Goober said to Tracey as they walked to class with Alfonso.

"Goober, would you mind if I sat with you two more often?" Tracey asked. "I really had fun too."

"I wouldn't mind," Goober said, making the biggest understatement of his life. Then he added even more enthusiastically, "I wouldn't mind at all. I LIKE having you around."

"I like being around you too, Goober" replied Tracey. And when she said that, Goober smiled and his heart did a dance!

"Any friend of Goob's is an amigo of mine," quipped Alfonso. And with that, Goober, Tracey and Alfonso became good friends. They began having lunch together every school day.

Saturday arrived and after morning chores, Goober went to J. C. Penney's and bought a birthday present for Tracey.

He spent a long time looking at costume jewelry before he settled on a really pretty blue-stoned locket.

After shopping, Goober went back home. He had planned for Alfonso to come over and shoot hoops with him in the afternoon. But then Alfonso phoned him and told Goober, "My dad wants me to stay home today and work with him in the garden. I'd ask you to come help us, but he said he wants to spend some special time with me alone."

"That's fine," Goober told him. "I think I'll clean my room. Mom's been after me to do that. Oh, and I bought a locket for Tracey that I hope she'll like."

"I know she will, Goob. She sure is nice."

"Yes she is. I wish you were going to her birthday party too. I know she would have invited you for sure if we'd been having lunch with her before this week."

"I'm just glad you're going, Goob. That will really be special."

There was no way for either of the boys to know at that moment that something else was happening in another part of Wake Up – something that would make Tracey's mom furious. Nor could Tracey's mom know what would happen to her as a result of her being so angry.

Elsie Dare was driving on Mountaintop Drive. She had stopped at a stop light at Greening Street when another car very lightly tapped the back end of her car.

Elsie wasn't hurt at all. She got out of her car and looked to see if any damage had been done. She saw a slight scratch on her bumper. A tall good-looking Mexican gentleman got out of his car and said, "I'm very sorry, Mam. Are you all right? I have insurance."

Had this man been anyone but a Mexican, Elsie would have laughed and told him, "Don't worry about this at all. You barely touched my car." Then she would have driven off. But Elsie Dare HATED all Mexicans, so she was outraged. "Are you blind, or stupid, or something?" she railed at the man. "You were obviously speeding or you would have stopped. I suppose you're an illegal immigrant and you're driving without a license! You ought to be in jail!"

All the time she was yelling at this poor man she grew louder and louder. "You Mexicans are all alike. Why don't you go back to your own country where you belong?"

"Mam, I assure you, I haven't snuck across your border. I was born in Omaha, Nebraska. My name is Ralph Guiterrez. I'm so sorry I didn't stop in time. I was distracted for just a moment and that's when I hit you. Are you sure that you're OK?" Elsie nodded yes. Ralph's car was larger than Elsie's, and the front end showed no marks either. "Looks like I created a bumper-thumper!" Ralph smiled. "Again, I'm very sorry."

Elsie didn't listen to his words, she saw his smile and it infuriated her. "There's nothing funny about this dented bumper," Elsie snapped. "You Mexicans always think it's funny to destroy *other* people's property and other *people* too."

Ralph Guiterrez understood prejudice. He had faced it many times. "No, Mam, I don't think this was funny. I'm so sorry it happened. Here is my driver's license and the name and number of my insurance company. I'm sure they'll take care of any damage very quickly."

Elsie angrily gave Ralph her driver's license and insurance information and then barked, "You need a lot more driving lessons!"

And that episode was over at least for awhile. But a very angry Elsie Dare glowered at Ralph as she got back into her car and drove away.

Monday came. Lunch hour found the three close friends sitting together again. None of them knew that Saturday's accident had been between Alfonso's dad and Tracey's mom. Tracey was talking about something else entirely: "Our neighbors, the Lottenblasters, got a new Fox Terrier. She's darling - all brown and white. They've named her 'Stinky' and she's really smart. You throw a ball and she'll go get it and bring it back to you for hours. And everytime someone comes to their door, she barks and barks." Then instantly, Tracey changed the subject. "My mom got her bumper hit on Saturday, but she wasn't hurt a bit."

Alfonso responded, "Wow! That's a coincidence. My dad got in some kind of a wreck on Saturday too. He wasn't hurt either." Then Alfonso began talking about something else.

All Tracey had heard her mom say was that it was a "stupid Mexican" who dented her bumper. Her mother never mentioned the driver's name. Tracey would have never used the word "stupid" to describe anyone. And it wasn't because Alfonso was Mexican that Tracey never would have mentioned his race. It was because his race had nothing at all to do with the fact that the bumper-thumper had occurred.

Talk among the three, as always, was fun. Near the end of their conversation, Tracey added, "I'm so sorry, Al, that I didn't invite you to my birthday party. It's amazing to think I only got to know you a week ago today. If I'd known you earlier, like I do now, you'd have been there for sure."

"Oh, that's OK, Tracey," Alfonso smiled. "You can tell me all about it when we get together for lunch Wednesday."

Tracey had asked her mother if she could invite one more person, but her mother had said, "Absolutely not. I have an eight piece dinner set, Sweetheart, not nine. I'm sorry, but there just won't be room for anyone else." And the subject was closed.

Tuesday came. Goober woke up excited, knowing that today after school he'd be going to Tracey's birthday party. He was just eating the last bite of his oatmeal when the phone rang. It was Tracey.

"Hi, Goob," Tracey said. "I'm calling to get Al's phone number. Nicky Jones has the flu. He was coming to my party, but with him sick he can't come. I'm going to invite Al to take his place."

Goober was delighted. "That's great, Tracey," he told her. Then quickly he thought of how that might have sounded. "I don't mean that's great that Nicky got the flu! I mean I'm glad Al can come to your party."

"I knew what you meant, Goob," she chuckled. "And I'm so glad Al can come too."

Goober gave Tracey Alfonso's number. "Thanks, Goob. I can hardly wait for lunchtime these days. See you at noon." Tracey smiled through the telephone.

Tracey was the only girl Goober had ever known who could actually smile through a telephone. He smiled back, "Food never tasted so good until you came and started sitting with us. Goodbye."

"Goodbye, Goob," Tracey said, still smiling.

As soon as she hung up, Tracey dialed Alfonso's number. Mrs. Guiterrez answered the phone with a cheery hello.

"Hello," answered Tracey, "is Al there?"

Sophia Guiterrez was a strikingly beautiful Mexican woman from Mexico City with long black hair and dark eyes. She was puzzled over who was on the other end of the telephone. "Is this a girl calling?" she asked with excitement.

"Yes," answered Tracey. "This is Tracey Dare. I'm in Al's class at school."

"Al, come quickly," his mother shouted. "There's a girl on the telephone calling for you and she sounds really pretty. Hurry!"

Tracey heard Sophia's remark and giggled quietly. She thought, "Mrs. Guiterrez must think I'm Al's girlfriend!"

There was silence for a minute and then Al spoke into the phone and asked, "Who is this please?"

Tracey told him, "Al, this is Tracey." She then told him about Nicky Jones getting the flu and asked him if he could come to her party instead.

Al answered eagerly, "Sure I'll come. Thanks for inviting me."

"I'm so glad you're coming. I'll talk with you at lunch. Bye."

"Bye, Tracey," he said.

Once he was off the phone his mother wanted to know all about Tracey. "What does she look like? What do her parents do? Where exactly does she live?"

Al was completely embarrassed by his mother's bombardment of questions. He explained, "Tracey is just a really nice girl in our class who has lunch with Goob and me every day."

"Well, that's just how your father and I met. We started having lunch together every day. Of course, we were in college. But we got to know each other just like that. After we got married we moved to Mexico City and had you. That's how these things happen!"

Alfonso didn't try any further to convince his mother that he had a very different relationship with Tracey than his mom and dad had in college. He knew she was just excited about the call.

Lunch hour was jam-packed with conversation among the three friends. Tracey couldn't believe the games she had to talk her mother out of for her party. "Mom thought we'd like to play Musical Chairs or Pin The Tail On The Donkey. I told her those were for her day, not for ours. Mom got kind of upset with me about saying that, but I told her, 'Mom, I'm turning thirteen. I'm not turning three!' So, she finally stopped trying to suggest games. She just warned me we're all going to get really bored just sitting around doing nothing."

Goober said, "Tracey, I don't think you'll have to worry that we'll get bored and have to play dorkey games. We talk so much every day right here that we're sure to have enough to talk about tonight, especially with your other friends there."

As soon as school was out, Alfonso asked Goober, "Can you come over to my house so we can go to the party together? I have a present for Tracey and I need to wrap it."

"Sure, Al," Goober replied. "My mom and dad went with friends to Burney Falls this afternoon. They didn't ask me to go because they knew I was going to Tracey's party."

It took longer to walk to Alfonso's home from school than to walk to Goober's. But the boys enjoyed the warmth of an unusual October day.

As they walked, Alfonso told Goober, "I didn't know I was buying a birthday present for Tracey when I bought it this week, but the package is still sealed. It's a DVD of the Disney movie *Prince Caspian* from *The Chronicles of Narnia*. Tracey told us the other day that she hadn't bought it yet and that it was one of her favorite movies. So I'm going to wrap it up and give it to her."

"Gosh, that's a great idea, Al. But that's one of your favorite movies too. Don't you want to keep it?"

"I'll get another one soon," Al said. "But getting invited to Tracey's party is fantastic. I'm happy knowing that she's going to like her gift from me. But she's REALLY going to love that locket you're giving her, Goob. I'll bet she wears it every day."

Goober smiled. He was carrying the brightly colored paper package that held the locket he had bought Tracey. "Well," he said, "both gifts come from our hearts. My mom says that's when gifts are best."

The boys reached Alfonso's house and Al wrapped the DVD for Tracey. Then they spent most of an hour watching a space galaxy movie on TV. At that point, Alfonso's dad came home from work. Seeing both boys all wrapped up in what they were watching, Mr. Guiterrez asked them, "Weren't you two supposed to be going to a birthday party this afternoon?"

"Yeah, Dad," Alfonso answered. Turning his head away from the TV for the first time since the movie began, he looked at his wristwatch. "Oh my gosh!" Alfonso exclaimed. "Goob, we've got to leave this minute to walk there, and we may have to run all the way!"

"Well," said Alfonso's father, "I think I've got a better idea. Just wait a minute and I'll drive you there instead. I'll stop and gas up the car as I'm driving back."

"Thanks, Dad," Alfonso said. "That would be great."

"Yes, thanks, Mr. Guiterrez," Goober echoed. "That sure would beat running."

"Right, Goober," Alfonso's father said with a smile. "And let me tell both you boys something to get you started right. Never be in a sweat when you are going to be with some girl. It looks bad, smells bad, and the girl will think you're in a sweat over *her*!"

Mr. Guiterrez changed into more comfortable shoes. Then he said, "Let's go boys. By the way, where does this girl live?"

Goober answered, "On Calico Court, Mr. Guiterrez."

"Oh no!" Mr. Guiterrez laughed, "Calico Court? Does Tracey's last name happen to be 'Dare'?"

Alfonso saw a strange look on his dad's face. He answered, "Yeah, Dad. How did you know?"

"And let me guess," his dad continued. "Is her mother's first name 'Elsie'?"

"I think that's her name," Goober answered. "Isn't that what she said her mom's name was, Al?"

"Yes, that's her mom's name, Dad."

Mr. Guiterrez thought a moment and then said, "I think maybe I'd better drop you at the end of their street and then peel out of there!"

Al was again surprised. "But why would you do that, Dad?"

"Because," said Mr. Guiterrez, chuckling, "it was Elsie Dare's bumper that I bumped last Saturday. And she hates me now!"

Mr. Guiterrez did let the boys off at the corner of Calico Court and Daffodil.

As they got out of the car he told Alfonso, "Phone me on your cell phone when you want me to pick you up. I'll be waiting right here at the end of the block. And I'd rather, Son, that she didn't know you and I are related. I don't want to have her react to you like she did to me."

"OK, Dad," Alfonso replied. "But I'm proud that you're my dad."

Mr. Guiterrez smiled at his son and said, "I'm so thankful for that, Son. But let's keep this all in the family!"

As Goober and Alfonso walked toward Tracey's house, neither one of them could imagine anything but fun ahead at Tracey's party. They greatly doubted they'd want to leave Tracey's house even after the party was over. But when they knocked on the door and Tracey's mother opened it, Goober soon began to have second thoughts.

Elsie Dare smiled at Goober when he entered and held out her hand to shake it. "You must be Goober," Mrs. Dare greeted him. "Tracey thinks you are *very* brave. And after the story she told me about you, I think so too."

Goober smiled and shook Mrs. Dare's hand, thanking her for her comment. But when Al walked in behind Goober, Mrs. Dare suddenly scowled at him and withdrew the hand she had almost offered him. "Are you a Mex....?" she asked, cutting off the word she nearly spit out of her mouth.

Alfonso knew what she was about to ask. He answered, "Yes, Mam."

Mrs. Dare turned and scowled directly at Tracey.

In the living room, bouncy Carrie Underwood was singing on a CD. On a table in the middle of the room sat several colorfully wrapped packages, including one huge long one.

Goober and Alfonso added their gifts to the table and then found seats quickly. Tracey made sure everyone was comfortable with each other. She got them talking.

The girls were freckled Shirley Obar and Clovella Stimple. Clovella lived on the same block with Tracey, the only girl who didn't attend Edison. She went instead to Amazing Grace Christian School. Clovella was fourteen, large-framed and tall. She had brown hair, brown eyes, and could play the cello.

At thirteen Shirley Obar was four foot eleven, a redhead with green eyes. Her freckles looked nice on her small face. She was full of energy, a real tomboy, and everybody chose her first, in spite of her size, for volleyball.

Goober sat down next to Willie Radner. Al sat next to Goober on his other side, right next to Larry Beale. All of the boys were classmates.

Willie Radner was muscular and extremely handsome. He had a great smile and was friendly to everybody. And Willie was a terrific baseball pitcher. He was already being scouted by the San Francisco Giants for his amazing strike-out record, which was unusual for someone only in the eighth grade. Willie made top grades too. All the teachers at Edison said that after high school, Willie would be getting an athletic scholarship from any university he chose.

Larry Beale was about the same height as Goober, but heavier. He had brown hair and brown eyes. He could beat anyone he played at chess. His greatest asset was a tremendously winning smile. His father owned Beale's Florist Shop in Wake Up.

Tracey's mother stood in the room for a moment or two after Goober and Al sat down. She was still scowling at Al and he wondered if maybe she had somehow seen his dad's car after all when his dad dropped the boys off, and if that was why she seemed so mad at him.

Jennifer Luden arrived and was warmly greeted by Tracey and her mother. Jennifer was also in Mrs. Plumpff's class. But to Goober, Jennifer always seemed a lot older than an eighth grader. She had black hair, but not as black as Willie's. She was exactly the same height as Tracey, had dark eyes, a marvelous smile, and in spite of the fact that she was very trim, loved to cook and eat exotic foods. In fact, she shared many recipes with Elsie Dare and had twice brought ethnic recipes to the Dare's home and cooked fabulous dinners for them. Tracey liked to cook too and loved learning how to cook new things from Jennifer.

Jennifer joined the group. Now all seven guests had arrived. Tracey's mom immediately asked, "Tracey, Dear, may I see you in the kitchen?"

Tracey smiled and said, "Sure, Mom," then followed her.

As soon as they were there and had the door closed, Elsie burst out angrily at Tracey. "Who on earth is that new boy who came with your friend Goob? And what on earth is he doing in MY house?"

"He's Al Guiterrez, Mom," Tracey answered calmly. "Goob and I have lunch with him every day at school. He's a friend."

Her mother exploded. "Well, you're NOT to have lunch with him ever again! First, 'Guiterrez' is the name of the man who crashed into my car on Saturday! That boy is probably related to him at least in some way. Second, and far more to the point, you've invited a MEXICAN to your party! I have taught you all your life about how to choose friends. You know what I feel about Mexicans! I do NOT want him near you again."

Tracey remained calm in spite of her mother's anger. But she was concerned that her mom's loud voice might be heard in the living room where her seven best friends sat talking. She said, "Just a minute, Mom." She walked into the living room, put on another Carrie Underwood CD, and turned the volume up as high as it would go. None of the seven sitting there cared that the sound had been raised. They loved Carrie Underwood's singing.

"Mom," Tracey said, closing the kitchen door behind her, "now I remember Al saying something about his dad getting in an accident too on Saturday. But Al is NOT his DAD! Al doesn't even have a car, and he couldn't drive it if he had one."

Tracey continued, "Second, Al isn't just a Mexican. He's Goob's best friend. I really like him. He is smart, and fun, and really really humble. He's tremendously brave too. In fact, he was the one who saved Goob's life the other day, but he'd never tell you that. You'd have to drag it out of him. Mom, Al isn't anything at all like you picture Mexicans. You're racially prejudiced, Mom. I love you, but racial prejudice is hate and it makes no sense at all."

"I can't believe my own daughter has just said that. Don't you dare try to lecture me about racial prejudice. You just don't want to understand the truth. He's a Mexican, and I want him out of this house RIGHT THIS MINUTE."

"Mom," Tracey answered. "I love you and I always try to do everything you ask me to do. But I won't order Al out of this house. It's my birthday. I'm asking you to please accept Al at least for today. I won't ever ask him here again after today, Mom, if you insist. For his sake, I wouldn't have asked him at all if I had thought about how you hate Mexicans. But I am asking you to consider my feelings too about him. He's a precious friend of mine. And I want you to allow him to stay for my birthday party."

Elsie understood her daughter's feelings, but she still didn't want to surrender her own feelings about Alfonso. She made an attempt to gain sympathy from Tracey. "But that boy's father could have killed me with his car."

"I know, Mom, but it was an accident. He didn't do it on purpose. And he didn't kill you. You aren't hurt at all. I can't even see that he did anything to your bumper. But his insurance company has already told you they will pay for any repairs. I don't know Mr. Guiterrez, but if he's even half as nice as Al, he must be a very good man."

Wallowing in self-pity and clinging to her prejudice, Elsie began to cry. She said, "It breaks my heart to think that you would take a Mexican's side against your own mother."

Tracey put her arms around her mother and held her as she wept. "I'm so sorry, Mom. I love you."

Seizing on this possible vulnerability in Tracey, Elsie pushed away from her daughter and said, "Then send him home NOW!"

Tracey replied, "I can't do that, Mom. Not now. It would ruin my whole party. And it would embarrass all my friends."

Elsie said, "Please sit down with me, Tracey. I want you to understand why I feel like I do."

When the two were seated, Elsie began. "It was when I was a teenager living in Reseda that a Mexican killed my brother Ted."

"I know, Mom. You've told me about it many times."

"Then let me tell you once more, Tracey. Maybe you'll finally understand why you should hate all Mexicans too. It happened when your Uncle Ted and I were growing up in Southern California. I was fifteen and your uncle was seventeen. I was so proud of my big brother. You'd have loved him, Tracey. One beautiful spring day we were sitting on the lawn just talking. All at once a car came down our street filled with Mexicans. When the car reached us, a teenage Mexican just like your so-called 'friend' sitting in our living room, stuck a gun out the window. He shot and killed Ted. Ted died in my arms. Your Uncle never got to grow up. That Mexican murdered him in cold blood. Mexicans have no soul. They are beasts."

"But AL didn't do that, Mom!" argued Tracey. "It was an entirely different person who killed Uncle Ted. Uncle Ted was in a gang too. And if the boy who killed him hadn't shot him first, Uncle Ted would have gladly killed *him*."

Elsie Dare looked at her daughter and it was as if Tracey had never before said those words to her, though she'd said them to her mother many times. Yet this time Tracey's simple statement penetrated the dark unforgiving bitterness in Mrs. Dare's soul. Elsie was startled. The truth began to dawn on her. Elsie fought it. She didn't want to change her mind at all.

Elsie put her right elbow on the table and leaned her forehead into the palm of her right hand. Tracey knew her mother was thinking hard. Tracey knew too that she shouldn't at all interrupt what was happening. So she stayed seated, praying silently for her mom.

Mrs. Dare stayed extremely silent. Tracey knew God was speaking to her mom.

Suddenly Elsie had a vision, though she would have never called it that. She could see herself crying at her brother's funeral. Many other people were crying too. Her mother was sobbing louder than them all. Elsie's seventeen-year-old brother lay absolutely still in a casket. Elsie had never known Ted to be quiet before. Ted loved to laugh, shout, and party all night long. Ted was her favorite brother who taught her how to dance, how to play cards, (even how to cheat!), and who would put her on the back of his motorcycle where they'd ride faster than the wind. Now Ted would be covered with dirt within an hour and his body would never move again. Ted would never come back to her, never laugh again, because some filthy Mexican had murdered him. That's how she had always thought of it from the time of her brother's death until the moment Tracey's words reached her hard heart. Tracey had said that it was just *one* Mexican, not all Mexicans, who had killed her brother. And now Elsie Dare realized what her daughter said was true.

Suddenly the vision changed. She was looking at the funeral of a young Mexican teenager who looked like he might be Ted's age. The boy's mother was sobbing hysterically.

New thoughts came to Elsie Dare. The truth was that teenagers like Ted were being murdered regularly in the area where they lived. Often girls were slaughtered too. And it wasn't just whites, but Mexicans who had lost their sons and daughters. After Ted was killed, and even before his death, she'd been glad about every one of the Mexicans who were murdered. Elsie's hard heart hadn't been moved a bit when others told her how loudly Mexican mothers sobbed over the loss of their children.

But now, with seven teenagers sitting in the Dare's living room - one of them a Mexican - Elsie for the first time began to feel a totally new sensation: Shame! She was ashamed that she had never felt sorry for those mothers and the children they had loved. They had never mattered at all to her until now. She thought it had served them right. But in hearing her daughter remind her again that her brother would have gladly killed this Mexican, the truth had finally broken through.

Mrs. Dare sat upright and brushed at her tears. When she sat they had first fallen for her dead brother. But now her tears had turned to guilt because of the fiery hatred she had carried in her heart for so many years for ALL Mexicans.

"I am so ashamed, Tracey. You're right. I've blindly hated every Mexican I've seen until today. I've felt that way even though Ted *would* have eagerly shot the one who shot him if he'd been given the chance. I don't know what just happened to me that has opened my eyes to this. I'm sure you've tried to tell me that before. But I see it now. And I feel so guilty."

"Mom, Jesus Christ died on the cross to take away all your guilt, shame, and every bit of your prejudice too. He paid in full for it with His own blood to set you completely free from sin. I see it happening with different friends of mine who join our youth group at church every week. Most of them aren't racially prejudiced at all, but they have other kinds of sins they know they need to be saved from. After they give their lives to Christ they're filled with His joy, the kind of joy I know even on my hardest days without Aunt Cheryl. You know you want to be with Aunt Cheryl again someday. Wouldn't this be a great time to give your life to Jesus Christ once and for all?"

"But what about your party, Tracey? We've spent a long time in this kitchen."

"Time never matters when you're giving your life to Christ. And you coming to Jesus would be my greatest birthday present ever."

There at the kitchen table, Tracey led her mother in a very simple prayer. "Jesus Christ, please forgive me for all my sins. I now believe you took them on the cross with You and I am no longer guilty of anything. Please come into my life and be my Savior forever. Amen."

After her mom prayed that prayer, Tracey hugged her again and said, "Mom, I know you meant every word you just said to God. And God absolutely knows it too. Romans 10:8 through 11 says because of what you just prayed you're born again. The angels in heaven are rejoicing right this minute because of what you just did."

"Gosh," Elsie admitted, "I didn't think it could be that simple."

Tracey smiled at her mom and told her, "Christ did all the hard part for you when He went to the cross."

"Tracey," her mother told her, "I probably wouldn't have prayed that prayer with you if I hadn't seen what your faith in God has done for you so many times."

"Praise the Lord!" Tracey replied. She leaned the side of her face into her mother's hair. "I love you so much, Mom. YOU are my mommy. And I just hope I can be half the mother you are when I grow up."

Elsie still had a concerned look on her face. She said, "Tracey, even though I'm a Christian now, I've lived hating Mexicans ever since your Uncle Ted was killed. How can I really be sure my prejudice won't come back?"

Tracey answered, "Because Christ removed all prejudice from your spirit just now when you asked Him to save you, Mom. The only place sin can ever try to tempt you again is in your mind. Whenever I find I've started thinking wrong thoughts that would be harmful to me or to others - like wanting to eat too many sweets, or watch a movie I know I shouldn't see - I go straight to God about it. I ask the Lord to take away that temptation, and then I call Clovella or one of my other Christian friends and talk with them about how great the Lord is. Or I pick up my Bible and I start studying it. That makes the tempter so mad he goes stomping away! When you say no to temptation and pray, God will always give you His supernatural power NOT to give in. That's what I John 4:7 and 8 promises."

Tracey's mom said, "I'm amazed, Tracey. I don't feel racially prejudiced towards anyone at all. It's just as if I'd NEVER felt that way."

"That's because it's not in you any more, Mom. It's gone."

"I guess I'd better read a Bible now and discover a whole lot of other things that I've never known before," Elsie said with a huge smile.

"Yep, Mom," Tracey agreed. "You'll love reading it. I sure do."

"I'm a Christian now!" Elsie declared in real surprise.

Tracey smiled, "Yes you are, Mom. You aren't going to be prejudiced anymore. And maybe something Mrs. Plumpff taught us in class will remind you why racial prejudice is always wrong."

"What was it, Tracey?" Mrs. Dare asked.

"Well, Mrs. Plumpff did a really smart thing when she began teaching us the history of the early West. She knew that if she just began by telling us about the war that Americans who had come from many countries fought against the Native American Indians there could be a lot of anger in our classroom. Our ancestors did a lot of horrible things to the Indians, and the Indians did a lot of horrible things to them. So to begin her teaching on that subject she asked our class a really funny question."

"What funny question?"

"She asked us, 'Did you know that all Indians who make phone calls from phone booths have only one leg?'"

"When she asked that we kids burst into laughter because we thought she was telling a joke. But Mrs. Plumpff stopped us and said, 'Don't laugh. I'm completely serious. Did you know all Indians who make phone calls from phone booths have only one leg?' All of us still wanted to laugh, but we knew she had told us not to."

"Finally, Willie Radner raised his hand and politely said, 'Mrs. Plumpff, you sound so serious and I don't mean to be rude. But every one of us knows what you're saying isn't true. Not every Indian who makes a phone call from a phone booth has only one leg.'"

"Mrs. Plumpff told him, 'The one I saw did!' And then she winked. Well, our whole class cracked up laughing. It still sounded like just a great joke. But then each one of us began to realize the point Mrs. Plumpff was making. Every human, white or any color, is an individual, and though there are some terrible people that are members of each race, most of them are really nice people. And that's why I said Al didn't kill Uncle Ted. Each Mexican is an individual person, just like each person in our race is."

"You're right, Dear" Tracey's mother admitted. "I've wrongly judged the entire Mexican race for what just one person did to your Uncle Ted. And there's something I've never told you - the boy who killed your uncle was killed by someone else in Ted's gang just three months later. I was very glad about it at the time, and have been ever since until a moment ago. Now I'm thoroughly ashamed that I ever felt that way."

Tracey said, "Mom, let it really dawn on you that your sins are COMPLETELY FORGIVEN AND GONE. Every one of them. You don't have any more guilt or shame. Jesus Christ took all those hideous feelings on the cross for you and replaced that junk with His love."

"I somehow know you're right, Tracey. All my shame and guilt ARE gone, and I *do* feel His love. I feel brand new inside. I have absolutely no more prejudice towards Mexicans or anyone else at all. It's amazing. Jesus Christ is real!"

"Jesus Christ rocks, Mom. If you'd like to study the Bible together with me every day, you'll find more and more how free you really are. And I can hardly wait to take you to church with me."

"I'd love to do both of those things with you, Darling," Mrs. Dare told her daughter. Then suddenly Elsie glanced at the kitchen clock and said, "Oh, I wonder what your friends are thinking. We've been in here for such a long time!"

Tracey smiled. "Clovella will be thrilled. She's prayed for you ever since I became a Christian. But they'd all be glad if they really understood what just happened in here, Mom. Time flies when you're having fun!"

"Thank you, Tracey," Elsie said, "I'll never forget what Christ and you just did for me. This is supposed to be YOUR birthday. But I'M the one who just got the best gift of all!" Then she stood up, continuing, "I'll just warm these three pizzas for a moment, Tracey. You go in and entertain the troops!"

Tracey laughed and headed for her friends. Elsie checked the pizzas in the oven, then again brushed the final tears from her eyes over what had just happened to her. She went to the bathroom so that she could look at her eyes in the mirror. She found God had given her another miracle. Her eyes weren't red!

Now she wanted to do something to absolutely prove to herself that every bit of her hatred for Mexicans was gone. She reached for her telephone.

When Tracey entered the living room all seven of her friends were happily laughing about movies they had seen and were acting out moments from several of them. Not a person in the room was the least bit bored. Each one of them had been having fun. Tracey had nothing to apologize about. "Never fear, the pizzas are here!" she announced.

Larry Beale said "Yum!" And, as Tracey promised, Mrs. Dare brought all three pizzas out, one at a time. Tracey served each of her friends the kind of pizza they enjoyed most from her mother's fancy dinner plates. Then all of them sat and ate their favorites with great gusto.

Mrs. Dare was beaming and specifically asked Alfonso, "Are you having a good time?"

"Oh yes, Mam," he answered politely.

Then she said, "I just had a wonderful talk with your father. He is such a nice man." Alfonso and Goober looked at each other quickly and couldn't believe she'd just said that.

"Thank you," Alfonso said, inwardly thinking there must have been some mistake.

Tracey followed her mother back to the kitchen and closed the door. "You phoned Al's dad, Mom? Why?"

As if it was the most natural phone call in the world that she had just made, Tracey's mom explained, "I just wanted to apologize to him for how I acted when he barely touched my bumper on Saturday. And I apologized for how silly I had acted about it."

"Wow, Mom," Tracey said, hugging her, "you sure have changed about Mexicans!"

"Yes, Dear, I certainly have," answered Elsie, still beaming.

The rest of the party went great. Maybe the only surprise besides opening Tracey's presents was that Willie suggested the group play Musical Chairs. Tracey's immediate answer was, "Oh, that would be great!" and they did.

It was no surprise that Willie won. He had simply suggested it to give himself some exercise. He explained, "I try to keep in shape every day for baseball season."

Tracey's opening of the presents was fun too. She took time to open each gift and tell the one who gave it to her how much it meant to her. She did get some lovely things to wear, play with, or hang. Goober knew instantly that she really loved the locket he gave her. And Al knew he'd given his best when Tracey exclaimed after opening it, "***Prince Caspian***! Al, this is my favorite movie and I didn't have it."

All three of her girlfriends had said even more about the locket. And Clovella at that moment couldn't resist saying in a teasing voice, "Somebody likes somebody!" But that comment dropped like a dead weight. Everyone else liked

Tracey too much to tease her. But only Clovella knew Tracey well enough to know she didn't mind at all being teased.

"This last huge present is from my Uncle Sylvester," Tracey announced. "He's lived all over the world. Right now he lives in Spain. But since I was a baby, Uncle Sylvester has sent me very expensive presents for every birthday and for every Christmas too. The funniest thing about his presents is that because he doesn't know me at all or even think of me as a girl, he always sends presents that I can't really use. When I was two he sent me a football signed by all the Chicago Bears. Now I cheer for the 49ers! Another time he sent me a painting worth a few thousand dollars and I couldn't even tell you what it was a picture of. Last birthday he sent me an egg that is supposed to be five thousand years old. I have it in a box. And last Christmas he was in India and he sent me a really elaborate boa constrictor cage! We looked really hard afterwards, but we don't think he enclosed a boa constrictor, thank goodness!" All the kids laughed.

Tracey continued, "So every birthday and every Christmas I keep Uncle Sylvester's present as the very last present I open. It's become a tradition for my mom and me. Even though it's always something I can't use, I think it's tons of fun to see what he's sent me. I always write him afterwards and tell him how wonderful it was for him to have sent it. I have his whole collection in my bedroom."

With that explanation from Tracey, all eyes were on the big long box. Goober whispered to Alfonso, "Do you think it might be the boa constrictor this time?"

"Man, I hope not!" he chuckled.

Tracey's fingers were already at the ribbon, then soon at the paper, then at the long box, and at last Uncle Sylvester's surprise was revealed in a long black case. "It's a musical instrument," volunteered Clovella, the cello player.

Tracey carefully unsnapped the case and inside lay a very beautiful guitar. "Oh!" gasped Tracey in amazement, "this is so beautiful. And it's the first time Uncle Sylvester has sent me something I'd really like to use!" She lifted the guitar out of its case and showed it first to her mother. "Mother, do you think I could take guitar lessons?"

Not even thinking before he spoke, Goober blurted out, "Al could teach you. He's great with a guitar, and he sings too."

Alfonso was embarrassed by Goober's quick statement, especially since he still wasn't sure what Tracey's mother thought of him. He said, "I just strum mine for the fun of it."

Tracey passed the guitar to Clovella who admired it, then she passed it to Alfonso who had stood to get a better look at it. He said, "Gosh, this must be one really expensive acoustic guitar. It's made from a very fine wood, and you can look at it and see so much detail has gone into it."

Mrs. Dare asked, "Al, would you play something for us? I'd love to hear my brother's gift played well. And I'd love to hear you sing."

Al was hesitant. He said, "Tracey, I've never seen such a fancy guitar. It's brand new, and it probably cost your uncle several thousand dollars. I can tune it for you, but you should be the first to play it. Let us watch."

"No," replied Tracey, "you play it for us. You know how. Tune it and then play it for us, Al. I'd just make noise. You'll make music."

Alfonso started to speak again, but Mrs. Dare stopped him by saying, "Oh yes, Al, please. Play something for us and sing."

Alfonso said, "Well, OK, if you both want me to." He quickly tuned Tracey's new guitar and said, "Then this is a birthday song for you, Tracey."

Alfonso sat down on a chair with the guitar and began to strum it. Only Goober, until this moment, knew how great Alfonso was with a guitar. Soon everyone, especially Mrs. Dare and Tracey, thrilled to the sounds Alfonso was producing.

Then Goober said, "Sing, Al." And Al sang to the music he was playing. He sang it in Spanish and the strength of his song moved Mrs. Dare to tears again.

Al was not only great with the guitar, but his voice was great too. Elsie leaned very close to Tracey and whispered, "To think how much I've missed because of my stupid prejudice towards people like Al." Tracey reached out and squeezed her mother's hand to let her know how much her mother meant to her.

When Alfonso finished the song, everyone applauded. Then Clovella shouted, "Please play another." The others eagerly agreed. In all, Alfonso played three songs at their request and then handed the guitar back to Tracey. "It's easy to play that guitar," Alfonso said. "It just about plays itself."

Mrs. Dare asked, "Al, would you teach Tracey to play that guitar? I'll gladly pay you for her lessons."

"Could Goob come with me when I teach her?" Al asked quickly.

"Of course he could, Al," Elsie Dare replied.

"But what could I do to help?" Goober asked him.

"Just being here with us will be great," Al answered.

"That would be fine, Goober," Mrs. Dare encouraged. "Tracey has told me you are a real inspiration to her." Goober was delighted.

"Would Tuesdays and Thursdays work well for you?" Alfonso asked both Goober and the Dares. All three agreed with Alfonso that those days would be perfect.

One by one, Tracey's friends left for home. Just before Clovella left, Tracey told her about her mom getting saved. Clovella said, "Wow! That's awesome. God answered our prayers, Tracey. Your mom is going to be a beautiful Christian."

"She sure is," Tracey agreed.

Goober and Alfonso were the last to leave. Tracey tried to explain to them the same thing she had told Clovella, but neither of them understood at all. The best Goober could say was, "I'm glad she changed her mind."

Finally, Mr. Guiterrez rang the bell at the Dare's home. Mrs. Dare greeted him warmly. "Hello, my friend. Your son has been such a delight, and he is SO talented."

Alfonso's father smiled at this woman who had so recently screamed at him. He said, "I'm so glad you enjoyed Alfonso. Tracey and you are going to have to come to our house really soon for the greatest Mexican dinner in Wake Up, Mrs. Dare."

Elsie beamed, "We'd love to. I've never tasted Mexican food, but I know I'll really enjoy it."

Ralph smiled, "Good, Mrs. Dare. Count on it."

"Oh, please, 'Mrs. Dare' is much too formal for my friends to call me. Call me Elsie," she beamed.

Mr. Guiterrez smiled back, "And you call me Ralph, Elsie. OK?"

"I'll do that from now on, Ralph!" Elsie told him as she waved to Alfonso's mother who was still sitting in the car. Mrs. Guiterrez waved back.

"We'd love to stay and visit with you, but we are hurrying to a movie," he explained. "And, Goober, I've got permission from your parents to take you along with us."

"Wow, that's great," Goober responded. He turned to Tracey and said, "You sure have awesome birthday parties! Thanks for inviting me."

Alfonso told her, "Yeah, thanks for inviting me too, Tracey. It's been an amazing day."

Tracey smiled, "The most amazing day of my life. Thanks for coming." Then Goober and Alfonso followed Mr. Guiterrez to his car.

When Ralph Guiterrez drove away, Elsie Dare turned to Tracey and asked her, "Did you know all Mexicans who make phone calls from phone booths have only one leg?" Then she winked.

Tracey laughed and said, "No, I didn't know that."

Her mom said, "Well the one who shot your Uncle Ted did." Then she grew serious and added, "And I feel so sorry for his mother now."

Tracey's birthday party had ended, and Tracey knew she would love having birthday parties all her life. But in her heart, Tracey knew that this one would always be her favorite birthday party of them all.

Five Real Friends

Chapter Three
A Rope Around The Heart

"Willie Radner has changed" announced Tracey, as the three close friends sat together after she had had her first guitar lesson.

"That's for sure," Goober agreed. "Did you hear how Freddie Melitt put it?" Freddie was twelve and the youngest student in their classroom. With brown hair that was never quite combed and an extreme love for desserts, his comment about Willie Radner carried weight. Goober quoted Freddie as saying, "Willie looks like he's been run over by an ice cream truck and didn't get any ice cream!" The three laughed, understanding how awful that would be. Then they all stopped laughing, knowing a friend of theirs was hurting.

Tracey said, "Ever since my birthday party Tuesday he just hasn't been the same. I said hello to him and he wouldn't even answer. I can't figure out what's wrong, but I hate to see him so unhappy."

"He was having a blast then. What could have happened that would have made him so sad?" Goober puzzled.

"Maybe he has a sick pet, or maybe his mom or dad is sick," Al suggested.

Not one of the three sitting at the lunchroom table was the kind of person who would talk behind a person's back. They weren't gossiping. They were honestly concerned for Willie.

"Did you know he got an F on that simple math test we took this morning?" Alfonso asked.

"NO!" both Goober and Tracey said at the same time. Willie made A's as easily as most people breathe, and all three knew for him to flunk this morning's test was unthinkable.

"I made an A on that test and I didn't even study that stuff,'" Tracey told them. "How did both of you do?"

Both boys answered that they had made A's too.

"It was a ridiculously easy test," Goober stated. "I'll bet no one in our class got less than a B except Willie, and he's smarter than the rest of our whole class put together!"

"Well, I don't know what's gone wrong with him," Tracey concluded. "But as his friends, I think we've got to find out. We need to help him through whatever it is."

"But how do we get Willie to talk?" Goober asked. "You just said yourself, Tracey, that he won't."

"Go to him, Goob," Al urged. "Willie and you talked a lot at the party. I bet he'll open up to you."

"Do it," Tracey further urged. "He's nice, and he's so gifted in sports, and so intelligent. We just can't let him hurt like this without finding out why and then seeing if we can help him."

"OK," Goober agreed. "I'll try to talk with him tomorrow. I'd phone him tonight, but I think I need to talk with him face to face. If I'm not with you two tomorrow for lunch, you'll know it's because I'm sitting with him at another table."

Tracey said, "I'll be praying a lot for both Willie and you between now and then, Goob."

"Thanks, Tracey," Goober responded.

Alfonso added before they left Tracey's house, "Be sure you're with us for lunch, Goob, if you don't get a chance to talk with him tomorrow."

"You know I'll be with you two if I can be, Amigo." Goober said with a smile.

The next day when the school bell rang for lunch hour, Goober hurried to the cafeteria where Willie was already sitting all alone at a small table. Goober quickly asked him, "Hey, Willie, are you sitting with anybody special today at lunch?"

Willie looked at him and rudely responded, "What's it to you, Goob? You lonely or something? How come you're not with your playmates?"

"Oh, they're fine," Goober smiled, ignoring the sarcasm. "But I had such a great time talking with you at Tracey's party that I thought I'd like to get to know you better."

"Well," said Willie with a smirk, "hand me a napkin and I'll give you my autograph!"

Goober laughed and sat down directly across the table from Willie.

"That Tracey is one hot looking chick," Willie began.

Goober answered, "Yes, she's very nice."

"Well," Willie said, "at least we agree about that."

"You'd really be welcome to come and sit with Tracey, Al, and me, any lunchtime."

"That's your thing, Goob," Willie replied quickly. "I don't like to be smothered by people. A lot of these kids in our class make me sick."

"Aren't you eating today?" Goober asked him. "You don't have any food in front of you."

"I'm not hungry," Willie scowled.

"Then do you mind if I go get some and come back and sit with you?"

"It's a free country," Willie answered sarcastically.

Goober went through the food line and then took his meal back to where Willie was sitting. This particular table was in the corner. Usually no one sat there. It was a table that was basically away from everyone.

"So what's on your mind, Goob? Have you started following Al to Tracey's house like her mother asked you to?"

Goober was unfazed by Willie's taunting. "Yep," he answered. "Al is teaching Tracey how to play that great guitar she got from her uncle. She's only had one lesson and she can already play a song. And she's got a great singing voice too, like Al does."

"That's just peachy," Willie sneered.

Goober leaned in and looked Willie straight in the eyes. "Willie, we think it's YOU who gets ALL the breaks. You're a fantastic pitcher, and smarter than any of us. You look like a movie star, and you have a great personality. But something's happened since Tracey's party that none of us understand. Look, I'm your friend. Tracey and Al are your friends too. Can you open with me and tell me what's happened to you?"

Willie snarled back, "It's none of your business, Goob. Just butt out!"

Goober was startled by Willie's anger, but he continued to probe with questions. "I know I don't hold a candle to you in any of the areas I've just mentioned. But if you can't tell me what's happening, can you tell somebody?"

Willie stiffened, "Nobody cares about me. They're all busy caring about themselves. Nothing really matters anyway. So what are you, Goob, a news reporter?"

"No, but I believe one day soon you'll be playing baseball at Giant Stadium. Then EVERYBODY will want to interview you, and I'll be boasting, 'I once had lunch with that superstar when I was in grade school!'"

In spite of himself, Willie gave a quick grin. Then he turned serious, "Well, Goob, don't hold your breath because I don't think that's ever going to happen."

"Why not, Willie?" Goober asked in surprise. "You've got the stuff for it. What would get in the way of that?"

"I don't want to play baseball anymore, or any other sport," Willie snarled again. "Sports are stupid. Take baseball - a bunch of guys go out on a field and throw a little ball around. If somebody hits it over a fence, everyone goes bananas. They think all that makes sense. And millions of stupid people who wish they were ballplayers cram stadiums or watch games on TV, screaming and hollering like a bunch of monkeys. It's stupid and I don't want to do it anymore. I don't want people to notice me. I want to be left alone."

"I don't get it, Willie" Goober told him. "You've never said anything like this at all before. At Tracey's party you told me you could hardly wait for baseball season to start."

"I've gotten a lot smarter since Tracey's party," Willie said in a bitter tone.

Goober went on, "Willie, think about it. If I could pitch like you, and you'd been cheering for me at every ballgame, just like I do for you, don't you think you'd find it really hard to understand if I told you Tuesday night I could hardly wait for baseball season, and on Thursday of the same week I told you I never want to play baseball again?"

"Maybe," Willie answered. "But I told you, it's none of your business."

Goober still tried to get Willie to tell him what was wrong. "You know, it's not only because you play baseball that your friendship means a lot to me. I want to get to know you if you'll let me. Just level with me. Tell me what's wrong."

"NOTHING is wrong," Willie shouted. "ABSOLUTELY NOTHING. Believe it, Goob, I've just wised up. Things have never been better in my life!" And with that Willie got up and walked away.

Goober rose slowly. He wished he'd said other things to Willie that might have made a difference. He figured he'd pushed him too hard and he had struck out. He spotted Tracey and Al, sitting where the three of them usually sat, and walked over to them. He sat down looking glum. Both of his friends looked up and saw his sad expression. "I blew it!" he told them. "I didn't find out anything from Willie and he probably won't ever speak to me again!"

"I'll keep praying hard," Tracey assured him.

"Good," replied Goober, "because this is going to take a miracle."

Miracles DO happen. At nearly 8 p.m. that same evening, Goober heard the telephone ringing at his house and was amazed to answer it and find Willie Radner on the other end.

"Hi," Willie began. "Is there any way you could meet me at McDonald's on River Boulevard in about twenty minutes? I'll buy you a burger. And I promise I'll open up and tell you what's going on with me."

"I think I can be there," Goober told him. "Let me check with my dad for a ride. Hold on. I'll be right back to you."

Goober went to his dad and said, "Dad, I've got kind of an emergency. A friend of mine needs to talk with me. Right now I think I'm the only one he'll open up to. Would you give me a ride to McDonalds on River and pick me up again at 9:30?"

"Is Al in some kind of trouble, Goober?" asked Mr. Boober.

"No, Dad," Goober answered. "It isn't Al. But it is one of the guys in my class."

"Sure I'll give you a ride. And I'll pick you up at 9:30. Do be outside waiting."

"I will," Goober agreed, "and thanks."

Goober returned to the phone and said, "I'll see you at McDonalds in a few minutes, Willie. I won't need a hamburger because I've already had dinner. But you can buy me a Coke."

"I'll be glad to," Willie responded. Quickly he added, "That meant a lot to me at lunchtime that you came and sat with me. Right now I think you're the only friend I have."

"Tracey and Al are your friends too, Willie, no matter what it is you're going through."

Willie said, "Thanks," and hung up.

Once Goober's dad found his car keys, the drive to McDonalds took less than ten minutes. Goober again thanked his dad for driving him there and walked in. Willie was already in the booth where he had been sitting when he had called Goober on his cell.

Willie said, "Let's go get those Cokes, Goob, and then I'll tell you what's been happening. I'm not a bit hungry either."

Willie was silent until he was asked by the woman behind the counter, "What'll you boys have?"

Willie answered, "Two super-sized Cokes, please."

The two boys were handed large cups. Willie paid for the Cokes and while they poured them from the fountain machine, Willie said in a very low voice, "I talked like a jerk today, Goob, and I wasn't sure you'd really come and talk with me again."

Goober answered in an equally low voice, "We're friends, Willie. This is what friends are for." When Goober said that it was the first time he had seen an honest smile on Willie since they'd both been together at Tracey's party.

Yet when they went back to the booth and sat down, Willie fell silent again. Goober waited. He could see how hard it was for Willie to say what was really on his mind. Finally Willie blurted it out, "My folks are getting a divorce!"

When Goober had entered the restaurant he had recognized how red Willie's eyes were. Now he knew why.

"I'd had such a great time at Tracey's party, Goob. I walked home whistling. But when I walked into my house my mom and dad were screaming at each other in the living room. When they saw me at the door, my dad said, 'Son, I'm done with being married to your mom. My things are already packed and in my car. I'll be back for a few more of my things tomorrow, but from this moment on I won't be living here anymore.' Then he said, 'I'm sorry, Son. I love you, but your mom and I are through.'"

Goober responded, "Well, parents sometimes say things they don't really mean, Willie. Maybe your dad thought he just needed some space and he'll come back even tonight or tomorrow."

"Thanks for trying to cheer me up, Goob, but I talked with my dad when I got home from school today. He was back to take more of his things and was just leaving again. He said he now has a really great apartment and that he wants me to come and stay with him whenever I can. I told him I wanted him to come back to Mom and stay married to her. He told me Mom and him don't have enough in common anymore. I can see what he means. Dad works late most nights and on Saturdays too. He sleeps Sundays til noon and then he's gone with friends to play golf. He hasn't been coming home from being with his friends until late Sunday nights. My mom used to cry a lot. Then she met this man, and I'm not going to go into that, but I'm alone in our house. We have a big house, and with everything falling apart I've talked to my mom or dad no more than five or ten lousy minutes since Tracey's party. I feel like I'm dying and nothing makes sense anymore."

"How long have your mom and dad been arguing with each other?" Goober asked.

"The worst part has been these last couple of weeks. It seems like they were yelling at each other every minute. I heard on TV that some moms and dads yell like that and that it's just a habit. They don't split. The guy on TV was talking about divorce and he sounded like he was talking about my mom and dad. But all the time I kept thinking MY mom and dad were BETTER than that. Sure they screamed at each other every day, but I thought as long as they were screaming, no one was leaving. I tried to believe it wasn't going to ever really happen because I HATE it. All their talk as I've been growing up about 'family' and 'morals' and 'choosing to do the right thing' has gone up in smoke."

"Were they always like that?" Goober asked him.

"Not at all. My dad and mom used to be best friends with each other, and my best friends too. They went to all my games and cheered their heads off for me. I wanted to please them more than I wanted to do any other thing in the whole world. And then all at once it stopped. Dad got too busy at work. Then Mom started going around with this other guy. And now my two best friends could care less about what happens to me."

"That must be really hard."

"It's the hardest thing that's ever hit me, Goob," Willie admitted. "And if they don't care what happens to me now, why should I?"

Goober knew the answer. He said, "Just because your mom and dad are messing up, doesn't mean *you've* got to mess up too. I know it must hurt like heck to suddenly know your folks don't care about how you feel. That probably hurts as much as if a knife got twisted in your heart. But you've got to do the right things whether they do them or not."

Willie was so deep into his troubles that he really didn't hear what Goober had just said. "I've thought of just walking out. I don't think they'd even notice I was gone."

"Yes, they'd notice," Goober declared. "But that's not the point, Willie. You can't run away from yourself. What's happening is happening whether you like it or not. Ducking your head in the sand like an ostrich won't make it go away. And if you run away, your mom and dad are going to think you really don't care about *them* any more."

Willie snarled, "They don't even WANT me."

Goober quickly answered, "Yes, they do. They might not know it right now, but they need you a lot."

Willie did a half-laugh, "What are you, Goob, some kind of a shrink?"

"Nope," Goober replied. "I'm just your friend who's hurting bigtime because you're hurting."

Willie looked down at the table before he looked back up and said, "Goob, you'll never know how much that means to me."

The two buddies were done with their deep conversation. They talked about nothing important for the next few minutes and then Goober said, "It's 9:25 and my dad wants me outside so he can pick me up. Are you OK?"

Willie answered, "Sure, Goob. I promise you I won't run away from home. Maybe you're right. Maybe after either my mom or dad wakes up, things will be different. I'll stick around. Thanks for caring."

Goober asked, "One more thing. Do you mind if I tell Tracey and Al? I know they won't tell anyone else, and they care a whole lot about you like I do."

"Sure, Goob," Willie agreed. "I know they're my friends."

Goober answered, "And I'm your friend 24/7, Willie. Phone me if you need me anytime of the day or night. I mean ANYTIME. Can we get lunch together again tomorrow and add Tracey and Al?"

Willie smiled, "Sure, Goob. Sure."

But when tomorrow came, Willie wasn't in class at all. At lunch Goober told Al and Tracey, "Maybe Willie's mom and dad made up last night. Otherwise, I know it sounds weird, but I sure hope Willie is sick with something unimportant. After our talk together last night it doesn't make sense that he didn't come to school."

Tracey replied, "Oh I hope his parents got back together. I prayed a long time last night for Willie and them after you phoned me."

Alfonso said, "Otherwise, he may have run away."

Goober had phoned Alfonso too the previous night and shared with him how sad and hopeless Willie had been at McDonald's. He told them nearly all of what Willie had said. He finished by saying, "I knew Willie wasn't going to walk home last night whistling, like he did right after being at your party, Tracey. But I did believe him when he said he wouldn't run away."

Alfonso said, "Well, maybe he caught a bad cold, or maybe his mom or dad did wake up and he's with them."

Tracey grew very quiet. Finally she spoke. "You know, I haven't told either of you that my dad and mom are divorced. It happened when I was three. I probably didn't feel the pain at that age that Willie's feeling right now, but I've felt it since SO many times."

Alfonso added, "I'm sorry, Tracey. It just seems so natural that every kid has both a mom and a dad."

"Well," sighed Tracey, "I can tell you, they don't. I wish I did. I really miss my dad. I don't even know where he lives."

Alfonso asked, "Do you remember much about him?"

Tracey sighed again, "No, I don't. But I really miss my dad anyway. He just disappeared. I do know he's a singer. My mom has told me he used to sing in Las Vegas with some rock groups."

Goober asked, "Does your mom know where he is?"

Tracey answered, "Nope. He just left."

Goober said, "Funny thing, until yesterday I never even thought about parents divorcing. The two sets of parents I know best are mine and Al's. Mine get into arguments at times, but I know they're best friends. Dad's loud; Mom's soft. But, Al, do your mom and dad ever get into any arguments at all?"

"Not around me," Alfonso answered. "So if they do, I never hear them."

"That's really great," Tracey sighed.

Then Al changed the subject. "Hey, Goob, I've been thinking. Suppose you and I go over to Willie's house after school and find out what's really happening. Maybe we can cheer him up if things are still bad for him."

Goober was immediately excited. "That's a great idea, Al. Let's do it."

After school, Goober and Alfonso went to Willie Radner's home. Goober knocked at the front door. No one answered. They waited. Goober knocked again. Still there was no answer. They found a very small doorbell and rang it twice. No one came.

Finally Alfonso asked, "Do you think it would be wrong to look in a window?"

Goober said, "No I don't. I think this is really important." The two boys looked through a window at the front of the Radner's house and could see part of the living room. They moved around the house to the side and looked through another window. They found Willie. "There he is, Al. But he looks like he's sleeping."

"Do you think we should wake him, Goob?" Alfonso asked.

"Sure. But I hope he doesn't get mad at us for waking him. Maybe it's a good thing there's a window between him and us!"

Goober tapped lightly on Willie's window. When that didn't wake him he tapped harder. Willie stirred on his bed. He rolled over, his face pointing towards the window, but he didn't wake up.

"Wow, he's really sleeping hard!" Alfonso noted.

Goober looked at his wristwatch. "Yeah, it's almost four o'clock. He must not have slept much last night."

"Maybe we ought to just leave," Alfonso suggested. "He might be angry as a bear if we wake him up."

"I hate to admit it, but sometimes I'm like that," Goober said. "I know curiosity killed the cat, and maybe it will get us killed too, but I feel like we should talk to Willie right now."

This time Goober tapped on the windowpane so hard that Alfonso warned, "Don't break it!"

The hard tapping did wake Willie. He woke slowly out of a deep but uncomfortable sleep and he knew someone or something was pounding on his window. Willie's head pounded too with every tap on the glass. He woke with the worst headache he had ever had. His tongue felt like he'd eaten a greasy dead rat, and he felt sicker than he'd ever felt.

Willie slowly opened his eyes, but shut them again quickly when they caught the sunlight. Goober shouted from outside his window, "Hey, Willie. Al and I came over to see how you're doing. We missed you at school."

Not wanting to rise, Willie shouted to Goober, "Goob, I'm fine." Then he grabbed his head because his shout made it hurt so badly.

Goober answered back, "You don't look fine. You look like you got hit by a bus! Can we just come in and talk?"

"OK, Goob," Willie responded reluctantly. "Come around front and I'll open the door for you guys."

It took nearly five minutes for Willie to even put on his robe and slippers. Every move made his head hurt worse. When he opened the door, handsome Willie looked the very worst he had ever looked.

"So," mumbled Willie, after letting the two boys in and obviously not caring what their answer was, "how was school today? Did I miss anything that would have changed my life?"

"You missed lunch with us, Willie," smiled Goober.

"I'm sorry about that, Goob. But I'll be there tomorrow."

With every step or movement, Willie felt like the Earth was shaking. He had to sit quickly to make his head stop pounding like a drum.

"Do you have the flu?" Alfonso asked him.

"No," Willie replied. "But any flu I've ever had felt better than this does now!"

"What have you got?" Goober asked.

"A hang-over!" came Willie's honest answer. "My mom and her 'boyfriend' left the liquor cabinet wide open last night. I didn't want to tell you at McDonald's, Goob, that this guy and my mom are drunk all the time. I've never seen my mom drunk before. She looks horrible. But when I got home from McDonald's I decided if I couldn't run away I'd drown myself in booze like they're doing!"

Goober slapped himself on his forehead. "But, Willie, that was just another kind of running away!"

"Well, it didn't work," Willie admitted. "I feel rotten. Now I know WHY they call it a 'hangover'! I was 'hanging over' the toilet a bunch of times last night, throwing up my guts!"

Goober repeated what his dad had told him many times, "You can never run away from a real problem. You need to run towards it and scare it to death!"

"Well," Willie moaned, "I'm not going to do ANY RUNNING at all today!"

Willie yawned, and even the yawn was painful. "I guess the only thing to do is sleep it off. Guys, trust me, I'm not going to do this again. I also may as well tell you two that I smoked a marijuana cigarette the night before last. It wasn't fun. I got a buzz from it, but I didn't feel good afterwards about doing it. I hate what's happening in my life right now.

But you're right, Goob, getting drunk or getting stoned are just other ways of running away. I'm completely done with both of them. I've never seen even one drunk or druggie that made me want to be what they've become. Excuse me right now though, guys. I've got to go puke again!" He hurried into the bathroom.

"Wow!" Alfonso gasped. "I sure wouldn't want to be Willie today!"

Willie looked very pale when he returned from the bathroom. He shook his head to try to clear it. Then he told his new friends, "Well, I've used up all my runaway tickets. I never ever thought I'd be one who had to sleep off a hangover. I never planned to get high or stoned. Now I want you guys to help me do something."

"What, Willie?" Goober asked him.

"I want you to help me dump every bit of the booze in this house into my kitchen sink!"

"Are you sure your mom won't get mad if she finds out you've done that?" Goober questioned.

"Probably," Willie answered him. "But I don't want her drinking that stuff and at least it will slow her down for a minute."

For the next ten minutes, Willie, Goober and Al, poured twenty bottles of alcohol into Willie's kitchen sink. At the end of all that pouring, Willie said, "You know what, guys? My head all of a sudden feels a whole lot better!"

"I wonder how your sink feels?" Goober laughed. That set both Willie and Alfonso off in laughter too, though Willie had to hold his throbbing head while he laughed.

Willie said, "When this hangover leaves me, I know I'm going to just go on hurting. There's nothing I can figure out to do."

Goober told him, "I know one thing you can do."

"What thing is that?" Willie asked him.

Goober replied, "When one of my mom's friends was going through a really hard time, I heard my mom tell her, 'Let time go by. This isn't the end of your life. It's just one really hard day in it.' It's the same thing for you, Willie. What happens with your parents has to be up to each of them. Give them time too."

The next day Willie was back in class. He joined his three new friends for lunch. "I've still kind of got a headache," Willie admitted. "I hope you three never drink ANY booze. It isn't worth it. From now on, if I *want* the flu I'll get the flu!"

Goober responded, "I saw an old movie on TV once called *The Days Of Wine And Roses*. It was really sad. It was about a lady who had never drunk any booze at all and a guy who was a lush. The guy started getting her drunk and the movie ended with her being a lush too. Then she left him to become a street person."

"Oh, I saw that movie," Tracey said. "After we saw it my mom was crying. She doesn't often talk about my dad, but she did then. She said what led to his leaving her was that he was so much into drinking. She kept saying how much she loved my father, but because he kept on getting drunk so much they could never get back together."

Willie said, "I keep hoping my mom will dump the loser she's with and stop drinking that garbage. And that dad will start loving her again."

Tracey continued, "I know what you mean. Of course, I was little when my dad walked out on my mom and me. Kids think funny thoughts when they're little. I know I sure did. I remember once I first started waking up to things and realizing my dad wasn't in my life at all, I wondered if I had put my toys away the night he left us if maybe daddy would have stayed with us and wouldn't have gone. Then I started pretending that my dad had just gone to the grocery store and that he'd be walking in any minute. But every time Mom cried, I knew he wouldn't."

Willie asked Tracey, "Tell me what you'd do if you were me."

Tracey prayed inwardly, then she told him, "I'd give my life to Jesus Christ and then leave everything in His hands. And I'd be there for my folks if either one of them wanted to talk to me. I guess I miss that most. I'd love to talk with my dad. I'd let him know I totally forgive him like my mom has. I love talking with my mom. It keeps us really close."

Willie admitted, "I'm afraid if I get into much of a talk with either my dad or my mom right now that I'll get angry over what they're doing and I'll drive them away from me even more than they are now."

Tracey replied, "That could happen I guess. That's what I mean about giving your life to Christ and praying. I'd ask the Holy Spirit to keep giving me *His* self-control. It's true if you don't talk to either of them with love, then you won't probably help your dad or mom until you do. Christ would give you the power to do that."

"Aw, Tracey," Willie said, "you are one terrific girl. But I'm not religious and Christ is just a swear word in my house."

"Christ died for you and for your parents. He lives to help each of you," Tracey answered.

"Well, that's good for you, Tracey. I'm glad you believe that. But what you're saying just sounds like a fairy tale to me. You talk about God like you know Him personally, like He's some big friend of yours. I don't even believe God exists."

Tracey finished the conversation with two words, "Ask Him!"

The first bell suddenly rang. All four friends cleared their lunch trays and slowly walked back to their classroom.

When Willie came home from school that day he found this note left for him by his dad:

Son: I love you. But your mom and I no longer want to be married to each other. We used to understand each other. Now we don't. I have now moved completely out of your mother's house. But I don't want to move out of your life. Can you plan from now on to spend at least part of every Sunday with me? I'd love to teach you how to play golf. I know you'd enjoy horseback riding too, and barbecues with great people who are my friends. I know you'll like my new apartment. It's big. I have a bedroom there for you as often as you want to stay overnight. Come join me.
I love you, Dad

Willie cried as he read his dad's letter. He knew his life was radically changing. Inside, he felt like a huge rope was tied around his heart. On the one end was his mother pulling one way, and on the other end was his father pulling the other way. Maybe that's why his heart was breaking. He loved them both and wanted to be together with them both. But he was afraid that would never be possible again. His best two friends in the world didn't like each other anymore.

The phone rang. It was Goober. Willie read to him the letter from his dad. Goober could hear the tears in Willie's voice. Afterwards, Willie asked him, "Goob, what am I going to do?"

Goober answered, "Love them both, Willie, just like you always have. They aren't divorcing you. They're divorcing each other. They still love you with all their hearts. Don't stop loving either of them."

"I won't," Willie agreed. "I CAN'T. I still love both of them with all MY heart too."

"I was calling," Goober continued, "to ask you out for pizza with Tracey, Al, and me. We're going to Pizza Hut on Mountaintop at 8 o'clock tonight. Will you come?"

"You bet I'll come," Willie said enthusiastically. "Maybe it sounds dumb for a *guy* to say it, but I feel like the three of you can get me through this."

"Your right, Willie. Now we're the FOUR Musketeers!" Goober declared.

Chapter Four
A Bomber Is Back!

Four pan-fried pizzas sat before four close friends as they discussed the letter in Willie's hands. It was the one he'd found from his dad. His dad had later left a message on Willie's cell:

"Skipper, I hope you found my letter. This is your dad. I love you. Call me."

Willie had read the letter aloud and had each of his three friends listen to his dad's recorded message on his cell. Then Willie asked them, "So what do I do now?"

"So, you are 'Skipper?'" Tracey asked.

"Yep," answered Willie. "That's me. Dad's always called me that."

"Why did he call you that? Have you gone sailing with him a lot?" Alfonso asked.

"No. It was because my mom and dad were going to skip having any children. But I came along anyway, so he called me 'Skipper!'"

"Well, you sure are here, Willie! And we sure are glad you're here," Goober encouraged.

"Man, you sure live in a great house, Willie," Alfonso added. "It's beautiful. It's almost like a palace. And your furniture is amazing. Add to all that all the things your folks have bought you and you must feel like a king."

"Al," Willie responded quickly, "I'd be glad to give away my house and all the junk I have TONIGHT if Dad would just come back to Mom. I don't even want to stay at my

105

house anymore. My mom is becoming a lush, and Lance, her 'boyfriend' - I HATE that word - is there all kinds of hours too. I don't want to see them, hear them, or be any part of of what they're doing."

Tracey reminded him, "Your dad seems to be saying you can stay with him."

"I don't want to do that either," Willie told her. "I don't want Dad to think I'm siding with him." A new thought hit Willie. "I've been torn in half, haven't I?"

"Yes," answered Tracey, thinking of how many times she'd felt that way about her own dad because she missed him, wherever he was. "I wish your mom and dad would go get help at my church."

"Aw, they'd never go to a church. They don't believe in that kind of stuff."

Tracey said, "I wish they'd try just once. But if they won't, I don't think your dad is asking you to move out of your house to get with him. He just wants to know if you'll give him some of your time too."

Goober suggested, "Why don't you read your dad's letter more slowly to us and we'll stop you if any of us has a question about it or thinks we have something worth saying."

Willie said, "OK", and began to read:

Son: I love you. But your mom and I no longer want to be married to each other. We used to understand each other. Now we don't.

"Man," Alfonso said, "it would kill me if my mom and dad split up." Willie looked at him with pain in his eyes. Alfonso suddenly realized how insensitive it was of him to have said such a thing in front of Willie. He apologized. "I'm sorry, Willie. You must feel the way I just said."

"Yep, I do," Willie answered. "But it's OK that you said that. I'm glad your parents are staying together."

Goober answered him. "We have lots of friends in our class from divorced homes. Since I found out about your parents, Willie, I began counting the ones I know of. I counted six, and there may be more I just don't know about."

"I'm so glad for those that never have to go through this," Tracey said. "It hurts too much."

"And right now I feel alone even with you three here," Willie admitted. "You're all great, but not one of you guys is like my mom and dad are to me."

"Well, Willie, I can sure see your dad loves you," Goober told him. "I'll betcha he wrote 'Son' instead of 'Skipper' because he wants you to know how he *really* thinks of you. He wants you to be sure you know you're still his *son*, no matter what's happening."

"I would have never thought of that," Willie admitted.

"Go on with the letter, Willie," Goober said with interest.

I have now moved completely out of your mother's house. But I don't want to move out of your life.

Tracey sighed and said, "I wish my dad had written that. It's awful missing a dad you can only see in your imagination. I've seen pictures of my mom and dad together when I was little, but I don't really remember him at all."

Willie read on:

Can you plan from now on to take at least part of every Sunday with me? I'd love to teach you how to play golf. I know you'd enjoy horseback riding too, and barbecues with great people who are my friends.

Goober said, "You've gotta say yes, Willie, if you're not going to run away from your dad. I know you hate to think about your mom and dad splitting up, but you have to face it. Your dad wants you to know he didn't leave you, he left your mom. That's lousy, but that's how it is. He needs you now bigtime because he's already missing you."

"But I don't want to become just another one of my dad's 'pals'. I'm NOT an adult. I just want to grow up from the age I am now. I'm only in the eighth grade. If he starts leaning on me, I don't have the answers for him. I just want him to come back home and be my dad."

"We don't always get what we want, Willie," Tracey reminded him.

Alfonso added, "Golf and horseback riding sound GREAT to me. Do you know any of your dad's friends?"

"Yeah," Willie said halfheartedly, "some of them. And they're a whole lot better than the creep whose dating my mom. She says he's her 'boyfriend'. You know, every time I even think of the word 'boyfriend' I want to punch that guy's lights out."

"But you do have to become a friend again to your mom, and to her friend too, Willie, because you love your mom. Maybe you can get your mom to quit drinking," Goober encouraged.

"You're asking me to do the impossible, Goob. How am I going to become friends with two drunks? I don't even want to try. I love my mom, but I HATE LANCE!" Willie said those last three words so loudly that a whole family at another table were startled. They turned quickly and looked at him. A baby being held by a woman at that table began crying. Embarrassed, Willie lowered his voice and told the three, "He only wants to be alone with my mom. He hasn't said a whole sentence to me since I saw him the first time."

"Then you're going to have to talk to him," Goober said. "Find out what he likes to do, where he likes to go, what floats his boat."

"I don't think that's possible, Goob. He likes taking my mom to a bar and bringing her home so full of booze that she hardly recognizes me. I hate him. He's completely destroying my mom. After he and mom drink I don't matter at all. I just want to disappear."

Alfonso suddenly said, "This looks like a job for Superman!" Goober and Tracey smiled. Even Willie smiled.

"No," Tracey said seriously, "this looks like a job for Jesus. I'm going to be praying even harder for you and your family, Willie."

"Thanks, Tracey," Willie replied. "But it would take Superman AND Jesus to work this thing out. I can't *make* it happen. I don't know how."

"But you do love your mom and your dad, Willie," Goober reminded him. "Even in my life, I have to kind of care about my folks friends just because my mom and dad like them."

"But WHAT IF SHE MARRIES THAT FREAK?" Willie responded. That was his greatest fear. The family from the other table looked at Willie again. The baby who had just stopped crying began crying again.

"Well," Goober answered, "My mom says, 'Ninety percent of what we worry about never happens. So there's no use worrying about the other ten percent because it's going to happen anyway.' If he's really a freak like you say, your mom will probably dump him before too long, especially if you pay her some attention. Probably they won't get married."

Willie read the final words of his dad's letter:

I know you'll like my new apartment. It's big. I have a bedroom there for you as often as you want to stay overnight. Come join me. I love you, Dad

"Phone him tonight, Willie," Goober advised, "and tell him that you love him and *want* to be with him on Sundays. He's going to be worried until you do call him. He doesn't want to lose you."

"OK," Willie answered. "I'll phone him. Thanks, guys, for sticking with me."

"We're the four amigos," Alfonso said cheerfully. "We stick together like gum sticks under tables!"

"Ugh!" Tracey said as she made a face. "I hope we're not that disgusting, Al!" Everyone, including Willie, laughed.

"I don't know what I'd do without you guys," Willie told them.

The four of them finished their pizzas and then their parents soon arrived to take Goober, Tracey and Al away. Only Willie was left alone. He walked home and phoned his dad.

Two weeks went by. In that time Tracey learned four more songs on her guitar and began singing two of them. Alfonso bought a goldfish because he always liked watching Goober's "Henry" swim around in his bowl. Goober got grounded for a full day because he forgot to feed Henry! And Willie shared time with his dad as well as his mom.

Even though Willie liked horseback riding and learning to play golf, he was finding it very hard to fit in to his parent's being apart. None of his feelings had changed. There had been no conversation between Willie and his mother's boyfriend. And he was finding his dad's friends didn't seem much interested in him either.

Willie was now at Goober's house, telling him about how he felt. "It's like I'm a half-person. I can't stand my mom's 'boyfriend'. I hate that word more every day. Mom and him together are disgusting. And remember, my mom never drank any booze at all until she got with him. My dad's friends crack jokes that aren't funny and everybody laughs except me."

"I know it stinks, Willie. But it's what's happening in your life right now. Things will get better."

"Or worse?" Willie responded.

"Well, isn't that what they say at weddings, Willie? At least they say it in movies that I've seen. 'For richer or for poorer, for better or for worse.' I guess that goes for their kids too if moms and dads split up."

Willie was about to say something in answer to that, but Mimi Goober had turned on Wake Up's all-music radio station and it was playing in the background. Suddenly a voice came on the radio that immediately caught both boys attention. Right in the middle of a song the music stopped and an announcer said:

"We interrupt this program to bring you this special news bulletin. Be on the lookout for fifteen-year-old Tinker Bomber. He has escaped from the Wake Up Youth Authority. He has red hair, is six foot four, and weighs 210 pounds. He was last seen wearing an orange cloth Youth Authority uniform. Tinker Bomber overpowered two Youth Authority guards this morning and is carrying one of their guns. He is considered armed and extremely dangerous. If you have any information that might lead to the capture of this young man, please call the Wake Up police station at once."

The announcer twice gave the number to call to make any report.

Goober thought immediately of the last words Tinker had said to him after being arrested:

"Just wait til we get back to school and grab you again! We'll pull more than your teeth! You'll wish you'd never been born!"

Goober shuddered. Quickly Willie said, "Oh, don't worry, Goob. Tinker would never be dumb enough to get anywhere near where you are. He knows the police would get him if he did."

Goober knew Willie was trying to encourage him at such an awful moment. But he also knew Tinker was absolutely dumb enough to come back and try to fulfill his threat. Willie asked, "Goob, do you think your folks would let me stay overnight here until Tinker is back behind bars? I'd still like to get away from my house and I'd be glad to stay. I'd be kind of like your own personal bodyguard."

Before Goober could answer, his cell phone rang. It was Alfonso. "Hey, Amigo, have you heard the news?"

Goober tried being light, "Yeah, Al, I guess I'd better guard my teeth!"

"What are you *really* going to do?" Alfonso asked him.

"There's not a whole lot that I can do about it. At least I know the police are already looking for him."

"Well," Alfonso said cheerfully, "do you need some company? Two are stronger than one and we could protect each other. I know Tinker threatened you, but he's probably real mad at me too. I know I'd feel better if I was with you. My folks might even let me stay overnight, knowing that your dad and Clyde will be near us too."

Goober felt a lot of his fear leave him. He realized he had two great friends who would stick with him even in his toughest moments. "Well," he said, "I'd like that a whole lot. And Willie thinks he might be able to stay here too. The three of us and my dad can whip anybody! I'm not sure about Clyde. He would probably sell me to Tinker if the price was right. Come if you can."

While Goober was talking to Al, Willie called his mom. His mom sounded woozy as she answered the phone and he could hardly bear it. She simply mumbled, "Yes, Willie. Do whatever you want."

Rex Boober was relaxing in his Lazy-Boy rocker and studying a computer manual when Alfonso knocked at the Boober's front door. After opening it he saw that Alfonso was carrying a sleeping bag and a small suitcase.

"Well, Al," Mr. Boober chuckled, "did you finally get kicked out of your house? Do you need a new home?"

"No, Mr. Boober. I thought you knew I was staying here for a couple of days with Goober."

"No, I didn't know, but that's fine. Goober and Willie are here somewhere."

"Yes," Alfonso said. "Willie's staying for a few days too."

Rex Boober scratched his head and laughed, "Are you three having a convention?"

"No, Mr. Boober," Alfonso answered, "but I'm sure Goober will explain it."

Rex Boober was interested now. "Yes, Al, when you find him, please have Goober come to me, will you?"

"Yes, Sir," replied Alfonso politely. "I'll do that right away."

Alfonso found Goober and Willie in Goober's room playing Battleship. He greeted Goober, "What's new, Bugaloo?"

"Lots of things," Goober smiled. "I'm sinking Willie's ships and Tinker Bomber wants to sink mine!"

Alfonso laughed and said, "Goob, your dad says he wants to see you."

"OK. Take over for me, Captain!" Goober answered, leaving his friends to go talk with his dad.

When Goober's father saw him he asked, "Son, why are Willie and Al planning on camping in your room?"

"Well, Dad" answered Goober, "I've got something to talk with you about, and I really need you to understand. Remember the Bomber brothers?"

"Who?" Goober's dad asked playfully.

"You know, Dad. The Bomber brothers," Goober said again.

"Of course, Son, I remember them. They stole computers from my store and tried to become your dentists."

"Those are the one's, Dad. Well, Tinker escaped from Youth Authority today. The newscaster says he's armed this time."

"Armed? Hmmmm," Goober's dad said thoughtfully, "I'd better check the batteries in our alarm system. But why do you need Willie and Al here, Goober? Do you feel you need them to protect you?"

"Not exactly, Dad," Goober answered. "But we just feel like Al might be as big a target in Tinker's mind as I am, to get even with him for his rescuing me and getting him and his brother arrested. And Willie just needs space from his own home for a little while. You know about his folks. All three of us would like to be together right now. Do you think that would be OK?"

"Yes, I do," Goober's dad answered. "I think that's fine. But you'd better tell your mother so that she can have two more places set for dinner. And after this you might want to ask me about having friends stay overnight before your whole tribe moves in."

"Thanks, Dad. I will. This just happened so fast," Goober said as he reached out and gave his dad a warm hug.

Before the day the Bomber brothers were first caught, Goober's dad would have most likely pulled away from being hugged by his son. But now he returned Goober's hug warmly and said, "Goober, you proved a lot to me when you weren't bawling on that ladder in the gymnasium when you were climbing it. And I've been watching you make a lot of wise choices ever since. Your friends are welcome here overnight as often as they'd like to be here. If it's OK with their folks it's fine with me, and I'm sure with your mom too."

No sooner had Goober's dad said that than their telephone rang. Mr. Boober answered it. It was Tracey Dare. She said, "Hello, Mr. Boober. Is Goober there?"

"Yes he is, Tracey," Mr. Boober answered. But before handing the phone to Goober, he put his hand over the receiver, grinned a big grin, and said, "NO! SHE is NOT staying overnight with you boys!"

Goober laughed, saying, "I know, Dad. I know."

When Goober greeted Tracey she immediately asked, "Have you heard the news about Tinker escaping from Youth Authority?"

"Yes, I have," Goober answered. Then he added, "Willie and Al are moving in with me until he's caught."

Tracey was delighted. "That makes me feel a lot better, Goob. It makes me feel you're going to be a whole lot safer."

"But what about you?" Goober asked. "I want you safe too. If Tinker somehow found out we were friends, he's the kind of guy who would hurt you just to hurt me."

"Well, you and I didn't really become close friends until after Tinker and his brother were caught. But just in case he has found out about us, my mom says she'll drive me to and from school each day until the police catch him."

"That'll be great, Tracey." Looking directly at his dad he said, "I think my dad will drive the three of us to school each day and pick us up afterwards too." Goober's dad nodded a yes from his Lazy-Boy. Goober smiled.

Tracey finished the conversation by saying, "I'll be praying hard for each of you, and for Tinker to be taken back to where he belongs."

"Thanks, Tracey. I'll talk with you soon."

"Son, would it help if I drove Willie to his house so he could get some clothes together?" Mr. Boober asked.

"It sure would, Dad. I'll tell him. Al and I will go too."

Mr. Boober laid down his manual, checked that he had his car keys, and the boys joined him for the short ride to Willie's house and back.

Once home again, Goober joined his two buddies in the den where they were happily playing Madden football. Then Mrs. Boober called all three of them to dinner. She was delighted to have two other boys in the house besides her own sons. She knew their being in their home meant even greater protection for each of them. She liked both Al and Willie and was so glad they were Goober's closest friends. She showed the boys where to sit and told them, "I do hope both of you like meatloaf. I planned it for tonight before I knew you two would be here."

Both boys assured Mrs. Boober that meatloaf was among their very favorite dishes. Only Clyde wasn't partial to meatloaf. But there were enough other foods on the table that when he took only a sliver of meat, he still later left the table more than satisfied. Peas, carrots, and a baked potato, went on everyone's dinner dish including his.

As everyone began eating, Clyde suddenly blurted out, "So, I guess Tinker's going to finish what he started. Hey, Goob?"

"You hush up right now, Clyde Boober!" Mimi ordered. "I'll have no talk like that in this house." Clyde knew she meant it and stopped instantly. Instead the conversation turned to happy thoughts and before long everyone, except Clyde, was having a very good time.

As she got up to get the dessert, Mimi said, "I've already phoned your mothers to thank them for sharing you boys with us like this. You both have lovely mothers." Willie hoped Mrs. Boober hadn't realized his mom had been drinking.

Dessert was homemade chocolate cake with vanilla ice cream. Clyde took the biggest slice, even bigger than Mr. Boober's enormous piece. As Clyde put it on his plate, Mrs. Boober teased him by saying, "Well, Son, I'm glad you left a little bit for the other boys!" There really was enough and everyone left the table full.

Goober told his friends, "Go into the den and play Madden some more while I help Mom with the dishes."

Immediately Alfonso volunteered, "Willie and I would be glad to help with the dishes too, Mrs. Boober."

She responded, "Not tonight, Al. But thank you. If you do stay longer I'll try to work you both into the dishwashing schedule." So the two boys played Madden's lateset game of video football instead.

Goober rinsed off the dirty dishes, bowls, and utensils. Then he loaded the dishwasher, stacking everything in the rack before adding detergent and starting the cycle going. After that he joined his friends on the video game and cheered for both of them.

The rest of the evening passed quickly. Ten o'clock was Goober's usual bedtime and at 9:30 Mimi called, "All right boys, time to get ready for bed." Alfonso had beaten Willie by two touch downs. With jokes and much laughter the three boys got their teeth brushed and took warm showers.

Goober had bunk beds. Willie took the top bunk and Goober the bottom. Alfonso put his sleeping bag down on the floor and crawled inside it.

Mimi came in to check that the boys were all right and said, "I'm so glad you three young men are together. Good night." Then she turned off the bedroom light. As she was closing the door she heard a trio of, "Good night, MOM!"

It was 3 a.m. Suddenly six eyes opened wide at the very same time. Six ears heard scratching at Goober's bedroom window. "It's Tinker!" Goober said loudly.

"Shhhh," Alfonso whispered.

Willie immediately tried to encourage his friends. He whispered too, saying, "Don't be afraid, guys. Close your eyes again so he doesn't realize we're awake. Just lie here for a minute until we see what he's going to do. He's all alone. But the three of us are together, so that makes us a lot more powerful than he is."

At that moment the strong beam of a flashlight cut across Goober's room from outside. It moved first to Goober's face, then to Willie's, and finally down to Alfonso's. All three boys lay still and pretended they were fast asleep.

The scratching began again at the window but suddenly stopped. Everything grew silent. Then the boys could hear footsteps moving away from the window and toward the front of the house.

About two minutes passed. Then all three boys could hear someone at the front door. They knew Goober's dad had carefully locked that door because he had showed them when he did it. But now Goober and Willie pushed aside their blankets, and Alfonso climbed out of his sleeping bag. They were all in pajamas. Goober told his friends, "Pick up something to clobber him with if he gets in."

Goober took the heavy flashlight that sat next to his bed every night. Alfonso picked up a heavy portable metal radio. Willie slung a baseball bat over his shoulder. Tiptoeing toward the front door, they stopped dead in their tracks whenever the doorknob was tried again. Each boy was thinking how glad he was that all of them were together and heavily armed.

Goober and Alfonso very quietly moved with Willie to the side of the door. Each got ready to hit Tinker hard as he entered. Willie carefully unlatched the door. A full minute passed that seemed much longer to them. But suddenly the door was flung wide open and WHAM! The intruder tripped on his own feet and immediately fell on his face on the living room carpet. Not one of the three landed a single blow because the unwelcome guest had tripped and fallen so quickly.

Instantly the light went on because Mimi had heard the noises too. If that light had not been turned on at that precise moment, the three boys might have committed a murder!

"CLYDE BOOBER!" Mrs. Boober shouted. "What in the name of toothbrushes are you doing?"

Clyde didn't have time to think up an alibi. "I was just trying to scare these guys, Mom! But when I swung the door open so fast, I tripped."

The three boys began roaring with laughter, but Mimi didn't. At 3 o'clock in the morning, Mimi was in no mood to think this was funny at all.

"Clyde Boober, you are grounded for a week with no car, no phone, and no television or computer privileges. Imagine you at your age trying to scare these innocent young men! I am SO ashamed of you."

"I'm sorry, Mom," Clyde whimpered. "I just thought it would be funny."

"Well you have a very sick sense of humor. And do you realize you could have gotten killed or seriously injured if these three boys had thought you were Tinker Bomber and started striking you? You must not realize how serious an armed enemy can be."

Clyde was staring directly at Willie holding a baseball bat as he said, "Oh yes I do!"

Mimi wasn't done chastising Clyde and added an even heavier sentence. "You are so lucky you weren't killed by Goober and his friends! They're very strong. Think about that this whole coming week while you're home doing yard work. Of course, if Willie had hit you with that baseball bat, maybe it would have knocked some sense into that absolutely empty noggin of yours!"

"I'm sorry, Mom," Clyde said with a voice full of self-pity.

"Don't sorry ME," Mimi responded. "Tell your brother and his two friends that you are sorry for trying to frighten them out of their wits."

Knowing that his mom was watching to see how he'd say it, Clyde said, "I'm sorry, guys."

Clyde was hoping a little bit of sympathy would come from his mom for the heavy fall he'd taken on the Boober carpet, but none came. In a couple more minutes everyone was headed back to bed.

The boys were laughing while honestly admitting how scared they were before they found out it was Clyde and not Tinker.

Willie said, "I learned a lesson tonight that I hadn't thought of before. No matter how bad Tinker is, I don't want to kill him!"

"Yeah," laughed Goober, "we'd ALL be in trouble if we messed up my mom's carpet with his blood!"

The boys could still hear Mimi lecturing Clyde for what he'd done. They could hear her loudly telling him, "You were downright mean. You'd just better be glad that your prank backfired!"

Clyde moaned, "Aw, Ma." He was even more unhappy knowing that his dad would totally agree with his mother in the morning.

But the happiest Boober at that moment was Mr. Boober, who slept through the whole thing dreaming he had swung a baseball bat, knocking a homerun over a wall that won the World Series!

Three days passed. A gas station, a convenience store, and a restaurant that was just closing for the evening, had each been robbed. In every case the thief was identified as a tall redheaded teenager who carried a gun. There was no doubt at all in anybody's mind who knew him, or in the minds of the police, that the thief was Tinker Bomber.

The four friends were having lunch together. Most of their talk was about other things, but they were friends and friends talk about everything. Tracey had roared with laughter when the three boys shared what happened when Clyde pretended he was Tinker. During Friday's lunch, Goober said, "I don't mind staying at home when my buddies are right there with me. It's a blast!"

Willie responded, "It's great. But you know, Tinker Bomber shouldn't be allowed to *make* us stay home. If we want to go somewhere together we ought to be able to go."

It was at that exact moment that Larry Beale came to the four of them as they sat at their table and said, "Hi, guys. I wonder if the four of you would do me a really big favor?"

"What kind of favor, Larry?" Willie asked him.

"Well," Larry began, "my dad is in a play tonight at the River Theater. It's a really big deal to him. Now suddenly the whole prop crew has been hit with the flu. There are a lot of props in this play and that leaves it with a big problem. I've got to go to the florist shop my dad owns right after school today and run it for him. I'll be there too late to do anything with the props at the beginning of the play. If my dad paid you ten dollars each for being backstage during the show so that you could set up the props that are needed at the opening and while the curtains are closed between scenes, would you do it for him, and for your old buddy Larry? I'll come help you as soon as I close up."

Willie asked, "What do you think, guys? Do you want to do it?"

Goober said, "We'd all have to ask our mom or dad first, but we could call them right now on our cells. Then we could give you your answer, Larry. I think we'd all like to do it. Right?"

The others said, "Right!" So the three of them phoned their parents while Larry waited. Willie didn't, because he knew it wouldn't matter to his mom whatever he did.

Very quickly the three had spoken to a parent, gotten approval, and then told Larry it was a deal.

"That's great, guys. I'll give your names to my dad so he'll know you're coming. Be there at 6:30. The stage manager will be there to explain everything to you. Oh, and give me your cell phone numbers so that my dad can call you if he needs to tell you anything more."

"See you at the River," Goober smiled.

When school was out, Tracey went to her house and all the boys went to Goober's to get freshened up for their big night at the theater.

What none of the four friends knew, and Larry didn't know either, was that Tinker Bomber, dressed totally as an old woman, had stood just inside the cafeteria at lunch hour and watched him talking with the four. A few of the kids sitting at tables nearest him laughed with each other when they saw Tinker, thinking he was a super tall old lady. But most of the kids were far too involved with each other to even look at where he stood.

Tinker was wearing a gadget on his ear that he hid under his Granny cap. It made it possible to hear some of what the four friends and Larry were saying to each other even at their distant table. His mother had bought this gadget when she had seen it advertised on TV. Immediately after Tinker broke out of Youth Authority he had gone straight to his mom's house. His mother wasn't there and this special hearing aid was sitting on her desk, so he took it.

He could hear the four friends talking and he saw Larry walking up to them. But loud kids happily walking out of the cafeteria and right by Tinker, drowned out some important parts of the rest of their conversation after Larry reached the table. Tinker knew something was going on involving the five of them. He saw the four friends hand Larry their cell phone numbers, and heard Larry say that he would be in charge of his dad's florist shop that afternoon. That's all Tinker heard, but it gave him his plan. His next robbery would be Beale's Florist Shop after Larry was out of school so that he could find out from Larry exactly what was going on.

Tinker knew about Beale's Florist Shop because once he and Morty had stayed away from home for three whole days and nights, thinking they would run away. But that was before they started robbing places and they grew VERY

123

hungry. Just before they returned to their house, Morty had said, "Let's buy Mom some really cheap flowers. That way when we come home she might not be mad at us for taking off like we did." Their scheme worked. She wasn't.

The Bombers told their mom they'd left a note for her about their leaving for a three-day camping trip, which of course was a lie. But she loved the flower they gave her. They had bought her a one dollar red rose, and she softened immediately and said while sniffing it, "Thank you boys for thinking about your mom like this. It means so much to me."

Tinker stayed dressed as a woman as he drove the car he'd stolen after his Youth Authority break to Beale's Florist Shop. It was a tan 1997 Chevrolet. He kept the car pretty well out of sight except at night. But he was willing to risk daylight now in order to get to Goober and his friends.

Tinker knew no one would ever think he would dress like he was dressed now. He hated smearing lipstick on his lips and smacking his cheeks with rouge. He wore a bonnet that covered all his red hair and the top part of his face. It was tied with a big white bow under his chin. In order not to be spotted in the very colorful clothes he usually wore, he had gone to a thrift shop the day before and bought a very dumpy plain-looking dress and a pair of Size 14 women's shoes. As he tried them on he had chuckled that he'd found any lady's shoes that would fit *his* feet.

This morning, after padding the top and bottom of his dress, and tightening the belt so that it could hide both his gun and his hunting knife inside his dress, he stepped back and looked to see himself in the cracked motel bathroom mirror. He instantly frowned and said to himself, "Tinker, for the first time in your life you look ugly! It's sure a good thing a handsome guy like you wasn't born a girl! Right now,

Tinker Bomber, you look like Little Red Riding Hood's grandmother. But, Granny, listen: If a wolf comes around to your house today, you are going to shoot it!"

Tinker had developed the habit of talking to himself very early in his life because no one else ever wanted to talk to him. Anyone who DID try to talk with him just made him mad because he believed everyone except he and his brother, Morty, were "stupid".

It was now 4 p.m. Tinker remembered exactly where Beale's Florist Shop was. He drove there, carefully keeping the speed limit so that no policeman would stop him for speeding.

Parking in an alley where a couple of other cars were parked, he made sure the gun he'd taken from one of the Youth Authority guards, and his hunting knife, were still well hidden. Then he practiced his "Granny voice" and laughed. "Hey, Tinker," he told himself, "you ought to be in the movies!"

Tinker made his way quietly to the florist shop and entered. He was glad to see Larry Beale was behind the counter taking money for a large bouquet of roses a man was buying.

The man had a little girl with him and was telling Larry, "My wife and I have been married twelve years. I'm crazy about her. Her birthday is today. These flowers are for her. I bought her an ice cream cake at Baskin Robbins for when we get home tonight. But Lucretia and I are taking her out for a scrumptious Italian dinner at Papa Luigi's. Then we're all going to see a play at the River Theater called *Arsenic And Old Lace*."

"My dad's in that play," Larry proudly told him. "He's the monster."

"I'll watch for him," the man told Larry.

All the time her daddy was talking with Larry, little Lucretia stood on one foot, then the other. Tinker thought, "Either she has to go to the bathroom or she's bored."

Tinker was delighted that Larry and the man had been so involved in conversation. It meant Larry hadn't looked away and spotted him. As soon as he entered the shop, Tinker moved quickly out of sight.

The man finished paying for the flowers. He then took the big bouquet in one hand, and Lucretia's hand in the other. Then thanking Larry, the man and Lucretia left. Now the only two humans in the shop were Larry and Tinker.

Tinker walked up to the counter and used his Granny voice, "Young man. Is there an adult here who could help me pick out some flowers?"

Larry couldn't believe how ugly this woman looked, but very politely he said, "No, Mam. No one is here except me. But I could help you. I know all about these flowers."

On hearing that, Tinker immediately pulled out the gun he carried and pointed it directly at Larry's chest. At the same time he pulled back his bonnet so that his red hair was exposed. Then he shouted, "SURPRISE!"

"TINKER!" Larry gasped, totally terrified.

"Yeah, Garbage Dump," he snarled, "aren't you tickled to see your old friend?"

Larry stuttered, "Sh sh sh sure. What do you want?" Larry immediately began to sweat.

Tinker told him, "First, I want all the money in that cash register, and if you have a safe I want all the money in it too."

Larry quickly took all the money out of the cash register and handed it to Tinker. "Here you are. But we don't have a safe. Dad just banks the money at the end of every day.

Honest, Tink."

"I'm TINKER to you, Stupe! Don't give me any of that 'Tink' stuff."

Larry was petrified as he looked at the gun Tinker was holding. "I'm sorry, Tinker. I didn't mean to insult you."

"OK, I'll overlook that ONE TIME since I'm such a nice guy. But I told you this money you just handed me is only the FIRST thing I want. And this is your lucky day. I only want TWO other things and then I'll waltz right out of here and you won't have a bullet hole in you for air conditioning!"

"What are the other two things, Tinker? You know I'll help you with them. But PLEASE DON'T SHOOT ME! PLEASE!"

Tinker saw how much Larry was shaking with fear and he loved it. "Well, we'll see, Larry. I haven't shot anybody at all today and I don't want to break my string of killing! After all, you are a really good target!"

"PLEASE DON'T, TINKER!" Larry pleaded, "PLEASE DON'T!"

"Aw, shut your trap, Potato Nose. Like I said, 'We'll see.' But if anyone walks into this florist shop while I'm still here, if I DON'T shoot you I'll shoot them! Is that a deal?"

"What do you want, Tinker? I don't want you to shoot *anybody*."

"Especially not you. Right, Braveheart?"

Larry was so scared he felt at any minute he might faint. He squeaked, "Tell me, Tinker. What else do you want?"

"I want to stop any way at all that you could let the police or your dad know I'm here. Give me your cell phone."

Larry didn't waste a moment. He handed Tinker his cell phone.

"Now, see this knife?" Tinker asked as he took it from his padding and showed it to Larry.

"PLEASE DON'T STAB ME EITHER!" Larry pleaded.

"Naw, I'm not going to stab you, unless you don't do what I say," Tinker sneered, continuing to feel great rushes of adrenalin from the joy of nearly scaring Larry to death. "I just want you to show me any wires that are hooked to your store's telephone, and show me any computer that you have here."

Larry said, "Dad has the computer at home. But here's our only telephone."

Tinker reached across the counter and swiftly cut the wire that connected the phone to the wall. Then he lifted off the receiver and shoved it and the knife into his padding.

"OK, Droopy Drawers, you're doing really good so far. Mrs. Plumpff would give you an A for how you've done, bless her ugly heart. But I want one more thing. And, if you give it to me, I promise you I will walk right out that door and you can start selling flowers again. Oh, and if you DON'T give it to me, your dad is going to be using these flowers for your casket!"

"ANYTHING Tinker! What's the third thing?" Larry was nearly wetting his pants.

Tinker pretended to moan. "I miss my classmates, Larry. I've been so lonely in Youth Authority just thinking about my best friend Goober. The only thing that makes me feel even a little bit worse is when I think of that really great kid Alfonso." Then Tinker quit pretending. "I haven't gotten to yank little boy Goober's teeth out yet. Not even one of them. And since that choirboy, Alfonso, ratted on my brother and me, I need to take his tonsils out too. Today at the cafeteria if you saw a sweet little old lady watching you from the door, that sweet little old lady was me. I've got great eyes, and that was Batboy Willie and Tinkerbell Tracey with them, wasn't it? Each one of those four must have had a great laugh over Morty and me getting locked up. This afternoon I want to make a social call on all of them. I'll shoot them if you won't let me shoot you!"

"NO!" Larry yelled.

"YES!" Tinker yelled louder. "I want the papers I saw you stuff in your pocket that I saw them handing you today. I know that you've got their cell phone numbers written on them."

Larry, in a state of total panic, was trying desperately to think of what to do. He knew if he didn't hand Tinker the papers in his pocket that the four friends had handed him, Tinker would most likely kill him then and there. But if he did give Tinker the papers he might still be able to warn the four and no one would get killed or even hurt. Very reluctantly, Larry fished into his pocket, pulled out all four slips of paper, and handed them to Tinker.

Tinker took the papers and carefully placed them in a pocket of his dress. "You are a really bright boy for a guy who looks like a monkey. I'm just about to turn and leave this sweet-smelling place. Just one more thing. Tell me where I can find the Four Stooges tonight."

"I don't know where they'll be, Tinker. They live at their houses," Larry lied.

"Oh oh," Tinker said. "I take it back about you being bright. You just lied to me. Just before I kill you, let me show you something my mom bought on TV. It's really handy. See you put this thing on your ear and you can hear conversations quite a distance away. You must not have seen me, but I was using it today at lunch while I was standing at the cafeteria door. I wanted to hear my old friends. You walked up and

129

said something to those guys about your dad being in a play tonight. Then you asked them something that meant they would be a part of that. The only problem is that just when I would have heard what they were going to do for ten bucks each, a bunch of loud-mouthed brats walked by yakking up a storm, and I couldn't make out clearly the rest of what they were agreeing to do for that dough. Now I'm going to count to maybe the last five numbers you will ever hear. Because if you don't tell me where your four buddies are going to be tonight before I say the number five, everybody is going to be able to look right through the big hole in your chest!"

Finding the last ounce of courage Larry had left in him, he wailed, "I CAN'T tell you, Tinker."

"That's fine," Tinker said. "I'm just going to start counting and you already know what will happen when I say five. That's fair isn't it?" Very slowly and deliberately Tinker Bomber began, "1……..2……3…….4…….."

"OK, TINKER, I'LL TELL YOU. But you've got to promise you won't hurt them."

"Hurt those rat-finks?" Tinker sneered again. "You know I'd never do anything like that! I'm their best friend."

"Do you promise me you won't shoot me or hurt me if I tell you?" Larry pleaded.

"Cross my heart and hope to die if I ever tell a lie," Tinker laughed.

"PLEASE!" Larry begged.

Tinker laughed even harder. "Scout's honor," he mocked.

Larry knew Tinker might shoot him whether he told him where his friends were or not. But if he didn't tell Tinker, it was almost certain Tinker would kill him right there in his dad's floral shop. He reasoned again that there was a much stronger chance he could somehow let his four friends know about what Tinker planned to do if he did tell Tinker. "OK," he agreed. "They are going to be backstage at the River Theater in charge of props tonight while my dad is in that play."

"What time will they be going there?" Tinker asked.

"At 7, when the play starts," Larry lied for a second time. He reasoned that a half hour would give him still more time to warn his friends and the police. This time, somehow, Tinker believed him.

"Well, you passed the test, Nut-case. In fact, you've been extremely helpful. Now, if you keep your yap shut about what just happened here, I won't kill you later either. Instead, in your honor I'm going to go buy dinner from the contribution your dad has made to me from his cash register. And Granny will be thinking of you all the time she's eating it, Dearie."

With that, Tinker pulled his bonnet into position and laced it again, hiding the gun and his knife. Then he turned and exited out the door. Right at that minute a man and woman walked in wanting to buy some carnations. The man said, "That sure was a funny looking lady that just walked out your door!"

Larry could barely find his voice. Finally he said, "Yeah, she sure was!"

As soon as the couple bought their flowers and left, Larry put a CLOSED sign on the shop door and ran to a friend's store nearby. Once there, Larry asked quickly, "Can I borrow your phone, Billy? I've got to phone my dad. It's an emergency."

"Sure," his friend told him, "but why don't you use your own cell?"

"I don't know where it is right now," Larry honestly told him, and dialed his dad.

"Tom Beale," his dad answered. Larry burst into tears as soon as he heard his father's voice.

"Son, what's wrong?" he said with concern and surprise.

Larry exploded with all the pent up energy he had held back all the time Tinker Bomber threatened him. "Dad, listen. Tinker Bomber came in dressed like an old lady this afternoon and robbed our store. He took my cell phone and he cut the wires on our store phone. I thought for sure he was going to kill me because he had a gun pointed straight at me all the time he was in the shop."

"I'm so sorry you had to go through that," his dad told him. "Are you all right?"

"Yes, Dad," Larry told him. "But I sure thought he'd shoot me all the time he was there."

"That must have been horrible for you, Son. Have you phoned the police?"

"No, Dad, I haven't had time. I wanted to tell you first because there's something that has happened that's even worse than all that."

"Son, what on earth could be worse than having your life threatened and my store robbed?"

"I had to tell Tinker where Goober and his friends will be tonight. He would have killed me if I hadn't told him. I think he plans to kill *them*."

"Oh my gosh!" Tom Beale said with alarm. "Those poor kids."

"Yeah, Dad, Tinker hates them, especially Goob and Al. And I'm sure he'll shoot at least them if he gets hold of them."

"Well, Son, close up the store. I'll call the police right now. We don't want your friends backstage at all. And I've got some good news. Louise and Sam have both phoned me. They say they just had slight cases of the flu and they think they're over it enough so that they can handle all the props themselves tonight. I'll warn them to keep an eye out for Tinker. And I'll ask the police for one of their men to be with them."

"That's great, Dad," Larry responded.

"I'll try to have as many police on hand at the theater as possible," he continued. "In fact, with the police there, if you can locate your friends before they come to the theater, they'd probably be safer in the audience tonight than anywhere else in Wake Up. Tell them I'll give them free tickets, plus the ten dollars each I promised them. I'll give them that because your friends were so ready to help me. I know the police will help all of us. Don't worry about a thing. Just phone your mother now. She'll come and get you and she can console you. Do you need me to come home and do that too?"

"No, Dad. You can console me later. But like I've heard you say a bunch of times, 'The show must go on!' Call the police. OK?"

"OK. Don't worry at all about your friends. Wake Up's police are outstanding. I know they'll keep them safe. And if any of your friend's parents want to come to the play with them, I'll make sure they all get comp tickets too.

"Thanks, Dad. You're the best," Larry told him. Larry's nightmare appeared to have ended. He let out a huge sigh of relief.

Rex and Mimi Boober, after hearing from Larry about what happened at the florist shop, and where a number of the Wake Up police planned to be, decided immediately that they wanted to accompany Goober and his three friends to the play. Ralph and Sophia Guiterrez felt the same way about Alfonso. And Elsie Dare said she definitely wanted to come with Tracey. Willie came alone. Comp tickets were arranged for all of them. Arriving at about the same time, the nine walked into the River Theater together. They were happy to see policemen standing outside the theater just as they'd been told they would be.

"Well," beamed Mimi Goober, "Larry's dad has really made this nice for us." It was 6:45.

"Have any of you ever seen this play?" Elsie asked.

"I got to see it on Broadway. It's a hoot," Ralph Guiterrez told her.

Elsie said, "I saw the movie version of it when I was a kid. Cary Grant starred in it. And I agree with you, Ralph, it's hilarious."

"Oh, my gosh," Sophia said in surprise. "Now I remember that movie. I saw it on Turner Movie Classics. Kids, you're going to love this play."

"I don't see any policeman inside the theater," Alfonso remarked. "Do you think they're only on the outside?"

"If there are any inside the theater, Al, they most likely are plainclothesmen," Mr. Boober told him. "They're just as equipped to handle anything that needs doing, but they're not as conspicuous this way."

"I hope they catch Tinker backstage," Mimi said to no one in particular. "He needs to be locked up again and have the key thrown away!"

At 7 p.m. the play began and soon everyone, including Goober's parents and friends, were laughing heartily. In fact, all of them forgot about Tinker entirely because they were so wrapped up in the play.

Tinker was feeling very bold. He was no longer wearing his Granny clothes. He'd scrubbed off all his makeup and he had on his much-preferred designer jeans and a black shirt. Still believing what Larry Beale had told him about Goober and his three friends being backstage at 7 in order to manage props for the play, Tinker tried the backstage doorknob. He cursed when he found the door locked. However, walking around the side of the theater he found an iron ladder fully attached to the building that led all the way up to the roof.

"There's more than one way to get those Scumbags," Tinker mused as he began climbing the ladder. He had watched carefully for police that might have been in the back or on the side of the theater. None seemed to be there.

Moving higher and higher, he thought of the ladder he and Morty made Goober climb at school. He started to laugh as he thought of it, but stopped when he suddenly remembered that awful moment when he knew his brother and him weren't going to make it to the top.

"Goober made us look like idiots that day," Tinker thought angrily. "But he and his stupid friends are going to be the idiots now."

Finally, after what seemed like a mile of climbing, he was nearly to the roof. He kept looking beneath him for any sign of human life, but he could see none.

Tinker stopped. He listened for voices on the roof, but all was silent. Slowly and carefully, Tinker rose to eye level of the roof. He could see the whole roof at once, even though it was quite long and quite wide. No one was there. No one at all.

Tinker pulled himself up and got on to the roof. Then he began to measure in his mind how big the front stage was compared to the back stage area. Deciding he'd found where the back part of the stage would be, the area where he thought Goober and his friends were managing props, he found a trap door and carefully lifted it. He was instantly excited. As he peered inside the trapdoor it was dark and he could see nothing except for light a long way down. He was certain he had found a way to get backstage.

Tinker felt around inside the hole. He found a rope. He felt its weight and it was heavy enough to make him feel sure that it would go all the way down to the backstage. "I'll shinny down that rope," Tinker decided, "and surprise those four losers. Then I'll deal with them one at a time."

Beginning to shinny, he was even more pleased with himself. He had his gun and knife hanging carefully on his belt. This was the night he was sure he'd use them. "The backstage in this big place must be huge and that's where I'll catch Goober and his pals," he told himself.

The fact that Tinker wasn't thinking clearly was obvious. If he had given any further thought to the situation he would have realized he really didn't know how far the rope would take him, and that he was gambling on being caught if he misjudged where the stage and backstage were. However, he was sure the guess he made would prove right. He believed he was ALWAYS right.

Tinker's hands began to burn as he continued down the rope and suddenly it was all he could do to hold on. He was very strong, but the longer he descended the more challenging his descent became. He was very glad for all the exercise he'd ever done. It gave him confidence that he could do this. But he also remembered that his climb up the ladder had been a very long one. Rope burns now made him angrier by the minute. He vowed, "Those clowns are going to pay for this when I get my hands on them!"

He descended one hand down and then the other. His hatred, especially for Goober, somehow seemed to make up for all the pain that his hands and body were going through. "Goober will hurt a whole lot more than this tonight," he assured himself.

He moved his hands carefully but quickly on the rope. Sweat was now drenching his whole body. He could hear people laughing from the audience and he was even more sure he was in the back area of the stage. Without his knowing it, the button on his gun holster came undone. Dangling in the darkness he felt the gun suddenly move and fall out of its holster. It hit the area below. CLANG!

"Oh NO," Tinker muttered, "I hope those brats didn't hear that." Tinker paused, afraid for just a moment - afraid either Goober or one of his friends would find the gun. He clung to the rope and waited. But he heard nothing below him and was confident he could find his gun again. Tinker's biceps bulged painfully with the strain of hanging onto the rope with all his weight and he knew he had to end this descent very soon. Sweat covered Tinker's face and forehead. More slowly and carefully now, he continued edging downward, concerned that he might fall. He could hear the actors speaking and the audience laughing every minute or so. This all grew louder as Tinker descended. Two minutes passed that seemed like ten.

Then in one awful moment there was light around Tinker's feet and legs! A whole audience of people began roaring with laughter. And the laugh got even louder as Tinker descended into even more light. The crowd was hysterical now. The audience had thought the gun that fell from Tinker was just another funny part of the play, and the actors had no idea why it had dropped out of the ceiling. Larry's dad, playing the part of someone who thought he was Count Dracula, had picked it up and put it on a table without even missing his next line. Now as Tinker looked beneath him he saw the actors staring up at him from the stage, and looked with horror at an audience roaring with laughter AT

HIM! Tinker hadn't found the back of the River Theater. He had found the stage itself!

Realizing his error, Tinker quickly tried to pull himself back up the rope, but his strength was gone. He wished with all his heart he was on the theater roof again. But his wish would not be granted. Suddenly the stage manager was yelling underneath him, "You come down here this instant! We know who you are, Tinker Bomber. The police want you!" Tinker had reached the end of his rope!

Sitting at Applebees on Mountaintop Drive at 10 p.m. that evening, Goober, his three friends, and all their parents except Willie's, were eating hot fudge sundaes and continually roaring with laughter as first one and then another gave their description of Tinker's "rope act". The manager of Applebees came to the table where they were sitting to find out why all of them were laughing so hard. He told them, "You HAVE TO let me in on your jokes!" When Goober and the others described what had happened with Tinker at the River, the manager began roaring with laughter too.

"All I can say," Mimi Goober said, "is that I have never attended a funnier play in all my life!"

As for Tinker, he was immediately arrested again, and after the various cashiers he had robbed at gunpoint identified him, a much longer sentence was added to the one he already was serving at Youth Authority. In fact, he would be doing a much longer prison stretch before ever being let out.

"Tinker," Morty yelled at him later, "you are such an IDIOT! I'm ASHAMED that you are my brother!" And THAT hurt Tinker even more than the further sentencing did.

Tinker was embarrassed too by the stage manager at the River Theater and what he said after Tinker let loose of that long rope. The manager pointed to the deep red rope burns across both of Tinker's palms and said to the two policemen who were hauling him away, "He was caught red-handed officers! Yep, RED-handed indeed!"

Five Real Friends

Chapter Five
Thanksgiving

Thanksgiving Day in Wake Up was spectacular. Leaves were showing off their brightest colors and it was just warm enough to be outdoors wearing lightweight sweaters or jackets.

Thanksgiving morning, Mr. Boober and Mr. Guiterrez got together to take the four friends to a football game at John Kennedy High. Both Rex and Ralph had been friends since their boys were in first grade.

Kennedy was behind by six points until the last two minutes of the game. Then Luke Benning, their left end, intercepted a pass and ran forty-three yards for a touchdown. Everyone for Kennedy was on their feet and screaming for Luke every second he was galloping to the end zone. Then, as the ball sailed over the goalpost for the extra point, John Kennedy won and everyone screamed even louder.

Rex, Ralph, and the friends, left feeling very proud of the friends' future high school.

The Guiterrez family, Tracey, her mother, and Willie, joined the Boobers to devour the scrumptious meal Mimi Boober had prepared.

The four friends had thought they would have to listen to the adults talk at the dining table during the Thanksgiving feast in order to be polite. But Mimi, knowing they'd have much more fun just talking together, seated them at a smaller second table.

As they gnawed on drumsticks the boys recapped the thrilling football game they'd seen that morning. Then all four used their vivid imaginations to describe what it would be like when they actually would be freshmen at John Kennedy. All agreed they could hardly wait.

Clyde Boober sat with the adults and was totally bored. Finally Mimi told him, "Chew all your food and swallow it BEFORE you yawn PLEASE!" He stopped yawning, but did a whole lot more eating.

Martinelli's Sparkling Grape Juice was the drink at everyone's plate. And after every person at both tables had their fill of turkey, cranberry, mashed potatoes and gravy, spinach, peas and carrots, and hot rolls. Mimi Goober served her prize-winning whipped cream pumpkin pie, accompanied by large scoops of vanilla ice cream.

Both Rex and Ralph were yawning after eating so much food just like Clyde was, though the two men had finished swallowing before they yawned. The three of them went into the Boober's cozy living room, sat down and watched a college football game on television.

The three women took the rest of both turkeys into the Boober kitchen and, talking merrily as they did it, carved off all the meat that was left on the turkey bones. Mimi split the meat into three packages and gave one each to Elsie and Sophia to take home. Then she put the bones, and the remaining meat hanging on the bones, into a large soup pot to make turkey soup.

Now it was the ladies' turn to relax while the four friends finished clearing the tables and loading the dishwasher. Then they went outside to play basketball. Goober and Alfonso were one team, Willie and Tracey the other. Tracey was a really great basketball player, scoring more baskets than any of the boys, so she and Willie won easily.

Elsie and Tracey then left to see a fun movie. The boys left to stay overnight at the Guiterrez home. They spent the evening throwing darts and playing ping pong. Al beat Willie in their first game of ping pong, but Willie got even. Then he played Goober, who had been making a spectacular show of his skill with darts. By bedtime they had all won a bunch of games and happily declared it a three-way tie.

After lights were out the boys got to talking about the night Clyde had pretended he was Tinker Bomber and how easily they might have bashed Clyde's skull in by mistake. But because they hadn't struck him at all, they roared and roared with laughter.

Alfonso laughed, "I'm glad we didn't end up pounding Clyde into the carpet!"

They continued howling with joy as they remembered how Goober's mother spoke to Clyde afterwards, and that it was nothing compared to what Mr. Boober said to him the next morning. Mr. Boober had extended all the sentences Mimi Boober had given Clyde for a whole second week.

Then they talked about Tinker Bomber climbing down the rope during the play at the River Theater. Goober described Tinker's legs and then his whole body dangling in front of the audience and the actors on the stage. "There he was," said Goober, "trying to climb back up that rope, but he couldn't!"

Willie roared, "Larry's dad was great in the play, but I think Tinker should get an Academy Award!" The boys agreed they were so glad Tinker was locked up again.

Finally the boys talked about how much had happened since eighth grade had started just three months before, and how Tracey and all of them had become such close friends.

Goober, thinking of Mrs. Dare, said, "Even our parents are friends now." Then thinking of Willie's parents he tried to encourage him by saying, "I'll bet your mom and dad will get back together and it will be even more fun next

Thanksgiving."

"I keep hoping that will happen, but I don't see any sign of it. Mom just keeps hanging on to her crazy boyfriend and they're partying all the time." Willie responded. "But I sure like all the adults who were at your house today, Goob. You guys have GREAT parents."

Just before they fell asleep, Alfonso said, "This was a great Thanksgiving, Goob. And we've sure got a lot to be thankful for."

"Yep," agreed Goober, "we sure do."

The next Monday, back in school, the four friends met at their usual table for lunch and each had had a great weekend.

Tracey's mother had taken her on a quick drive to Yosemite National Park. Tracey tried to describe it to the boys and ended up saying, "It is so beautiful that only God could have created it. It was a long drive and we were only there for a day. But Mom says we'll go back there and stay a whole week next summer."

Goober and Alfonso had gone to a carnival together. They rode the roller coaster six times. Goober said, "It was really scary."

"Then why on earth did you ride it six times?" Tracey asked.

Alfonso answered, as if hers was a really silly question, "Because we *like* being scared!"

The day after the carnival, Goober and Alfonso had gone hiking with Goober's dad up on White Mountain. Goober said, "I guess Tracey's God must have made White Mountain too, because it's amazing."

"He did," Tracey assured him.

Finally Goober asked Willie, "So how did things go for you since Friday?"

"Well," Willie said, "a lot has happened."

"WHAT?" the trio asked enthusiastically, seeing Willie was smiling.

"Tell us about it," Alfonso urged.

"It happened right after I got home from your house on Friday, Al. I was just putting my dirty clothes in the hamper when my mother's boyfriend, Lance, shocked me by asking me if we could sit down together in the living room and talk. For some reason I agreed, even though I didn't want to talk to him at all. But I could tell that for the first time since I'd seen him with Mom, he was completely sober and he was really down. I was hoping maybe he'd broken up with Mom and that's why he was so depressed. Instead he said something like, 'You're really lucky, Willie. You're just a kid. You've got your whole life ahead of you. I wish I did.'"

"That was a funny thing to tell you, wasn't it, Willie?" Goober asked. "If he's the same age as your mom, he can't be *really* old. And doesn't he realize how much he's messed up your life? Why would he say you were 'lucky'?"

"Well, he is a lot older than we are, that's for sure. But I thought exactly what you just said, Goob, 'Give me a break. You're not an *old* man.' And you're right, it really ticked me off when he said I was 'lucky'. I wanted to tell him, 'Yeah, I'm really 'lucky'. You broke up my mom and dad, and now I hate how my life is going because of you. Get lost!' But I didn't say that. See, it was like someone was suddenly telling me something I really hadn't thought of before. I realized that my mom *chose* to be with Lance. Their getting together wasn't all Lance's fault. It was hers too. So I didn't say anything."

"I never thought of that," Alfonso admitted. "I've been totally blaming Lance for hurting your mom."

"Lance kept talking. He asked me if I drank alcohol. I wanted to tell him, 'No. And my mom didn't drink it either until you forced it down her throat.' But then once again it was like I heard someone say, 'Your mom never had to take even one drink. She could have said no.' So I told Lance the truth. 'Not anymore. It makes me sick.'

"Lance said he wished he'd quit drinking when he was my age. Then he told me *why* he wished he'd quit. He had gone to his doctor that morning. He said, 'I found out today that alcohol makes me sick too. REALLY sick.'"

"How sick was he?" Alfonso asked.

"His doctor had told him straight out that morning that he was in big trouble with his liver because of all the booze he'd drunk in his life. He told Lance that if he drank even one more drink EVER, he would be 'committing suicide'! He told him he might die even now from all the booze in his body. I didn't like Lance, but I just wanted him to get out of my life, not die."

"You must have freaked," Goober told him.

"Yeah, I was really knocked out by his whole conversation. But I'll tell you something dumb. When Lance said 'liver', all I could think of was the one bite of yukky calf's liver I'd tried for the first time last year, and I knew I hated it. I pictured that liver and told him, 'Wow! That's really awful.'"

"I hate liver too," Tracey admitted.

"Lance said, 'I've got to stop drinking. But that's a lot harder to do than it sounds.' Then he told me he'd been drinking from the time he was ten years old."

"TEN YEARS OLD!" Goober gasped. "Where could he have gotten drunk when he was ten?"

"In his own house," Willie responded. "He said his folks didn't care. They were both alcoholics, so drinking alcohol

146

to them was a lot better than drinking milk. The first time they got Lance drunk they thought it was funny. They took a bunch of pictures of him and showed them to all their friends. Lance said he hated all the laughing over those pictures because he looked so stupid. But he kept on drinking."

"That was really mean of his parents," Tracey declared. "They should have been arrested for that."

"Yeah, Tracey, but they weren't. It was Lance himself who was arrested for drunk driving when he was fourteen. Of course he had no license. He got a suspended sentence and the judge told him he couldn't drive until he was eighteen. But he drove drunk lots of times after that and never got caught or he would have been sent to where Tinker and Morty are."

"That's amazing he didn't get caught," Alfonso said with astonishment. "The cops must have been somewhere else whenever he was driving." Then realizing Goober and Tracey were eager to hear the rest of Willie's story just like he was, he simply said, "Keep going."

"Lance told me he was twenty when he got into a really bad car wreck because he was drunk. Some girl he liked a whole lot got badly injured. The doctors thought she was going to die. She was unconscious for three weeks after having three surgeries. As soon as she was conscious he bought her a dozen red roses, took them to her hospital room, and she told him to get lost. He said he was really broken up about it. He felt real guilty about the accident. She did get well after about a year and a half, but the doctors told her she'd walk with a big limp for the rest of her life."

"Oh, I hope that girl has somehow forgiven him wherever she is." Tracey sighed. "Nobody should live life staying mad at anyone, no matter what they've done. That would make her as sick inside as all that drinking made him!"

147

"Lance said he talked with her just one more time for about two minutes when she finally got out of the hospital. She was still really mad at him. She showed him how badly she limped. Then she told him that limp would always remind her of him, and how much she hated him."

"She must have REALLY hated him," Goober responded.

"But even then Lance didn't stop drinking. He told me he had gotten drunk every night during the three weeks she was in a coma and even came to the hospital drunk when he brought the flowers."

"That's so sick," Tracey responded. "She should have stayed completely away from him, but not kept on hating him. Just like your mom with Lance, she didn't have to be with him in the first place."

Willie continued, "I could see, looking at Lance, that his doctor's words had really messed him up. He told me, 'I don't want to die.' Lance closed his eyes when he said that. Then he opened them again and changed the subject. He said, 'Hey, I haven't talked to you before.' Then he apologized to me for that. He said, 'It was pretty lousy of me to be dating your mom and not talking to you.'

"I told him that was OK. I didn't tell him that I had never wanted him to talk to me at all. But until he talked like that and opened up with me, you guys know I hadn't. Lance didn't shut up. He said, and I remember these words exactly, 'I guess if I don't die and I end up marrying your mom, you kind of come along with her as a package.'"

"That was a dumb thing to say," Goober sympathized. "Didn't he know saying that would hurt you?"

"Well, I honestly don't think he thought about how I would feel about anything he was saying. Sure, the idea of my mom and dad divorcing and Lance marrying my mom makes me sicker than his liver is. But for some reason I didn't say anything. I really didn't know what to say. Then Lance asked me, 'Do you suppose you and I can be friends?'"

Alfonso exploded, "FRIENDS? If someone else but my dad was dating my mom they could NEVER be my friend." Alfonso spoke so loudly that kids from other tables looked at him.

"Well, I still wanted to tell him to take a long walk on a short pier. But I didn't tell him that. Instead, I told him that I didn't know. But then I got blunt. I flat out said, 'I don't like you dating my mom.'"

Goober said, "I'd have told him the same thing, only a lot stronger."

"I would have been stronger, but wait until you hear the rest of it, Goob. He wasn't done honestly telling me his feelings. And I remember what he said next, word for word, it so shook me. He told me, 'I think I understand how you'd feel about that. But I'm sober now and I still want to marry your mom.'"

"NO!" Alfonso shouted. More kids started looking from other tables. Alfonso quieted down.

"It was like catching a bomb in my gut. I wanted to get up and walk away from him. But for some reason I just sat there. You know why? Because I really felt sorry for him for the very first time. And I know you guys are going to pound me for this, but I started to like him! I'd never heard any adult be as open with me as he was being."

"God is at work in this whole thing," Tracey said to encourage Willie.

Willie didn't respond to Tracey. Instead he said, "The next thing Lance told me was, 'Love's a funny thing.' He said, 'Take my dad and mom for example. I still love them.' He told me that for some reason both his mom and dad were totally sober one night. Then a drunk smashed into their car. They were killed and their bodies were taken straight to the morgue. Their bodies were so torn up, Lance never even got to see them in their caskets. Lance said he was sixteen and he cried his eyes out. But he'd never cried at all for them when they were alive, no matter how bad things were going for them. Once they were dead and couldn't hurt him anymore, he realized he really did love them."

"Gosh," Tracey sighed.

"Lance's honesty, and all that he was sharing with me, got to me. I realized what a hard life he must have lived growing up. The death of his father hit him hardest. I told him, 'I can't imagine how I'd take it if my dad died. We're really close.'"

"Yeah, if my dad died I couldn't stand it," Alfonso agreed.

Tracey said, "Without Jesus Christ in your life, the death of anyone you love wipes you out. It takes Him to get you through it."

"Well, I don't know where Lance stands with religion, Tracey," Willie told her. "But even you would hate it if your dad died."

"Yeah, I'd hate it if I found out. But my dad isn't in my life now, Willie," Tracey responded. "It's just as if my dad *is* dead. But I was really thinking about my Aunt Cheryl dying. It's really been hard, but Christ keeps me going. And I know *God* is my *real* Father."

Willie looked at Tracey as if she were talking about Santa Claus being her father. "Then Lance said something more I would have never expected him to say, and I knew he was trying to encourage me. He told me that my mom had told him that my dad doesn't drink any alcohol at all. And then he said something like, 'Your mom says your dad doesn't like alcohol. So I guess his liver and probably the rest of him is going to be just fine for a long, long time. You'll be able to keep your dad. That's good news!'"

"That IS good news," Alfonso agreed.

"After Lance had finished telling me this, I was quiet. I really didn't know what to say. Lance just smiled at me and said that he did hope we could be friends. He said maybe he could take my mom and me to a movie or something. He told me how proud mom is of me. She had told him I'm a scholar and an athlete. I told him I'm only in the eighth grade and games against other schools aren't probably all that important."

"They sure are!" Goober insisted. "You know you've already had a Giant scout check you out last year because of your strike-out record."

"And because you've never lost a game," Alfonso added.

"Well, Mom told him that too. He told me so. Then he completely bowled me over. He asked me if I'd let him come and watch me pitch this year."

"Are you going to let him?" Tracey asked.

"I told him I would, and then I couldn't believe I'd told him that. Until that talk I wouldn't have even wanted him *near* one of my ballgames."

"You're blowing my mind!" Goober told him.

Willie said, "It was at that minute that my mom walked in. Just like Lance, she was completely sober. And she said, 'Well, look at the two of you. You're talking to each other. I don't think I've ever seen you two do that before.'

"Lance spoke up and told her that was *his* fault. He said now he'd probably said too much. But he bragged on me and told mom she was right and that I WAS 'a great young man'. He said, 'No wonder you're so proud of him.' I've got to admit that felt good. With that, my mom walked over to me and gave me a big sloppy kiss on my cheek that embarrassed the heck out of me!"

Goober admitted, "My mom does that sometimes in front of company too. It embarrasses me, but I like it."

"Well, Lance saw how embarrassed I was, and I think in order to break my embarrassment he said, 'Hey, why don't we go out and have dinner, just the three of us. You pick the restaurant, Willie. I'll pay.'

"My mom was still standing next to me and hugging me. Guys, I was really afraid until then that I'd totally lost my mom. She said, 'Son, that's a great invitation if I've ever heard one. Will you go with us?'

"Well, I didn't want to let her down, and Lance had been so friendly, I thought 'What the heck'. Still I knew when I said yes that this was a really big change for me. Yet it was a whole lot better than seeing both of them drunk. So I told Lance that both my mom and I like the Thai food at High Thai. He said Thai was a favorite of his too. So that's where we went."

"My mom and I like High Thai too," Tracey agreed.

"Talk about miracles! The whole evening after that went great. Without booze, Lance is really nice. I learned that he manages a real estate company, and that he met my mom while they were waiting in line for lattes at Starbucks."

Goober asked, "Wasn't he sick or anything from not drinking when he'd been doing it all those years?"

Willie answered, "Well, that must have been another miracle. The doctor told him his body might start falling apart, and that he might even see weird things that weren't really there because his body was 'drowning' in all that booze. But he just sat there all evening talking with my mom and me, and nothing bad happened at all. In fact, what happened was pretty cool."

"I told you God is at work," Tracey told him. "He's great at miracles."

Willie asked her, "Do you really believe that, Tracey?"

Tracey answered, "I see them all the time. And I've really been praying hard for you, Willie."

"Well, keep it up," he told her. "Something is happening that I can't explain with Mom, Lance, and me. But I still want my dad to come back to my mom."

"I'm still praying hard for that too," Tracey assured him. "But you know, Willie, you could pray with me for it to happen."

Willie looked at her in disbelief, "ME? I'm sorry, but I'm just not religious."

"Me either," Tracey smiled. "But do you know who was talking to you in your mind?"

Willie said, "No."

Tracey said, "It was GOD, Willie. I pray for you all the time."

Willie said, "Thanks again, Tracey, but I think it was really just me talking to myself."

"Do you do that a lot?" she asked.

"No," he admitted. "I can't remember any other time in my life I heard myself like I did right then."

"Well," Tracey declared, "God DOES talk that way."

"OK," was all Willie could tell her, because God talking to Him wasn't something he could imagine in his wildest dreams. Goober and Alfonso were totally silent too because they couldn't imagine anything like that either.

Then Goober broke the silence by agreeing, "That does sound like a miracle, Willie. You didn't quit on your mom or your dad and now good things are happening. I knew they would if you didn't drop out."

The school bell rang.

"What a great weekend," Goober smiled. "We've all had Thanksgiving for sure!"

School, guitar practice, fun times together during lunchtimes, get togethers at each others homes, the boys having sleepovers at Goober's, Alfonso's, and now at Willie's house too, went quickly between Thanksgiving and Christmas vacations. It was the final day of school before Christmas break and again the four amigos were having lunch in the cafeteria. Tracey was the first to speak, "I know we'll all be doing things together at times, but what other special things are you three doing over Christmas?"

Willie answered, "Going three ways at once! I'll be spending time with Lance and my mom, and then with my dad and his friends, as well as with you guys. I found out his friends are OK. Not great, but OK. And I may have a job. Thanks to my dad, I may get to work for Mickey O'Rourke at his stables where I can go horseback riding free and help groom the horses after they've been out."

"Wow, that doesn't sound like work at all," Goober smiled.

Willie asked, "What are you going to be doing that's special, Al?"

"My dad is taking me fishing at White Mountain," Alfonso answered joyfully. "And we're going up in the woods to find our Christmas tree. You guys are going to have to come over to my house after we chop it down and decorate it. It's really going to look great."

"So how about you, Goob," Al asked. "What's your big Christmas adventure going to be like?"

Goober joyfully answered, "I'm going Christmas shopping. When my Great Aunt Gertrude died she left me two hundred dollars. It's all ready to spend. My folks have said I can spend it any way I want to. And I want to spend it on Christmas surprises that will make them happy, and also on three other friends who just happen to be sitting here right now."

"Oh, don't spend it on us, Goob," Tracey protested. "Spend it on your family and yourself. I get way too much for Christmas from my mom. And remember, Uncle Sylvester will be sending me a gift that will cost a small fortune! Let Christmas be a family time for you."

Willie spoke up, "Tracey's right, Goob, you've seen all the stuff I have at my house. I don't need anything more."

"And the same thing goes triple with me, Goob," Alfonso joined in. "I don't have room for anything more. Besides, my dad always says, 'Don't let money burn a hole in your wallet. Save it for something you'll really want sometime.'"

"My folks will be all the Santa I'll need," Goober responded.

"Well then, do something nice with the money for them if you feel you really want to spend it," Tracey suggested.

"OK, I'm listening to all of you," Goober smiled. "But don't be surprised if Santa-Goober comes 'ho ho hoing' down your chimneys on Christmas Eve."

"We don't have a chimney," Tracey chuckled. "You'd just have to stay up on our roof all night!"

Alfonso quickly said, "My folks are just like yours, Goober. They always go all out for me. We'll have plenty. And you might get shot on my roof because someone would think you were a burglar!"

Goober laughed, "Then maybe I'll just be the Grinch to each of you! After Santa leaves your presents, I'll snatch them away!"

Alfonso laughed. "Goob, you're not mean or green. You could never be the Grinch."

"That's for sure, Goob," Tracey added. "You care about people too much to steal anything."

"I guess you're right, Tracey," Goober answered. "I can't even imagine stealing anything. What's going to be extra special about *your* Christmas holidays?"

"It might not sound like fun to you guys, but the people who lived in our house before we did told us about some boxes of stuff they left in our attic. We're going to go through them. We don't know what we'll find in them, but Mom and I will make it an adventure."

"That does sound like fun," Goober told her. "We found lots of stuff in our attic that the other people left when they moved out, clothes and things. It was nothing we could use. But when we gave it to the Salvation Army they seemed really glad to get it."

"So, when do we all get together again?" Alfonso asked.

"Well," Goober answered, "you and I will probably be together a lot, Al. You too, Willie, as much as possible."

"And every Tuesday and Thursday you'll both be at my house for my guitar lessons," Tracey reminded them. "Could you join us at least one of those days each week, Willie? Maybe the four of us could go out afterwards and have pizza or go bowling or something."

"Part of it will depend on my mom and dad being in two different places and what I'll be doing with each of them. And a lot of it will depend on whether I go to work. But I'll sure try."

With that the four finished their lunch and headed back to class for a Christmas party.

The Saturday after school was out, Goober's mom drove her car to the White Mountain Mall so that he could do his Christmas shopping. He was really excited as he stepped out of the car. "I'll call you in an hour or so, Mom. Then you can drive me to the other stores where I can get the other things I'm buying."

"I'll be glad to be your chauffeur today, Goober. Have fun, Son," Goober's mother said cheerfully.

"I promise," Goober smiled.

Goober had actually been to the mall the Saturday before and picked out the presents he was now going to buy that day. He chose a leather wallet for Clyde, much nicer than his own. Tracey would get a pink silk scarf, Alfonso a Swiss knife, and Willie a great looking baseball bat.

Goober chuckled as he thought again of the bat Willie almost used on Clyde's head. Maybe this bat would remind Willie of that and make him laugh about it again.

He had seen a beautiful blue sweater that he wanted to get his mom, and a Navy blue dress-shirt for his dad. As he passed the Salvation Army bell-ringer before entering the mall he smiled and said hello. He thought to himself, "Any money I have left over, I'll have Mom bring me back here and I'll drop it in this lady's kettle." She smiled and wished him a Merry Christmas.

Entering the mall, Goober was flooded with the nostalgic joy of Christmas. Christmas music was playing throughout all the stores and Goober was going to J. C. Penney to get the presents for his own family.

He thought about his Great Aunt Gertrude. Goober was too young to remember the one time she had come to the Boober home. After that he had only seen photographs she had sent them. She looked like a nice old lady. She had moved to Ireland when Goober was two and that was where she had died this year. Even though he didn't remember her, he was still sorry she died. Goober's mom was very sad when she got a letter about it a couple of weeks ago. Great Aunt Gertrude had left two thousand dollars to her, and two hundred dollars each to Clyde and Goober. That represented a fortune in Goober's mind and all he wanted to do was use it to buy terrific gifts for his family and closest friends.

The mall was full of people buying presents. Goober passed the mall's Santa. Little children were standing in line. One little girl was in the prized position of sitting on Santa's lap. She was a curly-topped redhead of about five, very seriously telling him just what it was that she wanted for Christmas. Santa looked at her as if it was all in the bag. She'd get her Christmas wishes.

Goober remembered when he was little and would sit on Santa's lap. Usually he had gotten what he had requested, but the one time the gifts didn't come close to what he asked for he wondered whether Santa had simply forgotten what he'd said. When he asked his mom she agreed with him. She told him "Santa is getting older and he must have a lot on his mind, remembering every child in the whole world all at once."

Goober entered J. C. Penney to get the presents he had spotted there the week before. He knew right where they were and went first to get the sweater, then the shirt. After picking them up and comparing the colors with each other for a final time, he was convinced his mom and dad would look really great together in them. "They always look great," he thought to himself. "But I'll bet they'll especially like wearing *these* together."

Then Goober went to the wallet section and smiled as he found the one he wanted for Clyde. It was a really fine wallet. "He'll like it a lot," Goober thought to himself as he smiled again.

Finally Goober went to stand in the long line in front of the cash register. He took his place at the very back of it. The line moved very slowly, but Goober didn't mind. Under his breath he hummed along with each Christmas song as it was playing over their sound system.

After more than ten minutes, Goober stood before the cash register. He set the sweater and the shirt on the counter along with the wallet he was buying for Clyde. A lovely woman with brown hair smiled at him and said, "Hello, Son. Oh, what beautiful colors you've chosen. They look so nice together. Who are they for?"

Goober answered happily, "They're for my mom and dad." Then Goober reached for his wallet. It wasn't there! His mouth dropped open and his heart leapt into it. "My w w wallet", Goober stammered, "It's gone!"

When Goober turned around and looked at the long line, the couple right behind him had heard his words, saw the shock on his face, and the man asked "Are you sure your wallet's gone, Son?"

The lady at the counter immediately advised, "Go back to where you began the line and search the floor. Maybe you dropped it." Then she thought of something more and, speaking through a microphone, announced, "A young man up here has just lost his wallet. Would everyone look around near you on the floor and see if you can find it for him?"

People behind him in the line did look, but no one found his wallet. Goober was fighting back tears because he felt so helpless. He had left his mom and dad's beautiful Christmas presents with the lady, and Clyde's wallet too. Now he was looking frantically everywhere his eyes could search. There was no way at all to pay for those presents without the money in his wallet.

Finally, in great despair, he walked back to the lady at the counter. She was serving someone else, but stopped when she saw him and said, "If you dropped your wallet before you got in line, someone may have turned it in to the Security Office." Goober was feeling sick and empty. All his Christmas joy was gone. He felt instead as if he was having a nightmare. He was just sure he would have felt it if his wallet had worked it's way out of his back pocket and fallen. But he said, "Thank you, Mam," to the lady after she told him where the Security Office was, and he went there knowing in his heart it would not be found.

"No, young man, I'm sorry," a large security officer told him. "We have nothing at all that matches that description." The officer was very sympathetic and added, "This is a really busy day for Christmas shoppers. Someone may have found your wallet and will bring it here when they get their shopping done."

The officer took Goober's name, address, and phone number, and assured Goober, "We'll call you the minute your wallet is turned in."

Leaving the White Mountain Mall empty-handed was one of the hardest things Goober had ever done. All of his dreams for his family and his friends had been erased. Without the money he needed, all those gifts he'd planned to give had to be left with the lovely lady at the counter and someone else would no doubt put them back for other people to buy.

That morning when Goober left his house he had felt so happy. He knew the fun it really is to give. He had chuckled out loud as he had thought of the joy Tracey would have in receiving that pink scarf, and how much Al would like the

Swiss knife, and Willie the baseball bat. Now, less than an hour later, he was walking home feeling like a total failure. He didn't use his cell phone to call his mom. He knew he wasn't ready to talk with her, as miserable as he felt.

Goober didn't even look at the Salvation Army lady as he left. He couldn't face her, knowing he'd have nothing at all now to drop into her kettle. Goober wanted so much to give and he couldn't give anything. Why did this happen to him? Why did it have to happen now? "What a lousy Christmas," he said to himself as he kicked a can on the sidewalk. It came clanging to a halt under a bush.

As Goober walked he remembered a really old movie called *It's A Wonderful Life* that his parents had on a DVD. It was a movie that was mushy in parts, but it was a good story. A man had helped all the people in his town, but a bad man got all this man's money. Goober thought, "If that good man was real, he would have felt just like I feel now. He would have felt life just isn't worth living. That's when the good man screamed and jumped off a bridge and into the water to drown himself. But a really funny angel rescued him and the movie had a happy ending."

Goober grew more and more unhappy as he pictured someone taking his wallet. He wondered what kind of a person would do a thing like that. He knew in his heart that no one would return his wallet to the Security Office. "And no funny looking angel is going to show up and bring me back my wallet either. Angels are only for movies and Christmas tales."

When Goober returned home, neither his mom nor his dad were there. He was glad because he didn't want to talk to them. He went into the den and flipped on the TV. *Shrek II* was playing. He had seen it a bunch of times. Now he just stared at it. His brain was numb with disappointment and he didn't laugh at all, even in the funniest parts.

When his mom got home from grocery shopping she asked Goober why he hadn't called her. He told her he had just felt like walking and didn't say more. He didn't want to make her unhappy too about the missing wallet. So he asked his mom if he could eat and watch TV in the den and she had said yes. He stared blankly at the television set. *Akeela And The Bee* had begun playing. It was one of his very favorite movies, but it didn't capture his attention at all. Nothing could. He couldn't have told you later what he had watched or eaten. He finally told his mom he was extra tired and wanted to go to bed early. His mom was very surprised at that request and put her hand on his forehead to see if maybe he had a fever. Finding he wasn't hot, she gave him permission to go to his room.

In a little while, Mimi Boober knocked on Goober's door. Goober thought about pretending to be asleep, but realized that would be like telling a lie to his mother. So, Goober, in a weak voice said, "Come in."

Goober's mother did. It was dark in the room, except for the light coming from the partially opened door. She sat down on the edge of Goober's bed, then reached out and brushed the front of his hair back with her hand.

"Goober," she asked, "is anything wrong? Has somebody done something that's made you unhappy?" Goober still didn't want to tell her that he'd lost his wallet. He tried to think of something truthful that didn't uncover that fact. "It was really crowded in the mall, Mom. But everybody I talked to was nice to me."

"Then, come on, Goober, what's troubling you?" Goober was still hesitant. He was in such emotional pain that he was afraid to tell his mom, yet there was nothing left in him to hold the truth back. His mind raced, trying to think of something else to say. All at once he burst into tears and sobbed. He felt like a little boy again as his mom took him in her arms and hugged him, rocking him back and forth.

After a couple of minutes his mom asked, "Goober, do you want to tell me what's happened?"

Then it came flooding out, "Somebody must have pick-pocketed me, Mom. I picked out Daddy's, Clyde's and your presents, but when I got to the counter my wallet was gone."

"Oh my! Oh my!" Mimi Boober exclaimed. "Now I understand your tears. I know how excited you were to do something nice for your dad, Clyde, and me, and for your friends too, and I appreciate it more than I can tell you. I know your friends do too."

"Why did it happen, Mom? Why? It's SO unfair," Goober agonized.

"I know how you must feel," Mrs. Boober sympathized. "Once someone stole your dad's and my only car and we never got it back. That happened before you were born. We were devastated, and we didn't have it insured for theft. We went five months without a car. That was SO hard."

"But why do things like that happen, Mom? You and Dad are good people. Things like that shouldn't happen to you at all."

"We couldn't figure it out at the time either, Goober. But things like that do happen to lots and lots of people who are good."

"Well," Goober declared, "that sure proves there is no God. Tracey tries to tell me Jesus loves me. Heck, if He loved me He sure wouldn't let a pick-pocket steal my wallet. And he sure wouldn't let Dad and you lose a car."

"I don't know about God, Goober. But I do know that your dad and I learned a lot of things during those five months without a car. A retired neighbor man we hardly knew volunteered to drive your dad back and forth to work every day. We couldn't believe how kind he was, and through this we became good friends with his wife and him."

"Who was that man, Mom?" Goober asked her.

"You never met him, Goober. He and his wife have moved now, but he lived in San Jose where we lived before we moved here. We still exchange Christmas cards. But you mentioned God, and I know *he* was a Christian. He told us so, and he tried to tell us about what he believed about Jesus. Your father wasn't rude, but he told him we weren't really interested in hearing about his religion. He still remained our friend after that. Then five months later a friend of his from the church he attended drove up one day with a much finer car than the one that was stolen from us. This man told us that he'd heard we needed a car and he didn't need this one anymore. Then he handed us the keys and said, 'It's yours! God bless you.' We couldn't believe it."

"That's great, Mom, but it still doesn't answer my question. Why do bad things happen to people like us? Why did my wallet get stolen? I just wanted to make everybody happy."

"But, Goober, think about it. What got lost today? Just money. You didn't lose your dad, or Clyde, or me. You didn't lose one of your friends. We're still all here. And we're so happy because you're here too."

"But, Mom," Goober interrupted, "I don't have anything to give you for Christmas now. I had your present all picked out and now I can't give you anything."

"Goober," his mom told him, "I have YOU. YOU are my present. I love you. And no gift on earth could mean as much to me as you do."

Goober heard his mother's heart. "I love you too, Mom." he responded, hugging her extra hard.

It still hurt a lot that the money and the wallet were gone. But not as much as it had before. Goober knew his mom cared most that he was her son. And he knew too that his dad felt that way ever since Goober had been brave when the Bomber brothers nearly took him to the roof.

The next afternoon, feeling a whole lot better, Goober phoned Tracey. "Hi," he said when she answered. "How's the attic attack going at your house?"

"Mom and I are already done," Tracey answered. "There were all kinds of things for little children, stuff they'd really like. There were two big boxes that made me wish I was four years old again. There were toys and games that looked like they'd never even been used. Some of them were for boys and others were for girls. Funny, most of them were in boxes wrapped in cellophane and looked like they'd never been opened. I have no idea why they weren't. They're really nice."

Goober asked, "What are you going to do with them?"

"I'm not sure," Tracey replied. "We were going to take them to a thrift shop. But after we prayed about them we both suddenly felt like they'd be even more important to someone if we waited. I can't imagine what the Lord has in mind, but there's always time to give them to a thrift shop if we stop feeling that way."

Goober didn't mention to Tracey about losing his money at the mall. She sounded so happy about going through the boxes that he didn't see any reason to share his bad news.

Mickey O'Rourke owned O'Rourke Stables where Willie now worked. Mickey was only five feet tall, but he was every bit a man. He had been a jockey for fifteen years and his office was full of many of the trophies he had won. Pictures of him on winning thoroughbreds lined the walls.

Seven years ago, Mickey stopped jockeying. That was the day he had been in a race at the Santa Anita Racetrack and the horse he was on, Storm Cloud, fell and broke its leg. It had to be shot.

Mickey had broken his own leg in that fall too. He had fallen a few other times throughout his years of racing and this time he decided his racing days were over.

Even before the horse fell, Mickey had been thinking of stopping jockeying and buying a stable instead. He had found one he liked on a visit to Wake Up so he bought it. And from that time on he was very glad he did. Lots of people in the Wake Up area loved horseback riding and he did a thriving business.

Willie loved working at O'Rourke Stables and he liked Mickey immensely. Willie took to riding like ducks take to water, and to Willie, grooming the horses was hardly work at all. Each day after the paying riders were basically through, Willie would saddle up one of the horses and ride alone up into the hill country surrounding Wake Up. Sometimes Willie rode only a little while, but sometimes Mickey gave him permission to come back only when it started to get dark.

Mickey had allowed Willie to ride every horse at the stables except one. Firewall was new to the stables and Mickey hadn't really wanted to buy him at all. But the friend he first visited in Wake Up needed the money. So, very reluctantly, Mickey bought Firewall from him with the intention of quickly selling him again.

Mickey knew before he bought him that Firewall was too wild to be used by the customers who rented horses from him. He himself had only ridden him twice. Because he was an extremely skilled rider, Mickey was able to keep Firewall under control. The horse bucked and kicked, but Mickey just braced himself and stayed on.

Willie walked into Mickey's office and said, "I think our customers are through for the day, Mr. O'Rourke."

Mickey looked up at him, proud of this strong young man. He smiled and said, "Well then, take any of the horses and have some fun."

Willie smiled back, "Thanks, Mr. O'Rourke." Then he asked him, "How long shall I ride?"

Mickey glanced at his watch, remembering that he had a dinner date with his wife and some friends that would begin in about an hour. So he said, "Ride for just a few minutes, Willie. I'm going home early tonight."

Willie was thankful for any minutes he'd get to ride. He went out to the stables to saddle up. As he was walking into the barn it suddenly dawned on him that every one of the riding horses had been on the trail all day. The Boy Scouts had been holding a Jamboree in Wake Up, and Scouts had been arriving ever since morning to ride. Willie knew he should let the stable horses rest. It wasn't good for them to be ridden as tired as they were. They'd labored enough that day.

Then suddenly, Willie heard a loud whinny. It was Firewall. "Hey, boy," Willie called to him and walked toward the horse that began to shy immediately.

Willie knew Mr. O'Rourke had said he could ride ANY horse, and Firewall was *definitely* a horse. He grabbed a saddle and started toward him. But Firewall didn't want to be ridden. He made that very clear by snorting and backing into a corner of his stall.

Jack Lester, another one of the stable hands, smiled at Willie. "Do you think THAT horse will let you ride him? He's got a mind of his own and he's mean clear through."

Willie smiled back. "He's the only horse in the stables that hasn't been ridden all day, Jack. It's his turn."

"But he'll buck you, Willie," Jack warned. "You sure you can stay on him?"

"I'm pretty sure I can," Willie responded.

"Do you think you ought to ask Mr. O'Rourke about it first?" Jack asked, concerned for Willie's safety.

"He's already told me I could ride ANY horse. This is the one that isn't worn out."

Jack smiled and said, "Well, I wish he *was* worn out, for your sake!"

Firewall would have nothing to do with being brushed, but since Willie knew the ride would be very brief, he figured that would be OK. Firewall puffed out his stomach, trying to keep from having the saddle placed on him. He snorted like a dragon and kept moving his feet. He tried to push Willie away, but Willie was fast and, amazingly, got the saddle on him and the blanket underneath it.

Firewall tried to bite Willie, but when he opened his mouth to do it, Willie slipped the bit inside.

Jack smiled again, shaking his head. "OK, Willie, I see you can dress him. The question remains whether you can ride him."

The moment Willie swung into the saddle, Firewall bucked. His purpose was obvious. He wanted to get rid of this unwelcome rider who now was on top of him.

Jack opened the stall gate into the paddock and Firewall didn't wait at all. He was galloping before he got out of the barn. As soon as he reached a clearing he did more than buck with his hind feet. He switched his weight and reared into the air. Firewall did everything he could to throw his rider, and Willie did everything he knew to stay on.

Willie held the stirrups and the reins just tightly enough to let Firewall know he didn't plan to leave the saddle. The battle raged for eight long minutes.

Willie was twisted like a pretzel over and over again. He had never felt anything like it and it took everything he had in him to stay mounted. Arching his back, standing on his hind hooves and bellowing loudly like a horse on fire, Firewall did everything he could to get Willie off his back.

Then, all at once, Firewall gave up. Willie had mastered him and Firewall knew it. Suddenly the horse quieted down and stood solidly in defeat. But when Firewall stopped fighting, Willie wasn't vain about it. He moved forward in the saddle and patted Firewall's mane saying, "You're a beauty, Firewall. That was real fun!"

Two things had happened during the eight long minutes of contest between a boy and a horse. First, Mickey O'Rourke had come out of his office because he'd heard all the ruckus. When Mickey saw what was happening he was totally alarmed. He hollered, "Careful, Willie, careful!" But as he watched he suddenly knew Willie was indeed a match for the horse. He wasn't really surprised to see Firewall finally give up.

The second thing that happened was that two separate cars had pulled up outside the stables just in time to watch Willie's amazing feat. One car was driven by Willie's dad. The other was driven by Lance. Both men hurried out of their cars to see Willie flying into the air, but holding fast to the reins and finally conquering Firewall. Both men stood in stunned silence through the whole eight minute explosion. It wasn't until it was all over that the three men realized the other two were there.

Mickey turned first to Willie's dad. "I hope that didn't scare you, Jim. I told Willie he could ride for a few minutes. I didn't know he was going to fly instead! I had no idea he'd try that horse. Fact is, a lot of skilled riders would have been thrown off of Firewall just now."

"It was all pretty exciting," Willie's dad answered. "I didn't know he could ride like that."

"Neither did I!" Mickey admitted.

Lance introduced himself to Mickey. Then he told Willie's dad, "I didn't know you'd be here just now. But I'm glad you were so you could see that. You must be really proud of your son. I've never seen anything like that in my life. I always wanted to go to a rodeo. I just never got around to it. Now I feel like I've been to one!"

Willie's dad smiled and said, "Willie and I have been doing a lot of riding recently. But we weren't riding bucking broncos. Willie did that all on his own."

"Willie's a born rider," Mickey said. "If he were a lot shorter I'd do everything to help him become a jockey. He could have made a profession of that."

"Well, my son IS a born athlete," Jim Radner answered. "I expect he'll be in the Big Leagues one day. I'm really proud of him."

Lance said, "You've got a lot of reasons to be proud of him. I sure am."

"And I'm thankful he really likes you, Lance," Willie's dad replied. "He's told me he does."

Now Willie walked up and joined the three men after taking Firewall back to the corral and taking off the saddle and the blanket. "Hi," he greeted them. "I guess you saw that horse make me dance!"

Lance laughed, "You're a real Spiderman, Willie! Well done."

"Yes, Son," exclaimed Willie's dad. "I didn't know which one of you was going to win." Then he laughed, "I'm glad it ended up with you on top of him and not him on top of you!"

"Are you going to be able to sit down when you have a meal, Willie?" Lance chuckled. "Your bottom took quite a beating!"

"It sure did," Willie agreed.

Mickey asked, "Willie, what on earth were you doing on Firewall? I had no idea at all that you'd try to ride him."

Willie was immediately apologetic. "I'm sorry, Mr. O'Rourke, if I misunderstood you. It's just that when I realized all of the regular horses had been ridden all day, I figured Firewall was the only horse left."

Mickey looked very seriously at Willie. "Well," he said, "you could have been killed or badly injured if Firewall had thrown you. But I do remember telling you that you could ride *any* of the horses. And I'm awfully glad you were ready for Firewall's rock and roll!" Everyone laughed.

"I wouldn't have sued you, Mickey, if Willie had been hurt or if something worse had happened," Jim Radner assured him. "I know the risk he takes around any horse. They're big animals."

"Yes, they are," Mickey agreed. "But none of the others are even close to being as risky as Firewall. Still, I was just about Willie's age when I had my first try at a horse as wild as him. It ended a lot differently. I broke an arm!"

"Your pitching arm?" asked Willie's dad.

"I guess so," answered Mickey. "But remember, I wasn't a baseball player. I always knew I'd be a jockey."

"Thanks for not being mad about me riding Firewall, Mr. O'Rourke," Willie apologized. "He was the only horse that didn't look tired."

Mickey O'Rourke laughed and said, "Well I guarantee you, Firewall is tired now!"

Five Real Friends

Chapter Six
Merry Christmess!

SMOKE!

There was smoke in the air. Alfonso could smell it, but there was one big problem. Alfonso was asleep!

It was 2 a.m. and Alfonso had been asleep for three hours. Not wanting to wake up, Alfonso, with his eyes still closed, pulled his pillow out from beneath his head and covered his face with it. Aside from that, he didn't move. That felt better for a moment, but then he coughed. It was hard to cough underneath his pillow and the cough woke him up. Alfonso sat bolt upright and his pillow fell to the floor. Now he could really smell the smoke and he knew something had to be on fire. Throwing on his robe, he ran out of his bedroom into the living room. He looked out the side window and was horrified by what he saw. The house next door was on fire.

"FIRE!" Alfonso shouted. He shouted again, adding, 'THE RITTER'S HOUSE IS ON FIRE!"

Suddenly his mom came running out of her bedroom in her robe too. She gasped, ran to the phone, and called 911. They told her they had already been called.

The next thing Alfonso saw mystified him. Ralph Guiterrez, his dad, was standing next door where the fire was, using a large rock to break all the glass in the window where Alfonso knew Luke and Suzie Ritter's two young children slept.

His question about what his dad was doing was quickly answered by the next terrifying sight. Ralph boosted himself through the shattered window and disappeared. "Dad!" was all that Alfonso could utter. His heart was in his mouth and he was terrified.

Sophia gasped as she watched her husband dive into that room and she instinctively covered her mouth with her hands. Then she dropped her hands, and in a quivering voice tried to assure Alfonso, "He'll be all right." But her voice was full of fear. She put an arm on Alfonso's shoulder and hugged him, wanting to do anything to make herself believe her husband was somehow going to come out of that window with the two children and be fine.

Three minutes passed that seemed much more like hours. Alfonso and his mother could see Mr. and Mrs. Ritter rush to just outside the broken window. They could see them calling out what were probably their children's names. A very few moments later, Suzie Ritter held out her hands and received three-year-old Mary Lou in her arms. She held her and kissed her as Luke Ritter extended his hands and received five year old Teddy. Both children were crying.

At that point, Ralph Guiterrez appeared, pushing himself out through the broken window. Everyone moved quickly away from the burning house. The Ritters followed Ralph in a daze. The children somehow stopped crying and stared wide-eyed at their house which was now totally engulfed in flames. A moment later there was a loud crashing sound as the second story of the Ritter's home fell on top of the first. If the timing hadn't been perfect, the children and Mr. Guiterrez would have most certainly been killed or badly injured by the collapse. And if they had survived that, they would almost certainly have been trapped beyond rescue by the fallen debris.

Now that Alfonso knew his dad was safe, he could breathe again. Yet it was still horrifying to see the Ritter's home being reduced to rubble by a raging fire. The flames showed no mercy as they licked away at the house. Ralph had phoned 911 before hurrying next door, but the firemen arrived too late.

The front door opened at the Guiterrez home and the whole Ritter family walked in, followed by Ralph. They were obviously badly shaken. Sophia Guiterrez greeted the Ritters as she rushed to throw her arms around her husband. She told him, "I love you, and I was SO scared."

Wiping his brow, Ralph smiled at her and said, "It WAS a bit warm in there! But we made it."

Finally she let go of her husband to hug Suzie Ritter. Sophia told her, "I'm so sorry for what has happened to your house. Would you all like some hot chocolate while you try to start recovering from this?"

Little Mary Lou spoke up, "Yes, please. Do you have any marshmallows?"

"Mary Lou!" her mother said in embarrassment.

But Mrs. Guiterrez smiled, "Oh, that's fine. Hot chocolate is always best with a marshmallow."

"Can I help you make it?" Suzie asked.

"Oh no, Suzie," Sophia told her, "you've been through enough. Just sit and try your best to relax. I know you must have a whirlwind going on in your mind right now. I can't imagine this happening."

Suzie sat and drew her children to her side. "Everything we own inside our house is gone," she declared. "But thanks to the bravery of your husband, our most important two possessions are right here."

"Where did you find the children, Ralph?" Luke asked.

"They were hiding in their closet with the closet door closed. It's the worst place they could have hidden. I was trying to find them and almost didn't. But then one of them

175

started coughing, and when I threw open the closet door, there they were."

Suzie gasped, "The closet! Why did you hide in the closet?"

"Because the fire was burning our bedroom," five-year-old Teddy answered matter-of-factly. "I thought it couldn't burn the closet if we closed the closet door!"

"Oh, but it easily could have," Luke gasped.

"Yes, it could have," Ralph agreed.

"Ralph," Luke told him, "I'll never know how to do enough for you to thank you for saving my children."

"You don't owe me a thing," Ralph answered. "This is what neighbors are for."

After a very few minutes, the adults who had been outside washed the ashes away from their bodies and Suzie got her children clean. The hot chocolate was served and drunk gratefully. It warmed everybody's insides. And Mary Lou was right, the marshmallow in each cup was delicious.

A heavy smell of smoke had come to every room in the Guiterrez home, but no one had anything at all to complain about as they looked at the two children.

"Now," Ralph said, "we have an extra bedroom, bathroom, and an extra shower too. And we have two great sleeping bags for the children. Why not sleep here tonight, even longer if you'd like? You can all get hot showers. And tomorrow you can assess the damage and find out what your insurance company will do."

"It is insured," Luke answered. "Every bit of it. But I've got a feeling it will take quite a long time to rebuild it. I don't want to be in your way. I'm sure our insurance company will move us into a house until ours is rebuilt."

Ralph said, "Good. But know that you won't be in our way at all. It's the least we could do for you."

"Yes, of course you'll stay with us for however long," Sophia agreed. "We love you and we want you to be as comfortable as possible."

The Ritters could only agree. They knew the Guiterrez invitation would not only be the quickest way they would ever get some sleep that night, but exactly what their children needed immediately.

A few minutes later Luke said, "I think I should go to our house now that the firemen have the fire nearly out. I need to talk with the fire chief."

Ralph said, "Let me come with you, Luke. "

"I'd be glad to have your company, Ralph," Luke answered. "My brain is kind of muddled right now. Maybe you can listen to the fire chief too, and together we can remember everything he says."

The firemen were dousing the last embers as Luke and Ralph spotted the fire chief. They walked up to him and Luke asked, "So, what do I do now?"

The chief said, "I wish I had better news for you, but you can see that your house is absolutely totaled. Nothing in it could be saved."

"Well," Luke responded, "I'd be lying if I didn't say that makes me really sad. But we'll make it. My wife and I got out just fine." Pointing to Ralph, he said, "So did my two children, thanks to this neighbor of mine who broke in their bedroom window and rescued them."

"Thank you, Sir," the fireman said to Mr. Guiterrez. "You're a hero. Some families aren't lucky enough to have someone like you around. Three weeks ago two children under six died because they hid themselves in their closet when fire took their house. The guys on my crew are very tough, but several of them cried when the charred bodies of the children were discovered."

Both Luke and Ralph shuddered. "That's where my kids were," Luke told him.

"Well," the fire chief told him, "it's the major death-trap for kids in any house fire."

Luke was silent for a moment, thinking how horrible it would have been to have lost his children. Then refocusing his thoughts he asked, "What's the next step in getting my house rebuilt?"

The chief answered, "Well, I'll have a full report on what caused this fire by tomorrow noon. Your insurance company will do their own inspection too. Then you'll need to deal with them as to what they're going to do about all this. You do have fire insurance, don't you?"

"Yes," Luke answered, "the house is completely insured."

"Great!" the chief responded. "I've got to go help my men, but the best of luck to you."

Luke told the Captain, "I know you and your crew did everything you could to save my house. Thanks, and please thank your whole crew for me."

Ralph asked Luke, "Ready to go get some sleep?"

"I sure am," Luke responded. "I feel like I'm a hundred years old."

As they walked into the Guiterrez home the smell of smoke from the fire was even more noticeable. Luke said, "I hope smoke damage doesn't ruin your house, Ralph. I'm so sorry."

"No worries," Ralph answered. "Even though it's a bit unpleasant now, I doubt this smell will remain long. I want you to know that you and your family are a tremendous gift to our home. We'll love having you here as you sort out all the legal work to get you a brand new home right next door. Hey, Merry Christmas!"

"Christmas!" Luke exclaimed, and he suddenly looked unhappier than he'd even been about the fire. "I'd forgotten all about that with this fire keeping my mind so occupied. What on earth are we going to do for Mary Lou and Teddy to replace their burned up presents?"

Ralph had no good answer. "Even Wal-Mart is closed because it's after midnight. And that's about it, Luke. Everything else is basically closed until the day after tomorrow."

"Everybody will be celebrating Christmas," Luke moaned. "Everybody but Teddy and Mary Lou. And they were so looking forward to opening their presents."

Ralph put his hand on his neighbor's shoulder, "You're tired, Luke. This will all work out. Besides, because your house is gone, Santa might get mixed up and bring their presents to our house instead of yours."

"I wish he could," Luke said seriously. "But I know this is one Christmas none of us will ever forget."

"I'll bet Teddy and Mary Lou will still get some surprises."

"Christmas presents for my kids? I don't think so," Luke despaired.

"Something good will happen," Ralph smiled, though he had no idea how the children's need for presents could be met with all the stores closed on Christmas day in Wake Up.

Early Christmas morning, Alfonso was awake before anyone else. Knowing that the opening of presents in his house was still a couple of hours away he phoned Goober, who always got up early, to tell him about the fire.

Goober's parents weren't up yet either and Clyde always slept late. Goober had been watching the Christmas parade from New York on television. When Alfonso called him, Goober answered on the second ring, "Ho! Ho! Ho! Merry Christmas. Santa Claus speaking!" not even knowing who was calling, but guessing it was one of his friends. Goober was jam-full of the joy of Christmas from watching the parade.

In the days leading up to Christmas, Goober had told his friends about being pick-pocketed. Now it was just as if it had only been a bad dream.

Alfonso was full of news about the fire next door and about how his dad had saved the Ritter children. "The whole house burned to ashes. They lost everything. Mr. and Mrs. Ritter and their little kids, Teddy and Mary Lou, are staying at our house right now."

Goober said, "Man, your dad is really amazing!" But instantly another idea hit him. "Did the Ritters rescue the presents they had under the Christmas tree for Teddy and Mary Lou?"

"No, everything burned up," Alfonso answered. "This morning is going to be pretty sad for those kids."

A smile came quickly to Goober's face. "I don't think so. Al, I've got an idea. I think they can get all the presents those kids could imagine. What I'm thinking about involves Tracey. Let me phone you back as soon as I call her."

"OK, Amigo," Alfonso said, "I don't know what plan you've got. But if you can do anything for these kids it would be great."

"I don't want to say anything until I can make sure about this with Tracey. I'll phone you right back after I talk with her. Bye," replied Goober, as he hung up and immediately dialed Tracey. He knew she'd be awake because she was an early riser too. She answered the phone quickly.

"Hi, Tracey. Merry Christmas."

"Merry Christmas, Goob," Tracey replied. "Were your stockings hung by your chimney with care?"

"They sure were," he chuckled. Then, in a more excited tone he said, "I've got a really big question to ask you. Have you given away those two boxes of toys that you found in your attic?"

"Not yet, Goob," she answered.

Now Goober was really excited. "If I told you of two little kids who will get no presents at all this year because their house burned down last night, do you think you'd want to give all that stuff to them?"

"Well, sure. I know my mom would feel great about that. We just want to give them away to some kids who will really enjoy them."

Then Goober told Tracey about the fire at the Ritter's home that wiped out everything the family had. He explained, "I've got a bunch of Christmas wrapping paper my mom gave me to wrap the presents I'm not giving. It's all underneath my bed. Maybe Al, and even Willie, could join us at your house, I can bring the paper and we can wrap all those presents for the Ritter kids really quickly."

"That's a GREAT idea, Goob," Tracey said excitedly. "Call them and I'll see you soon. Bye."

"Bye, Tracey," Goober replied.

As soon as he was off the phone to her, Goober called Alfonso back. "You won't have to worry at all about presents for the Ritter kids. Tracey has a bunch of little kids' things she and her mom found — toys and stuff - when they went through those boxes in their attic. It's all new stuff and I know Teddy and Mary Lou will love them."

Alfonso was instantly as excited as Goober was. "That's great. Mom had hardly anything to give them. She'd given away my old toys and stuff a long time ago and she was feeling really bad about it."

"Can you get your dad to take you to Tracey's house, Al? I'm going to ask Willie to join us too. With all hands on deck we should be able to wrap all those presents in record time."

Alfonso beamed, "Yeah, sure. If Teddy and Mary Lou can have a merry Christmas I know my dad will be glad to take me to Tracey's."

Then Goober called Willie. Willie said he'd be glad to go to Tracey's to help wrap the gifts.

Finally Goober went to his bedroom. He had five rolls of Christmas wrapping paper underneath his bed. The first four he reached easily. But then he had to grope around under the bed, trying to find the fifth. All at once his hand struck something small and hard that wasn't Christmas wrapping at all. He pulled it out. There in his hand was his wallet containing two hundred dollar bills! Awestruck, he realized his wallet must have fallen under his bed without his ever knowing it.

Goober smiled ear to ear as a brand new idea came to him about what to do with the money. He was even more excited now. He phoned Alfonso.

Alfonso answered the phone, "Feliz Navidad."

"Hey, Al, it's me again. But I want to know something else. Did Mr. and Mrs. Ritter's presents for each other burn up in that fire too?"

Alfonso answered, "Yeah, they did. Nothing they owned was left."

"Well, I've got great presents for *them* too!" Goober told him.

"Wow!" exclaimed Alfonso, "they'll think you ARE Santa Claus if you can pull that off!"

"The big thing right now," said Goober, "is that the gifts for the Ritter kids have to be wrapped. How soon can you join me at Tracey's? Willie is coming too. We can walk to your house afterwards. Tracey has an old Coaster Wagon in her garage and we can carry all the gifts in it."

Alfonso responded, "Dad is up and dressed, and Mom is fixing breakfast. Dad's ready to drive me to Tracey's right now. They were really happy to know about the gifts for Teddy and Mary Lou. And they'll be extra excited when I tell them you've got something for their mom and dad too. I'll go to Tracey's house right now, then I'll unwrap my presents and eat when I get back."

Goober next phoned Willie back to check on timing and his mother said he had already left.

As Goober hung up the phone, Mimi Boober suddenly appeared. She had a cup of hot chocolate in her hand for Goober, with a marshmallow sitting on top. "How's my favorite Christmas elf?" she asked, smiling at him.

"Great, Mom, great," he smiled at her. Then Goober took a sip of the hot chocolate and told his mother all about the Ritter's fire, and about Tracey and her mother finding "a ton" of kid's stuff in their attic. "They're perfect presents for the Ritter kids, Mom. It was just like someone put them in their attic for them."

"Oh, my! Oh, my!" Mimi exclaimed.

Then Goober grinned. "And I found something else under my bed this morning. Look!" Goober held out the two hundred dollar bills he thought had been pick-pocketed from him at the mall. "Mom, my wallet was under my bed all this time." He held it up for her to see.

"Oh my! Oh, my!" Mimi said again. "Isn't that amazing!"

Goober felt his mom would understand as he told her, "I've changed my mind about what I want to do with that money if it's OK with you. I want to put a hundred dollars each inside cards for the Ritters. Would that be all right? I won't have any more money to buy you, Dad, or Clyde a present. But it will be just the little extra that I think will mean a lot to them for Christmas after that fire."

Mimi Boober reached out and carefully hugged Goober so that his hot chocolate wouldn't spill. Then she said, "Oh, Son, of course it's all right with me. We've got much more than enough. And I'm so moved that you would think of doing something loving like that." She added, "I'll get the box of Christmas cards I have left. You can put a hundred dollar bill in two of them."

She left and soon returned. Goober very quickly chose the two Christmas cards for the Ritters. He simply wrote, "Merry Christmas from Santa Claus" on the inside of each of them. He then explained, "I've got to go to Tracey's, Mom. Willie and Al are probably there already. But I've never been this excited about Christmas before."

"I can see that, Son," she told him. "I'm SO PROUD of you. Let me drive you there."

Just as he'd predicted, Alfonso and Willie were already waiting for Goober at Tracey's. Soon they were all buried in gift paper, wrapping up the toys. And the toys were just as Tracey had described them - like brand new. Each toy, after being wrapped, was signed by Tracey, "To Teddy" or "To Mary Lou". And by the time the last present was completed there was a very huge pile.

"Wow!" Alfonso exclaimed. "I never got that many presents *any* Christmas! Teddy and Mary Lou will have so much fun opening these." He was having so much fun too that he'd forgotten all about Goober's telling him he had presents for Mr. and Mrs. Ritter. Goober said nothing to any of them about the two hundred dollars of his that he'd found. He simply buried the two cards his mother had given him in amongst the children's presents.

Tracey stayed home to be with her mom so that they could unwrap their own presents. Willie went back home to be with his mom and Lance. So, Goober and Alfonso dragged Tracey's huge wagon-full of presents to Alfonso's home. When they reached his house the door was locked. Goober rang the doorbell and Sophia came to open it.

"Oh my gosh!" Sophia exclaimed with glee as she saw the wagon-full of presents. "Come children and see what Santa has brought you!" Teddy and Mary Lou, along with their mom and dad, came quickly to the door.

Goober laughed and said, "Santa couldn't find your house last night so he asked us to see that you got these gifts from him." The children's eyes bulged with excitement.

Suzie Ritter wiped tears away as she told Goober and Alfonso. "We'll never know how to thank you boys enough."

"I hope Teddy grows up to be as fine a man as you two are already," Luke Ritter added.

"Well, Mrs. Dare and Tracey had all these things to give," Goober explained. "We're just the delivery boys."

Alfonso smiled, "Besides, this really made *our* Christmas special."

"Stay, Goober, and watch the children unwrap their gifts," Sophia urged.

But Goober said, "Thanks so much, but I've got to get home to open the presents Santa brought me. I hope everybody here has a very merry Christmas."

"Thanks to you and your friends, everyone here will be able to celebrate in style," Mrs. Guiterrez smiled. "Merry

Christmas, Goober."

"Merry Christmas everybody," Goober warmly replied.

"I'll see that this wagon is properly returned to Tracey," Mr. Guiterrez told him. "But right now, let me drive you home." Goober had planned to walk home, but with his parents and brother probably waiting, he accepted the ride.

As he left the car, Mr. Guiterrez told him, "Goober, you are a fine young man. I'm so glad you are such a close friend to my son."

He replied, "Well, Mr. Guiterrez, I'm the lucky one. I'm really glad Al is such a close friend of mine." Then Goober wished him, "Merry Christmas!"

Willie had whistled as he rode his bike home. He felt "Christmassy", whatever THAT meant. He'd deeply enjoyed the fun of wrapping all those presents with his friends. But all that happy feeling left him as soon as he entered his house.

Willie's mother ran to him and gushed, "Look, Willie, at the engagement ring Lance gave me for Christmas!"

To Willie, in that one moment his home had been destroyed even more than the Ritter's home had been. Only it wasn't fire that had totaled it. It was his mother's announcement.

Frieda continued, "We're going to be married. Isn't that a beautiful diamond?" She wiggled the sparkling jewel in front of his eyes.

"Uh huh," answered Willie as grief hit him. He smiled a half smile to try to be kind to his mom, but now every hope Willie had for his mom and dad ever getting back together was shattered. Still, Willie didn't want his mom to know how badly he was hurting because of what had just happened. He told her, "I'm glad for you, Mom." He was numb as he went through the motions of opening presents with his mom and

Lance.

Willie had presents from his mom, Lance, and from his own dad too. "See Willie," his mom said cheerfully, "it pays to have two dads."

Willie didn't answer her. There was too much pain in him that she just didn't understand.

He said all the right things while he unwrapped each of his gifts. But as the last present was unwrapped, Willie excused himself and went to his room. There the tears began to flow non-stop.

It wasn't that he didn't like Lance. True, he hadn't liked him at all at first, during the days his mom and Lance were drunk. But ever since the first day Lance started talking to him and telling him about his liver, the boozing had stopped. He knew Lance sincerely liked him and, in spite of himself, he liked Lance - but NOT as a dad. As long as Lance was just a close friend of his mom's there was still the possibility in Willie's mind that his dad would somehow come back. Now that possibility was shot to smithereens.

Ever since Lance had talked with Willie so honestly, he had thought good thoughts about Lance. Yet whenever he had such thoughts and realized he was thinking them, he instantly felt totally disloyal to his dad. He knew Lance could never replace his dad in his heart. No human on Earth could do that. His dad simply wasn't replaceable. And to fully guard against that ever even possibly happening, Willie felt he couldn't risk letting Lance have any place at all in his heart.

He was broken-hearted when his mom and dad filed for divorce, but he still held out some hope. One of them could still wake up and come back to the other. Now, this Christmas day, Lance, by giving his mom a ring, had formed an irremovable blockade that stood totally in the way of his mom and dad EVER coming back together. It was hideous. And there was nothing at all he could do to stop his mom

187

from forcing Lance into his life.

Frieda Radner knocked on Willie's door. "Honey," she said, "come have dinner. It's really going to be yummy."

Willie dried his eyes, forced a happy face on, and went to the dining table to have Christmas lunch with his mom and Lance. His mom was right, the food looked yummy. But Willie picked at it and ate hardly anything. He said hardly anything either.

Afterward, Willie sat in a living room chair in front of the television set. He hurt too much to pay attention to the movie Lance and his mother were watching from the couch. But they kept laughing as they watched it. Once in awhile they'd kiss. The night before, all three of them were laughing and putting tinsel on the beautifully decorated Christmas tree that was in the living room too. It was just fun then. But it wasn't fun at all now.

Trying to put a smile on his face, Willie finally asked to be excused. He told them he was tired because he'd gotten up so early. They both smiled at him and said, "Fine".

Willie went to his bed, lay down on it, and tears flooded his eyes again. Then he fell asleep and had a nightmare. A ferocious looking monster had come to the Radner front door. Willie could see it through the window. It began to pound on the door. Neither his mom nor his dad could hear the deafening knocks, but Willie was terrified by the sound. Each knock sounded like huge explosions in his ears. He tried to shout to his parents, but it was as if his voice could make no sound at all. He watched his dad put his arms around his mother and hold her. Suddenly their front door burst open with a huge crash. The hideous monster stepped inside their living room. The monster's head nearly touched their ceiling. It had a totally hairy body like an ape, but its arms and legs were made of steel. It was terribly, terribly strong. Terrified, his mom tried to hide behind Willie's dad. His dad did everything he could to shield her from the monster. But the monster was far too strong for even his dad. It picked his dad up, threw him out the open door of their house, and quickly closed the door and locked it. At that moment the monster took off his hairy mask. The monster was Lance!

That's when Willie woke up. His whole body was shaking and he was covered with sweat. Now his tears were mixed with horrible fear. "Why wasn't I smart enough to hate Lance all the time? Just because a guy's nice to you, doesn't mean he can have your mother!"

Willie knew Lance was the monster who was throwing his dad out of his own house. And Willie could only let it happen because he was absolutely helpless to deal with the monster himself. If even his dad couldn't stop that monster, then, in Willie's mind, no one could.

He lay there in the dark, feeling lonelier than he had ever been in his life. His tears began again. Then he remembered one of the angry old Ebenezer Scrooge lines from a play a long dead writer named Charles Dickens had written. It was called *A Christmas Carol*. Willie shouted Scrooge's line in anger too - "Christmas! Bah, humbug!"

Five Real Friends

Chapter Seven
Meaner Than A Junkyard Dog!

The telephone rang and Goober answered it, "Hello."

"Goober," Sophia Guiterrez said, "don't be alarmed, but Alfonso is in the hospital. I wanted to let you know."

"WHAT?" gasped Goober, "THE HOSPITAL? What's wrong with him?"

There was a long silence on the other end of the telephone. Then Sophia said with tears in her voice, "Alfonso was beaten up!"

"BEATEN UP?" Goober said, even louder than his first response. Tears began to form in his voice too.

"Yes, Goober, a gang of men did it when he was coming home from the grocery store. They dragged him into an alley and beat him up. When he was so long in coming home, Ralph and I drove to the store to see if he was OK. When we got there and didn't see him we drove around until we found him lying alone in that alley. He said it happened so fast and it was so dark in the alley that he couldn't say what any of his attackers looked like. He doesn't know how many did this, but he said there were too many for him to defend himself, and that they smelled like they'd all been drinking. That's all he could tell the police."

"Is he hurt badly, Mrs. Guiterrez?" Goober asked her.

"Our doctor doesn't think so. He's bruised and he's limping and his voice is strained. But the doctor thinks he'll be OK. I'm staying with him overnight here at White Mountain Hospital. They are keeping him here for observation. But he whispered to me to call you and to ask you 'What's new, Bugaloo?' I've heard both of you say that sometimes to each other, but he's never told me what it means. He said you'd know."

"Yes, I do, Mrs. Guiterrez," Goober told her.

Then she said, "Goober, I need to get back to him. But would you call Willie and Tracey to let them know what's happened?"

"Yes, I will," Goober assured her. "But WHY would anyone want to beat Al up?"

Again there was a long pause before Mrs. Guiterrez answered. "Whoever did it made a sign and left it lying on Alfonso's chest. It read, GO HOME YOU MEXICAN."

"NO!" Goober cried loudly again. "Who could have done a thing like that?"

"The police told us that it's extremely rare for something like this to happen in Wake Up. Wake Up is a town with barely any racial prejudice in it at all. But the fact that the ones who did beat him up were smelling heavily of alcohol means they were drunk. The police said it is officially a 'Hate Crime', but that in Wake Up they consider it more of a 'Drunk Crime'."

"Whatever it was," Goober responded, "I wish I'd been with Al and could have helped him fight."

"I know, Goober," Sophia comforted him. "Ralph and I wish we'd been there too. But now it's just like a bad dream. I think Alfonso will be home tomorrow and you can come and visit him then."

"I will, Mrs. Guiterrez," Goober assured her. "And I'll phone Tracey and Willie right now and let them know what's happened. Is there anything my parents or I could do for you or Mr. Guiterrez tonight or before I come over tomorrow?"

"No, Goober, we're fine," Sophia answered. "We're just VERY thankful Alfonso wasn't hurt worse."

"Me too," Goober agreed. "Thanks for calling."

As soon as that phone call was completed, Goober first phoned Willie then Tracey. Both of them were stunned by what had happened to their friend. Tracey said that she'd be praying for Alfonso to heal quickly.

All three went together to visit Alfonso at his house as soon as he was home from the hospital and they were out of school. Willie had made a sign too, and the three of them laid it on Alfonso's chest. It read *ALFONSO IS A HERO. STAY IN WAKE UP.*

Alfonso laughed as he read the sign. The four had a great visit. Before Alfonso's three friends left, Tracey asked Alfonso if she could lay hands on him and pray for him. Alfonso said, "If it would make you feel better, Tracey."

Tracey laughed and said, "It will make YOU feel better, Al."

He told her, "OK, whatever."

Two days later Alfonso was back in school without any limp at all, with his voice fully back to normal, and leaving the nightmare behind him.

Pee Wee Fritz was really no "Pee Wee" at all. In fact, with the Bomber Brothers forever gone from school, Pee Wee was the tallest student in his class. He was also the meanest too, and a bully.

Pee Wee was absolutely unteachable. Every teacher passed him on to the next grade only because they wanted to be totally sure he was never in *their* classroom again.

Pee Wee got his nickname in kindergarten where he was the smallest boy in his class. But by the second grade he began to grow by inches throughout the year. And by the third grade "little" Pee Wee was "BIG" Pee Wee. He just kept growing and didn't stop.

Pee Wee really enjoyed his height. But even in kindergarten he was the type of kid who loved to walk up behind other students - boys or girls - and punch them hard on the arm, then laugh.

Now in the eighth grade, all the other kids tried to stay totally clear of Pee Wee so that they didn't get punched and go home with sore arms. No other boy felt he could finish any fight Pee Wee started. Willie could, but Willie didn't fight *anyone*.

Now a particular problem had arisen. Pee Wee had picked out Rodney Toole as his major punching bag. Rodney was the smallest boy in class, a little under five feet tall. Ever since Christmas vacation was over and school had begun again in January, Pee Wee had started teasing and then tormenting Rodney in front of other classmates. He gave Rodney the nickname "Weenie Head". And he not only pounded him daily, but twice slapped him across the face while saying, "Wake up, Weenie Head!"

The four friends discussed this over lunch one day. A moment before, Pee Wee had walked by them and purposely brushed Goober hard. Pee Wee then laughed and walked on. Tracey was the first to speak up and ask, "What can be done about that jerk?"

"Funny thing is," Goober began, "he has a great Mom and Dad. My dad and mom know them and they like them a lot. He's not like any of the other guys I've seen whose parents are mean to them or don't show them any love so they just try to get attention from us. I've been to his house for dinner. His parents are kind of poor and they don't live in a house as nice as any of ours. But his mom and dad really care about him. Yet he's mean to them too. I heard him say things to them that would have gotten me grounded for a month if I had ever said them to *my* parents, which I wouldn't. The thing is, they must not know how to stop him either because his dad whispered to me to keep an eye on him and to help him if I could. I've tried to do that, but he doesn't want to be helped. He's not looking for friends. He'd rather bloody some little kid's nose or tear up some girl's homework than do anything else."

Tracey suggested, "We have really great parenting classes at our church. If his mom and dad would come, Pee Wee wouldn't act like that any more."

"I'm sure," Willie responded sarcastically.

Goober glanced at Pee Wee. He was now sitting at a table three rows away from him. Pee Wee caught Goober's glance and stuck his tongue out at him. The next thing Pee Wee did was reach over and snatch another kid's dessert, laughing as he did it. The boy did nothing in return, not wanting to get punched.

"He's just like a rattlesnake!" Goober ventured. "He just sits there to make trouble."

"He's got a tongue like a rattlesnake too," Alfonso added.

"It's strange," Tracey said, "he isn't like either of the Bomber brothers. They were evil. Pee Wee Fritz is just meaner than a junkyard dog!"

Alfonso spoke again. "He's a bully. He knows he's big and he takes full advantage of it."

"So," asked Willie, "what can we do to change that?"

Goober got an idea. "Willie, remember when Al and I came to your house the first time and talked with you after you'd found out that your mom and dad were divorcing?"

Willie answered, "I sure do. I was really miserable until you guys came over. Now we've become good friends. I still hate the idea of Lance and my mother getting married. I keep hoping something will happen to change that. But that was a really great day."

"Well," Goober suggested, "why don't we go to Pee Wee's house and do the same kind of thing? I don't think you should come, Tracey, because if he starts hitting us I know he'd hit you too. But just maybe our visit would cause him to change just like you did, Willie."

Alfonso spoke up. "But there's a big difference between Willie and Pee Wee, Goober. Willie was nice to begin with. He just needed to know he had friends. But I've never known a minute when Pee Wee wasn't mean and looking for a fight. He LIKES being that way. The change you're talking about, Goob, would take a whole makeover like I saw once on TV with some lady that was really ugly and they made her look better with surgery and stuff. Pee Wee would have to have that happen somewhere inside him. Even surgery wouldn't do it. It would mean he'd have to become a whole different person."

"That wouldn't take much," Tracey chimed in. "All Pee Wee would have to do is get saved."

"Saved from what?" Willie asked her.

"Saved from what he's like now. Jesus Christ does makeovers all the time!"

"I haven't got a clue in the world what you're talking about," Willie told her. "I really like you until you start getting religious."

"I'm not religious, Willie," Tracey replied, "I'm saved."

Goober kidded her, "So Tracey, tell us. Did YOU used to be meaner than a junkyard dog?" All three of the boys laughed.

"No," Tracey answered honestly, "not like Pee Wee. But I used to have a really bad temper until I was ten and got saved. And I used to always feel sorry for myself because my dad was gone."

"I still do that, Tracey. Does that mean I ought to get 'saved'?" Willie asked her.

"Yes, Willie, all three of you should," Tracey responded. "It would make such a big difference in your lives."

"Because it's you," Willie promised, "I'm not going to get mad. But let's drop that and talk about Pee Wee. OK?"

Alfonso began, "What do you think we ought to do when we get to Pee Wee's house, guys? Don't you think he knows already why other kids don't like him?"

Goober replied, "Yes, he probably does. But I can't believe he really thinks it's cool to not be liked by anybody."

Tracey said, "I don't think he thinks about that. He's in his own world. In his world it doesn't matter if kids don't like you if you can beat them up. No one ever stops him by beating *him* up. Nobody in school is big enough except you Willie, and you're too kind to do it."

"Even if I'm not 'saved'?" Willie sneered.

Tracey realized she'd offended Willie and simply said, "Yes."

Goober wanted to stop Tracey's "religious talk" too. He said to the other two boys, "Pee Wee likes fights. But if we three guys went to his house just to let him know we really cared about him, maybe it would be enough to change him."

Alfonso put his hand on Goober's shoulder. "You know I'm always with you, Amigo. And if you want to go to Pee Wee's house, I'll go with you."

"Me too," smiled Willie. "I don't know anybody who can make a friend quicker than you can, Goob."

And so it was decided that after school the three friends would go to Pee Wee's house for a visit.

"I'll be praying for you guys *and* for Pee Wee," Tracey assured them.

"Well," Willie said to her sarcastically, "if we get Pee Wee 'saved', we'll know just who to thank for it!"

As the boys walked to Pee Wee's house, Willie told them, "OK, we're going to knock on Pee Wee's door and be real friendly when he opens it. But if he greets us with a baseball bat, RUN!"

Goober did the knocking. There was a long pause. "Maybe he didn't come home from school," Alfonso remarked hopefully. Alfonso was only there because Goober wanted to be there. After being beaten up and having to spend a night in the hospital, Alfonso was nervous about what might happen if they disturbed a bully like Pee Wee. He was really glad Willie was with them.

Finally Pee Wee opened his door just a crack and peered out. He was immediately surprised to find Willie, Alfonso and Goober standing there.

"What the heck do ya freaks want?" Pee Wee growled. "Are ya sellin Girl Scout cookies?"

Goober overlooked Pee Wee's growl and in a very friendly tone he answered, "No, we just wanted to come by and see if you'd like to go to the basketball court with us and shoot some hoops."

Pee Wee sneered. "I don't play basketball, Dummy. That's a game only fer jerks."

"Well then," injected Willie, "what if we all went to Cold Stone for some ice cream? I'll treat."

Pee Wee sneered again, "Too many calories. Besides, I'd get sick lookin at ya."

Alfonso now spoke up, "Look, Pee Wee, we just came by to tell you we'd like to be friends with you."

"FRIENDS?" Pee Wee laughed. "FRIENDS with saps like ya losers? I pick my own friends and ya Gooberheads pick yer noses!"

Goober repeated what Alfonso had said, "Well, we really DO want to be your friends, Pee Wee."

Pee Wee looked straight into Goober's eyes and said in a mocking tone, "Friends with pea-brains like ya creeps, Gumball? I'd be fraid if we shoot hoops I'd step on yer stupid faces! And, Al, I ain't got no friends who ain't white like me. Go eat a taco!"

"I'll share it with you," Alfonso smiled, still trying any way possible to be friendly to Pee Wee.

"Forget it," Pee Wee snapped, "I don' wanna catch yer dizeez."

Pee Wee turned to Willie. "So that leaves you, Wormy Willie. Yer more my size, but yer brain ain't. I can't stand the sight of none of ya guys. So why don't ya all go stand in the street and let the cars run over ya! THAT'S the most 'friendly' thing ya could do for me!" On saying that he slammed the door in their faces.

The three friends stood for a moment stunned and silent. Then Goober said, "I don't think that went very well!" Both Alfonso and Willie laughed.

Then Alfonso commented sadly as they turned to go, "You know, the truth is that Pee Wee doesn't like ANY color of human skin. He hates EVERYBODY."

As they continued walking, Willie said, "Wouldn't it be terrible to be Pee-wee? I don't think he really has *any* friends. I don't think he even likes himself!"

"Well," Goober said, "I still think something could change his mind. I just don't know what could do it."

"It would take a miracle" Alfonso declared.

Willie quickly responded, "Well, don't tell Tracey that. She'll go lay hands on him!" The boys laughed again.

Goober said, "I guess, at least for now, Tracey IS right about one thing. Pee Wee Fritz is STILL 'meaner than a junkyard dog'!"

"And he DID make me hungry, guys," Alfonso said cheerily. "I'm going to go have that taco!"

Goober, Alfonso, and Willie, walked back to school. Then each rode his own bike home.

That same evening Willie sat in his bedroom doing homework on his computer. There was a knock on his door and his mom called, "Willie?"

He invited her in. She came, walked up to him, put her arms around him from the back and hugged him. Then she sat down on his bed. "Do you have a moment to talk with me?" she asked.

"Sure, Mom," Willie said, and turned his chair towards her to give her his full attention.

"Willie," she said, "I know things haven't been easy for you with your dad and me divorcing and Lance coming into your life."

Willie looked at her seriously and said, "I know there's nothing I can do about it. I still love you, Mom. That hasn't changed. But this is really hard."

Mrs. Radner hesitated, but she didn't stop. "Honey, I want to ask you something. Do you like Lance?"

Then Willie hesitated and finally answered, "He's OK."

She went on quickly, "Because he really likes you."

Willie leveled with his mom. "Mom, he's not my dad. I like him all right. But I LOVE my dad."

"Willie," his mom exclaimed, "I never want your love for your father to stop. Your dad is your dad. I wish I still loved him for your sake. But for some reason your dad got too busy to keep loving me and so I quit loving him. I love Lance. I've come to tell you that as soon as your dad's and my divorce is final I'm going to marry Lance. We've set the date for May 15th."

Willie sat quietly and said nothing. There was nothing to say. He was paralyzed with the impossibility of fighting back. Her announcement sealed the coffin lid shut and there was nothing at all he could do about it.

"Congratulations," came out of his mouth, but not his heart. It sounded very hollow and his mother knew it. She knew Willie was devastated by the news.

"Are you OK, Son?" his mom asked.

"Yes," he answered in a hollow tone.

His mother kissed him on the forehead and left the room.

As soon as she was gone, Willie went to the lightswitch on his bedroom wall and snapped the light off. Then he found his bed and sat on the edge of it. His head had suddenly begun hurting. He wished he could switch his brain off as easily as he had just switched off the light. But he couldn't. Instead he felt every bit of the security he'd ever known while he was growing up, slip away as if through quicksand. It was gone.

Tears filled Willie's eyes and he cried silently with a broken heart. He knew there was no one who could see him cry and he let the tears fall wherever they wanted to.

It was the night of the annual talent contest at Thomas Edison. Goober went backstage to see his two favorite contestants - Alfonso and Tracey.

A month earlier, while the four friends were having lunch, Alfonso had talked about the contest. Then he said, "I've got a great idea, Tracey. Why don't the two of us enter as contestants? We could play our guitars and sing."

Tracey swallowed hard. Then she said, "Al, do you really think I'm ready for something like that?"

"You're more than ready, Tracey. You're really good. You have been for a long time now."

Goober and Willie both hollered, "YES!"

"Al's right," Goober told her. "I've been listening to you two for months now and you're hot!"

"OK," Tracey dared. "I'll do it if we pass the audition."

Al and Tracey were among the twenty-one groups or singles who tried out. Twelve were chosen. They passed their audition with flying colors. Mrs. Plumpff had been there to watch. Afterward, she complimented both Tracey and Al. "My goodness," she exclaimed, "you two are wonderful! I never realized either of you had that kind of talent. You could be on television."

Now it was the night of the show. "How are you two?" Goober asked as he entered the waiting room where all the contestants were gathering.

"Not good," Alfonso answered. Both Tracey and Alfonso looked unhappy.

Tracey explained, "I've broken a guitar string. It looks like we're going to have to drop out of the contest."

"No way," Goober said in disbelief. "Can't you find another guitar string somewhere? There must be some around."

"Not this late, Goob," Alfonso declared with disappointment. "Tracey's mom and my mom and dad won't be here until the show starts, so *they* can't help us. We don't have another set. And with one string gone on her guitar it means she needs to replace all six strings."

"Won't one of your guitars be enough for the two of you?" Goober asked him.

"If we'd practiced other songs, one guitar would have worked. But it takes both our guitars to do the songs we planned to do. The song titles are already printed in the program."

"Well," Goober grinned, "haven't you ever heard the old saying 'The show must go on'? You two are already the winners in my book. You've got to perform. If I left right now, Al, where could I go to get a new set of strings for you?"

"The only place would be a music store," Alfonso answered. "But it's too late for you to walk to any of them. You'd never get back before we're supposed to go on."

Goober thought a moment and said, "The Salvation Army Thrift Shop! That's a block from here. Let me run to it and see if, just maybe, they'd have the strings you need."

"But they don't sell guitar strings, Goob," Alfonso replied. "It's a second-hand store."

"And besides, it's probably closed by now," Tracey added.

"Tracey," Goober gently chided, "how good is that God of yours doing tonight? You're always telling us He can do

203

miracles. Well, can your God get you the strings you need for your guitar before you two are scheduled to go on stage and sing?"

Tracey looked at Goober with astonishment. "Yes, Goober, He can. I should have thought to pray."

"Well, you pray, Tracey. And you relax, Al. And it's Goober Boober to the rescue!" With those words, Goober dashed out the backstage door and began running with all his might toward the Salvation Army Thrift Shop.

A kind-looking black-haired lady with glasses had just put a CLOSED sign on the front entrance door when he reached it. It was a glass door and she could see Goober through it on the other side. "Mam, I've got an emergency," he hollered to her. "Would you let me come in?"

The lady smiled and opened the door. She said, "Now if it was anybody other than a handsome young boy like you I'd have stayed closed. But you look like you do need something. What is your 'emergency'?"

Goober thanked the lady for opening for him and then quickly asked, "Do you happen to have a set of acoustic guitar strings for sale? THAT'S the emergency!"

The lady looked at him with sympathy. She shook her head and said, "No, I'm sorry. I'm sure we don't even have any guitars for sale right now, let alone strings."

For some reason, Goober still felt confident. He asked, "Is it OK if I look around in your store for a minute just in case?"

"Oh," the lady said, "of course you can. If we did have anything like a guitar it would be over in THAT section." She pointed to the music section of the store where she knew only three instruments were sitting. "But I worked on that section less than an hour ago and I know there's absolutely no guitar there. I wish there was one for you."

Goober hurried to the music section anyway. All he saw was a kid's drum set, a faded yellow tuba, and a really worn-out looking flute. For a moment he felt discouraged. But suddenly it was as if a voice told him, "Look behind the drum set."

He looked, and there it was. "There IS a guitar, Mam!" Goober shouted to her in joy. "A really nice looking guitar. And it's got a full set of strings."

"Let me see what you're talking about," the lady said in surprise. "I KNOW there was no guitar there. I put those instruments there myself." When she came to where Goober was standing she said, "Why, my stars! That IS a guitar. It's a VERY NICE LOOKING guitar."

Suddenly fear hit Goober. Until that moment he hadn't thought about the price. He had a five dollar bill in his wallet and that was it.

"Mam," Goober asked her, "how much does this guitar cost?"

"Well, let me see if there's a price tag on it," the lady answered as she turned the guitar around to look at the back. "Nope," she told Goober. "Whoever put this guitar here forgot to put a tag on it at all. But tell me, why do you need this guitar so badly young man?"

Goober hurriedly explained. "Two of my best friends are in a talent contest tonight at Edison. And one of them had a guitar string break. They said that means they'd need a whole set of strings to replace the broken one so that they can perform."

"Well, my goodness," said the cheery lady, "we can't let them miss their big moment. I remember when my grandson was your age. I wouldn't have let him down either."

Goober was still worried that the price of the guitar would be way beyond the money that he had on him. "The price, Mam?" he asked again. "What would it be?"

"Well, since it wasn't marked, I'll just have to set the price myself. How much did you want to pay for it?"

"I just have five dollars on me right now," Goober told her honestly.

"Well for goodness sakes. THAT'S the exact price of this guitar!"

Goober asked, "Really?"

She smiled at him again, "Really. Is it a deal?"

"It sure is, Mam. Thank you SO MUCH," Goober smiled.

"My grandson is overseas fighting in a war to keep America free, young man. Just say a prayer when you think of him, will you?"

"Yes, Mam, I will," he told her, knowing Tracey was really the only friend he had who believed in prayer. Then he thought of Tracey who had begun to pray as he'd left to try to find the strings. He now was carrying back to them a whole guitar! He knew it was kind of a miracle, but he didn't have any time to think about that. Goober ran all the way back to Edison, hanging tightly to it.

The talent contest had already begun and Alfonso had all but given up thinking he and Tracey would get to be a part of it. But suddenly there Goober stood clutching a guitar.

Alfonso was stunned. "Where did you ever get THAT guitar, Goob?" he asked him.

"From a really nice lady at the Salvation Army Thrift Shop," he answered.

"But THAT'S a GREAT looking guitar. It looks brand new. How much money did you have to pay to buy it?"

"Five dollars," Goober told him.

Alfonso's mouth flew open, "FIVE DOLLARS! Goob, if that guitar sounds like it looks its worth several HUNDRED dollars! How did you get it for FIVE?"

"It was a miracle, wasn't it, Goob?" Tracey smiled.

"Yes, it *was* a miracle, Tracey. A really BIG miracle," Goober agreed.

"Well, I'm really thankful to God and you for it," Tracey said. "That was really great of you to go get this for us."

Alfonso began to strum the guitar. He couldn't believe what he heard. "This guitar is perfectly tuned. But that's impossible. This guitar should need tuning."

"A really BIG miracle," Tracey grinned. "All things are possible with God."

"Well something happened that doesn't make sense," Alfonso admitted.

"Anyhow, you've got your strings, Tracey," Goober reminded her. "Or do you want to play this new guitar tonight?"

"No," Tracey answered, "Al should play it. He's my teacher. And I'll play yours, Al, if that's all right with you. I know I can play it because I've practiced with it a bunch of times. I'm sure Uncle Sylvester won't mind. I'll get new strings for mine tomorrow."

"Great," Goober responded. "Oh, and there's something else you need to do, Tracey. The lady at the store asked for prayer for her grandson who is in a war overseas. You know I don't pray, but you do. Would you shoot some prayers up to your God for that lady and her son?"

"Sure I will, Goob," Tracey answered.

Suddenly Mrs. Plumpff walked in and asked, "Are you two ready? You're next."

Goober said, "I can hardly wait to hear you two. You'll knock everybody's socks off. I'd better get to my seat. Willie will be out there now, saving it for me."

Willie was sitting right where he said he'd be and asked Goober what had taken him so long.

"It was one of Tracey's miracles, Willie. I'll tell you all about it later," Goober said as he sat down.

When the winners of the talent show were announced, third place went to the four friend's classmate, Billy Birch, who recited *The Midnight Ride Of Paul Revere*. Second place went to three sixth grade girls who sang and acted out, *Happy Working Song* from the Disney movie *Enchanted*. I'll let you guess who won first place and I'll give you a clue. Goober and Willie's hands were nearly as red after all the applauding they did for the winners as Tinker Bomber's had been when he was caught shinnying down the rope at the River Theater!

Chapter Eight
A Winning Team

The Boobers were in shock. It happened all of a sudden at the dinner table one night when Clyde announced, "I've just joined the Army!"

Goober immediately thought about the thrift shop where he'd purchased the guitar for Tracey and Al. "The Salvation Army?" he asked.

"No, Dork," Clyde responded, "the United States Army!"

A gasp came from Mrs. Boober, and Mr. Boober's mouth dropped open even though there was food in it.

Clyde said it just as his mother was dishing out the potatoes. "Greg Dugan and I went into the recruiting office this afternoon and signed up."

"But….!" Mrs. Boober began to say something that died with that one word. She instantly knew that if Clyde had signed the papers and was over eighteen, which he was, there was nothing in the world she could do to stop him.

"Just as soon as I put in my years of service they'll help me financially get through college," he explained to his stunned parents.

"That makes sense," Goober encouraged.

The dish of potatoes was frozen in mid-air because Mimi Boober had stood stark still like a statue from the moment Clyde made his first statement. Suddenly she placed the dish hard on the dinner table and said, "Oh my! Oh my! Excuse me." Then she ran into her kitchen to cry.

There was a heavy silence at the table. Mr. Boober, just like his wife, wanted to talk his son out of joining the Army, but he knew as well as she did that it was too late. So he stayed silent and began reasoning with himself. He knew that Clyde was of age and if he wanted to join the Army he had every right to do so. Clyde and Goober had kept on eating, but Rex Boober just picked at his food, unable to enjoy it. He said nothing.

At least ten minutes later, Mrs. Boober returned red-eyed to the table. She had a question for Clyde. "But what about Lucy Flipp? You've been dating her and I really thought you two might be in love."

Clyde answered. "Well, Mom, I like Lucy. She's fine. But after a whole lot of thinking I realized I don't love her enough to marry her. I don't want to get tied down."

Now Mr. Boober finally spoke. He said, "Son, I'm really proud of you. But why didn't you talk with us about joining the Army before you did such a permanent thing?"

"Because I didn't want Mom and you to talk me out of it, Dad," he honestly answered.

Mimi said, "I know I should be proud of you too, Clyde. And I guess I am. But I don't mind admitting that I'm scared. I love you and I don't want anything terrible to happen to you."

"Mom," Clyde answered, and it was the only time Goober could ever remember that Clyde used the word 'love'. "I love you too. But I have no more protection here than I will there. Anything could happen to anybody at any time, anywhere at all. I could stay home and a building could fall on me, or I could get run over by a bus!"

Clyde's mom was afraid to ask her next question. Finally she blurted it out, "Are they going to keep you near Wake Up for your boot camp training?"

Realizing the pain he saw in his mother's eyes, he knew his answer would hurt her. "No, Mom, I'll be in training in Georgia."

"GEORGIA!" she wailed.

Clyde hesitated before adding, "I leave in thirty days."

No one ate much after that. Goober had eaten enough and asked if he could be excused. His mother nodded yes. Before he walked away he turned to Clyde and said, "I'm going to miss you."

Goober meant it. Clyde had always been his big brother. He knew his brother liked to tease him, and sometimes torment him, but he thought, "What does that matter? He's my brother." He knew he was going to miss him. It didn't matter why.

Goober had felt the pain of his parents too. He felt sad for them. "Man," he said to himself, "sometimes this is a really crummy world!"

"Hey, guys, it's baseball season," Willie said enthusiastically. The four friends were seated again having lunch at school and Willie went on, "I need you three with me this year."

"Oh," Goober said, "I'm always with you every year. I haven't missed a game you've pitched since the sixth grade."

"That's not what I mean," Willie answered. "This year our team is down in numbers. We aren't going to be a team at all unless you guys do more than sit in the bleachers yelling for me. You've got to play too."

"ME?" responded Alfonso, shocked at the idea because he'd never thought of it before.

"And what about me?" Tracey asked. "You want ME on the team to play baseball with you boys?"

Willie smiled, "Well, we've all played together bunches of times for fun. I actually think you'd feel more awkward than we would, Tracey, about you being on the team. You'd probably outplay us. But Coach Coopoo told me yesterday that we need an announcer for all the home games. I suggested you. I told him you have a great voice. He was really happy about that. He asked me to ask you if you'd do it."

"Whoa!" Tracey replied. "That would be a real honor. I've just got to ask my mom first."

"Great! Now, what about you guys?" he asked, looking at Goober and Alfonso. "Can I count on you to make our team happen?"

The two looked at each other and in a moment nodded. "Yeah," Goober grinned, "we'll help any way we can."

Willie was excited. "To tell you the truth, you guys are already better than most of the others on the team. And the guys you're replacing from last year couldn't hit, couldn't throw, and couldn't catch. You'll be great."

"YOU'RE the one who's great, Amigo," Alfonso declared.

"You sure are," Goober agreed.

Willie smiled and said, "Well, I can't do it all by myself. The coach will be holding tryouts tomorrow afternoon."

"We'll be there," Goober confirmed. "I know mom and dad will say yes."

Alfonso said the same thing about his mom and dad. "They'll think it's a GREAT idea."

Tracey's mom said yes, and Goober and Alfonso were right about their parents agreeing. The next day all three joined Willie for tryouts.

Coach Coopoo was impressed with each of them. Tracey sounded great on the microphone and wasn't shy at all. And Willie was right about Goober and Alfonso – they could hit, they could throw, and they could catch. They were enthusiastic players too. They showed up day after day for practice and got noticeably better the longer they practiced.

When it finally came time to assign permanent positions, the coach said, "Goober, you'll play second base. And, Al, I'm putting you in left field." Both boys were delighted with their assignments, not only because they were actually going to play, but because they knew if they hadn't played there wouldn't have been enough players and Willie would have been without a team.

"OK guys," Willie joyfully told his three friends, "all we have to wait for now is an umpire to shout, "PLAY BALL!"

The umpire shouted, "PLAY BALL!" It was the first game of the season. Goober and Alfonso had grown confident with their success in practicing and Willie's constant encouragement.

Clyde was there just to watch Goober play. That really pleased Goober, especially because one of his times at the plate he hit a triple. He looked to the bleachers after landing on third base and saw Clyde standing on his feet. He was clapping his hands and yelling excitedly. He was also telling somebody sitting next to him, "That's my little brother who hit that ball!" But Goober couldn't hear him.

Alfonso hit two singles. Tracey was a really good announcer. Willie pitched a shutout. Thomas Edison won 5-0.

Clyde left for Georgia two days after that. His mom and dad were there with Goober to see him off. His mom handed him a basket filled with food, kissed him, and cried. Clyde was embarrassed and said, "Aw, Ma!" But he had expected she'd do that.

Now that he was leaving, he wouldn't have admitted it to a single soul, but inside himself he was crying too. He knew all of his points of reference, everything he had known since he had been born, would vanish when the bus he would be riding pulled away. He was sure he'd made the right decision, but leaving his parents and Goober was unexpectedly rough for him.

Mimi in the midst of her tears told Clyde, "Don't forget to brush your teeth twice a day and change your underwear *every* day." She had been his mother close to nineteen years and letting go of him was to her like letting go of one of her arms.

Clyde just told her whatever he thought she'd want to hear. She handed him two freshly ironed handkerchiefs. "Thanks, Mom," he told her as he crammed them into his two front pockets, fully knowing he'd never use either one.

Clyde's dad told him, "Go be all that you can be, Son. But write to us. You hear me, Clyde? Write to us."

Clyde answered, "I will, Dad," and hugged him, but not as tightly as he'd hugged his mom.

Finally Clyde turned to Goober. He suddenly reached out and hugged him too. Goober had never been hugged by Clyde before. It felt so warm and friendly. "You know," Clyde told him, "I think I'm going to miss you, Peanut." Then he added, "Who else can I pick on all the time?"

Goober told him, "I'm going to miss you too, Clyde. It's going to feel really strange not to have my big brother around."

Finally Clyde boarded the bus. He got a window seat and opened the window to shout one more time to his family the words Goober only remembered him using that night at the dinner table - "I LOVE YOU!". The bus quickly moved away, rounded a corner and was gone.

Mimi Boober continued to cry for another three minutes. More than once she said, "Oh my! Oh my!" Then she blew her nose on her handkerchief, gave a half-hearted smile to her husband, and turned to Goober, saying, "Son, let's the three of us go drown our sorrows in hot fudge sundaes at Cold Stone." They did. It was a sweet way to fill the empty places now in each of them.

Once again, as he'd done in earlier grades, Willie continued shutting out the other teams. And it wasn't simply that he shut them out, but how he pitched. He had a remarkable ability to throw with a great variety of change-ups and curves. His fastball alone was faster than most high school seniors could throw.

Sitting in class one day as Mrs. Plumpff was drilling her students in math, an announcement came over the loudspeaker in her classroom. The announcer said, "Willie Radner is wanted in the principal's office immediately."

The announcement startled Willie. He quickly tried to think if he'd done anything that would have gotten him into trouble. Unable to think of anything, he then wondered if there was a problem at home and he was being called to the office to be given a message about it. "May I be excused, Mrs. Plumpff?" Willie asked politely.

"Why, of course, Willie," she smiled, already knowing what Mr. Hirkshire was about to tell this boy.

All of his classmates watched him as he got up and left the room. He glanced quickly at Goober, then at Alfonso and Tracey, giving them a quizzical look and shrugging his shoulders as he went out the door.

When Willie entered the principal's office, Mr. Hirkshire was waiting for him. He offered Willie a chair and Willie sat down. Mr. Hirkshire came right to the point. "Willie, I've called you into the office to privately tell you just how proud the faculty of Thomas Edison and I are of you. I can honestly say that some of the loudest shouts from the bleachers when you're pitching come from me. I thought my private office would give me a good place to tell you that. You're very popular, and finding you somewhere else on the campus to talk with you alone is nearly impossible."

"Well, I do have close friends who are usually with me," Willie agreed. "We're kind of like a team ourselves. But if I'd known you wanted to talk with me about anything at all, I would have made it happen. And telling me you cheer for me means a lot. I do see you at the games and I've heard you shouting. That really feels good when you do that, Mr. Hirkshire."

"Well, that's not everything I wanted to tell you, Willie. Yesterday I was at a faculty meeting and all of your former teachers and Mrs. Plumpff too, were commending your written and verbal scores as well as talking about your wonderful personality. I know each of them has worked to help you. But it's really YOU who has accomplished all you've done. No one can really take the credit for that except you. That's why I'm so very proud of you. I wanted you to know we have chosen you to be our valedictorian. We want you to give a speech at graduation."

Willie responded, "Gosh, that's a real honor. Thank you, Sir."

Mr. Hirkshire cleared his throat and asked, "Willie, do you know of a newspaper that calls itself U.S.A. Today?"

"Yes, Sir," Willie answered. "It's a national newspaper. I used it last month for part of some research I was doing for a debate."

Mr. Hirkshire handed Willie a copy of this day's issue, opened it to the Sports section, and Willie gasped.

"How does it feel to be nationally known, Willie?" he asked him.

"Wow!" Willie exclaimed, as he looked at a picture of himself in the paper. It was a picture that must have been snapped by someone while he was pitching last Friday's game. His name was underneath it, and so was a short write-up about him.

"I want you to realize how extremely rare an honor this is for an eighth grader," his principal explained. "Usually you'd have to be at least a junior in high school to get any possible recognition by USA Today. Even then you'd have to be a VERY GREAT player. But you have EXTREME talent. That's clearly why this national newspaper has written about you and shown your picture."

Willie was overwhelmed. "I don't know what to say, Sir. I just like to pitch."

"Well, I'm sure all of Wake Up is proud of you today, Son. And your parents must be the proudest. How are your mom and dad?"

With all the praise Mr. Hirkshire had heaped on him, Willie found it very hard to answer. Finally, and very quietly, he said, "They're divorcing, Sir."

Mr. Hirkshire could see the pain in Willie's eyes as he told him what his parents were doing. "I'm so sorry, Son," he said. "I've just put my foot in it. I wouldn't have asked if I had known. I meant for this time together in my office to be a wonderful one for you."

"It's OK, Sir," Willie quickly responded. "It has been wonderful. I'm excited about everything you've shared with me. I hate it that my parents are divorcing and I know you must not have heard about it."

Mr. Hirkshire stood. "No, I hadn't. If there's anything I can do to help them or you, please let me know, Willie."

217

"Thanks Mr. Hirkshire for everything. I will let you know. But I don't think anything will help them now. My mom is marrying someone else."

Now Willie's principal felt even more uneasy. For a moment he couldn't think of anything at all to say. Then finally he did speak again. "Well, I know this kind of thing happens, Willie. I'm just sorry it's happened to you." He put his arm on Willie's shoulder, smiled at him, and escorted him out of his office.

Both Goober's and Alfonso's parents were at every game all season long. Tracey's mom too, who had never been interested in baseball, came and sat with them in order to hear her daughter announce each player and to watch the boys play. Lance and Willie's mom were there for every game, and Willie's dad showed up for three of them.

Throughout the baseball season, college scouts had off and on come to the Edison High games too, expressly to see Willie pitch. Twice a scout from the San Francisco Giants came. It was small wonder these scouts wanted to watch this amazing kid. By the end of the season, Willie had pitched fourteen shut-outs in fourteen games. In six of those games he struck out every rival player for the entire seven innings. And he had only given up seven scattered hits throughout the season. Willie was a phenomenon.

At times, varous sports writers across America wrote articles about Willie because of what they read from a syndicated sports writer who lived in Wake Up and often attended Willie's games. That's how USA Today had picked up the story.

The day after the final game of the season, Mr. Hirkshire again asked Willie to come to his office. Just as in their earlier meeting, the announcement that Willie was wanted there was broadcast through the loudspeaker into his classroom.

This time Willie wasn't concerned about why he was being called. He thought Mr. Hirkshire probably just wanted to talk to him about Edison's great baseball season. He had felt as awkward as Mr. Hirkshire did about how things had ended the last time he was in his office and he was glad to get a second chance to talk alone with him.

But when Willie entered the principal's office this time, both Mr. Hirkshire and Coach Coopoo were seated and smiling up at him. "Hello, Willie," Mr. Hirkshire welcomed him. "You've had another magnificent season. I am totally amazed at how you handle a ball."

"Thank you, Sir," Willie replied. "And hello Coach." Willie smiled warmly back at both men as he took the seat offered him.

"Hello Willie," Coach Coopoo returned. "I'm really glad you're here."

Mr. Hirkshire came right to the point. "The purpose of my calling you here this time, Willie, is just as unusual as you finding your picture and that article about you in USA Today a month ago. This time you're wanted on television."

"Television, Sir?" Willie questioned.

"Yes, Willie, television. I was amazed to have a phone call waiting for me when I walked in here this morning from none other than ESPN."

"The sports channel?" Willie asked in surprise.

"Yes, Willie," Mr. Hirkshire answered, "that's the one. And that's why I called Coach Coopoo in before I called you. I felt I had to have his OK first before I approached you with this subject."

"Willie, you don't have to do what ESPN has asked unless you absolutely want to," Coach Coopoo assured him.

Willie was curious. "What do they want, Mr. Hirkshire?"

"Well, they realize you have an amazing strikeout record and that you're only in the eighth grade. The six perfect games you've pitched this year, striking out everyone on the other team for seven whole innings, plus your consistent strikeout record in every game you pitch, is equal in their mind to an eighth grader bowling a bunch of perfect 300's while in a bowling league against fourteen other schools."

"Wow," Willie exclaimed honestly, "I don't look at it that way at all, Sir. I just like to pitch."

"I'm glad you do, Willie," his principal told him. "But you have more and more fans throughout America who because of what someone wrote about you in a national newspaper or in their local one, would like to watch you do it."

"How could they do that?" Willie asked.

"ESPN wants to know if they can come to Thomas Edison and do a live broadcast of your final game."

"But we just played our final game yesterday, Sir," Willie responded.

"Well," Mr. Hirkshire explained, "they're not talking about the final game of your regular season, the one you won yesterday. They want your team to play an additional game against a middle school from Flagstaff, Arizona."

Willie wanted to know, "What team is that, Mr. Hirkshire?"

"It's a team called the Mesquite Roadrunners. Like Edison, it's been unbeaten in three years, mostly because of the tremendous pitcher who strikes out players kind of like you do. ESPN says his record nearly equals yours. Their network has never shown two middle schools playing against each other, but they are willing to spend a bunch of money to come and do a live telecast of the game if you are willing. Their pitcher is eager to throw against Edison, and mostly against you."

"Who is this pitcher, Sir?" Willie asked again.

"His name is Stanley Strom, but everyone calls him 'Pork Chop'. He's got a great throwing arm and uses a strong variety of pitches like you do. He's got an amazing strike-out record too. Their team hasn't lost a game in three years with Pork Chop pitching, just as Edison hasn't with you. Willie, here's what I need to know. If I allowed ESPN to come and film a live baseball game here, especially against as strong a team as Mesquite, would it make you too nervous and throw your pitching off at all? I'd never let that happen if I could help it. And I have to tell you that if anything went wrong with your pitching during this game it could possibly decrease the opportunities you are going to otherwise continue to have with scouts. I told ESPN that I'd phone them back only after I talked with you, and only then if I get the whole team's approval as well. I can certainly call and tell them no, and that wouldn't make a bit of difference about how your coach or I feel about you. We just want to know how you'd feel about this, Willie."

Willie answered, "I think it would be great. And no, it won't throw my game off at all. I think the rest of the guys on the team are going to feel the same way about it. If they do, let's do it."

Mr. Hirkshire and the coach both smiled broadly. Then Coach Coopoo said, "I told Mr. Hirkshire that's how you would feel about it, Willie."

A few minutes later the whole baseball team for Edison jammed into Mr. Hirkshire's office, Goober and Alfonso among them. Willie had asked Mr. Hirkshire to bring Tracey into his office with the baseball team too, "Because she's done such a great job announcing for us all season."

After Tracey and the whole team arrived, the principal explained to them what ESPN wanted to do. They were ecstatic and said "SURE!"

"Then the game will take place two weeks from today," Mr. Hirkshire told them. "Congratulations on winning this entire season. Now you have one more game to win!"

When the four friends sat down for lunch in the cafeteria that day they were exploding with excitement. "We're going to be on television!" Goober began. "I hope I don't have to wear make-up!" That cracked everybody up.

Willie kidded Goober and Alfonso, "You two haven't made an error all season. So don't start tripping over the camera wires now!" Again the four laughed.

"We won't, Willie," Alfonso chuckled. "But don't you start grinning into the camera every time you're going to make a pitch!" More gales of laughter.

Tracey laughed, "How will a 'Pork Chop' look, pitching on TV?" Goober and Alfonso laughed again, but that question brought a serious response from Willie.

"You know guys, this isn't going to be an easy win like the kinds we've had all season. I've already looked at Pork Chop's stats. This guy really mows the batters down."

"So do you, Willie," Goober reminded him.

"Yeah, I know," he said, seriously. "But I mean THIS ballgame won't be a piece of cake."

"I'll bet you pitch another perfect game, Willie" Alfonso encouraged. "What Goob, the rest of the team, and I have to do is play a perfect game too."

Willie responded, "You guys do great. I'm not worried about that. But with a pitcher like Pork Chop, the game could easily go into extra innings. Their team has some really heavy hitters. Remember, they've never lost a game either."

Goober smiled, "That just means we won't be able to lie down and take a nap during the game because people are going to be watching us all over America!"

"It's the biggest game we might ever play in," Willie declared. "Each of us has got to be on our toes."

"I'm praying for you guys," Tracey told them.

"Thanks, Tracey," Willie said quickly. "We wouldn't want GOD to miss the game!" The boys laughed. Tracey knew they just didn't understand.

When Willie's dad heard about the thirteenth and final game of the season being televised, he told Willie, "How I wish I could be there to see you play. But I can't because I've got two really important meetings that day." Then he told Willie he'd make sure the game got videotaped so that he could watch it afterwards with him.

Willie wished with all his heart that his dad could be at his game, but he had often in the past two years heard his father explain why he couldn't be somewhere important with him or his mom. He'd say, 'Business before pleasure'. And that's what he told Willie now. He did add, "Skipper, I'll try to sneak peeks at it on television every few minutes while I'm working, and I'm aiming to be there for at least the last two innings to watch you. Then you and I will go out to dinner and catch a movie. What do you say?"

"Sure, Dad," Willie responded. "That'll be great." But in his heart, Willie wished with everything in him that his dad would say he'd put aside all of his work for just a couple of hours and come see him pitch this big game.

The day of the game arrived. ESPN had come to Edison the day before to search out camera angles, set up the television announcer's booth, and prepare to televise the game. The production crew was there early in the morning to be certain their cameras and equipment were in the right spots and get all final filming ready.

Mesquite High had been in Wake Up for three days and practiced on the Edison ball field every day. They practiced when Edison had school in session, then Willie and his team practiced after school.

Willie had gone to bed extra early the night before so that he would feel totally fresh for the game. But something went terribly wrong. When Willie woke the morning of the game he immediately felt a sharp pain in his pitching arm. Wincing, he got out of bed and tried working what he thought must be a kink out of it. He thought he must have slept on that arm in some way that had cramped a muscle.

The more Willie tried to relieve the pain, the more definite the pain remained. It just grew sharper.

Willie took a hot shower, hoping the heat would help his arm. It didn't. Then he went to his mom with the problem and she suggested he take two of her pain pills. "I can't do that, Mom," he told her. "They could throw me off when I pitch today."

She answered, "Well, Willie, if your arm remains in pain you won't be pitching anyway. How about trying a heating pad on it? That sometimes works for me."

Willie tried the pad, but it did nothing for his arm. He began to worry. He thought about phoning Goober or Alfonso, but knew both of them were going to be playing in the game too in just four hours. He didn't want them worrying about his arm at all.

Willie also thought about phoning Coach Coopoo or Mr. Hirkshire, but he knew how excited they were about this game and didn't want them to worry about him either.

Finally he decided to tell Tracey. "Nothing shakes her up," he said to himself as he punched her number on his cell phone. "Maybe she'll have a suggestion for me."

As soon as Tracey answered her phone, Willie said, "Hi, Tracey. I've got a problem. I only told my mom about it, but she didn't know what to do." Then Willie paused, thinking to himself, "Why in heck have I called Tracey?"

"What's your problem, Willie?" Tracey asked him. "You know I'll help you if I can."

Willie suddenly felt silly about what he was going to tell her. He couldn't see any way at all how she could help him with his sore arm. But since they were already talking, Willie said, "It's my arm, Tracey - my pitching arm. I've got a really sharp pain in it. If this pain keeps up I won't be able to pitch this afternoon."

"Oh, a pain in an arm is NO PROBLEM AT ALL," Tracey assured him. "I'll just pray and your pain will disappear."

If it hadn't been that Tracey was such a good friend, Willie would have laughed her off when she said that and gotten off the phone. But Willie knew he was fresh out of answers. He had thought about seeing a chiropractor, but knew there wouldn't be time to do that before the game. And because this was just a middle school game, there were no sports doctors on hand to help him. So, feeling totally helpless, Willie asked Tracey, "So what do I do, start humming ohmmmm?"

"No, Silly," Tracey laughed. "Just sit there or stand there, whatever you're doing, and let me pray for you. We Christians do this all the time."

"OK," Willie told her, "I'm standing with my cell phone in my hand, talking with you. Pray." Willie couldn't believe he was asking Tracey to do this.

"Lord Jesus," Tracey prayed, "take the pain completely away from Willie's arm right now and don't ever let it come back."

Willie still waited. Finally he said, "Isn't there a whole bunch more stuff you've got to say, Tracey?"

"No, that's it," Tracey told him. "The Lord heard me. Now, move your pitching arm. Check it out and then tell me what you feel."

Willie said, "Just a minute. I'm going to put my phone down."

Willie set his phone on the bed and then moved his pitching arm, still fully expecting it to be in pain, but it wasn't. He moved it more, stretching it to see if he could feel any soreness. There was none. Then he struck a pose as if he were standing on the pitcher's mound and went through all the motions he'd use in pitching. His pitching arm felt perfectly normal, just as if there had been no pain in it EVER!

Amazed, Willie picked his phone up off the bed and told Tracey, "I can't believe this. That pain in my arm is completely gone. What the heck did you just do?"

"I prayed to Jesus Christ, the One who loves you and gave His life for you, Willie," Tracey explained. "He just healed you."

"I'd almost believe that," Willie responded. "Almost. But maybe when I started moving my arm like I did, somehow the kink just left on its own. I'm sorry, Tracey, but I still don't believe in God."

"That's OK, Willie," Tracey assured him. "God believes in YOU!"

Every member of each family, except for Willie's dad, was in the Edison stand long before game time. Willie was disappointed that his dad had other commitments, but was happy that his mom was there. He was even glad to see Lance with her. There was just one stand and it was small. And with so many relatives and friends of each ball player coming to cheer, and others coming because they knew the game was being televised, there was standing room only very quickly.

"You're going to eat up that Pork Chop!" Goober told Willie as they were putting on their uniforms.

"You'll cut him up and have him for lunch," Alfonso agreed. Willie just smiled.

But the game didn't start well for Willie. In fact, it was like no other game he'd ever pitched.

Tracey announced the first player up for Mesquite: "Now batting, Tommy Leopard, third base." WHAM! Tommy's hit sent the ball over Goober's head and into right field. It was a clear single. Willie couldn't believe it. He shook his whole body and tried to get himself loosened up and mentally ready to pitch to the second batter.

Tracey spoke again: "Now batting, Larry Braxton, first base." WHAM! Larry sent the ball flying deep into left field. Alfonso was on it and cut it off quickly, but by the time he was able to throw, he had to throw to third where Tommy had made it easily. In just two pitches, Willie had put runners on first and third base with no one out.

"It's OK, Willie," Lance yelled from the stand. "You'll get them out. Don't worry."

Goober, always the encourager, strode from second base to Willie and told him, "I can see what you're doing, Willie. You're going to strike out the next three batters and leave those guys stranded on those bases and looking silly. You're proving to the world you're a real star!"

Coach Coopoo and Mr. Hirkshire were extremely concerned, especially after the second single. But after

Goober walked back to second base, Willie did exactly what Goober had predicted. He struck out the next three batters in a row.

As the game proceeded, Pork Chop gave up a double in the fourth inning, but then again retired the side.

It was in the top half of the fifth inning with one away that a commotion began. Willie was pitching when the ESPN announcer suddenly said, "I don't know what this young fellow is doing, but he's come on to the ball field and he's carrying a bag. Something is in that bag. This could be interesting. Let's watch." The camera zoomed in, but the kids from Edison knew immediately that the boy carrying the bag was none other than Pee Wee Fritz!

Pee Wee walked as quickly as he could towards the pitcher's mound. He was carrying a sack with something obviously inside it. Then Pee Wee opened the sack and a SKUNK crawled out!

Willie stood still as a statue as the skunk eyed him. But then the skunk scampered away, out past the shortstop, Jerry Ribaldi and straight toward Manny Bookalooski in centerfield.

The people, especially in the stand and on the field, were breathless as they watched what was about to happen. But there was no way to stop it. Poor Manny tried to stand still, as Willie and Jerry had, but the nearer the skunk came towards him, the more scared Manny became. Manny finally started to run and the skunk let him know just exactly what he thought of that. He raised his tail and sprayed the center fielder. Manny let out a howl.

The game had to be held up while Coach Coopoo and Manny's dad, who had both been standing and watching it all, ran to help the now-stinking boy off the field. They took him to the showers and after ten minutes had passed allowing the worst of the odor to die down on the field itself, Freddy Lawson, the last possible Edison player, was sent off the bench to take over for the still-stinking center fielder. You could smell the odor of skunk spray on the field and in the stand too, but the game had to go on.

The frightened skunk had disappeared quickly through a hole in the fence. Mr. Hirkshire ran and caught Pee Wee, who wasn't as lucky as the skunk, and sent him home with a three-day suspension from school for playing such a prank.

Although Pork Chop gave up another double in the seventh inning, at the end of the seventh there was no score at all in the ballgame. Usually middle school games would end after seven innings, but it had already been agreed that since this game was being televised, and because of the awesome pitching duel between Pork Chop and Willie, it would go into extra innings if there was a tie at the end of the seventh.

The eighth inning went by with no score. Both Willie and Pork Chop struck out their side. They did the same in the ninth, and Willie fanned all three batters in the tenth. Now it was the bottom of the tenth. Pork Chop continued as great as ever. Both Jimmy Drust and Matt Ricardo, the first two boys up for Edison, struck out.

But then Alfonso connected solidly with his bat and sent the ball towering far out into right field. Don Dominic went way back for the ball and up against the fence. He couldn't get it. The ball hit the top of the fence and bounced several yards in front of Don. He finally got to the ball and threw it hard to third. By that time, Alfonso was standing happily on third base with his cap off, wiping sweat from his brow.

The four friend's parents and Lance were all on their feet shouting for Alfonso, thrilled with what he'd just done. All of the Edison fans in the stand were standing and yelling too. Many of the students were jumping up and down as they whooped. And the loudest cheers of all came from Alfonso's mom and dad who were hugging each other as they watched their son round the bases.

Goober, who was standing on deck, Willie from the dug-out, and Coach Coopoo standing just off third base, were jumping up and down too as Alfonso was coming into third. When Alfonso's foot hit the bag, Coach Coopoo stopped jumping and told him, "Great hit, Al. Now, just stay there until I signal you home." Coach Coopoo had quickly left Manny and his dad so that Manny could take a long shower and the coach could get back to the game. Fortunately, he got away from Manny quickly enough to not smell at all of skunk spray. Alfonso was glad about that. So was Coach Coopoo!

Goober knew that this was now one of the most important moments in his life. Tracey took a deep breath and announced, "Next batter, Goober Boober. Second base."

The first time Tracey had announced "Goober Boober" that day there had been a strong ripple of laughter from any in the crowd who hadn't known who Goober was. But now there was no laughter at all. Everyone in the stand, on the field, or in both dug-outs, was silent and watching either Goober or Pork Chop.

Goober stepped into the batter's box. "I only need to get a single," he told himself. "Just a single and Al will score."

On the pitcher's mound, Pork Chop was angry with himself for giving up that triple. "Well," he thought, "it isn't going to happen again." Pork Chop had struck Goober out his last time to the plate and had caused him to ground out his first time up. He could hear his team chattering all around him. From first base, Larry Braxton hollered, "Easy out!"

Goober swung at Pork Chop's first pitch and the ball went whizzing by into the catcher's mitt. "Strike One," the umpire called.

The catcher mocked Goober's name: "Scooby Dooby Doo, loser." The plate umpire warned the catcher to be quiet. Pork Chop threw the ball a second time to Goober and Goober swung. He missed the ball. "Strike two!"

Mimi Goober sat in the stand saying, "Oh my! Oh my!"

Goober knew he was now in deep trouble. But he reminded himself again, "I only need a single."

With two strikes on Goober, Pork Chop knew he could waste a couple of pitches just teasing Goober, hoping to get him to swing. His next pitch was high and outside. Goober let it go by. Then Pork Chop threw a change-up that went by Goober too low.

Pork Chop watched his catcher's signals carefully and shrugged off a couple of them before agreeing that he'd put another one right over the plate, but far too fast for Goober to hit. However, when he threw it, it was high and this time inside. Goober backed up quickly and the ball flew past him.

Pork Chop had thrown three balls and two strikes, a full count. Goober told himself again, "I only need a single."

Once again, Pork Chop decided to throw his fastball right over the plate. He had used it earlier and it was the pitch that got Goober to strike out.

Pork Chop reared back and threw. WHAM! The ball went high over Pork Chop's head, high out into right field, and high over the fence. A HOME RUN! The crowd went wild!

As Alfonso ran in easily from third, and Goober rounded the bases heading home, Goober knew this was one of those miracle moments he would remember all his life. The crowd for Edison poured out on to the field as Goober rounded first, then second, then third. Alfonso threw his arms around his friend, hugging him fiercely, right after Goober's foot touched home plate. Then his team mobbed him. It was only the second homerun Goober had hit the whole season, but it was by far the most important. Tracey came down from the announcer's box. Goober's parents rushed to get with him, and his friends did too. Coach Coopoo and Mr. Hirkshire also hurried from the sidelines to congratulate him.

Before Willie went to Goober, he walked straight out to Pork Chop who was still standing on the pitcher's mound with tears running down his face. Willie told him, "You pitched a great game. I sure thought you might beat us. Keep that arm going. You're going to be awesome in high school. I hope we're on the same team in the Big Leagues."

Pork Chop thanked him and said, "You're a great pitcher, Willie. I wanted to beat you with everything in me. But you won this game. I hope we pitch together in the Big Leagues too because I never want to pitch against you again!"

It was then that Willie ran back to Goober and joined the crowd to tell him how great he was. As soon as the crowd saw Willie, they lifted him up in the air and walked with him, knowing that he was the only reason ESPN had wanted to televise this game on their network. When the crowd put him down, a sports announcer from ESPN interviewed Willie immediately. Willie just kept telling the interviewer how great his other teammates had done, and what an amazing pitcher Pork Chop was. Willie's dad stood beaming as his son talked with the announcer.

Willie's mom and Lance had already hugged him and were leaving with the crowd. Willie had told them about the plans his dad had made with him to go to dinner and see a movie.

After Willie's national interview, his dad walked up to him, gave him a hug, and said, "Wow, ESPN! Skipper, what an important moment in your life this is! You were spectacular and you've made me very proud. One day when you still get a lot more famous, I'm going to be able to say that I watched the very beginning moment of all that. I got here to watch the tenth inning." Willie just smiled.

"Son," Mr. Radner continued, "I need to talk with you. Can we go sit in my car?"

Willie said, "Sure, Dad. But aren't we going out for dinner?"

"That's what I need to talk with you about, Skipper. That and a couple of other things."

Willie and his father walked to Mr. Radner's BMW. Willie got in on the passenger side of the front seat and his dad sat at the wheel.

"Willie, I've got some good news and I've got some bad news. Of course to me, both things I'm going to share with you are good news."

"What are they, Dad?" Willie asked.

"Well, let me tell you the good news first. You're going to be with me to see a lot of New York City."

"New York City, Dad?"

"Yep, because, and my guess is this is what will at first seem to you to be bad news - I'm moving there tomorrow."

Willie was stunned. "What do you mean tomorrow? Why do you have to move to New York City?"

"Son, I've just received a large promotion at work. I'm actually going to be the company manager in New York. It means a whole lot more money. I'll have a huge office. Instead of working for others, others will be working for me. You wouldn't keep me from all that by insisting that I stay here in Wake Up would you?"

"No, Dad," Willie said with an instant ache in his heart. "Not if it means that much to you."

"It sure does. And there is one other piece of bad news. I can't take you to dinner tonight. We'll have to postpone that. I've got to get home and pack. There are a million things that need to be done before I leave on the plane at 5 p.m. tomorrow."

Willie was confused. He definitely didn't want his dad to leave or to live anywhere but in Wake Up. There had never been a greater time in his young life that he needed his dad to stay and be close and available than he did now. His mom and Lance would marry tomorrow, but until this very moment he had at least thought that if things got to be too much for him at home he could count on going to his dad to talk about it. Now his dad wasn't going to be there at all for him.

"Skipper," his dad went on, "I've been thinking a lot about this since I found out today. I know you may feel I'm throwing you to the sharks, but I'm not. I wouldn't make this move at all if I didn't know you're a young man who can swim with the best of them. There are a lot of advantages to this if you look at things the way I see them. First, I want to show you New York City. I want to take you to Broadway plays and to watch the Yankees and the Mets play. You'll get to see the Statue of Liberty, the Empire State Building, Ellis Island, and Times Square. I'll take you to fabulous restaurants, and we'll even ride in a horse and buggy carriage in Central Park."

Willie could tell by the way his dad was presenting New York to him that he had memorized this whole sales spiel. He sounded like a tourist guide as he rattled off those points of interest. But Willie knew he still very much wanted his dad in his life and that he would be going to New York City as often as possible to be with him.

"Second," Willie's dad told him, "Lance is a really great guy and he really likes you. Give him a break, Willie. He's promised me he'll be there for you."

"Third, about us, there's our cell phones, e-mail, and my video conference line. So in a lot of ways it will be like I'm still right here in Wake Up. If you call me and I'm tied up, I'll call you back as soon as I can get free. And I mean it about bringing you to New York. I know you'll enjoy the airplane rides. You'll even start racking up frequent flyer miles. Your life is going to be more exciting BY FAR because I'm making this move. So, do you see what I mean when I say that even the bad news part of this is really good news?"

Willie wanted to let his dad know he was glad for his promotion. He knew it was what his dad wanted, and Willie didn't want to spoil his dad's joy. So he said, "Sure, Dad."

But inside, Willie felt sick. He wanted his dad to say, "So I was offered all that and I turned it down because you're a whole lot more important than all that would be to me." But he knew his dad would never say such a thing. His dad's work and money were far more important to him than Willie or his mom and there was nothing Willie could do about it. He knew these were the reasons why his dad had divorced his mom. His dad had run totally out of time for her and for him.

But Willie was now hit with another feeling too – guilt. He thought he shouldn't feel that his dad was shoving him out of his life. He guessed he was just being selfish to wish his dad was any other way. After all, this was how his dad was and Willie still loved him. It was just that moving to New York in Willie's mind was like having his dad move to the moon.

"So, Son," his dad continued, "I'm really sorry, but I've got to get going. I can't waste a minute. I do have something for you." And saying that he reached into his wallet and handed

Willie a hundred dollar bill. "Take this, and here's an extra twenty to get some dinner. Do you want me to drive you home or to a restaurant?"

Willie replied, "No, Dad. Thanks for this money, but I think I'll walk. It will do my legs good and save you some time."

"Well, OK, Skipper. Just know I'm always as close as that cell phone. I love you, Son. Everything's going to be great."

Mr. Radner reached over and gave Willie a hug. Willie kissed his dad's cheek, got out of the car, and his dad drove away without him.

The day after his final ballgame for Edison, Willie's mom and Lance married. Tank Smith, a sophomore at White Mountain College, who had done some office work for Willie's dad, picked Willie up at his house that morning and dropped him off at the River City Church on Churn Creek Road in Redding. Tank had tried to make conversation with Willie while driving him to the church, but Willie was very quiet and said hardly anything. "Hope it's a great wedding," Tank said cheerily as Willie stepped out of his car.

"Thanks," Willie responded sadly.

Tank had driven Willie there because Mr. Radner had asked him to. As he drove away he said out loud, "That Willie Radner is one unhappy dude."

Willie quietly entered the sanctuary of the church. Lance had asked him to come. Willie didn't know why. Willie had asked both his mother and Lance if he could be excused from actually participating in their wedding. He explained that he just wasn't ready to be an active part of it. Lance and his mom understood.

Willie had planned to stay with his dad the whole week during his mom and Lance's honeymoon, but with his dad suddenly moving to New York, Willie phoned Goober and made arrangements to stay with him and his family instead. They were glad to have him come. And with all that was happening in Willie's life, he felt a deep need to be with a happy family.

Willie was sitting in the first pew when Lance approached him. "Hi, Willie," Lance smiled. "Thanks for coming. That means a lot to me. Do you mind if I slide in next to you?"

Willie told him, "OK," but he felt rigid.

Lance sat and then said, "I just wanted to talk with you for a moment before the few other people get here. Your dad phoned me yesterday that he'd just found out his company was moving him to New York today. I know that must be rough on you in spite of his success. But he told me he'll still try to be there for you even in New York. He reminded me to tell you that he's always as close to you as your cell phone."

"Yeah, he told me that last night too," Willie responded.

Lance continued, "Willie, I want you to know I really love your mom. That's why we're marrying. I know we'll be living in the same house, all three of us. But though I'm there, I promise you right now that I'm never going to try to fill your dad's shoes with you. You only have one dad and I know that. And I'll work hard to always give you alone time with your mom too."

"Thanks," Willie said quietly.

Lance went on. "I like everything I know about you, Willie. I feel so lucky to have even a little place in your life. Except for your mom, I've never been much in anybody's life. I want to be someone you respect, and I'm going to do everything in my power to keep that happening. If you ever want to talk with me about anything at all, I'll be more than glad to hear you quickly. And if I do something wrong, tell me what it is. Maybe somehow whatever you fear about your mom and me marrying will go away if you do that. Again,

237

I'll never try to be your dad. But I do hope there will come a time when we can be good friends."

Willie realized a lot of kids who had talked with him at school didn't even have real dads that seemed to care about them as much as Lance seemed to care about him. But it was so hard to think that after all the years of being with his dad and mom together, this stranger would suddenly be at his home every day in the place his dad should be. Willie wanted to say something, but he couldn't find the words.

After an awkward silence, Lance said, "Well, I guess I better go get ready."

Willie sat for a long time after Lance was gone, just staring into space. His mind was numb. And he still felt so terribly alone. Then Goober, Alfonso, and Tracey, arrived to sit with him. That made things a bit more cheerful. He felt less lonely with them there.

There were only thirty-one people who attended the wedding including Willie and his three friends. Lance wore a gray suit with a blue tie and Willie's mom wore a pretty blue dress. There was no wedding march. Lance and Mrs. Radner simply came to the front of the church to stand with the pastor who was going to perform the ceremony.

The pastor was an older man, short, bald, and had a white mustache. He wore glasses. Willie, who knew no pastors at all, was surprised to see how friendly this man was. "Hi," he said to the people, "I'm Wendell McGowan, the pastor here at River City Church. I've talked with this young couple about God and I believe God has brought them together for a great purpose. I know He has magnificent plans for their future. God has great plans for anyone who will give their life to Jesus Christ. I'd be glad to talk with any of you about that following this happy ceremony."

Willie asked himself, "How could this guy know God has 'magnificent plans' for Lance and my mom? I don't think God has anything to do with my mom and Lance getting married. I don't even believe in God. My mom and Lance don't believe in Him either."

Pastor McGowan finished speaking to the group that had gathered, by saying, "I have the extreme joy of helping this beautiful couple tie the knot now with God's blessings."

"Yeah," thought Willie, "you're going to tie a hangman's knot around *my* neck!"

The four friends sat in silence as the wedding proceeded. Tracey especially loved weddings, and she loved Pastor McGowan. She had been to some great meetings at his church. The music was beautiful, and even Willie noticed how good both his mom and Lance looked.

The couple exchanged their vows, were pronounced husband and wife, kissed, and then were introduced to the crowd as Mr. and Mrs. Amos. The music played again and the couple walked to a reception room where the handful of relatives and friends who had come could greet them and share wedding cake and ice cream with them.

When Willie and his friends had finished eating, Willie went to his mom and Lance to say goodbye for the week. He hugged his mom and told her how pretty she looked. He simply shook Lance's hand.

Willie's mother told him, "We'll be back before you know it. Thank you for being here with us today. That meant a lot to us. Things are going to be a lot better in our home now."

He hugged his mom again and said, "Have fun." Then he left the church with his three friends.

Within an hour the four friends were eating sandwiches at Subway. After they'd placed their orders, Alfonso, in an attempt to thank Willie for inviting him, said, "That was a really nice wedding."

Willie shrugged, "I guess so. My mom's happy, and I guess that's what's important."

"You really are lucky, Willie," stated Tracey.

"Lucky?!" Willie exclaimed, "What do you mean I'm 'lucky'?"

"Simple," said Tracey, "you've got two dads and I haven't even got one." Willie would have never expected Tracey to say such a thing.

"Do you know, Tracey," Willie asked her, "that until the wedding this morning I didn't even know what Lance's last name was? I never thought to ask. 'Amos'! That sounds funny and it feels funny. I'm still Willie Radner, so I'm the only Radner who will now be living at my house! That's pretty weird."

Tracey continued, "I'd gladly see my mom get a new last name if she could get a new better life with it. She never complains to me about it, but I know how lonely she gets sometimes. And from now on, Willie, Lance is going to be your step-dad. That's really neat. So many times I wish I had a step-dad to care about me. With your dad having to move to New York, I'll bet there'll be days when Lance is going to become very important in your life."

"Don't hold your breath waiting for *that*," Willie responded.

Goober entered the conversation, "Willie, I know how you feel because you've told us a bunch of times. But everything I've seen about Lance since he and your mom gave up booze tells me if you give him half a chance you're going to really like your step-dad. But let me ask you something. Are you afraid that if you do find that you really like your step-dad, it will make you feel like you might hurt your real dad's feelings?"

Willie answered truthfully. "Yeah, I guess so."

Goober reminded him, "But didn't you tell me that your dad said Lance was 'a nice guy'? That sounds to me like your dad wants you to like him."

"Yeah," responded Willie as he thought about that.

Tracey added, "And as busy as your own dad sounds like he's going to be, I'll bet he's hoping your mom and Lance are really happy, and that you fit right in as part of your new family. That'll make it so much easier on your dad."

Willie was quiet, thinking about all the things his friends had said. Then he began, "You know, I've never thought about what you guys are saying. I've been angry and feeling sorry for myself. Today, before the three of you got to the church, Lance came and sat with me. He told me he won't ever try to become my dad because I already have one. But that he loves my mother and will try to be my friend."

"Wow," Tracey said, "that's sounds really nice to me."

"You know," Willie responded, "I guess you're right, Tracey. I am kind of lucky. I should have told Lance thanks instead of shining him off."

Goober smiled, "Well, there will be plenty of time to tell him that once your mom and him are back. Hey, and if it really doesn't work out for you, you can come live at our house. My mom said this morning she's really glad you're going to be spending a week with us now. She misses Clyde a lot and you'll kind of make up for him being gone while you're with us."

"I'm looking forward to it too," Willie said, finally smiling.

Alfonso added, "And, Willie, Lance knows he's on thin ice with you about being your step-dad and moving into your house. He sounds like he's making it as easy on you as he can."

"Yeah," Willie responded, "I guess he is. Pass me the mayonnaise."

Chapter Nine
The Biggest Surprise Of All

It was a lazy Saturday afternoon. Now that baseball season was over for sure, the four best friends were at Alfonso's house just hanging out. They'd been talking about going to a movie, but they couldn't decide what to see. Mr. Guiterrez told them that when they did decide, he'd be glad to drive them to the theater where the movie they chose was playing.

"I'm in the mood for something funny," Goober said yawning. "I want to laugh."

"Well, I'm in the mood for something fun, but romantic," Tracey told the boys. "I don't mean some mushy gooey love story. But something that shows how special we girls are."

Willie disagreed with them both. "I'd like to see something with some real action in it. Maybe a war movie, or something with monsters."

And Alfonso, who seldom disagreed with his friends, said, "I'm in the mood for a cartoon movie. I like those."

Willie spoke again, "Wow! We all want to see something different, but we want to see a movie together. How can we decide what to see?"

"Hey, I know what would be fun," Goober answered. "Let's throw darts. We'll each find the particular movie we want to see, then we'll look and see if our type of movie is playing. If it is, we'll each tear that movie's title out of the newspaper and then we'll tape it to the dart board. Whichever gets the most darts, that's the movie we'll see."

Alfonso laughed. "Hey," he said, "that's a great idea. But let's make it even harder. When it's each of our turns to throw a dart, let's do it blindfolded! Whichever movie gets the most darts, that's the one we'll go see."

"Let's do it!" the other three agreed enthusiastically. Alfonso found the scissors and a large enough piece of cloth to blindfold each of the four. Each one cut out the movie ad from the newspaper for the particular movie title that looked most like what they'd want to see. Then they did exactly what Goober and Alfonso had suggested.

"Ladies first," Goober smiled. He handed a dart to Tracey and Alfonso blindfolded her. The two boys turned her all the way around twice and then lined her up with the dartboard. All three boys laughed when Tracey threw her dart and it went whizzing by the dart board and hit a large piece of cardboard that Alfonso had set up behind it so that no darts would ever hurt the wall. But the boys soon stopped laughing because the same thing happened to each of them.

"Maybe we're too far away," Al suggested.

"Maybe we're just lousy dart throwers!" Willie volunteered.

"Well," Goober said, "I do think we could all stand a little closer to the board since we're wearing a blind-fold when we throw."

They chose a new closer place from which to throw. This time when Tracey threw blindfolded she hit the cartoon movie that Alfonso wanted to see.

"Yay!" Alfonso cheered. "Now we're getting somewhere!"

However, when all darts had hit the board it was Tracey's amazing girl story that all three boys had hit.

"Ugh!," Willie grimaced. "We're going to see a chick flick, guys. And we're the ones who chose it!"

"Groan," kidded Alfonso, half-serious.

"A deal's a deal," Goober stated.

"You're right, Goob," Alfonso agreed. "Congratulations, Tracey. I'll go ask my dad to drive us to Anderson to see it."

Soon the four amigos were happily seated in Ralph Guiterrez' Honda CRV and riding along Collar Drive, headed for the theater. Alfonso was seated next to his dad and his other three friends were on the back seat. All four were enjoying their conversation.

Alfonso laughed, "When we get to the movie we'll get two tubs of popcorn and we'll mix M&M's all through them and our tummies will be SO happy." All at once his dad jammed his brake. All conversation ceased. An auto accident had happened on Butter Creek Road at the exit off River Boulevard. All five in Ralph's car immediately saw that it must be a very serious accident because ambulances and a fire truck were already on the scene and traffic was beginning to back up. Alfonso's dad decided he'd better take a side street.

As he made the turn to Allison Road, there to his surprise he saw a tall boy sobbing on the side of the road who was holding a scruffy looking multi-colored dog that was bleeding heavily. Ralph stopped to see if he could help both the boy and his dog. Alfonso rolled down his window. The dog was whimpering and obviously had just been hit by a car.

Just as quickly as they'd seen the dog they recognized who it was that carried him. Five voices from the car said the same name at the very same time, "Pee Wee!"

Goober confirmed, "It's him. It's Pee Wee!"

As soon as Pee Wee Fritz looked inside the car and saw the four friends he turned his back on them quickly and tried to run away. Everyone in the car could hear him sobbing as he ran. But then Pee Wee slowed down to a fast walk because his dog was groaning and was too heavy for him to hold and continue running.

All Pee Wee could think about now was how he'd gotten some drunks to beat up Alfonso, how he'd tried to ruin Willie's big baseball game by letting a skunk loose right next to him, how he'd told Goober and the other guys to get away from his house, how he'd said awful things to each of those guys, and how Tracey and Alfonso's dad must hate him because he had been so mean to these three boys. He knew no one in that car was going to help him at all. But as usual, Pee Wee was wrong.

Alfonso tried to stop him. He hollered, "Pee Wee, come back. Let us know what's wrong. Maybe we can help you."

Pee Wee stopped walking away and turned in desperation but disbelief. Only because his dog was so badly injured did he walk back to the car that, to him, held his four mortal enemies.

When he reached the car, Alfonso asked him, "What happened?"

Pee Wee tried to stop crying in front of these kids he hated. But he was only partly successful. "Spike got smashed by a car jest now. Some dame was racin an didn't stop at all." Letting out a huge moan, Pee Wee said, "I think Spike's gonna die. There ain't nobody in this world that could help him now." Pee Wee began crying harder than ever, in spite of his enemies, at the thought of losing Spike. "I can't take him to no vet," he sobbed. "Vets cost big bucks and I ain't got no dough." Pee Wee's tears were falling hard onto his dog's wet and bloody fur.

"Well," said Mr. Guiterrez, "this is your lucky day, Pee Wee. I just happen to have enough money IF I include all the money from the kids in this car who were going to spend theirs on a movie and popcorn with M&M's to make their tummies happy. All together we could pay a veterinarian to look at Spike."

"YES!" all four friends echoed, immediately handing Alfonso's dad all their money.

"None of us would care if we missed a movie if we can help your dog," Goober told the totally confused boy.

"Wait a minute," Pee Wee responded. "What's the catch? Why would ya help *my* dog?"

"Because we like you, Pee Wee," Willie said as sincerely as he could. "We've been trying to tell you that."

"This ain't no joke?" Pee Wee asked. "Ya ain't gonna drive us somewhere an then dump Spike an me an leave us in the boonies?"

"We wouldn't do that," Mr. Guiterrez assured him. "We want to help Spike and you."

Pee Wee hesitated just a moment more. "But my dog's bleedin. He's going to get blood in yer car, Mister," he warned Ralph.

"A little blood never hurt anything," Alfonso's father told him. "If you were bleeding I'd take you to a doctor in my car. Your dog is important to you. So bring him in."

Still doubtful, but knowing his dog was in great pain and had to have help, Pee Wee decided to take the risk that the five in the car were sincere. "Let me open up the back end of my car," Ralph volunteered, "and you can hold Spike until we reach the vet."

Alfonso's dad went to the back of the CRV and opened it. Pee Wee, still crying, and hating the fact he thought he must look like a sissy in front of his enemies, slid in, still holding Spike.

The dog gave off a terrible odor, but nobody cared. Ralph started up the engine again and headed for Fisher's Animal Hospital on Fisher's Peak. Tracey asked Pee Wee, "Could I pray for Spike by laying my hand on him."

Pee Wee barked, "No," and pulled the injured dog further away from her. The boys snickered.

Turning away from the traffic jam that had made him turn his car in the first place, Ralph drove quickly and was there within ten minutes.

There was blood all over Pee Wee's jeans, all over his shirt, and all over the back end of the car. Spike lay very still and Pee Wee was afraid his dog had died. Then all at once Spike opened his eyes and closed them again as if to say, "I'm still here."

Ralph quickly parked his car and rushed to open Pee Wee's door. Alfonso held out his arms for the dog so that Pee Wee could get out. Pee Wee handed Spike to Alfonso very carefully saying, "Be real careful with Spike. He's hurt awful bad."

A receptionist took one look at the six entering the clinic and said, "Your dog is bleeding!" Then she pushed a buzzer.

A woman veterinarian came right out. Very carefully she took the dog from Alfonso. Pee Wee said, "Spike got smashed by a car, Doc. Whaddaya think? Is he gonna live?"

The veterinarian looked at the dog in her arms and said, "I won't lie to you, Son. This dog has been seriously injured. I don't know whether he will live. I'll have to thoroughly examine him first."

"But what'll that cost?" Pee-wee asked immediately.

"Fifty-five dollars for the examination. But probably a couple hundred dollars at least if I have to operate - perhaps more. And this dog definitely appears to need surgery," she told him.

"A couple hundred bucks?" Pee Wee repeated. "But I ain't got no dough."

"Yes, but I do, Doctor," Ralph Guiterrez told her. "If you can save Spike we want him saved. Do whatever needs to be done."

The doctor said, "I'll let you know as soon as I know," and she took Spike away.

Pee Wee didn't know what to say or what to do. Why was this Mexican being nice to him? Why were all these kids acting like he was their long lost buddy? He knew all that any of them owed him was a hard kick in the pants for everything he'd done and said to them.

For the next two hours the animal surgeon first carefully examined and then operated on Spike. In the waiting room the four friends tried to engage Pee Wee in conversation.

Goober asked, "Where were you born, Pee Wee?"

Until this moment, Pee Wee would have sarcastically answered, "In a hospital," if he answered at all. But Pee Wee wasn't feeling a bit sarcastic now. He answered, "Somewhere in the mountains of Tennessee. We didn't have no town."

Alfonso asked, "Do you have any brothers or sisters?"

Pee Wee hesitated before answering Alfonso's question, but finally did. "I hadda twin brother, but he got drowned before I started goin to school with ya guys."

Goober was shocked. He said, "I'm sorry, Pee Wee. I've been to dinner at your house and I never knew that."

Pee Wee lowered his head and said, "Well, my mom and pop, they don' talk bout it very much. In fact, we don' talk about it atall."

Goober asked another question, trying to keep Pee Wee talking and his mind at least somewhat off his dog. "Do you like school, Pee Wee?"

Pee Wee answered in one short word, "Nope."

Tracey asked, "What do you like to do?"

Pee Wee thought for a moment, then he said, "Not much. I play puter games. And Spike and I like ta walk together."

Pee Wee was immediately silent. He couldn't imagine what life would be like without Spike and knew now that was a real possibility. Pee Wee didn't want to talk at all after that.

Finally, after what seemed to be an eternity, the veterinarian came out. Pee Wee jumped up immediately. "How's he doin', Doc?"

"I think Spike is going to be fine," she told him. "But we are going to have to keep him until the day after tomorrow to be sure he stays fine. I'll examine him both days. I think you can have him back then."

"I don' wanna leave Spike, Doc," Pee Wee argued, "not even overnite. Ain't there any way he cun come home with me now? I'll take real good care of him and I'll do whadever ya tell me."

The veterinarian explained, "Your dog was hit by a car today and has just been through surgery. He needs to sleep. And he needs to be examined again for the next two days. He'll still need you to take very good care of him when he goes home with you."

"Could I sleep out here PLEASE if I don't make no noise?" Pee Wee pleaded.

"No, I'm sorry" she answered. "You're going to need to sleep well too to be ready to take care of your dog when he does come home."

"Be real honest with me, Lady. How long da ya think Spike'll live?"

The surgeon smiled and answered Pee Wee, "Well, if you take real good care of him, Son, your dog will probably live

250

for many more years."

Pee Wee tried one more argument to stay. "I ain't got no way to get back here in two days. I'd be real quiet if ya'd let me stay."

Ralph spoke up, "Pee Wee, they have rules here. But I promise to bring you back for Spike just as soon as he's ready to come home."

With that promise, Pee Wee gave up. "OK," he told the veterinarian, "but I'm sure gonna miss him." Pee Wee hadn't slept without his dog since his dad brought him home for him when Pee Wee was eight. But he knew Mr. Guiterrez wouldn't have gone to all this trouble if he was going to quit on him now.

"Take real good care of him, lady," Pee Wee told the doctor. "He means an awful lot ta me."

"I know," she answered. "He'll be fine."

As Mr. Guiterrez drove away from Pee Wee's house after dropping him off without Spike, all four friends told Alfonso's dad how great he was for rescuing Pee Wee's dog. Then Goober shouted, "Yahoooo! We didn't give up on him, guys. I'll bet there won't be anymore skunks!"

Two days later the veterinarian gently placed Spike in Pee Wee's arms. Spike had a large bandage over his stomach.

Pee Wee hugged his dog and told him, "Aw Spike, I thought ya was a goner." Then he said, "Thank you, Doc, for savin Spike."

"What do I owe you for all the good work you've done, Doctor?" Mr. Guiterrez asked.

"The bill comes to three hundred and thirty-three dollars," she answered.

Pee Wee nearly fell over. "Oh, ya can't pay that much, Mr. Guiterrez," he blurted. "That's a fortune and ya don't even know me."

"Oh I know you all right, Pee Wee," Ralph chuckled. "I saw you at a baseball game. You were carrying a sack!" Pee Wee looked very guilty and was silent. He couldn't think of anything to say.

The veterinarian told Ralph, "That dog was about to die when you brought him in." Then she turned to Pee Wee and said, "Here are the pills you need to give your dog every six hours. They are anti-biotics. You must not forget even once to give Spike a pill until this bottle runs out. And for the first three days, Spike should be kept indoors and not run or play. Can you take care of him like that?"

Pee Wee said, "You betcha I can. Thank ya."

The doctor continued, "Once Spike has taken all those pills you can very carefully remove that big bandage. That should be a rather simple procedure. And if your dog shows any signs of discomfort, or if he bleeds at all after that, bring Spike back to me and it won't cost you anything more."

As he was writing out the check, Ralph thanked the doctor, "I'm so glad you could save this dog for the boy. You've done a great job."

Pee Wee continued to hug his dog carefully all the way back home. When Ralph reached Pee Wee's house and stopped the car so that Pee Wee could get out with Spike, Pee Wee hesitated in the car for a moment. Then he looked directly at Ralph and said, "I wanna thank ya, Mr. Guiterrez. I can't believe ya spent all that money on Spike. Or that ya even took Spike an me to the vet at all. I don't get it why ya did it. And I don't get why yer kid an his frenz treated me so nice. I know if I was any of ya, I wouldn'ta helped me at all. Thanks."

"Have any of you ever heard of Bo Branders?" It was Tracey who asked the question as the four friends sat together for lunch in the cafeteria.

"Of course," Willie answered. "He plays second base for the San Francisco Giants, been an All-star all four years, and has a batting average right now of .387."

"Well," Tracey asked, "would you like to hear him in person?"

"Yeah, sure," Willie answered eagerly.

"Me too," chimed in Goober.

"Me three!" Alfonso chuckled.

"OK. But there's a catch to hearing him," Tracey told them. "You have to go to a youth rally at my church Thursday night. Bo Branders is a Christian. He's going to be speaking at a Larry Jack Youth Night at Amazing Grace. Larry says Bo is a GREAT speaker. Want to come?"

"Well, I went to church already this year and my mom changed her name," Willie said.

"And that's working out OK for you, right?" Tracey smiled.

"Yeah, better than I thought it would anyway," Willie answered.

"Al and I did you one better, Willie," Goober smiled. "We not only went to church for that wedding, but we went to a funeral too."

Tracey said, "I remember. That was so nice of you two. But what about church this coming Thursday night? Will you go to hear Bo?"

"Well," smiled Goober, "I'd sure like to hear from another second baseman. He might have some tips for me. I guess I could put up with going to church again just this once. Sure

I'll go."

"And," Tracey added, "my mom threw in an offer to make it fun even if you don't like what he says. Afterward the four of us can go to Applebees and she'll pay our whole bill."

"Count me in," said Willie. "I'd just about crawl on my hands and knees to hear Bo Branders. Oh, and I've got a confession to make since we're talking about church." Looking at Goober, then at Alfonso, Willie said, "I've never told you guys what Tracey did for me the morning of our ESPN baseball game."

"What?" Goober asked, delighted to be let in on a secret.

"I woke up that day with my arm in too much pain to pitch. Tracey healed it."

"WHAT?!" both boys gasped.

"What do you mean 'Tracey healed it'?" Goober asked.

Tracey spoke up, "Well, Willie, I didn't really heal it. The Holy Spirit healed it when I prayed for you over the phone."

"Whatever happened, Tracey, my pitching arm was totally back and I haven't had a pain in it since. I've never really thanked you for that prayer."

"Thank Jesus Christ, Willie," Tracey urged. "He paid for that pain to be taken from you when he was beaten bloody before He was crucified. I Peter 2:24 explains it. Peter said, 'By His stripes you were healed'."

"Oh no," Goober mocked, "now we have a preacher sitting with us!"

Tracey said, "I apologize. I was just trying to explain how Willie got his healing."

"Well, however it got done," Willie told her, "I'm sure glad I got to pitch that game. But me going to church on purpose, I can hardly believe it."

"Stranger things than that have happened," Tracey laughed. "A LOT stranger things!"

Thursday night came and the three boys were amazed to find Tracey's church full of excited teenagers. As they entered the church, Goober and Alfonso saw the big gate was opened in front of IS REAL and kids were lined up buying everything from lattes to Cokes. "Why do they call it 'IS REAL', Tracey?" Goober asked.

She explained, "It's a play on words. Jesus Christ IS REAL. And IS REAL is where He was born."

A man with gray hair stood at the door welcoming the youth. Tracey greeted him, "Hi, Ron. These are three of my very best friends."

The man named Ron welcomed the boys. Smiling, he said, "I know you're going to really enjoy this evening." The boys followed Tracey.

There were a few older people there like Ron, but very few. Everywhere the boys looked, they saw and heard kids talking loudly and smiling. Ripples of laughter often exploded from various sections of the crowd It was obvious these kids LIKED being in this church. It seemed like a really friendly place.

The four friends walked down the middle aisle and found four seats in the sixth row. "That's our first miracle tonight!" Tracey told them. "Sometimes I have to sit in the Overflow Room because this sanctuary is absolutely packed. It will probably get that way before we start worshipping at 7. That's why my mom brought us early."

"We're going to 'worship'?" Willie asked. "What are we going to 'worship'?"

"The Lord, Willie. The One who healed your pitching arm," she reminded him.

"Is He going to appear or anything?" Goober asked.

"He could if He wanted to, Goober," Tracey replied. "But if you know Him and you really get into worship, you'll know He's here whether you see Him or not."

"What's an 'Overflow Room'? Alfonso asked.

"It's the room we use at church if this main sanctuary gets too full for people to find seats. Everybody watches what's happening on a big screen in there."

Some of the kids were praying. Willie watched them for awhile. Then he told Tracy, "I've always thought the whole idea of prayer is really dumb. I mean, if there was a God, how could He hear everybody praying to Him at the same time? I don't think anybody could do that. And if they did, wouldn't it just sound like a bunch of noise to Him? That is, if there even was a God."

Tracey answered, "Willie, trying to figure out how God does everything He does just isn't possible. It's like trying to figure out electricity. God is God and we're only humans. After all, He's the Creator of the universe, and electricity, and our Creator too. But I can tell you from my own experiences that it isn't just that we can talk to God, but that God will talk to us as clearly as I'm talking to you."

"OK, if you say so," Willie told her. But at the same moment he was thinking, "I think these people must be nuttier than fruitcakes!"

Fabulous sounds were coming from the stage in front of them. A full piece youth band made up of teenage boys and girls, most of them looking more like college age, was practicing there. The music sounded somewhat like the kind of music each boy was used to hearing, yet there was something very different about it too. "That's a great band," Willie declared.

A young woman singer joined in to rehearse with the band.

"Who is that?" Goober asked. "She's amazing."

"That's Kimina Runner," Tracey told him. "She's a Christian recording artist who sings all over America and overseas too. She leads worship here lots of times when she's not on tour and she has several CD's out. Christian radio stations are playing them, and I have her latest DVD."

"Wow!" Alfonso responded. "She can REALLY sing. No wonder people want to hear her. I didn't even know there was such a thing as 'Christian' radio stations."

"Sure, they're all over America. You can hear this kind of music every day on your computer too."

The boys quit asking questions and looked around, wondering if they would see any of their other friends from Edison. Suddenly Goober spotted Manny Bookalooski two rows ahead of him. "Hey, guys, there's Manny," Goober told them.

"He sure has had to take a lot of kidding from everyone about his getting sprayed by that skunk," Willie said.

"Yes, he has," Tracey agreed. "But he told me that because he's a Christian, the jokes haven't bothered him all that much."

"And there's your friend, Clovella Stimple," Alfonso pointed.

"Yep," Tracey smiled, "the gang's all here."

At 7 p.m. the atmosphere changed. With four beats of the drummer's drumsticks, wildly joyful music broke loose from the band and everyone stood and began to do what Tracey had described - everyone worshipped the Lord.

The three boys stood wide-eyed as young people spilled out into the aisles with all the enthusiasm of a rock concert. They entered into total celebration, raising their hands and singing.

Kimina Runner sang, and the words she was singing were projected on two large screens at either side of the stage so that everyone who wanted to could sing right along with her.

Some of the youth went into the aisles and towards the front of the stage. They began to dance to the beat with tremendous joy. Many of those standing, but not joining those in the aisle, had their hands raised too.

The boys didn't understand much of what they were seeing and hearing, but they liked it. Goober shouted to Tracey, hoping he'd be heard above all the music, "I saw part of a rock concert on TV once with a really fabulous band. But THIS band is A LOT BETTER than THAT one was! It feels really good."

Tracey smiled and said, "It ALWAYS feels good when Jesus Christ is in the room!"

Goober looked hard to see if he could see Jesus, but he couldn't. He stayed quiet after that, just watching, because he wasn't sure exactly what Tracey meant.

The worship went on for an hour. Tracey often raised her hands as she sang. The boys didn't mind. This was all new to them and they were getting an eye-full as well as an ear-full. They liked the songs being sung and even began to join in on some of the lyrics.

Alfonso tapped Willie on the shoulder about three-fourths through the hour and said, "Look at Manny!"

Manny Bookalooski had his hands raised just like many of the people in the room did. He was looking up at the ceiling as if he really could see Jesus.

At 8 p.m. Larry Jack came to the microphone on the stage. Tracey had already explained to the boys that Larry was the head of all the youth departments at the church.

"Tonight," Larry began, "we have spent a great time worshipping Jesus Christ. So we can absolutely expect this to be a night of miracles because the Bible tells us 'God INHABITS the praises of His people'. We worship Him like this at all of our services at Amazing Grace."

Larry asked, "How many of you love Jesus Christ and actually feel better than you did when you got here because you've spent this time telling God and reminding yourselves how really great He is?" Hands went up all over the church sanctuary. Larry added, "Do that at home too or wherever you are. Whenever you do, He'll make you stronger."

The three boys hadn't raised their hands because they knew they weren't Christians and they didn't want to pretend. But each of them thought to themselves that they really could have raised their hands because they did enjoy the music and watching these people at Amazing Grace worshipping their invisible Jesus Christ.

The boys had liked everything they saw and heard for the whole hour of worship - all the cool music - Kimina Runner's beautiful singing - the mass of kids who danced to every beat - people who kept raising their hands - people on stage who waved different colored flags in time with the music - ballerinas on stage who were marvelously graceful and danced while carrying different colored cloths - and artists on one side of the stage actually painting awesome paintings all the time the worship continued. It was totally new to them and extremely interesting. Goober described it later by saying he thought it was like what he might feel if he was in a foreign country watching people celebrate their nation's dances.

Larry continued, "For any of you who are new to Amazing Grace or haven't met Jesus Christ yet, WELCOME. This is going to be a fabulous night for you. If you're curious about why so many of us at Amazing Grace love Christ it's because He lived for us, died for us, rose for us, and is at the right hand of Father God praying right now for us so that He can minister miracles through us and for us."

"Normally we would have held this meeting at the Municipal Auditorium and there would have been tons more room. But the Auditorium was booked for tonight so we didn't advertise our speaker or even let anyone but the youth of our church know who our speaker was going to be. That means all of you who are here and new to us were invited by one of your friends who are part of Amazing Grace's Youth Culture. Thanks, Gang," Larry told those who did the inviting, "you've done a great job." The crowd applauded.

"This whole sanctuary is packed. The bleachers in the back are full, and the overflow room is jam packed too." Tracey gave a big smile to the boys. They were really thankful to be sitting in the sixth row.

Now Larry began to introduce this night's speaker. "Again, tonight will be a night of miracles. 'Miracle' pretty well describes our speaker. I was personally blown away when our pastor, Sky Smith, told me that my favorite baseball player, a Major League star who is totally sold out to Jesus Christ, wanted to come speak to us at Amazing Grace. I phoned him, he was available for tonight, and I asked him to come. I know you're glad I did. And you'll be far more glad after you hear him."

"We get a lot of amazing speakers here, but tonight's speaker is one probably everyone in this room knows from watching him on television or at the baseball stadium during a game, seeing him interviewed on TV, or reading tremendous stories about him in magazines, newspapers, and on the internet. Because of his constantly amazing baseball stats it would be really hard NOT to know who he is if you care at all about baseball."

"Until tonight you, at very least, have known his name and what he does so powerfully at second base for our neighbors, the San Francisco Giants. This is the Christian who has been an All-Star all four years he has played for the Giants. As of last night he has a batting average of .388. He guards second base like a Pit Bull, throws a ball faster than you can blink, and catches as if he had a magnet in his glove. It's my great pleasure to introduce to you a Giant among baseball players - Bo Branders."

Everyone, including Tracey's three friends, jumped to their feet applauding wildly as Bo Branders came to the microphone to speak to them.

But Bo didn't begin by speaking to the crowd. Instead he began by speaking to God. He bowed his head and prayed, "Heavenly Father, this church is full of young people who came tonight to see a professional baseball player. Let them know I will sign all the autographs they want after this service is over. But that's not why they're really here. Holy Spirit, You brought them so that You could talk through me to them. Please don't let my flesh get in the way of that. Tonight bring many miracles of salvation, healing, and whatever other miracles You've got in mind. There are absolutely no limits to Your power. Thanks for dying for us and living for us now. In Jesus Name, Amen."

Not one of the three boys really understood what Bo had just prayed. They'd never heard anyone pray that way. In fact, except for Willie, when Tracey had prayed for his sore arm, and for the wedding the boys attended, and the funeral Goober and Alfonso had also attended for Tracey's sake, neither Goober nor Willie had heard anyone pray at all. Alfonso had also heard a priest pray a couple of times, but he didn't sound anything at all like what Bo had just said.

Now Bo began speaking to the crowd, "I want to thank each and every one of you for coming out tonight. What a great looking crowd! Right now I'm a baseball player in the Major Leagues. That is something God has done, and God is using it to bring people together so that I can share His Son with them."

"I've prayed, but the prayer of my heart is that you'll be really glad you came to be with me tonight AFTER I've spoken to you. I pray you'll feel it was worth your time, and even more important that GOD will feel it was worth your time. I love playing baseball and I always have. It amazes me that I get paid to play it. But it amazes me far more that God has given me the privilege of talking to great groups like you and watching miracles happen wherever I go. Let me show you what I mean."

Bo pointed to a boy who looked to be about sixteen, sitting in the third row to his left. He asked the boy to stand and then he spoke directly to him. "Two months ago you dropped something really heavy on your right foot and you've been walking with a limp and lots of pain ever since. Is that right?"

The boy looked at Bo in amazement and said, "Yes."

Bo asked, "What did you drop on your foot, Son?"

The boy told him, "A television set! It didn't break, but my right foot did." Some in the crowd laughed.

Bo pointed to the boy again, "In the Name of Jesus, be healed. Now test that. I know you're wearing a cast, but stomp with all your might with your right foot."

The boy stomped and then gasped. "THERE'S NO PAIN!" he shouted. "THERE'S NO PAIN AT ALL!"

Bo asked the boy, "Do you know Jesus Christ as your personal Lord and Savior?"

The boy said, "Yes sir. I got saved here at Amazing Grace a month ago."

"Well," Bo smiled, "Jesus Christ took your pain on the cross two thousand years ago and it has had no right to you at all. Pain was illegally parked on your foot until this minute. Aren't you glad God towed that pain away? Doesn't that feel great to do the stomp?" More happy laughter.

The boy still standing and stomping his right foot on the floor over and over again, shouted up to Bo, "IT SURE DOES." He finally sat after four more stomps.

Willie was staring at Tracey and realizing that the healing of his pitching arm *wasn't* just an unexplained happening and that it wasn't Tracey who had healed him. Tracey could see Willie was beginning to understand it was Jesus Christ who had healed his arm. Tracey continued praying for Willie and her other two friends to be saved.

After that Bo called three other people to stand, one at a time and prayed for them to be healed. They were. One eighteen year old girl had a left thumb that had throbbed with pain for more than a year until Bo prayed. The pain instantly stopped.

A man who was twenty-three was sitting in the eleventh row to Bo's right, and Bo had him stand. Bo said, "You've been deaf in your right ear from birth." The man said that was true. When Bo prayed for him from the stage the young man began crying because for the first time in his life he could hear perfectly out of his right ear. Bo explained, "You've just had a re-creative healing. Christ restored missing body parts in your ear, just as He restored the ear of a Roman soldier after Peter chopped it off." Bo urged everyone to memorize and believe Hebrews 13:8 - "Jesus Christ is THE SAME yesterday and today and forever."

Finally Bo pointed to the bleachers and had a thirteen year old blonde girl stand up. He said, "I always love bleachers because that's where the baseball fans sit." Everyone laughed. "You have been blind in your left eye ever since a piece of metal hit it when you were five years old. I believe that happened on your birthday."

Her mother shouted from the bleacher where she'd been sitting and was now standing, "Yes, it was!" Bo prayed and everyone in the bleachers around the girl began to shout because the girl's sight in her left eye had instantly returned to her.

Now all three of the boys were realizing that what happened to Willie's arm was a miracle and that Jesus Christ must be alive if He was answering Bo Branders' prayers like that. Tracey continued silently praying for each of them.

Bo continued, "The danger always of my praying for healings as I've just done is for you to think one of two things. First, you might think I'm some kind of a magic man and that these people you've just seen healed got healed by hocus-pocus. Second, you might think all this is totally fake and that I snuck these three people into the crowd and paid them to say they were healed. If you believe either of these things I grieve for you because there is not one bit of magic or fakery involved in what just happened here. These healings happened because Jesus Christ is alive and answers the prayers of His believers.

"I'm going to say it again – and have you repeat it after me – 'Jesus Christ is THE SAME yesterday and today and forever.' The crowd, including the four friends, repeated that verse. "Now remember where that came from – Hebrews 13:8.

"One day an angel appeared to Jesus' mom and told her in Luke 1:37 - 'NOTHING is impossible with God'. Mary believed it and that's all it took for her to have a baby, our Savior, Jesus Christ.

"So, how much is impossible for God? NOTHING! NADA!

"So, what do you need in your life that He can't give you? NOTHING! NADA!"

Willie thought about his dad and mom and their divorce. He knew Tracey had prayed a lot for them to come back together. He thought, "If NOTHING is impossible with God, how come they stayed divorced and Lance ended up marrying my mom?

Then Bo said, "The Bible doesn't tell you that everyone around you is going to do what you want them to do. There's no doubt that sometimes kids at school, your mom or dad, or someone else, has terribly hurt your feelings or even broken your heart. You see, without the love of Christ in ANY person's heart, a person will do their own thing. People without Christ are sometimes very self-centered, even very cruel. Sadly, there are even some messed up Christians like that. They're only interested in themselves and whatever it is that *they* like or want to do. If their decision is something that crushes you, they'll do their own thing anyway. They don't care how much it hurts you. If you know any people who are calling themselves 'Christians' but are doing that - pray for them. Let them know you love them. Do good to them. But know what they are like, and know that they will keep on doing exactly what they are doing until they fully repent or get saved. And if they are being cruel, you'd be wise to love and pray for them at a distance."

Willie was now thinking of his father. Whenever Willie really faced the truth, he knew his dad just left his mom and him because he loved his work and money more than he loved them. Willie thought, "My dad needs to get saved".

Goober was now thinking about his brother, and how Clyde hadn't even talked with his mom and dad about joining the army before he did it. He knew that really hurt his parents, even though they probably would have agreed with Clyde after he explained all the things the army would do for him after he spent his time in the service. Goober thought, "Clyde needs to get saved."

Alfonso was thinking about Pee Wee Fritz. Pee Wee was totally into his self and he didn't care about any other human. He'd proved that from kindergarten until now. Alfonso thought, "Pee Wee needs to get saved."

Bo went on, "People like that need the Holy Spirit to come and live in them so that their whole attitude and way they have thought about life becomes radically changed. That can happen faster than you can blink. A guy named Saul, who was galloping his horse as fast as it would go so that he could kill more Christians, got knocked off his horse by God. Then God changed him from killer Saul to apostle Paul, faster than you can blow your nose!"

"All a person has to do to have their whole life made new and get rid of all the selfishness and stinking thinking inside them is to honestly ask Jesus Christ to come into their life. If they're a Christian they need to repent. In a moment I'm going to ask you who realize you've only lived for yourself and want to change that tonight forever, to come forward and let me pray with you. Just like the miracle healings a few minutes ago, you'll see the miracle of a brand new you with love, joy, and peace in your heart, beginning tonight. That miracle is called 'salvation'. For a Christian it's called 'restoration'.

"But just before I invite the ones of you to the front who know you have a selfish heart and haven't cared about all the people that you've hurt, I want to talk about one other kind of people who need Jesus Christ to save them as much as you do. They're what people usually call 'The Good People'. They are really nice to be around. They are your best friends at school who only want to help you. They act almost like a Christian, but they're not one. The Holy Spirit isn't living inside them. I'm talking about anyone you know who has never invited Christ into their life and they aren't following Him. They just like being good. They've found out that it feels good to do good. They're so good you don't have to pay them. In other words, they're good for nothing!" The crowd roared.

"But here's the problem: they are doing all their 'good works' with only their own human strength because they don't know Jesus Christ. And many Christians are doing 'good works' with only their human strength too, even though they DO know Him.

"No thinking Christian can read the first five Books of the New Testament and see Christ and His believers CONSTANTLY healing the sick, raising the dead, casting out demons - and once Christ rose from the dead, telling everyone about Him and helping them become born again - and then think they AREN'T supposed to be doing the same things themself. If you really want to do what Jesus would do - GET PEOPLE SAVED and HEAL THE SICK.

"Paul healed a whole island of sick people in Acts 28. Then in First Corinthians 11:1 this same Paul told us, 'Be imitators of me, even as I am of Christ Jesus'. How can we Christians say we are being imitators of Paul or Jesus Christ if we aren't healing the sick, raising the dead, casting out demons, and telling everyone about Christ and leading people to Him wherever we are? It's not enough for a Christian to try to be 'good'. Eagle Scouts try to be 'good'. Christians ARE to try to be good AND WALK IN THE LOVE AND MIRACLE POWER OF JESUS CHRIST.

"I love to read the writings of Paul, Peter, and the rest of the New Testament authors. They were powerful men of God. But Peter, who in Acts 9:36 through 41 raised a dead lady back to life, told us in Acts 10:24 and 25 NOT to worship him because he was just another human like we are. Jesus Christ had raised her and he can do the same thing through you.

"How many sick people, crippled people, people in pain, people who are deaf or blind or who are dying do you know? How much do you really care about them? It's great to bring flowers to sick friends, but it's FAR GREATER to bring HEALING to sick friends and to people wherever you go. And the Holy Spirit WANTS to release Jesus Christ's healing power through EVERY Christian, no matter what their age. You're not "too young' or 'too old' to be doing the 'GREATER WORKS' Christ promised you would do if you believed Him.

"Jesus Christ doesn't live in some far-off galaxy where cell phones can't reach! He wants to have powerful conversations with you and let His power out through you EVERY DAY. These kinds of conversations with Him are called 'prayer'.

"WARNING: Without spending quality time in prayer every day, and getting megadoses of Holy Spirit oxygen from the Bible as you study it, it gets easier and easier for any Christian to feel like God is further and further away from them until they begin to wonder if they really are a Christian at all.

"You know, I never really got good at baseball until my senior year of high school. That happened because in my junior year I had a coach come to me whose name is Jim Blessing. He was a real 'blessing' to me all right. He saw my heart and knew how seriously I REALLY wanted to be a baseball player. So he spent my whole junior year training me. He had me study every part of baseball like God wants you to study the Bible. He told me not to look for the things I already knew, but for new things I hadn't realized before. I had to change a lot of my thinking. I studied and studied and studied. Then I practiced and practiced and practiced what I was learning. THAT'S what God wants you to do with the Bible. Don't look for what you think you already know. Look for new things, especially in the New Testament - things like healing, miracles, signs and wonders, how to care for the poor, how to love people, how to lead them to Christ. Realize these are the kind of things the Bible says that we should be involved with every day. Study and study and study the Bible, then practice and practice and practice what you learn. I'm still doing that with *my* Bible and I'll do it every day of my life.

"I'm often asked if every person that I pray for is instantly healed. The answer is no. But I won't quit praying because I don't have a 100% healing average. Tonight Pastor Jack told you that I only have a .388 batting average right now for the Giants. I've had times during games when I've struck out every single time I've gone to the plate. That's frustrating. But I won't quit trying to get a higher average because of my strikeouts. And I won't quit praying for the sick and expecting a higher average of miracles because some people I pray for aren't healed.

"If you who are a Christian aren't praying for the sick, START NOW AND NEVER QUIT. Keep on praying for the sick, and more and more of the people you pray for WILL be healed. Your "batting average" will get better and better all the time!"

Since Goober, Alfonso, and Willie, weren't churchgoers and they only knew one Christian - Tracey - they weren't sure what Bo was talking about. They knew Tracey definitely prayed, and she definitely prayed for people to be healed too. Willie was especially glad about that.

Bo continued, "Then there is another kind of 'Good People' without Jesus Christ at all. They're really nice people, friendly, loving, they make great parents. How many nice people do you know who aren't Christians? There are millions and millions of people like that. Kids at school who will help you any way they can. Parents who are so nice their kids never want to leave home!

"Are you the kind of person who would do anything you could for anybody you know? You're not mean. You don't like to fight. You try not to hurt anybody's feelings. You deserve an A+ for goodness. Yet Jesus Christ said in Mark 10:17 that no one is to call any human 'good' because only GOD is good. And Jesus said in John 14:6, I am the way, the truth, and the life, and no one can get to God except through Me."

Suddenly all three boys realized THEY always liked doing good things for people. People sometimes called each of them "a nice boy" or "a nice young man". But they had never asked Jesus Christ into their lives to save them eternally.

Bo went on: "Wouldn't it be horrible to waste all your life trying by yourself to be good and then never get to heaven after you die because you never asked Jesus Christ to get you there? THAT would be committing the unforgiveable sin!

"Jesus said in John 3:3 'I tell you the truth, no one can see the kingdom of God unless they are born again'. Hey, the kingdom of God is the real Christian life. It is the high adventure of being led by the Holy Spirit and bringing Christ's love and miracles to people who are hurting at your school, in your neighborhood, and to the uttermost parts of the world. Christ's love and power can heal anyone spiritually, emotionally, or physically. And though I've got to get back to second base, I love knowing that you are right here at

Amazing Grace. This is a church of continuous miracles with pastors and a staff that can quickly, biblically, teach you how to do all the things our Lord means for you to be doing.

"Remember, being saved by Christ is only the beginning of what will happen with you when you take God seriously. There's SO MUCH MORE. And it's ALL GOOD because GOD IS ALL GOOD. Christ has been waiting all this time for you to receive His great love and His awesome power. But if you've never asked Jesus Christ to save you, until you do you'll just stay the same self-centered or cruel you, or the same loving, nice you, who will never go to heaven. And I think something nearly as terrible as that is that you'll never have the absolute fun and thrilling adventure of doing what Pastor Sky Smith calls, 'Bringing heaven to Earth'.

"You've seen God bring heaven to Earth tonight by healing people. Now, remember this always: No other major religion has a Savior - none at all - who died to take away your sins, sicknesses, infirmities, diseases, emotional pain, and every other rotten thing about yourself that makes you unhappy. Follow any other religious leader in any other major or minor religion and you are still in your sins. Only Jesus Christ died and rose again to take away all that and fill you full of His joy.

"And tonight I know because the Holy Spirit has been working in your heart as I've been speaking that you, whether you think of yourself as bad or think of yourself as good, absolutely need to be saved. So, will all you 'bad' people and all of you 'good' people who haven't asked Jesus Christ to save you, give your life to Jesus Christ right now? And will you who consider yourself a Christian, but know you've been doing your own thing, or know that you aren't following Christ, come join me here. Come to Jesus Christ now.

"And will all of you who haven't entered into all the joy and miracle power God has for you, stand up and come down here to the front along with these others and let me pray with you? For those of you making a decision for Christ for the very first time, Jesus Christ will become your Savior and your Lord right now and forever. And for you who have been missing out on all the joy and supernatural power in the kingdom of God, I'm going to pray a separate prayer with you.

"Excuse me, Tracey," Willie said as he stood to move out of their row. Goober and Alfonso had sat closer to the aisle and were already on their way. Tracey stood and let Willie by while tears ran down her face. Goober, Alfonso, and Willie, made their way out to the aisle and walked down to the front to ask Jesus Christ to save them. "Thank you, Jesus," she told Him. "I am so happy. Praise the Lord! YOU did it!"

Nearly two hundred young people made their way to the front of the sanctuary, including the three boys. Then Bo asked, "So, how do you make the connection? How does a mere human like you or me get in touch with the Almighty God who created heaven and Earth? How do you really give your life to Jesus Christ so that you can follow Him? The answer is the greatest weapon in the universe - prayer. Real prayer is talking with God. No cell-phone, telephone, computer, or any other form of communication, can do what prayer can do. It's absolutely true that your salvation is just a prayer away. And that's what you're going to do right now. You're going to talk to God by praying this prayer with me."

"Pray these words after me: 'Lord Jesus Christ.....forgive me for all my sins.....Forgive me for ever thinking I was good enough to not need You.....or too bad for You to ever want me......Create a clean heart in me this very minute.....Right now and forever, become my only Lord and Savior.....I'll follow You, Lord, because You are the only One who knows all You've planned for me to do on this Earth..... and the only One who knows the way to heaven.....Bring heaven

272

to Earth right now.....Send the Holy Spirit to live inside me.....Thank you, Lord..... In Jesus Name, Amen.' He's there if you meant what you just prayed. Welcome to the kingdom of God!"

(To the reader: If you haven't been born again you can honestly pray this very same prayer and you'll be saved. To understand this even more read Romans 10:8-11 in the Bible.)

"Those of you who are here because you know you are a Christian, but you've been doing your own thing rather than His, pray to Him right now with me. Remember, Jesus Christ's blood cleanses from ALL sin. He makes ALL things new. He'll do that with you. He isn't angry with you at all for what you've done, no matter how horrible you know it was. He loves you 24/7. He knows what you've been doing has been messing up your life and it's grieved Him, and it's grieved the Holy Spirit, to see you hurting. But God promises in James 4:7 through 8 that if you will say no to the one tempting you, God Himself WILL draw close to you. Take your stand with Christ right now. NOTHING you have done could disqualify you from His love and forgiveness. He has never left you even for a second. Let Him know that you really want to follow Him from this moment on. Pray this prayer with me right now:

"Lord Jesus Christ.....forgive me for sinning against You.....I know I've been wrongly doing my own thing.....I know You've said that if I confess my sins to You, You WILL forgive me completely for WHATEVER I've done.....I ask You to do that now.....I love You.....You've promised me in Your Bible that You will never leave me EVER.....I repent of all my sins this very minute.....and I fully accept the forgiveness You died and rose to give me.....I will follow You.....because no one on Earth will ever love me or care about me as much as You do.....Thanks, Lord.....Amen."

(To the reader: If you know you are a Christian, but have been walking away from God and doing your own thing, honestly pray the above prayer now. If you prayed a similar prayer before, but you still want a closer walk with Christ, pray it again. Then read 1 John 1:8 through 2:1 and know that God keeps ALL of His promises. Praying this kind of prayer WILL restore your walk with Him. Then with His power, get away from whatever has been causing you to sin.)

"Now I'm going to pray for those of you who want all the joy and miracle power that is rightly yours to help others because you are saved. How many of you want EVERYTHING Christ died and lives to give you?" Everyone standing before Bo raised their hands. Many others in the crowd raised theirs too.

Then Bo said, "Pray these words after me. 'Lord Jesus Christ.....I ask You to give me far greater faith in the Holy Spirit's miracle power within me.....I promise You I'll use Your miracle power to honor YOU and make Your Name known.....and to lead others to You wherever I am.....I will begin praying for the sick and not stop.....I believe You are the God of love and of miracles.....In Your mighty Name, Amen."

(To the reader: If you want MUCH more of the joy and miracle power of God in your life as a Christian, pray the above prayer now. Age has NOTHING to do with it. What Jesus Christ and His first disciples did when they were on Earth is a small taste of what YOU, as Christ's believer, can do. Read and believe John 14:12 through 14 and Acts 10:37 and 38. God is with YOU too. Do what Jesus Christ would do from now on. Let the Holy Spirit do it through you.)

As soon as Bo stopped praying Alfonso felt a large hand on his back. He looked behind him into the face of Pee Wee Fritz! There were tears in Pee Wee's eyes and Pee Wee said,

"I'm sorry, Al, fer bein sech a jerk!"

Five Real Friends

Chapter Ten
Applebee's!

Tracey's mother couldn't drive for several minutes after Tracey told her about each of the boys being saved at the rally. She was crying too hard. She told Goober, Alfonso, and Willie, "Tracey and I have prayed together for each of you to be saved every single day since I realized you were such an important part of Tracey's life. Now God has answered our prayers and I'm SO happy."

Then Pee Wee entered the car and being as tall as he was he bumped his head on the roof. Mrs. Dare told him, "Every day since I saw you at the baseball game when you let out that skunk, Tracey and I must have been praying for you in tongues, Pee Wee. But we didn't know we were. It turns out it wasn't any harder to get you saved than it was for her other three friends!"

"Thank ya fer yer prayers, Mrs. Dare," Pee Wee told her. "Gosh, I cun hardly believe it maself!"

As they rode to Mountaintop Drive, Willie held up a piece of paper that was autographed by Bo Branders. He said, "I never in my life until tonight would have thought I'd ever say what I'm about to say. Bo Branders signed this piece of paper and even talked with me for a minute, but that wasn't the most exciting thing that happened to me tonight. The most exciting thing was when I asked Jesus Christ into my life. I know I'm saved. I feel so different."

Goober said, "Yeah, I don't understand everything that happened, but when I prayed that prayer Bo led us in I felt like my whole insides came alive."

Alfonso stayed silent for a moment, but then decided he had to know the answer. "I want to be truthful, Mrs. Dare, I prayed the very same prayer the other guys prayed, but I don't feel any different. Does that mean Jesus didn't save me?"

"Not at all," Mrs. Dare assured him. "When you or however many others honestly prayed to receive Jesus Christ as Savior, the Holy Spirit came into you and into them and He won't leave. How a person feels or doesn't feel after they've asked Christ to save them makes no difference. God saw your hearts and answered your prayers. Did you honestly pray and ask Jesus Christ to be your Savior, Al?"

Al answered, "Yes, Mam."

"Then you're saved, Al, no matter how you feel."

"Boy, my mom and dad are reely gonna be surprised that the Holy Spirit came inside ME tonight!" Pee Wee said. "I guess the devil's been in me til now!"

Mrs. Dare said, "Well, the devil can only be in one place on Earth at any single moment, Pee Wee. So I'm sure he wasn't spending his time living inside you. But none of his demons are in you anymore, if they ever were inside you until tonight. The Holy Spirit wouldn't allow it. Your spirit is like a lock-box and the Holy Spirit is the only One in there now. You could only decide with your mind to sin from now on. That's why one of my favorite authors, Joyce Meyers, wrote a great book called, ***Battlefield Of The Mind.***"

"I LOVE that book, guys," Tracey said enthusiastically, "If any of you want to borrow it, you sure can."

Elsie Dare pulled into Applebees' parking lot and let all the kids out of the car. She was glowing with joy. "Have fun you Christians!" she told them. Then she handed Tracey her Bible, saying, "If the boys have any further questions you might need this Sword. Of course, since God gave you a photographic memory when you were born, you can probably quote any verses you need anyway. Phone me whenever you're ready to come home, Honey. I'm so proud of you."

Tracey said, "This is thrilling, Mom. Thanks." She gave her mom a kiss and walked with the boys into Applebees. It was crowded, but a waitress led them to a table right away.

Before Pee Wee sat with his four new friends he asked Alfonso, "Cun ya an me go back outside fer just a minute so I cun talk with ya about somethin'?"

Alfonso had started to sit down next to Goober. But now, puzzled, he told Pee Wee, "Sure."

The other three looked with surprise at each other and wondered why Pee Wee wanted to talk with Alfonso alone.

As soon as Pee Wee and Alfonso were outside, Pee Wee said, "I'm goin' to tell ya somethin that I never ever thought I'd tell ya. And after I tell ya I give ya permission to break my nose!"

"What do you want to tell me, Pee Wee?" Alfonso asked, totally surprised by his statement.

Pee Wee started, "Member the night ya was taken to an alley an sum drunks beat ya up real bad?"

"Yes," Alfonso responded.

"Well, I was the guy who gottem to do that to ya! I lied an told them yud beat up my dad. And I made that sign we left on top of ya. I even kicked ya a couple of times after ya was already hurt bad and was layin on the ground. I thought I hated ya. But I don't hate ya at all tonight, Al. I'm real sorry I did all that to ya. So I'm just standin here. Poke my nose hard. Or beat me up bad. I won't defend maself. I know I got it comin."

For a moment Alfonso was speechless. He was totally stunned that Pee Wee Fritz, of all people, would ever be brave enough and honest enough to say what he had just said. Finally Alfonso told Pee Wee, "Hey, I really respect you for telling me that. I'm glad you guys didn't kill me that night. But didn't you hear Bo Branders say that Christ died for ALL our sins? That was sin inside you that made you do that, Pee Wee. And sin isn't inside you anymore. Like Mrs. Dare just told us in the car, the Holy Spirit kicked all the sin out of you when He came in. None of us but Tracey are the same person we were when we came to that rally at Amazing Grace tonight. You're my amigo now." Alfonso added, "But even if you hadn't been saved and I found out you and those guys pulverized me, I would have forgiven all of you because now I know I really *did* get saved tonight. I'm really glad you did too."

"Wow!" Pee Wee told him. "You sure must be a Christian alright!" He felt his nose. "My nose is glad yurra Christian too!"

When Alfonso and Pee Wee returned to their table at Applebees, Tracey immediately asked, "Is everything OK?"

"It sure is," Pee Wee responded while touching his nose, amazed that Alfonso hadn't punched it.

"Yeah," Alfonso added, "things are more OK than they've ever been!"

"I'm glad," Tracey told them, not wanting to make them feel they had to tell her and the other boys what it was that had just happened.

"Yeah, we prayed for you two," Goober grinned. "And that's the first time in my life I've ever prayed at Applebees!" Everyone laughed. Alfonso and Pee Wee slid in to opposite sides of the booth to join their friends.

Tracey said, "Pee Wee, I'm SO sorry I didn't invite you to hear Bo. Who did?"

"I herd about it at school. Manny was talkin to sum other kids and he said a big crowd of kids was gonna be at yer church. So, I came cuz I hadda cuppla frogs in my pockits that I was gonna let loose. But the minnit I walked inta yer church I got a reel funny feeling I never had befor, like I didn't want to mess things up. I took those frogs back outside and lettum loose in sum bushes. Then I jest set down and watched and lissend. And when Bo started talkin, I felt like he was talkin jest to me!"

"Praise the Lord," Tracey smiled.

"Yep," Pee Wee responded, "Praize the Lord!"

After the waitress had come and taken all their orders, Willie was the first one to speak. He said, "OK. We're all Christians now. I know I feel really great, Tracey. But you're the expert about this Christian stuff. I want to know how all this worked."

"Well," Tracey answered, "let me try to explain just a little of it. Jesus Christ died for you on the cross. He is God's only begotten Son. When He came to Earth He was born a human baby. So He was both God and human."

"How can someone be both God *and* human, Tracey?" Alfonso asked. "Wouldn't they have to be one or the other?"

"No," Tracey explained, "because God is always God. That didn't and couldn't change. But the interesting thing is that although He was God and perfect, He lived His life as a human from the time He was born in a manger and did only things that any other human who is saved and full of the Holy Spirit can do. He spent His first thirty years having great visits with His Father every day and studying the God-Book, the Bible, which was at that time the Old Testament. He understood every single part of it. Then He spent His final three and a half years doing what it said He would do. You'll be able to talk with God too and discover the great adventures He has planned for *your* lives as you enter in to daily conversations with Him. It's SO exciting. Jesus knew the Bible so well that when the Holy Spirit took Him to be tempted in the desert He was able to totally stop the devil by quoting just three Scripture verses to him! As you guys get God's Word inside you, you'll be able to stop the devil that very same way."

"That'll be cool," Pee Wee smiled.

"Jesus Christ had a terrific prayer life with His Father. He prayed bunches of times throughout the day, into the night, and early in the mornings. When Jesus prayed He got instant directions from His Father, just like you and I can do."

"Prayer really is amazing, isn't it?" Willie thought out loud.

"Yes, Willie. Prayer is the most powerful force we humans have been given by God."

"Keep going about Jesus, Tracey," Goober urged.

"Jesus Christ was perfect in every way. He never sinned even once. Like Bo said tonight, the apostle Paul said we're to 'imitate Him'. That means we're to quit doing sinful stuff and keep on letting loose His love and power that's inside us so that others will see it and want what we've got. We've got Christ! And Christ in us is the hope of glory."

"I know that Christ got butchered by some Roman soldiers and hung on a cross," Goober said. "My grandma took me to see Mel Gibson's movie, *Passion Of The Christ*, and neither of us could even sit through it. It was so gory we got up and left. We couldn't even eat our popcorn!"

"My mom and I saw it too," Tracey told him. "We bought a DVD of it and watched it. We cried all through it. But it was nothing compared to what really happened when the Roman soldiers took Christ from the garden where He'd sweat great drops of blood just thinking about what was going to happen to Him. The Bible tells us that all the blood He lost while being tortured, and all the blood He lost while hanging on that cross, totally and forever paid for our sins and all of our sicknesses too. I know we're in a restaurant and I don't want to spoil your appetites, but imagine a trillion tons of maggots crawling all over your skin."

Picturing a trillion tons of maggots crawling all over his skin, Alfonso responded, "Ugh! That's gross!"

"Yes it was," Tracey agreed. "But Christ did that for you and they didn't show our sins in the movie. The sins of every human who would ever live, including ours, got dumped on Him all at once when He was nailed to that cross. Every human's sins combined were FAR WORSE than a trillion tons of maggots. He died on that cross of a broken heart. His greatest pain wasn't the nails in His hands and feet, or even hanging there on the cross while His life ran out of Him, but it was all those sins. God, His Father, had to turn His back on His own Son because He couldn't stand to look at all that sin on Him. It broke Christ's heart that all the humans He created would sin like that. And yet He, clearly knowing what would happen to Him, let that sin come all over Him for you and for me and for everyone who has or ever will live."

Goober asked, "So does that mean everyone who has ever lived is saved because He died for them?"

"No, but it means everyone has been if they honestly asked Jesus Christ to be their Savior like you did tonight. Probably the most famous verse of Scripture in the Bible is the one Bo quoted tonight, John 3:16. Even lots of unsaved people can quote it. But they need to understand what it means and do it. That verse says, 'For God so loved the world that He gave His only begotten Son, that whosoever believes in Him will not perish, but have everlasting life.'"

"I know that verse," Alfonso said in surprise. "I heard it somewhere, maybe on television. But what does 'begotten' mean?"

"It means Jesus Christ is God the Father's only God-Son and is God too. We're God's children, but we'll never be God" Tracey answered. "And the rest of that verse means what you've done tonight will last forever. That's what 'will not perish but have everlasting life' means. All of us will be in heaven together forever. Won't that be awesome? Right now though, here on Earth, we need to do what Pastor Sky Smith calls 'bringing heaven to Earth'. See, people often call another famous few verses from the New Testament 'The Lord's Prayer'. In part of that prayer, Jesus said we're to pray to God, our Father - 'Thy kingdom come' - 'Kingdom' is another word for the amazing Christian life - 'Thy will be done on Earth as it is in heaven.' You saw a bunch of healings tonight because nobody's ever sick in heaven. So when Bo had those people stand and they were healed, Bo was bringing heaven to Earth and the Holy Spirit was healing them through Bo."

"That was amazing," Alfonso said, awestruck again as he thought about the healings he had seen that night.

Tracey went on, "Like Bo said, because we're Christians we should bring healing too. That's because after Christ rose from the dead and taught His disciples for forty days about 'the kingdom of God' – which means the abundant life He came to bring to all His followers - He went back to heaven, to Command Center at the right hand of His Father, where He's been ever since. Ephesians 2:10 and a bunch of other verses tells you He sets up miracles and awesome experiences so that at the right time you, me, and all other Christians, can work the works of God wherever each of us are. Now you're like His very first twelve disciples because you have become followers of His and you really want to get to know Him."

Pee Wee said, "I reely do, Tracey. I wanna do whatever He wants."

"I know that, Pee Wee," Tracey told him, "and I'm SO glad."

Goober said, "Count me in. I've got to admit when Willie told us about you praying for his healing and his pitching arm being healed I couldn't believe it. But tonight I saw the healing of those people with my own eyes. Tracey, how did Bo know about those people the Holy Spirit healed through him?"

"Well, Goob, prayer should be hearing from God as much as talking with God. Bo must talk with God a lot to hear Him so clearly. He also really loves studying the Bible. I do too. Doing what the Bible says to do and not doing what it tells you not to do, keeps us in the will of God so that we're at our best for Him. Because you'll be taught by pastors and leaders at our church who have been walking in God's miracles for many years, they can show you how to release miracles in no time. All your life God will keep using you to bring more and more people to His Son. Miracles of healing and a whole lot more should be normal for every Christian, and they're a blast too. Wasn't it awesome to see Bo minister healing to those people tonight?" The boys eagerly agreed. "I'm used to seeing God do those kinds of things at Amazing Grace and I love it."

Goober said, "OK. Let me see if I've got this straight. Jesus Christ is in heaven with His Father, waiting to give me my directions. And the Holy Spirit is living inside me now?"

"That's right, Goob. The Holy Spirit is God, just as much as God, the Father, and God, the Son, are. We call 'The Trinity.' The Holy Spirit is not an 'it'. The Holy Spirit is a He. He lives inside you now. In John 16:5 through 15, Jesus was really excited that He was going to die and get back with

His Father so that the Holy Spirit could come and be inside all Christians like He is in you and me."

"He was 'excited' that He was going to die, Tracey?" Willie asked. "So it wasn't the Romans or the Jews who just grabbed Him and killed Him? He knew before that happened that He was going to die on the cross for us?"

"Yes," Tracey answered, "Revelation 13:8 says that Jesus Christ was the sacrificial Lamb 'slain from the creation of the world'. So this was something God, the Son, always knew, ever since Adam and Eve blew it in the garden. Christ came to Earth knowing He would die to pay for all human sin. God used the Jewish leaders and the Roman soldiers to make it happen."

"Wow!" Alfonso exclaimed. "Jesus Christ must have loved the people on this planet a whole lot to let Himself be born here knowing He was going to be tortured and die like that for 'whosoever'."

"Yes He did, and He still does, Al," she answered.

The waitress brought hamburgers, French fries, Cokes, milkshakes, and onion rings, to the table. As she served them to the five friends she said, "I see you have a Bible. Are you kids Christians?"

"We sure are," Goober smiled. "All of us guys accepted Jesus Christ tonight."

The waitress smiled back. "That's the greatest decision you'll ever make. I'm a Christian too. I was in a terrible car accident on River Boulevard at Butter Creek Road last week."

Alfonso said, "Wow! You must have been in one of those cars we saw that day my dad turned away from your accident because of the ambulances and the fire truck blocking him. That's when we found you and Spike, Pee Wee."

"Yep," Pee Wee responded. "That's right where Spike got smashed."

The waitress admitted, "I was the one who hit him. I jammed my brakes when I saw him crossing the street, but I couldn't stop in time. I'm so sorry."

"It's OK," Pee Wee assured her. "He's jus bout good as new."

The waitress said, "I'm so glad. I'm still awfully sorry I hit him. But when I stopped so fast after hitting your dog, another car crashed right into the back of my car. No one was hurt in that car. But I got thrown into my steering wheel. The Paramedics rushed me to White Mountain Hospital where the doctor did an X-ray and said I'd need surgery right away. I was screaming in pain. But just before I was to be wheeled in, some guy named Chris walked up and asked if he could pray for me. He said he was from Amazing Grace Church."

"Gosh," Willie exclaimed, "that's where all of us guys got saved tonight."

"Praise the Lord!" the waitress responded. Then she went on, "This man prayed for me. Then the nurse checked me almost immediately afterwards. She was shocked and called the doctor. Neither of them could explain it. I was perfectly well again. It was as if the accident had never happened. Do you have any idea at all who this man was?"

Tracey asked, "What color hair did he have?"

The waitress answered, "He had short brown hair, and I'm sure he had an accent of some kind."

"Oh, then that was Chris Gore. He's from New Zealand. I thought it might have been Chris Overstreet because both of those guys bring a lot of healing in hospitals or wherever they go. I'll tell Chris what you've said."

The waitress said, "Thanks. I've got to keep working. But tell Mr. Gore that my name is Sandy. And tell him to come see me at Applebees and I'll treat him to a really great meal!"

"I'll tell him," Tracey assured her.

When the waitress walked away, Willie quickly asked, "Is Amazing Grace church the only great church?"

Tracey laughed, "Goodness no. Amazing Grace isn't the only great church even in Wake Up. There are some wonderful churches here, all over America, and throughout the whole world. I'm just hooked on Amazing Grace so I talk a lot about it. I'm thrilled to be in a church that follows the Bible and does what it tells us to do – feed the poor, help and love people every way we can, lead people to Him, heal the sick, cast out demons, and raise the dead."

Willie said, "You don't mean raising dead people, do you?"

Tracey simply answered, "Yes."

Goober declared, "I guess we've got a lot to learn about miracles, Tracey. That sure sounds exciting."

"It really IS, Goob," Tracey replied.

Alfonso asked her, "Will everyone be healed when we pray for them?"

"Well," Tracey answered, "you heard Bo talk about that tonight. THAT'S our goal. Right now not everyone I pray for - or anyone else at Amazing Grace prays for - is instantly healed like Sandy was or like you were, Willie. But lots of them are. Sometimes it takes time for a healing to take place after a person is prayed for. The New Testament tells of a time when Jesus healed ten lepers, and it says, 'As they were going they were healed'. And some people don't get healed when one Christian prays for them, but when some other

Christian prays for them they do. We don't know why. If a person doesn't get healed, or isn't a whole lot better after we pray for them, we know it sure isn't God's fault. Christ's blood that gushed out of Him the night He was crucified was enough to heal everyone in every century since then and until He comes back for His Church. Still, some people aren't healed at all. We wonder about that. But we don't feel guilty about them not getting healed after we pray for them because we've done all we knew to do and they've done all they knew to do. We just keep believing for their healing while we keep praying for more and more people. And we keep asking Christ to give us more of His wisdom and power. We need to keep doing whatever He tells us to do. So does every Christian."

Alfonso said, "I can't imagine ever standing before a crowd like Bo did tonight. It was great singing with you at the talent show, but giving a report in front of our class totally shakes me up. Am I going to have to do what Bo did?"

"No," Tracey assured him. "Not unless the Lord does what He did with Moses when Moses didn't think he could speak in front of people either. God knows you better than you or anyone else in this world could ever know you. He knows what He's made you to be. As you pray, He'll prepare you for anything He'll ever call you to do. Bo has been called by God to be a speaker in front of crowds. But like a scared believer named Ananias in Acts 9, who was no apostle at all, brought miracle healings to Paul that rocked his whole life, YOU might always pray for other people to be healed just one person at a time."

"Well," Goober admitted, "I did hear what Bo said about that, but I think if I started praying for a couple of people and nothing happened I'd probably get really embarrassed and stop praying for anyone else."

"Oh, Goob, never stop praying for sick people just because somebody you pray for doesn't get healed. Remember that old saying that Mrs. Plumff keeps telling us, 'If at first you don't succeed, try, try, again'? Look, if you pray for ten people believing for their healing and even one is healed, then something thrilling has happened that wouldn't have happened if you hadn't prayed. And most often when you pray for ten people, a lot more than one will be healed. A great Bible teacher named Randy Clark says, 'Pray for two hundred people and you'll be hooked for life!' It's really important to keep on praying for the sick no matter how many people you pray for aren't healed. All of a sudden someone will be. And then more and more will be."

Alfonso admitted, "I'd really be scared to pray for someone who was blind or in a wheelchair."

Tracey smiled, "Then start with people who have headaches and work your way up."

Willie suggested, "There sure must be a lot of sick people at Amazing Grace."

"There are, because a lot of people come from all over the world to be prayed for at our church. Lots of them have been told by their doctors that they're going to die. Many of them return back to their homes completely healed after we pray. And God often restores missing body parts or builds new ones when we pray too. Our Creator designed the human body. He knows how to fix it. Blind eyes, deaf ears, missing arms or legs, paralysis, autism, and things like that - NOTHING is impossible with God. But we don't just pray for people there. We look for people all over Wake Up who need healing or may be open to salvation - in the mall, in the post office, quietly in the library, or on the streets and other places, or in our homes. Our pastor says you can't judge how great a church is by how many come to hear a pastor preach. But a great church is one where people go out from that church to heal lives all over their town. He says, 'every real church service should begin when the people go out the door.'"

Alfonso said, "Tracey, you talk a lot about laying hands on people. Is that the only way people can be healed?"

Tracey said, "No, Al. But Jesus healed a whole lot of people that way, and so did His disciples in the Book of Acts. Yet, Willie, you got healed the day of the ESPN game when I prayed for you over a cell phone. That happens a lot. And lots of people who are sick just walk into the Healing Room at Amazing Grace and are instantly healed with no one laying hands on them at all. That's true all over our church's grounds. Lots of people get healed while they're inside the Prayer Chapel or wherever they're walking. So much prayer and worship to God comes from our church that the Holy Spirit loves being there. He knows we love Him. God means that to be the way it is in EVERY church. *How* He heals doesn't make any difference."

Goober asked, "So how do you know exactly how God wants you to pray for each person?"

"Before I pray I ask the Lord just how He wants me to bring healing to this particular sick person that I'm about to pray for. Sometimes He tells me to lay hands. Other times he tells me not to, but to minister in some other way. Jesus once healed a blind man with spit and mud. I'm glad He hasn't told me to do THAT, but I would if He told me to. Acts 19:11 and 12 says the apostle Paul laid His hands on cloths and aprons and then sent them to people who were sick to heal them. I've done that by laying my hand on a cloth and then sending it to a friend by mail who had a sore kneecap. She was healed when she touched her leg with it."

"That's awesome," Alfonso marveled.

Willie said, "It really is awesome. Can you tell us what Bo was talking about when he said we Christians could do 'GREATER WORKS' than Christ did on Earth? That seems impossible to me."

Tracey explained, "Bo was quoting Jesus Christ Himself in John 14:12 through 14. That's where Jesus told us we Christians would do GREATER miracles than He did. You'll learn about them and see them as you keep growing in your faith in Him. Acts 10:38 and 39 tells us Jesus didn't use His God-power while He was on Earth, He did everything as a human. Jesus Christ is right now at Command Center in heaven to work those works through us. He's done it through every century for those who would receive Him and believe Him. I could spend hour after hour blowing your minds over things I've seen with my own eyes or that I've read about Christians who were alive to the Holy Spirit from the very First Century on. Remind me some time to tell you about Saint Francis of Assissi and about the real Saint Patrick. But let me just tell you right now about one of those things that *I* was a part of. A few Friday nights ago I decided to go on a 'Night Strike' after worship instead of staying for the service."

Pee Wee asked, "What's a 'Night Strike'?"

"It's when a bunch of us get together and pray about where the fishing for souls will be best. Then we go wherever God sends us and gather all kinds of people into God's net. Sometimes it's just one person the Holy Spirit sends us to lead to Christ or to bring healing. One particular night during football season last year we all felt led to go to a high school football game at John Kennedy. When we got there a couple of people in our group felt we were to go to the football field where the cheerleaders were getting ready for a game."

"Well," Pee Wee said, "I betcha Jesus never went to a high school football game!"

"He has now!" Tracey responded. "We started talking with a couple of the cheerleaders, asking them if any of them needed healing. They told us one of the other cheerleaders had hurt herself in practice and was going to have to sit on the sidelines during the game. We asked if we could all pray for her. One of them said, 'If she wants you to', and took us to where she was. She was more than glad to have us pray for her and, like Willie, she was instantly healed. We all began to praise the Lord. The game started and the Holy Spirit suddenly fell on thirty people in the stands who immediately gave their lives to Christ. That's just a little piece of the 'greater works than Christ' I've seen. And God is moving in different ways like this all over the world. God loves to have fun with His kids. We Christians *are* His kids and Christ is the miracle doer."

Goober said, "And all my life I've thought I *was* having fun. Man, I can't imagine all the fun I've been missing out on!"

Tracey smiled, "Yep, your adventure is just beginning."

Willie said, "I never in my life thought I'd WANT to go to church. But if your pastors are anything like Bo was tonight, wild horses couldn't keep me away."

"Not even Firewall?" Tracey smiled.

"Not even Firewall," Willie smiled back.

Goober said, "I'll be there too, Tracey. Now that I know what prayer can do I'm going after God with all my heart."

Alfonso agreed. "Count me in. How about you, Pee Wee?"

"Yep," he said. "But I cun sure see I'm gonna REELY be diffrunt from now on!"

Willie spoke up again. "I was glued to what Bo was saying. He said getting saved is just the first step. What's the next thing we need to do?"

"You need to get water baptized," Tracey answered.

"What's 'water baptized' mean?" Pee Wee asked. "Does it mean we gotta take a bath?"

Tracey smiled, "No, Pee Wee. But Christ told his disciples that this is really important once you're saved. It's the moment of being buried with Christ and then totally risen with Him. One of our pastors will dunk you completely under water and then raise you right back up. The 'old you' gets drowned, and the 'new you' comes to life. The Holy Spirit shows up BIGTIME during water baptisms."

Tracey moved her plate with a hamburger and some French Fries on it. Then she said, 'Here, let me read it to you in Romans 6:4: 'We were buried with Christ through baptism into death in order that, just as Christ was raised from the dead through the glory of the Father, we too may live a new life.' Water baptism shows everyone else what you already know – you really love Jesus Christ and you plan to follow Him forever."

Goober said, "I feel like I just came alive for the first time tonight after I prayed, Tracey. You mean there's more that God's going to do inside me?"

"MUCH MUCH MORE," smiled Tracey.

"Wow!" Goober gasped.

Pee Wee said, "I know I sure am difrent. I'm listenin to ya read from the Bible, Tracey. I'd of never let ya do that before tonight! If you'd have started doin that I would have cussed you out and walked away. Or I might've grabbed your Bible and torn pages out of it!"

"I know what you mean, Pee Wee," Goober agreed. "I would have been bored stiff listening to Tracey talk about Jesus and the Bible. Now I can't get enough of it!"

"I'm even thinking differently about Lance now," Willie joined in. "I mean, I've been polite to him and all, but now I've been thinking about how great he's been treating me, and when I get home tonight if he's still up I'm going to apologize to him. I'll tell both Mom and him about what Christ did for me tonight. And I can't wait to tell my dad too."

"I want to tell my mom and dad about all this too," Alfonso agreed. "They're going to be as surprised as I am. All I told them before I left with you and your mom, Tracey, was that I was going to hear Bo Branders speak. I didn't tell them I was going to CHURCH to hear him! Now I want to get water baptized right away."

Goober asked, "What else do we need to do right away?"

"Read the New Testament all the way through," Tracey answered. "Then you'll understand what the Christian life is all about. After that you should read the Old Testament through. And if you keep coming to church, everything you read from the Bible will mean more and more to you."

"Won't that take years to read the whole New Testament through?" Alfonso asked.

"No, not at all," Tracey answered. "You need to keep reading at least a small part of it every day for the rest of your life. But even a slow reader can read the New Testament through in a week or two, depending of course on how much time they spend reading it every day. I've read the whole New Testament in a day."

"I hate ta read ANYTHIN," Pee Wee declared. "Aren't Bibles real hard ta understan?"

295

"Some are easier to understand than others, Pee Wee, but they all say the very same things in different words. And, Pee Wee, if you don't want to *read* the Bible you can listen to someone else read it to you on CD's. They even have some really neat audios with sound effects. You'll like them, Pee Wee."

"Great!" Pee Wee responded.

Goober said, "I'd like to hear those too."

"Anything more, besides those things that we need to do right away?" Alfonso asked.

"Yes," Tracey answered. "You all need to get baptized in the Holy Spirit."

"What does that mean?" Goober asked her.

"Well, when we go outside, I'll lay hands on each of your heads and pray for you to receive the baptism in the Holy Spirit. When I pray, Christ will pour out His Holy Spirit on you and give you greater and greater miracle power for the rest of your lives as you continue releasing His power to others. And when the Holy Spirit comes upon you, God is going to give you a prayer language. That prayer language is a code God has set up between you and Him. That code is called 'tongues'. It's the only code satan can't crack."

"A code?" Goober responded. "Man, that's great!"

"You're right, Goob. It IS. The more you pray in tongues every day, the more of God's power will be released in you and from you, and the more miraculous your life will get. I do it a lot every day and this is the most miraculous night I can remember in my whole life. All five of us being here and all of us saved is more than I ever asked for. You guys are beautiful. But I prayed in English for only three of you to be saved. I apologize, Pee Wee, but I never once prayed in English for *you* to be saved. I guess I just thought you were too mean."

"That's OK, Tracey. I woulda thought I was too mean too," Pee Wee responded.

"It was just like my mom told you in the car. We must've prayed in tongues for you, Pee Wee, but neither of us knew we were doing that. The Holy Spirit prayed through code to God what we wouldn't even have thought to pray in English. We never knew we were praying for you at all."

"Now I see what you mean by 'praying in code'," Willie told her.

"So what is this code all about, Tracey?" Alfonso asked.

"Well, it was on the day the Bible calls 'Pentecost' in Acts 2:1 through 4 that the very first Christians who ever lived found the very same thing I've found. Speaking in tongues is like a rocket launcher that is yours to use all your life. Pray to God in tongues before you get out of your bedroom for breakfast and it will give you a kick-start with Christ for that day. Then listen for God to speak to you then or at any other time. And you need to find real times while you're wide awake every day or night to hang out with God. Praise Him and talk to Him, then pray in tongues. After you do that, get real quiet and listen for Him to speak to you. Our Prayer Chapel is open twenty-four hours a day so that people can pray and wait silently before Him. Sometimes I go there, and sometimes I just get with God in my room. Still other times Mom or I put on worship music and just wait on God together, praising Him. We call that 'soaking'. Often during times like that He'll give my mom or me a feeling about something we should or shouldn't do. Usually He speaks to us in our thoughts. But He can speak out loud any time He wants."

"What happens if Christians don't pray like that, Tracey?" Goober wanted to know.

"Usually they start pooping out and not feeling the spiritual zip Christ wants them to feel. You should pray in code whenever you think of it all through the day or night. That will get you through even your toughest moments. Really, without doing that you pretty much have to work out everything on your own - problems included - just HOPING you're doing the right thing. Or you'll be carrying problems all by yourself because you won't know how to give them to God and leave them with Him. Like my mom says about it, 'Too many Christians never let the Holy Spirit get a word in edgewise!'"

Willie suggested, "But if I just wake up and pray in English, won't that do the same thing?"

Tracey answered, "Well, you should say 'Hi' to God and praise Him the first thing every morning. And you can tell Him how things are going in your life and ask Him for His help for others or for yourself while you're praying. But tongues isn't praying from your own feelings about things or about people. Tongues is praying from your spirit where the Holy Spirit lives inside you. Tongues is the language of the Spirit talking directly to God and telling Him everything you really need or don't need. That's why I call it 'praying in code'. And you've got to have a lot of trust in God to pray this way because God knows what's good or bad for us, and too often we don't know the difference.

"But don't I know what I need or don't need, Tracey?" Goober asked. "I mean, I'm ME."

"Well," Tracey answered him, "sometimes you know and sometimes you don't. The Holy Spirit wants you to trust Him with your tongue. Your prayer language keeps you on the right track with God if you'll keep your mind on Him while you're praying."

Goober said, "Let's see if I've got this right then. The Bible should be every Christian's roadmap. Prayer in my own language tells God how *I'm* seeing things. Praying in code should be every Christian's GPS. We get our prayer language in other tongues so that the Holy Spirit can speak through us and tell Command Center in heaven where Christ is just how *He* sees things should be *for me* every day. And God will always agree with Himself."

Tracey beamed, "That's straight out of the New Testament, Goob. You're right about everything you just said. But tongues is even more than that. It's a great way to praise the Lord when you're worshipping Him. I Corinthians 14:15 says you can sing in tongues too."

"Oh, no," Goober responded. "I leave the singing up to Al and you. I can't even carry a tune."

"Well, Goob, God doesn't mind at all how you sound when you sing. Psalm 98:4 is one of my favorite psalms. It says, 'Make a joyful *noise* unto the Lord all the earth, make a loud noise unto Him with psalms.'"

"That's how it sounz when I try to sing, Tracey," Pee Wee told her, "jest a loud noise."

"That's fine, Pee Wee. And God wants all three of you to sing to Him in Psalms, songs and tongues. God made every human mouth to praise Him. But when you just do it in your own language you soon run out of words. That's true about ANYTHING when you are praying in your own language. You'll never run out when you praise Him in tongues."

Willie said, "So this speaking in code thing is to keep me on the right track with God and to give me a great way to praise Him. Anything else tongues is for?"

"It's great for intercession," Tracey answered. "That's when you're praying for people, nations, bringing heaven to Earth, all kinds of things. Most of the time when you're using the Holy Spirit's code you don't even know who or what you're praying for, but God sure does. Pastor Smith's wife will teach you how to intercede. She's taught me SO MUCH about how to talk with God. She's awesome."

Willie wanted to know, "Will we understand what the words mean that we're praying in tongues?"

"Not usually," Tracey replied. "The apostle Paul in First Corinthians 14:14 explained why. He said, 'If I pray in a tongue, my spirit - where the Holy Spirit is - prays, but my mind is unfruitful'. 'Unfruitful', means your mind *doesn't* understand what you're praying."

Alfonso asked, "Does every Christian speak in tongues as soon as they're saved?"

Tracey told him, "No, but every Christian could. Some churches even teach against it. They say all of the things the Holy Spirit did in the First Century stopped when the writers of the Bible finished writing it. But that's not what the Bible says. Instead a bunch of verses in both the Old and New Testament say just the opposite. Think about it: Would our Lord have only talked to people - healed - did miracles, signs and wonders - in crowds and alone with people for three and a half years - then stopped doing that for every century up until now? Of course not. He loves us just as much as He loved the people of the First Century. He said we believers would do 'greater works' than Him BECAUSE HE'LL WORK THEM THROUGH US. All of these things are happening now and completely available to every believer."

"So there are Christians who don't speak in tongues, and don't lay hands on their sick friends to get them healed?" Goober marveled. "Why not, Tracey?"

"I don't understand it. Christ healed and healed while He was here. Like I said, would He put a cork in all that healing after He rose and sent the Holy Spirit? Nope. You saw that tonight, and I've seen God healing almost every day since I've been a Christian. He healed you, Willie, because that's God's M.O. He's so full of love that First John 4:8 says God IS love! When you read the Book of Acts you'll see for sure that His healing and His miracles never stopped when Christ went to be with His Father. The Book of Acts comes alive through people in our church every day. This is happening with Christians all over the world. I'm so thrilled you guys are going to be a part of it now."

Willie admitted, "I wish I had listened to you about being saved when I first met you instead of just pushing you away, Tracey. I remember when we guys laughed at you because you said we needed this to happen to us and how it would change us. If I had been able to pray in tongues to God when my mom and dad were divorcing, and Lance was dating and then marrying my mom, I think it would have been a whole lot easier on everybody. I know it would if I felt then like I feel now."

"Yes it would have, Willie. You're going to see a humongous difference in your life from now on. I've mentioned the apostle Paul. He went through all kinds of trouble too. In fact, he was in prison for a total of seven whole years while he was a powerful Christian leader. And it was Paul who told us in First Corinthians 14:18, 'I thank my God that I speak in tongues more than you all.' He must've prayed and prayed in tongues while he was chained in there, and he didn't stop praying in tongues whenever he was out. All the time he kept writing about how full of joy he was no matter how bad things got. God knew He could trust Paul anywhere. You're going to have that same power, and you'll be able to pray in tongues every day so that the Holy Spirit can speak through you to God."

"Wow!" Pee Wee smiled. "This gits better all the time!"

Goober admitted, "I still have a question for you, Tracey. Bo, your mom, and you, all said that when we received Christ as our Savior, the Holy Spirit came in and will stay forever.

So are we going to get a second Holy Spirit when you pray for us to receive the baptism in the Holy Spirit now?"

"No, Goob, not at all," Tracey smiled. "There's just one Holy Spirit. But let me see if I can make this clearer. The Holy Spirit was inside Jesus while He was in His mother's womb and all the time that He was growing up. That's obvious. But the Holy Spirit came 'upon' Jesus in Luke 3:21 and 22 when He was baptized in water and baptized in the Holy Spirit at the very same time. From the moment the Holy Spirit came upon Him when He was thirty years old, Christ healed people and did miracles in the power of the Holy Spirit that God, the Father, poured out on Him at His baptism. When you guys begin to study the New Testament you should notice that every time it's talking about salvation, the Bible says that the Holy Spirit is 'in' a Christian. But every time the Bible is talking about the baptism in the Holy Spirit, it says the Holy Spirit is 'on' or 'upon' a Christian. That's exactly what will happen with each of you. The Holy Spirit's going to come upon you. You'll receive God's full anointing to do healing and miracles."

Pee Wee was amazed. He said, "Gosh, my ma, pop, an Spike, are REELY goin to be s'prized when I git home! Do ya think they'll know who I am?"

"Yes, Pee Wee," Tracey assured him. "You'll still look like you do now. But you're really different inside."

"What if I furget ta pray in code, Tracey? I furget things."

"The Lord would understand, Pee Wee. He knows your heart. He might let you go through some things that would remind you how much more of His help you really need so that you'd pray in code again. He pretty well does that with all of His people. The apostle Paul's friend, Timothy, in II Timothy 1:6 must have been going through some big problems that got him down. That's where Paul told him to 'stir up the gift that is within you that was put there with the laying on of hands'. So you'd just start praying in tongues again like Timothy did. God never gets mad at you, and He'll ALWAYS hear your prayers. He loves you every second and says, 'Let's get started again RIGHT NOW'."

Willie wanted to be sure. He asked, "Tracey, we're brand-new Christians tonight. How do you know we're ready for the baptism in the Holy Spirit?"

"Because you're saved, Willie. When you read the book of Acts you'll see that tongues is the very next thing, along with water baptism, for EVERY Christian after they're saved. And you'll see that sometimes people got water baptized first and other times people got baptized in the Holy Spirit first. We may as well get started tonight with my best friends getting baptized in the Holy Spirit. You are saved, Willie, right?"

Willie smiled, "I sure am, Tracey. I sure am."

Tracey could hardly wait. She stood and asked the boys, "So, are you all ready to receive your rocket launching code?"

"YES," four boys said all at once.

Goober said, "You've hardly gotten a bite out of your hamburger, Tracey. Wouldn't you like to finish it first?"

Tracey responded, "No, Goob. Jesus told His disciples, 'I have food you can't even imagine'. Now I know what He meant. I can have a hamburger anytime. Right now I can hardly wait to see what God is going to do."

Five Real Friends

Chapter Eleven
Graduation

Out in the dark of the parking lot and away from anyone who might look and not understand, the four boys and Tracey talked more. It was a wonderfully warm evening. If anyone went in or came out of the restaurant the five didn't notice them at all. They sat down on a lawn. A sky full of stars and a bright yellow moon caused Tracey to say, "Look what our Creator made for us."

"Wow!" Goober said looking up. "I sure never thought about that before. Thank You God for making the sky so beautiful."

Tracey then said, "Now there's nothing weird about what we're about to do. I just want you to concentrate on God like you will whenever you pray to Him because I'm going to pray to Him in just a minute and ask Him to baptize each of you in the Holy Spirit and give you the power to speak in code to Him. The moment I lay hands on each of you guys, one at a time, the one I'm praying for should open his mouth and speak any language that isn't one you already know. It will be tongues."

Willie said, "It still sounds kind of strange that we have to say words we don't understand."

Tracey explained, "Isaiah 55:8 tells us God's ways AREN'T our ways and His thoughts AREN'T our thoughts. So what might seem 'strange' to us isn't 'strange' at all to God. Some Christians even think speaking in tongues is 'foolish'. But I Corinthians 1:27 says, 'God chose the foolish things of the world to shame the wise'."

Pee Wee chuckled, "That verse musta been ritten bout me."

Alfonso asked, "But couldn't we just fake ourselves out, thinking we're praying in tongues but just making up the words?"

"Not if you really have your heart set on Jesus Christ when you're praying, Al," Tracey answered. "I'm going to pray for each of you and God answers prayer."

"But," Goober asked, "how do we know we're really going to get our prayer language when we ask Him for it? How can we be sure it's tongues?"

Tracey smiled, "Because, Goob, He's promised this gift to us. Like I've said millions and millions of Christians all over the world pray in tongues. When Peter got baptized in the Holy Spirit he explained to a whole lot of people that this experience was promised by the Prophet Joel in Joel 2:28 and 29 and by Jesus in Luke 24:49. Then Peter told them, 'Repent, and each of you be baptized in the name of Jesus Christ for the forgiveness of your sins' - in other words, get saved, 'AND YOU WILL RECEIVE THE GIFT OF THE HOLY SPIRIT.' Speaking in tongues IS that gift. It's for ALL Christians. Then he said, 'For the promise' that Joel and our Lord made is for you, and your children, and for all who are far off, as many as the Lord our God will call to Him.' You three were called by the Lord tonight. Now I'm going to ask our Heavenly Father to baptize each of you in the Holy Spirit and God always keeps His promises. He's not going to let some demon bug you or let something silly happen. This is a really big moment for each of you just like it was for me when I got baptized in the Holy Spirit."

"So, whadda we do, Tracey?" Pee Wee asked. "I reely wanna pray in code."

"I'm going to lay hands on each of your heads and pray. That's what Christ's believers did in the Book of Acts." Tracey explained, "In Acts 8:14 through 17, where Peter and John came to pray for a bunch of new Christians who had already been water baptized and definitely had the Holy Spirit in them, they laid hands on them and they received their prayer language just like you're going to do now. A magician watching them was so impressed with what was happening that he offended Peter and John by trying to buy what he thought was a magic trick they were doing that gave the power to these new Christians to speak in other tongues. But this is no magic trick. Our living God wants to release every Christian to pray in code. So let's stand up. Oh, and Pee Wee and Willie, you're both going to have to bend your heads down because I sure can't reach them when you're standing straight."

"I'll bend," Pee Wee agreed.

"I'm ready," Willie said. "Being a Christian is really exciting!"

"It sure is," Goober agreed.

"OK. Put your whole attention now on Jesus Christ, your Savior, and begin to tell Him how much you love Him. Then start speaking any words that aren't English or some other language that you already know and it will be tongues. Don't stop what God is going to do. Use new words no matter how you feel after I pray for you. And I hope you don't think I'm just trying to impress you with all the Bible verses I remember. I hope you'll all start memorizing a bunch of Scriptures. But Acts 2:4 clearly tells you *how* this is going to happen. It says, 'All of them were filled with the Holy Spirit and began to speak in other tongues as the Spirit gave them the words to say'. God is going to answer my prayer to Him and give you the words to say from the Holy Spirit right now."

She went to Pee Wee first. "Bend your head down here, Pee Wee," she told him. Pee Wee bent. Tracey prayed, "Lord Jesus, please baptize Pee Wee in the Holy Spirit."

Pee Wee had just been saying, "Thank ya Jesus fer savin' me," and his whole language changed, "Lana seepa la cuz me peeria. Donpa le glorio en palatana." The words poured out of Pee Wee. He straightened up and raised his hands into the air. "I love ya Jesus Christ," he cried out as he then spoke again in tongues non-stop. Tracey was thrilled. So was Pee Wee.

(To the reader: If you aren't baptized in the Holy Spirit, pray and ask the Lord to baptize you in the Holy Spirit right now. Then follow the directions Tracey gave and God will give you His code too so that *you* can start praying to God in tongues.)

Tracey turned to Willie and he bent so that she could lay hands on his head. She prayed again, "Lord, please baptize Willie in the Holy Spirit." Willie had been praising God too. He grew silent and just stood there. No language seemed to come. He suddenly asked Tracey in a worried tone, "What's wrong? I'm not getting a prayer language."

"Willie," Tracey responded, "get your mind right back on God. Don't concentrate on what you don't have yet. Concentrate on what you DO have. Praise God, Willie. You know you were saved tonight."

"Yes," Willie responded, "I know that for sure."

Tracey added, "You know, Willie, when I first prayed to be baptized in the Holy Spirit, I had the same problem you did. No language came. I had to wait for God to do it."

"O.K." Willie agreed. "But how come Pee Wee got tongues and I didn't?"

All the time Tracey had been sharing God's promises with Willie, Pee Wee still stood with his hands raised, praising

God in code.

Tracey prayed again for Willie, but though Willie praised the Lord he felt nothing had come in the way of a new language.

"Willie," Tracey told him, "look what Pee Wee is doing. Do it too. I'll pray for Goob and Al, and then I'll come back and help you some more. Keep praising God in English and then be totally willing to speak what might even seem like gibberish to you. It WILL be tongues."

"OK," Willie said, and he began praising God and waiting for his breakthrough.

Tracey moved to Alfonso and he shot off like a rocket! He burst right into his new language. "Shinka moosha shaba broast," the Holy Spirit told God through Alfonso. "Meistar librido lakshan fooroo." He continued to speak brand new words that he had never heard to the God he had just met that evening.

Now Tracey moved to Goober. She prayed and Goober kept his mouth closed. "Goober," she smiled, "do you always talk with your mouth closed?"

Goober smiled back and said, "No. But I've just been silently praising God in my mind."

"That's a great thing to do, Goob. But you need the baptism in the Holy Spirit right now, and to get it you've got to pray out loud. Remember, praise the Lord out loud and then speak the new language that the Holy Spirit will give you."

Goober began praising the Lord out loud. Only Tracey was watching him. Pee Wee and Alfonso were happily praying in their new language. Willie was still praising God in English.

Pee Wee kept his hands raised and Alfonso stood with his face towards the sky looking into the heavens God had made. Both boys knew the Holy Spirit was for sure talking to God through them.

Goober's praise was loud and clear. Then Goober grew silent and Tracey said, "Let the tongues out." Goober's lips quivered, but nothing came.

"You have to put your breath to it, Goob. It's just like talking. Your breath pushes your words out. You have to use your breath whenever you speak. You're used to speaking in English. But the Holy Spirit is ready right now to give you new words."

Goober said, "I've got two funny words in my mind. But I don't want to get this wrong, it's too important. I'm afraid I'll be making tongues up."

"I've shared God's Word with you on that, Goob," Tracey reminded him. "Trust God. Even if you think at first that you're making the words up, speak them anyway. Those words will be from the Holy Spirit and you just need to let them out."

"But they sound really dumb!" Goober told her.

"Any foreign language sounds dumb, Goob, if you want to look at it that way. But it's NOT dumb. It's just that you don't understand it. Believe me, GOD'S words are NEVER dumb," Tracey declared.

"OK," Goober told her, "Here goes. "Pooloo magoshic. That's it."

"Say it again," Tracey urged.

"Pooloo magoshic. Pooloo magoshic. Pooloo magoshic," Goober said three times. "I told you it sounded dumb!"

Tracey said, "No, Goob, that's beautiful. It's not unusual at all for someone being baptized in the Holy Spirit to only get one or two words at the start. Just keep saying those words to God. He'll give you more in His timing. Just don't stop praying those two words every day until He gives you more or changes your words entirely. Those are beautiful words because they come from the Holy Spirit and God knows what they mean."

"I wish I had two words to speak to God in code," Willie told Goober. "I'd say them all night."

Tracey said, "Guys, let's all pray for Willie some more to receive his prayer language." The four friends prayed for Willie for another ten minutes. Willie kept praising God in English, but nothing else happened.

Willie became frustrated. "Maybe I didn't get saved tonight. Maybe God doesn't love me like He loves you guys. Maybe that's why He didn't give me tongues."

Goober told him, "You're as saved as any of us are, Willie. You know that."

Willie stopped and thought about what he'd just said. "I'm sorry. Yes, I *am* saved," Willie responded. "But maybe He's saved me, but He doesn't plan to use me."

Tracey told him, "That's a lie, Willie. The devil would love for you to believe it. He's the father of lies. He knows how powerful you're going to be and you scare him to death. The truth is, Jesus Christ loves you so much that if you were the only human on this planet He would have died for you to save you. And God's going to use you amazingly."

"Then why doesn't He give me tongues?" Willie asked. "You prayed for me to get them. I prayed for me to get them. I did everything you told me. And I'm the only one of the five of us who doesn't pray in tongues."

"I only got two words, Willie," Goober reminded him. "But I'm not going to stop using them. Don't stop praising and believing God. He'll give you your code."

"Oh my gosh!" Tracey said with joy. "You've been a Christian a couple of hours, Goob, and I couldn't have said that better myself!" It was nearly midnight.

"Willie, all I can tell you is to keep praising God and expect Him to give you your code. I've told you I had the same problem you're having. I wish I could stay out all night to help you, but it's a little after midnight and I don't want to keep my mom awake waiting to come and get us. I've got to call her."

"It's OK," Willie said, "but I sure don't understand why I didn't get my code."

Tracey used her cell phone to call her mother and very quickly she arrived to take everyone to their homes. Everyone but Willie was bursting with joy over being baptized in the Holy Spirit. Tracey's mother was ecstatic. Only Willie was quiet and withdrawn. He said a quick goodnight when Tracey's mother dropped him off at his house. Everyone knew Willie's feelings had really been hurt in spite of every one of his friends trying to encourage him.

Tracey told him as he left the car, "Jesus Christ has saved you, Willie. Just keep praising Him and you'll get your code."

"OK, sure," he said, and walked away.

The next day at school Goober, Tracey, and Pee Wee, sat at a table to have lunch. Goober said, "I don't get it. After all the great things Christ did last night, Willie walked away from us looking like he'd lost his best friend. But today I looked over at him in class and he grinned back at me every single time. Al is even harder to figure out. He was really turned on last night. Yet he hardly said a word to me before class this morning and he looks like someone who got all F's on his report card!"

Suddenly Willie joined his three friends at the lunch table. "Hi guys," he beamed. "Isn't it a beautiful day?"

"Willie, what's happened?" Tracey asked him. "Did you get your prayer language?"

"Yes! Last night in my bedroom!" Willie announced.

All three of Willie's friends shouted so loudly that they drew the attention of kids at other tables. "Tell us about it," Goober smiled. "What happened?"

"Well," he began, "I left you guys and walked into my house. I was so glad Mom and Lance had already gone to bed. I didn't want to talk to anybody. I was all mixed up and mad. I figured I'd followed all your instructions, Tracey, and they just didn't work for me. Then I thought I must have let God down. Finally, I even started wondering again whether I really was a Christian. I went to my bedroom and yanked my clothes off, threw on my pajamas and went to bed feeling really sorry for myself. I did kind of mumble, 'Thank you, Lord, for saving me', but I knew that He understood how I felt about Him not giving me my code and I wondered if He even heard what I said or if He even cared. Guess what happened?"

'WHAT?" all three shouted, and kids from other tables looked at them again.

"God spoke to Me! He didn't speak out loud, but I know the way that I was feeling it HAD to be God. It was like a small voice inside my head saying, 'I LOVE you, Willie Radner, and I HAVE saved you. You are a man after My own heart' - whatever THAT means!"

"Oh my gosh!" Tracey exclaimed. "That's what God said about King David. He's in the Old Testament. But in Acts 13:22, God said about him what He's now said about you!"

Willie said, "That's amazing. I had no idea at all that was in the Bible. But when He said that I was shocked that God was speaking straight to me. I pulled the covers back and jumped out of bed. I felt like kneeling by my bed so that's what I did. Then I asked Him, 'God, do you have anything else to tell me?' Well, He sure did! He said, 'Willie Radner, I have called you to be My close friend and My believer. Always know that I love you and will give you everything I've promised and MORE! I will do the same thing for any other Christian who gives Me their whole heart and keeps Me first in their life no matter how badly things appear to be going for them at the moment. Continuing to believe Me is faith. And I will use your faith in Me to give this message to crowds, just like you saw My son, Bo Branders, do. Now speak, Willie, and I will hear your code.' I didn't wait a second. I just opened my mouth and I spoke funny words I'd never heard before. I haven't got a clue what they meant. I spoke and spoke in tongues. New words just poured out of me just like you said they would, Tracey. And just like they poured out of you guys last night. All that meant so much to me that I grabbed a notebook on my desk and He helped me write down everything He'd said to me. Then I memorized it."

"Oh my gosh," Goober responded, "That's awesome. I haven't heard God speak to *me* like that at all. And my prayer language is only three words."

"God only gave ya *two* words last night, Goob," Pee Wee reminded him.

"Yeah," Goober told him, "but as I was walking to school this morning and praying them, God added a word to 'Pooloo magoshic'. Now I'm praying, 'Mopow pooloo magoshic'. And just like you, Willie, I don't know at all what I'm praying. I'm just trusting God and praying what He's giving me."

"He'll add more words, Goob, in His time," Tracey encouraged. "But it's great that you're trusting Him like that."

"I've given Him my life, Tracey, to do with me whatever He wants to do. He's GOD. I want Him close every day of my life from now on. I'll keep praying 'Mopow pooloo magoshic' and expecting more."

"He will give you more, Goob. MUCH more." Tracey assured him. "But what He loves about you already is how much faith you have in Him."

Alfonso arrived at the table looking really blue. "What's new, Bugaloo?" he asked Goober, looking like he wasn't at all sure he should sit down with his friends.

"A brand new word added to my amazing dictionary of God's code, Al. 'Mopow!'" Goober answered. "What's new with you?"

Alfonso finally sat down with a worried look. He hesitated and then said, "I think I'm in trouble with God, guys. Something has messed up my prayer code!"

"WHAT?" all four of his friends responded at once. Yet again other students looked at where the five friends were sitting together and wondered why they were being so noisy.

Alfonso explained, "Well, while I was walking to school this morning I tried to pray in my prayer language again. I couldn't do it. A whole different language came out. I don't know what that language was, just like I don't know what language I was speaking last night. But I knew they weren't the same language at all. This morning I sounded more like Chinese or something. I just shut up and wouldn't pray in code anymore. I think I've lost my code."

"Oh, Al, your code to God hasn't been short-circuited at all," Tracey assured him. "And you haven't lost your code. What happened is fine. I Corinthians 12:10 tells us there are 'various kinds of tongues'. Sometimes when I'm praying I think I sound German. Other times I think I sound more like

315

Indian or Chinese. Still other times I haven't got a clue in the world what kind of language I'm praying. I Corinthians 13:1 says Christians might even 'speak in the tongues of angels'. It's all good. And since you're praying in code, the Holy Spirit knows how you should sound at any time. Remember, the Holy Spirit is talking straight to God through you any time you speak in tongues."

"Wow!" Alfonso exclaimed in relief. "I was worried I'd messed things up somehow and I'd never get my real prayer language back. I thought I'd failed God."

Willie smiled at him and said, "Al, that just shows how much even us Christians can worry about nothing. But I apologize to all of you for freaking out when I didn't get my code like God gave each of you last night. And Pee Wee, I especially apologize to you because I was actually mad that God would give you tongues and not give them to me. Even when I left the car last night I felt that I deserved them more than you did."

"Oh, that's OK, Willie," Pee Wee said. "Yer still my pal."

Tracey said, "Willie, let me tell you something I didn't tell you last night because you were so discouraged. I didn't speak in tongues for three whole months after my Aunt Cheryl prayed for me to receive them."

"THREE MONTHS!" Willie exclaimed. "You REALLY must have believed God to hang on to His promise THAT long."

Tracey told him, "Sometimes God's promises take a whole lot longer than that to be fulfilled, Willie. Just keep on believing Him even at times when everything is going exactly opposite to what you're believing for. Keep your faith in spite of everything. God so often pulls off His miracles at the very last minute. And sometimes things turn out differently than you think they should. Look what's happened now with

Lance and your mom. I prayed and prayed for your dad to come back home. I know God wanted him to, but he's not listening to God yet. Even Christians sometimes won't listen to God or obey Him. I think I could have spoken in tongues much sooner than three months, but I was too sure of how I thought my prayer language had to come. I was SO wrong. I laugh about it now, but I was dead serious about it then. It didn't come at all like I thought it would. If I hadn't been going to the meetings at Amazing Grace I might have quit on the whole idea of praying in tongues. But I kept seeing what the Holy Spirit's prayer language did for a whole bunch of my friends there. If Mom had become a Christian when I did I'm sure she would have sent me to Amazing Grace's Christian school. That school is SO AMAZING. But if I'd gone I might never have met you guys."

After Tracey said that there was a moment when all five just sat there silently. Tracey thought about how much she would have missed not knowing these boys. The boys were thinking the same thing about her. Finally, Goober asked, "So how did you get your prayer language, Tracey?"

"I went to church with a friend. Only this friend had already been on drugs. She'd even been arrested by the police and her mom thought she was going to end up in prison. I took her to Amazing Grace for one meeting, completely surprised she'd go to church with me at all. There is always a big crowd at our church. Pastor Smith was speaking. Suddenly he stopped and began to call out healings that the Holy Spirit was doing right in front of him. People were being rocked by the Lord's healing touch just like you saw when Bo Branders was there last night. Only there weren't four or five people being healed, but more like a hundred or even more than that. I was so thrilled. I was praising God and watching what was happening to a person being healed in the row in front of me. So I didn't notice my friend for a minute. But when she started sobbing I looked at her. She said, 'The pain in my stomach is gone.' ! I asked her, 'What pain?' She said, 'I've had a horrible pain in my stomach since I was little. It's never stopped at all until just now. Doctors said they couldn't find anything wrong so they couldn't help me. I think Jesus Christ just healed me!' She kept sobbing for a minute or so and then she started praising God instead. Suddenly she cried out, 'Come into my life, Lord Jesus.' He came. Then we both kept praising God. That pain has never come back to her stomach. She's moved to Phoenix, but I still talk with her on my cell phone. She really loves Jesus."

"That's terrific," Goober said. "But what did your friend getting saved have to do with you speaking in tongues?"

"Well," Tracey explained, "I was so excited when I saw my friend receive Christ that I began to praise Him in English. And as if He'd only been waiting for me to praise Him while I was thrilled about something He'd done, I began praising Him in a whole new language. She began right there to speak in a whole new language too. Both of us have been speaking in code ever since."

Each of them fell silent again. Now they were thinking about all the miracles God had done for them since they had gone to church the night before. Alfonso broke the silence, saying, "Tracey, I'm so glad you pray in tongues and that you have a photographic memory like you do so that you could share all those Scriptures with us like you did last night. I'm going to be memorizing the same Scriptures.

Tracey smiled, "You're going to love the Bible like I do, Al."

"I know that's true," Alfonso agreed.

Goober asked, "How come we feel so much like raising our hands when we praise the Lord now?"

Tracey answered, "Well, sometimes it's just the natural thing to do. It's like fully surrendering to God when we put our hands in the air. And sometimes I think of raising my hands being like a football referee raising his hands when our team scores the winning touchdown over satan. The apostle Paul in I Timothy 2:8 said Christians everywhere should pray and lift up holy hands without getting mad about it or getting mad at anyone else who does it."

Pee Wee added, "I liked the guys wavin flags with diffrant colors up on stage last night. They were great."

"All of that is a part of our worship to God, Pee Wee," Tracey told him.

"It's cool," Pee Wee smiled.

First bell rang and the five friends started back to their classroom.

Willie had written his valedictorian speech and had asked his four friends to come and help him change anything they thought needed changing. Everyone but Willie was sitting on the large couch in his living room. Willie was standing in front of the fireplace. He said, "I really thank you guys for coming to hear this right now. I'm sure it's still rough in spots. But I've been so caught up in writing it that I don't honestly know where the rough spots are. That's why you guys are here. Stop me while I'm speaking if you hear something that I could say better. Here goes:"

"Mr. Hirkshire, teachers, and staff of Thomas Edison Middle School, I am sure that I speak for every student here when I tell you that we are really going to miss you. I especially want to honor Mr. Bozzknobber for the way he's kept this school sparkling clean. I also want to thank my mom and dad, and Lance Amos, because you, plus my closest friends, are the ones who made me want to succeed. I still think 'valedictorian' is too high an honor for me, but I've got to admit I like it!" The four friends laughed.

"Everyone here, students and faculty alike, face an unknown future. Every human does, no matter what age they are and no matter where they are. Each of us faces a future that we shouldn't even try to face alone. We need friends, REAL friends, all the time.

"I want to be extremely honest. I went through some really hard times this year. I'm sure many of you have too. And the dumbest thing I did at first was to start closing into myself and keeping everyone else at a distance. I thought somehow if nobody knew how awful things were in my life then I could just carry all the pain of my problems alone and no one would ever know. The trouble was that when I did that I stood out like a sore thumb. Those who really cared about me and knew what I was doing reached out to help me FAST!

"There are two kinds of 'friends'. I'm going to call them 'Good friends' and 'Bad friends'. You only have to look at anyone's life who says they want to be your friend and ask yourself if you really want to be like them, to know if they should be your close friend or not. If they are wrecking their life in any way – by hating their parents - or using drugs - or getting drunk - or lying to you that whatever they're doing that could mess up your or their life is 'really cool' - or telling you that sex before marriage is the way to go, and that marriage itself doesn't matter - or by telling you some other way is right that you know in your heart is wrong - NEVER let them suck *you* into their lifestyle.

"'Good friends' won't steal your life from you or lie to you. 'Good friends' tell you the truth even when it hurts, so that they can help you, NOT so that they can use you or abuse you. I'm thankful for every word I've heard this year that has helped me see a far more wonderful way to live than I'd been living.

"Whether you choose good friends or bad ones, I guarantee they're going to change your life. The good ones will help you keep doing the right thing even when things go wrong around you. But the bad ones won't care. They'll leave you when your boat begins to sink, even though they're the ones who helped make the hole in the bottom of it.

"I want to close by taking a risk. A local pastor in this town, Sky Smith, has taught me that faith requires risk. So here I go – Willie Radner stepping out on the water! Here are just a few facts that I'm sure we can all agree about. I got all of them from my very best Friend. I'll tell you who He is in just a moment.

"Let me ask you a question. If you were sitting at home and waiting for dinner and your mom brought you a plate of food, you would think she or someone else prepared that food. Right? But why would you think that? It's because SOMETHING CAN'T COME FROM NOTHING. It never has and it never will.

"Take your eyes for example. Each of your two tiny retinas contain about 130 million rod-shaped cells. They transmit signals to your brain through one million nerve fibres. That's happening while nearly six million cone-shaped cells give you color variations. Your eyes can handle 500,000 messages, all at the same time. Both eyes are kept clean at the very same instant by ducts that continually produce exactly the right amount of fluid all your life, cleaning both of your eyes in one-five-thousandth of a second.

"Evolutionary scientists say that this world wasn't designed by a Designer. They say this world just 'happened', and that everything on Earth just 'evolved' after that. But would you believe your dinner just 'happened' or 'evolved'? Or that those amazing eyes of yours just 'happened' or 'evolved'? Even Charles Darwin had a hard time believing that. In 1859 he wrote on page 170 of his famous book, *On*

The Origin Of Species, 'To suppose that the eye with all its inimitable contrivances for adjusting the focus to different distances, for admitting different amounts of light, and for the correction of spherical and chromatic aberration, could have been formed by natural selection, seems, I freely confess, **absurd in the highest sense**.'

"How could things that weren't alive produce things that came to life at the beginning of this world or at any other time since then?

"Evolutionists have a really tough time trying to explain away the Bombardier Beetle. That's a fascinating little insect that whenever it's scared by another insect protects itself by shooting fire from its bottom to stop that insect from harming it. If the Bombardier Beetle didn't have the EXACT amount of fire inside itself each time it couldn't defend itself, or it would blow itself up, or it would blow its bottom off!" Willie's four friends laughed. "No other animal, bird, or insect, that ANY scientist knows about has ever shot fire from its bottom. And no *honest* scientist can explain it away."

"As soon as this ceremony is over you can go to the internet and find out EXACTLY when the sun is going to rise tomorrow and EXACTLY when it is going to set. Any scientist can do that too, whether they believe in the One who created the sun or not. People have done that from the beginning of creation. You can count on the sun and moon's perfect timing and set your wristwatch by it. Did a perfectly controlled sun and moon just 'happen'? That's like believing your dinner just 'happened'!

"I could go on and on with these kinds of facts. But let me ask you another question instead. How many of you were there when ESPN televised our baseball game?" All four friends raised their hands and Willie grinned. He went on, "Well, I never could have pitched that game at all if my friend, Tracey Dare, hadn't prayed for my arm to be healed. It was so sore when I woke up that day that I thought I might never get to pitch. But she asked my new best Friend, Jesus Christ, to heal it and He did. I now know Jesus Christ as my Savior and Lord. And if you'd like Tracey, Goober Boober, Alfonso Guiterrez, Pee Wee Fritz, or me, to pray for any pain or sickness you have, we'll be more than glad to do it because Jesus Christ is alive and He is the Great Physician. He loves you!

"I've been told there are certain things no one can say at a graduation or somebody's going to pull the plug on them. But if nuclear bombs start dropping on America, the very ones who are trying to censor me now will cry out 'God help me!' as everything in their world falls apart. I wish they'd pray that NOW. God is the only Friend who is ready to help each of us in ways no humans can ever do. His Son, Jesus Christ, is the One who died and rose again for you. I want all of you to know HE'S ALIVE! He makes life worth living. I wish with all my heart that you would come and let my friends and me introduce you to our very best Friend of all, Jesus Christ. Thank you."

"Don't change a thing Willie. That's BRILLIANT!" Goober said in response to Willie's speech.

"It's FANTASTIC!" Alfonso agreed.

"WOW! I wish I cudda ritta speech like that," Pee Wee told him.

Tracey had one question. "Are you sure you'll be able to give the last part of your speech without having the plug pulled on you?"

Willie smiled. "Mr. Hirkshire, Mr. Bozzknobber and I, talked about it. They said freedom of speech is a 'First Amendment Right', and that they'll conveniently find something real urgent to do somewhere else so that they won't be able to get to the plug in time to stop me!"

"Good old Mr. Hirkshire and Mr. Bozzknobber," Tracey laughed with the others. "They really are wonderful."

Willie's four friends agreed that not a single word of Willie's speech should be changed. Then they prayed.

It was the final day of school. The awards celebration had already been held. Goober was surprised with a trophy that read "Friend Of The Year" with his name engraved on it. Mrs. Plumpff had Tracey present it to him.

The graduation ceremony would take place that night and Willie would be giving his valedictorian speech. Report cards had already been given out and a party atmosphere was all that was left in Mrs. Plumpff's room.

As the four friends walked to the cafeteria, Pee Wee stopped them for a moment in the hallway. He said, "Hi, guys. I'd cum an eat with ya, but I promist I'd have lunch with Billy Gottenber. I'm gonna tellum bout Jesus."

The four friends stopped and prayed for Pee Wee and for Billy. "Jesus Christ, our Savior" Willie prayed, "give Pee Wee the words from You that will get Billy saved." Pee Wee thanked them and left them to join Billy.

As he walked away Tracey smiled. "Well, I guess the junkyard dog is dead!"

The four friends entered the food line and got their trays of food. Then they sat down for a final lunch at Edison Middle School. "So, what are we doing this summer besides growing in Christ together at Amazing Grace?" asked Goober.

Willie had news. "Right before we all start high school, I'm taking my first airplane trip to New York City to visit my dad. I talked to him before school this morning. He told me again how sorry he was that he couldn't make our graduation.

But he's taking two weeks off to just spend that time with me. I'll actually get to see a double-header with the Yankees and a game with the Mets too. And I'm going to share with him what's happened with Christ and me. I want to tell him while we're together."

"Wow!" responded Tracey. "We'll all be praying for you."

"Yeah, I'll really need your prayers. And I'm going to be working for Mr. O'Rourke again at his stables this summer until I go get with my dad. Of course, there will be a few get-together days for baseball practice at John Kennedy too. I'll need a great second baseman and a great left fielder to back me up." Then glancing at Goober and Al, he said, "You guys do plan to play freshman ball with me, don't you?"

"Sure," they joyfully agreed.

"What about you, Tracey? What's the summer hold for you?" Goober asked.

"Well," she answered, "Mom and I are going to spend her vacation at Yosemite National Park for a week. The rest of the time we'll be here. So we can all get together and just hang out."

Goober said, "I think all of us are going to be reading our Bibles a lot. School is going to be out, but I've got a whole lot of learning to do."

Willie said, "Me too. You know, I've never asked you how you got saved, Tracey. How did that happen, and when?"

"It happened three years ago during the summer. I was staying for a week with my Aunt Cheryl while my mom was in Atlanta being trained by the company she sells online for. I was bored. I told Aunt Cheryl I needed something to do. I thought maybe she'd have me peel potatoes or mow the lawn. Instead she handed me a book called *The Message*. It's written by a man named Eugene Peterson. I didn't notice until I got into it that it said on the cover in lighter print *The*

Bible In Contemporary Language. She suggested I read the Book of John. I did and I couldn't put it down. The way this Bible is written is more like a fabulous novel. I know you'll love it too. When I finished reading John, I asked if I could read the whole Bible all the way through. She was thrilled that I wanted to do that.

"Well, that same night, Aunt Cheryl and I talked together and she asked me if I'd understood what I'd read in the Bible so far. I told her I thought I did. Then she asked me if I wanted to know the Author of this Book. I thought she meant she was going to introduce me to Eugene Peterson. But that wasn't what she meant at all. She introduced me to Jesus Christ. I prayed and received Him. Then she prayed for me to receive the baptism in the Holy Spirit too, but I wasn't at all as quick to speak in code as you guys were. My life has never been the same since."

Willie said, "I apologize to you, Tracey, for not listening to you about Christ for such a long time. I really thought you were one French Fry short of a Happy Meal!"

"Me too," Goober told her.

"Me three," Alfonso chimed in.

"How come you never told me about Aunt Cheryl leading you to Christ the day we first walked together after your Aunt Cheryl died?" Goober asked her.

"I wanted to, Goob," Tracey responded, "but I felt a check in my spirit about doing that."

Alfonso wanted to know, "What's 'a check in your spirit'?"

"It's when you want to do or say something, but the Lord doesn't want you to do it or say it. You just 'know' you shouldn't, just like I knew that day."

"You're right Tracey," Goober agreed. "I apologize for joking with the guys that I knew you had a photographic memory, but that you must keep leaving your camera at home. Until the night we got saved I thought you were just religious, Now I know you're not religious. You're in a lifestyle with your living Savior. Can you believe it, so are we!"

"We haven't heard yet from you, Al," Willie reminded him. "Got any big plans for the summer besides hanging out with us and going to Amazing Grace?"

"Yeah," Alfonso answered. "I'm going to keep going on Treasure Hunts. They're incredible. I was at church last night and Larry Jack had just read a book by a guy named Kevin Dedmon. He told us how the Treasure Hunts work. And then he and I and five others went on one. I know you're all going to want to do this too. Here's what Larry taught us: We prayed and then the Lord put in our minds clues about someone we were going to meet and pray for. First, Larry heard God say, 'A green shirt'. Then a girl who was with us heard Him say, 'Tennis shoes'. Another guy with us got the impression, 'Someone who walks with a limp'. And then I saw the word 'Costco' in my mind. So we all jumped into Larry's car and he drove us to Costco. As soon as we got out of his car a man started walking right towards us who was limping and wore a green shirt and tennis shoes. We walked up to him and told him what we were doing. We told him we were on a Treasure Hunt and that he was 'our treasure'. He was really surprised. We asked him if he knew the Lord, and he did. Then we asked him if we could pray for his limp to be healed. He said, 'Sure'. We prayed and that guy started walking and had no limp at all! He was shocked. He said he'd limped for the last five years. I guess none of us should have been surprised. God was the one who sent us to that man in the first place. You guys have got to read Kevin's books and join me on a Treasure Hunt. You'll be blown away with all the miracles that happen."

"I think you can count all of us in," Goober smiled. The others agreed.

"We'll be really busy with our youth group too," Willie added. The others agreed again.

Goober said, "You know, we're all going to be kind of busy, sometimes together, sometimes apart, until we start our freshman year. But I was just thinking about the surprises that have come into our lives this year, including the surprise of the four of us being together."

"That was a really great surprise for me," Willie said. "I don't know what I'd have done without you three as my buddies."

"I had guitar lessons taught to me by the expert himself," Tracey said as she smiled at Alfonso.

"And you have a voice that made even *me* sound good at the talent show," Alfonso smiled back.

Goober reminded them, "Oh, and the Bomber Brothers didn't make me toothless, thanks to you, Al!"

Alfonso chimed in, "There was the fire next to my house. And thanks to you, Tracey, we had heaps of presents for the Ritter kids. And thanks to you, Goob, even for Mr. and Mrs. Ritter. Now their house is completely rebuilt and it's even better than the first one."

Tracey looked at Goober and said, "You and Al came to my Aunt Cheryl's funeral. You'll never know how much that meant to me."

"And," smiled Willie, "you three came to what I thought was MY funeral. Now you've made me see that it wasn't."

"Hey, how about Pee-wee chasing you three away from his house. Grrrrrrr!" laughed Tracey.

"And that skunk!" Willie laughed, "Man, I thought I was going to lose it when I saw that thing coming out of that bag. Poor Manny!" Everyone laughed just remembering that moment.

"The baseball season, and especially the last game," Tracey said. "I was never so proud of three guys in my whole life."

"It took all three of us to win that game," Willie said. "And, Tracey, you were a first-class announcer. Just think, it was right here in this cafeteria that all three of you agreed to join the team."

Goober responded, "You're the star, Willie. Thanks for asking us."

Willie pointed at Tracey and Alfonso – "YOU were the stars of the talent show. You two were terrific."

"Well, we couldn't have even performed if you hadn't brought us that new guitar, Goob," Tracey smiled. "And now you know where that guitar you brought us really came from. It came from God!"

"You're right," Goober agreed. "And God had us hatch another plot right in this cafeteria. Now Pee Wee is a great new friend, saved and getting others saved!"

"Hey," Tracey smiled, "How about Pee Wee's dog? Your dad was a hero to save that dog's life and to pay that huge bill for him," she told Alfonso.

"I know," Alfonso agreed. "When my dad told my mom how much the bill for Spike's surgery was she almost fainted. But she started laughing instead and she couldn't stop!"

"I've worn this locket every day since my birthday, Goob. I love it."

"It looks really beautiful on you, Tracey. I still think you're the prettiest girl I've ever seen."

"We ALL do, Tracey," Willie agreed.

Ray Mossholder traveled nearly non-stop in ministry for 34 years. He taught healing seminars and marriage and singles seminars all over the United States and in 22 foreign countries. His list of friends and mentors reads like a Who's Who in ministry.

Ray has been Dr. Jack Hayford's associate pastor, staff evangelist for Dr. Tommy Barnett, a national representative for Youth With A Mission and Loren Cunningham, did constant appearances with Dr. Jim Bakker during the television days of PTL, taught more than fifty marriage seminars for Dr. Pat Robertson at CBN, and had his own two international television programs – "Marriage Plus" and "Singles Plus" for six years with Cornerstone Television Network and Sky Angel.

Then in 2001 Ray burned out and was out of ministry for four and half years, living his life as a castaway. In 2006, Pastor Bill Johnson, the pastor of Bethel Church in Redding, California, offered Ray restoration. Ray brought his new wife, Georgia Mae, who had nothing at all to do with his past ministry or failure to Redding and to Bethel Church. After three years of careful restoring and fresh revelation, including a year of this couple attending Bethel's marvelous School of the Supernatural, Ray's ministry is fully endorsed by Bill and the leaders of Bethel. Ray taught courses at Bethel on The Timeline of the Holy Spirit from Pentecost to Today and on the Book of Philippians. He also taught a constantly growing home Bible study called the "The Gathering". Finally Ray ministered to the congregation at Bethel.

In February of 2010 Ray and Georgia Mae, moved to Fort Worth, Texas, where Ray has fully returned to evangelism and ministry. Ray not only teaches God's Word, but demostates the power of it with signs and wonders following.

Five Real Friends is Ray's fifth published book. A complete professionally recorded audio version of this book is also available by contacting Ray at his e-mail address.

If you would like to have Ray and Georgia come to where you are for <u>minitery</u>, contact them by e-mail. Ray invites you to get in touch with him at his e-mail address: raymossholder@holyhugs.com

For Book orders contact:

Accent Digital Publishing, Inc

2932 Churn Creek Rd

Redding, CA 96002

accentdigitalpublishing.com

email accentdigital@gmail.com